Sweet Dreams Publishing of Massachusetts

# Chicken Fried Steak

## Steven I. Dahl, M.D.

A Novel

Sweet Dreams Publishing
of Massachusetts

Other books by

Steven I. Dahl, M.D.

*HOA Gold*, Action-Adventure

*Picasso's Zipline*, Adventure/Medical Mystery

*Kick the Can*, Murder-Mystery

*Rattlesnake*, Wait and "See"

In the words of his father, "Son, be careful what you wish for," Dr. Bryson Bender, Ob/Gyn has the ride of his life when his dream of retiring and being a trucker and hitting the road with his cousin, Jack, come to fruition. It is a rollicking tale from a guy's perspective that gave this gal some delightful reading time.

—Sherry Young
Columnist for *Deseret News*
Salt Lake City, Utah

Chicken Fried Steak
Published by Sweet Dreams Publishing of Massachusetts, May 2010
5 Federal Street
Weymouth, MA 02188

*Cover & Interior Design:* Lisa Akoury-Ross
*Photo Credits:*
*Front Cover:* "Paved Rural Road Along Green Countryside and Blue Skies" (Background image), iStockphoto; "Highway Star," (Truck image, bottom right), iStockphoto.
*Back Cover:* "Country Diner" (Top), iStockphoto; "On The Road" (Faded Truck, background screen), iStockphoto.

For more information about this book contact Sweet Dreams Publishing of MA by email at info@PublishAtSweetDreams.com

Library of Congress Control Number: 2010920323

ISBN-10: 0-9824461-3-6
ISBN-13: 978-0-9824461-3-3

Printed in the United States of America
Copyright © 2010, Steven I. Dahl, M.D.

*My Paula*
*Who, when asked to come share my life, agreed.*

Other books published by

Sweet Dreams Publishing of Massachusetts

*HOA Gold*, Action-Adventure
by Steven I. Dahl, M.D.

*A Wayward Oath*, Crime/Detective Novella
by Bill Jacques, Writer, Actor

*Streets of Rage*, A Novella
by Richard Chandler, Writer/Film Director

*Oodle Van Boodle and The Great Cake Adventure*,
A Children's Story
by Kim Shanley-Peretti, Olivia and Luke's Mom

Visit us at:
www.PublishAtSweetDreams.com
or
Contact us at:
info@PublishAtSweetDreams.com

# Chapter One

# THE BLAZE

It all started with a leaky old X-ray machine and chicken fried steak.

It was impractical—maybe impossible—to count the number of times Bryson Bender had been told that the world's best chicken fried steak was always found at truck stop cafés or small mom-and-pop restaurants along America's highways. Growing up in the Southwest, food words such as escargot, chateaubriand and étouffée had never touched his tympanic membranes, let alone his palate, and thus had never become a part of his culinary vocabulary. Chicken fried steak, however, was a sound that evoked the most primitive instincts and responses, including salivation, increased respiratory rate and the darting of eyes as he searched for any signs that the gustatory delight might be near.

"If you want the real thing, then you've got to eat at a real truck stop," his Uncle Bill would say. "Not those gigantic trucking centers along the freeways, with two hundred pumps, junk food shops and hydro-massages. Find the truck stops the local truckers use, the ones on two-lane highways with gravel parking lots and neon signs that say CAFE. That's where a man finds the best chicken fried steak. Careful that you don't eat too much 'cause they usually have good homemade cherry pies, too."

Bryson had been asleep in the back of the family sedan when his dad once stopped at just such a place. Though the location and circumstances of the trip were soon forgotten, the smell, taste and texture of a hot bite of chicken fried steak was still with him to this day.

His uncle's advice years before, along with those wonderful smells and tastes, held an indelible niche in the recesses of Bryson's cluttered brain. As many times as he had heard the advice and repeated it to his patient wife, Marisa, and to his not-so-patient five kids, he never—not even once—took the time to heed that advice. Often, while blitzing down the Interstate at law-breaking speeds on forgettable road trips, Bryson would think about his uncle's advice and would start mental plans to turn off onto the Route 66s of America's heartland. Then he would check his watch, glance at the odometer, or look down at the ever-present excess of abdominal fat above his belt line, and change his mind.

For those who have never enjoyed biting into a morsel of the hot, crispy delicacy, perfectly seasoned with French's black pepper and Morton's iodized salt, the rest of the world should feel pity. In creating the delicacy, only the best cuts of fresh flank steak, trimmed and pounded beyond butter-knife tenderness, should ever be used. The breading recipe is age-old, so old that no cook worth their keep would dare to write it down. Yes, there are cooks who prepare and serve chicken fried steak. Chefs, on the other hand, arrange tiny portions of weed-like vegetables and insufficient amounts of rich sauces made from yesterday's leftover specials, fancifully displayed around expensive pieces of way-too-lean flesh. They serve it with six-dollar-a-bottle water and thirty-dollar-a-bottle grape juice that had set too long in someone's root cellar.

Getting back to the cook's secrets. The cooking oil—usually lard, but any grease will work—must be just the right depth in the frying pan and exactly the correct temperature. Ladling the scalding oil onto the meat as it cooks is an art form in itself. If one ladles too often, the result is a burned piece of cheap shoe leather. Ladle too seldom and the grease soaks in and makes a gooey slime covering the meat. Whether one serves biscuits, mashed potatoes, or grits with the meat is irrelevant—yet for some that remains a matter of strong debate. The gravy, however, is as important as the savory steak. It must be thin enough to flow at a steaming hot temperature and thick enough to stick in luscious globs to the morsels of meat as they cross the abyss from dinner plate to the anticipating palate. Gravy must not be too dark in color and never so salty that one can't safely add their own habitual dashes before digging in.

Bryson woke after dreaming about such a meal. He lay in his comfortable bed hoping for a whiff of sizzling beef; even bacon would have sufficed. He smelled nothing and heard only the soft breathing of his sleeping wife.

"No breakfast, again?" his wife asked a short while later. Dressed in her robe, Marisa stood at the door to give him a kiss.

"I'll get a doughnut and OJ at the doctor's lounge," he said, smiling at the smudge of toothpaste on her nose.

✻✻✻

For the thirty long years of his career, Bryson Bender, M.D., had been the renter, not an owner, of the medical building where he practiced. The Samaritan Hospital next door was the landlord. His office, an easy three-minute walk from the modern hospital, still had the manufacturer's paper stickers on its windows the day Bryson saw his first pregnant private patient.

Many were the times he had considered buying his own office building. Tax deductions, appreciation and pride of ownership sounded good, but the decision to buy took time, effort and cash. All were scarce in Dr. Bender's life. It had been so easy and hassle-free to just write a rent check once a month. Let someone else worry about upkeep, cleaning, leaking hot water heaters and painting the parking lot stripes. He walked out of the office at five each evening knowing that at nine the next morning, the place would be freshly cleaned, the burned-out lights replaced and someone would be on duty to unstop the toilets or mop up spilled sodas.

Bryson had recently signed a new contract renewing his office lease for five years with an option of renewal for an additional five. He hoped that renewal wouldn't be necessary—he would be in a wheelchair, straightjacket or pine box if he had to work another ten years. Five years, he might be able to tolerate. The physical and mental toil of late night deliveries, difficult hysterectomies and the life-and-death decisions he faced each day were taking a harder toll each year.

Every doctor he knew dreamed of early retirement. The idea of not having to get up every morning to face patients' problems, coupled with living a life of lavish and leisure like all of their pension managers promised years ago, sounded wonderful. But for most, the increasing strangulation of managed care and decreasing reimbursement payments made an early death seem more likely than early retirement.

Recently his attorney, Brian, had talked him into upping the insurance replacement value of his Ob/Gyn practice to one point five million big ones. He had balked at the idea, but Brian had caught Marisa's ear and the two had prevailed on Bryson's weakness of wanting to overprotect his family. The fat premium check had been mailed the previous week. Bryson considered insurance to be the cost of business. His various insurance policy premiums had been draining his pockets for years with only a Christmas card or a stupid cubic calendar from the brokers. He, like most doctors and their wives, was a sucker for a good insurance sales pitch.

***

"What a great day to be outdoors. The forecast calls for crisp air and sunshine . . . "

Bryson changed the station. He would be stuck in the office, not outdoors. Driving to work, he thought about doughnuts, and then a Geico commercial aired. It fueled his anger over the recent insurance premium he had paid. The thought jumped into his head to punch the insurance agent's phone number into his car's cell phone. He was seriously considering telling the man he had changed his mind and would cancel the new office insurance policy.

Then he saw the smoke.

He glanced through the windshield and saw a distinct trail of black smoke snaking its way into the sky ahead. As he stopped for a red light close to his office building, a sense of foreboding infiltrated the atmosphere of his car. Chills went up his spine as he turned the last corner leading toward his parking garage and saw flashing lights of police cars and fire trucks. The smoke was right there in front of him and was very real.

Bryson's office building was on fire!

He parked his car at an odd angle along one of the building's tree-lined staff picnic areas and stared out the window. He couldn't believe what he was seeing. It wasn't just a little curl of smoke anymore. His entire office building, all four stories of the two-hundred-foot-long building, was ablaze.

There was total chaos around the parking lot and the adjacent buildings of the hospital complex as police and firemen tried to get cars and people moved away from the roaring blaze.

A sharp rapping sound on his window took his attention away from the flames. A policeman yelled at him to move his car to allow additional fire trucks into the parking area. By the time he drove across the main street into a church parking lot where the cars and trucks were parked helter-skelter, Bryson could feel the heat from the fire inside his air-conditioned car. He got out of his car, shielding his face with his hand and headed across the street. He stopped in the middle of the road to run back and grab his cell phone.

Bryson found himself standing in a crowd of familiar doctors, nurses and office staffers, many wearing their matching scrub tops with the logos of their respective clinics. All were watching the chaos unfold. Several women in the crowd were his patients and friends. Many of the doctors had started their practice careers about the same time as Bryson. Over the years, they had built up their practices and lived their lives up and down the hallways beside his office. Now, right there in front of their eyes, the fire was consuming the entire four-story office complex. Their office complex. His office complex.

Everyone stood, frozen in shock. Sobs rose over the roar of the fire. Not only were the furniture and medical records going up in smoke, but jobs, friendships and the doctors' practices as well.

The heat from the fire soon grew so intense that once the fire chief had been assured that the building was clear of people, he ordered his crews to back away from the inferno. The building contained storage rooms full of oxygen tanks and other explosive gases. Luckily, the prevailing easterly wind was carrying the dense smoke away from the crowd and away from the adjacent hospital just four hundred feet to the north.

"Can you believe this disaster, Bender?" The voice was a familiar one—John Southwick—the orthopedic surgeon who headed the group of bone crunchers, occupying the space on the floor immediately above Bryson's. Gripping his arm and leaning close, he whispered, "Sorry, Bender."

Southwick was one of the old school docs. He was habitually grouchy but smarter and more talented than any of the new high-tech orthopedic doctors in town. He was a man who dedicated his life to building a strong medical community, always with the welfare of his patients foremost in his thoughts. Recently he, like many his age, had seen many of his regular patients abandon him for the new generation of corporate-owned doctors working in big, impersonal groups. The new guys all had fancy waiting rooms full of aquariums and glossy magazines. They had advertisements on the TV paid for by the hospitals. To make things worse, the big insurance companies short-changed him and the other small practice docs on every payment claim.

Southwick had been forced to accept the lower pay and stay in practice to support a young second family after his first wife had died of breast cancer.

"It looks like your office suite is gone with all the rest of us," Bryson said to the slump-shouldered Southwick, not yet really comprehending what *gone* would actually mean to the sixty-some-odd doctors, health practitioners and their four or five hundred employees.

"Yep, looks like they're all gone."

"It's nice of you to feel sorry for me, John, but we're all in the same boat."

"I said sorry, Bender, because I was here early and I know that the fire started in your office."

"That can't be true! There is no way that it could have started there."

Bryson couldn't believe what he had just heard. What in the world could have started a fire in his office? There weren't any flammables except a couple of bottles of rubbing alcohol.

He looked around for Teri, his secretary, and finally saw her and his nurse standing with a group of women from the office next door. It appeared that all the women were crying. Heading in their direction, he was gently grabbed by the arm. It was Dr. Southwick again.

"Well, don't say anything to anyone," Southwick whispered, "but I wouldn't doubt it if that damn X-ray developer in my back room . . . you know the one that has been leaking down the wall into your exam rooms for the last twenty years? I think your nurse called it the 'Love Canal on a wall.' I wouldn't be surprised if it leaked down into your office and started the fire."

Bryson stopped in his tracks and turned toward

Southwick. "Yeah, I know the machine and the leaking all right. What a piece of crap! I thought you replaced it with some expensive digital computer." Turning again toward the burning building, he was now listening intently, but kept his eyes glued on the fire.

"We have a new digital unit waiting in another room. We have been asking for months, but our wonderful landlord, the hospital, hasn't removed the old unit yet. Finally, Thursday, after almost daily nagging from my office manager, the hospital sent somebody up with a crowbar, a hammer and a double-digit IQ. When I left the office last Friday night there was a pounding noise coming from the room and the strong smell of chemicals . . . something really nasty. Maybe it was some kind of solvent. All of us left the office early because it smelled so toxic."

Southwick's explanation was interrupted by Bryson's cell phone. By the time he checked the number on the caller ID, Southwick had walked away into the growing crowd of spectators.

"Did you hear about the fire? Is the hospital really on fire?" Marisa asked in an excited voice.

"Do you mean the fire I'm standing here watching? The one that is burning up all of my patients' charts and all the records of money the insurance companies owe us? It's not the hospital, sweetheart. Our whole office building will soon be a pile of ashes."

✳✳✳

"You are there? I thought you had an appointment with Don to do your annual corporate report. Hey, I think I can see you on the news. Yes, it's you! Wave at me. My gosh, Bryson, it is your office building."

"Okay, I'll wave at you, and when I do, you can wave back and say goodbye to the office that feeds and clothes us. Then you better turn off the TV and go look through your closet for anything you can return to Nordstrom's. Our whole income stream has just vaporized in front of our eyes."

Bryson hated himself for his sarcasm. It was a recurring problem, which Marisa usually ignored. This time he worried that it had hurt her feelings. He tried to apologize but she was too upset about the fire to listen or care.

He said goodbye and watched the roof of the building collapse, crushing the floors and parking garage below and shooting out an enormous cloud of soot and sparks. Nauseated and dizzy, he turned away from the fire toward the crowd of onlookers, which had now grown to thousands. His brain felt fried right along with his office building. Maybe he had been standing too close to the fire. His head was spinning and he felt short of breath. Questions were shuffling through his mind like a deck of cards. How would he begin trying to make plans for the rest of the day—the week—the month—his life?

When he had finished speaking with his wife of thirty-nine terrific years, he started searching again for his secretary and nursing assistants and found them standing in the shade of a cluster of palm trees. Walking closer, he confirmed that they had been crying. Red eyes and smeared mascara along with the tissues in hand made him stop thinking about himself for a minute and focus on what a huge catastrophe this fire would be for his employees. They had run from the building earlier, carrying just their purses and a few picture frames.

Leaning against a tree trunk was a stack of framed diplomas, which he recognized as his. They had saved them for him. The computers and patient records were left behind to the incinerating heat.

Bryson tried his best to reassure his staff that things would work out for them. He thanked them again for rescuing his cherished sheepskins and they all agreed on a meeting at his home later in the afternoon. Teri volunteered to get a hold of the answering service to let them know what to tell patients. He would decide the specifics later, when he figured out what the heck to do next. They had over a hundred patients scheduled for office visits the next five days, many of them pregnant. Some were at or near term.

He tried to reassure his staff, who were his friends as well as his employees. He could sense the fear, both theirs and his own, as they watched the anticlimactic firefighting and then parted. As he tried to remember where he had parked his car in all the confusion, a sense of déjà vu struck him. When he was eleven years old, his family had been victims of a middle-of-the-night house fire. He had long since forgotten about it until this moment. For the last forty-five years, he had taken the attitude that those things were somebody else's problems. Now, right now, they were his problems.

***

Dealing with his pregnant patients would be the hardest thing. As soon as those lucky doctors who still had offices could finish up the morning clinics and surgeries, he and his call partners held an emergency meeting in the hospital cafeteria. Two of the other Ob/Gyn groups had watched their offices go up in smoke right along with Bryson's. All the men and women were in shock and were trying to work out a solution to the enormous problem of not having a physical office. Meanwhile, patients would be going into labor in the middle of the night, just like always. His patients would expect their doctor to be there for them, not to be out looking for office space.

Trying to get a group of doctors to agree on anything had always seemed to be nearly impossible. However, the afternoon of the fire, every one of the doctors in the hospital conference room was in too much shock to argue.

The three obstetric groups, representing about fifteen doctors, with intact off-campus offices, had only enough office space for themselves. They were sympathetic to those who had lost offices in the fire and did offer to help out by seeing the "nearly due" pregnant women. For the other forty-plus thousand obstetrical and gynecological female patients in the remaining three practices, something else had to be found.

As the meeting drew to an inconclusive close, Bryson was not just exasperated and exhausted, but had received a call informing him that he had two patients in early labor. It was going to be a very long twenty-four hours. By the time he walked from the conference room to labor and delivery, he had adopted a fatalistic attitude and told himself that he might as well be working because sleep would be impossible.

Bryson's cell would not stop ringing. Later he learned that Marisa, too, was spending every minute answering calls from frantic patients, concerned friends and nosey neighbors.

✳✳✳

A mid-afternoon delivery of a healthy baby girl postponed the planned meeting with his staff until the next day. A second delivery resulted in an emergency C-section, which spared the mother a long labor, saved the baby any risk of oxygen deprivation, and allowed Bryson to finish both of his deliveries in time to head home for dinner with Marisa and his youngest daughter, Madeline. When he pulled into his garage at home, he realized that he couldn't even remember driving there.

Dinner at the kitchen table was interrupted by more phone calls and dozens of questions from his wife and daughter. For most of them, Bryson had no good answers. The frequency of calls finally started to diminish as the meal ended. Bryson avoided helping with the dishes by taking another call then ducking off to the bedroom and putting on his swimsuit. He found the LeCarré novel he had started the week before and escaped into the backyard to sit in his hot tub. He could still hear the phone ring occasionally, but had handed the question answering over to Marisa. As his body sank into the swirling hot water, his brain finally stopped spinning. He took several deep breaths, leaned his head back against a foam pad and began to daydream about a life away from medicine and work. He tried to lose himself in the book, but finally laid it aside and stared up at the starlit sky. For a little while, at least, he pretended that work didn't exist.

*** 

Competition in business, even in medicine, can be cruel, but once in a blue moon humanity can redeem herself. For Bryson, that night it was like manna from heaven. At about nine thirty, Marisa brought the phone out to him. He dried off his hands and took a conference call. Two of the new kids in town—women just months out of their Ob/Gyn specialty training and hungry to get a bigger piece of the patient market—were on the line offering to take over the care of any of the patients Bryson was willing to share. In addition, he could use their office part-time to see his own patients. He could start that very week if he wanted. He would be expected—and rightly so—to share a portion of the rent, utilities, office staff costs and any other expenses they might decide to charge to his tab. That was just fine with him. His own office overhead had just come to a screeching halt. As frosting on the cake, they offered to do any deliveries he might have that night or any other night until they could work out a regular rotation. They all agreed that he would start seeing his patients in their office in two days. When he turned off the phone, he was elated.

\*\*\*

The next morning, Bryson slept in for the first time in forty years. Marisa had shut off the phone in the bedroom and had snuck out, skipping her usual morning bathroom routines so she wouldn't awaken him. He got up around ten thirty feeling somewhat stiff and sore from lying in the bed for so long. He went for a swim and ate a real breakfast of pancakes, eggs and crisp bacon. As he sat over the tailings of his breakfast, boring Marisa with a laundry list of things to do, he realized that his malpractice insurance was the only big-dollar money meter still running. He was starting to relax. He thanked his wife for breakfast with a kiss and was headed for his study to catch up on the list of messages Marisa had saved for him when the phone rang again.

"Backup discs," Teri said to him. "Everything is on backup discs in the office safe. I was too distraught yesterday to think of it. But I couldn't stop thinking about it all night. You probably didn't sleep either. If we can get into the safe and it's held up to its fireproof warranty, things might just be fine with the insurance collections and the schedule of appointments."

Sensing his secretary's stress and worry, Bryson had a wave of guilt for having slept so long and for not worrying enough. Teri was the best! Not only was she efficient and loyal, she had a brain for organization equal only to Marisa's. She had already gone online that morning and put a notice in the newspaper for patients with appointments to call her to reschedule. A friend of a friend had notified her of the new arrangement with the young female doctors. She had forwarded the office number to her own home phone.

Bryson thanked her, and they agreed to meet later in the day at the old burned-down office to see if they could get into the fireproof safe.

\*\*\*

When Bryson arrived at the charred office that afternoon, he found the demolition crews already waiting to go to work with their giant excavators and backhoes. Everyone was standing around waiting for the fire department to finish its investigation and take down the yellow crime scene tape. Other doctors and their staff were there as well, many with the same hopes Bryson and Teri had: Please, let the office records be saved.

Most were wearing old clothes and hiking boots in anticipation of having to wade through the soggy, sooty debris left from the charred building and thousands of gallons of fire-hose water. Bryson had on his usual office attire, not having thought about ruining his clothes. Marisa showed up to help, dressed in a casual hiker's outfit.

It was nearly dusk before the yellow police-barrier tape came down. By then rumors were running rampant. One was that there was absolutely nothing left to be salvaged from the rubble. Another rumor made the rounds telling of a body being found among all the muck. A lab technician's husband, a senior fire fighter, had told his wife that the fire had started on the third floor and was chemically ignited. This started another round of rumors eventually evolving into a terrorism scenario. No one really knew what to believe.

When permission to approach the building was given, Bryson, Marisa, Teri and the rest of the varied staffs tiptoed into, climbed over and looked under debris until their eyes burned from the mixture of chemical toxins created by the fire. They were never able to get even close to the area of the rubble where they guessed Bryson's office had ended up. Fallen slabs of concrete and heat-twisted steel beams were everywhere. The best they could figure, Bryson's office contents were in the basement parking garage buried under at least one layer of crushed concrete flooring and what remained of the building's roof. Bryson assembled his group and headed back to the hospital parking lot. "It's a lost cause," he told the teary-eyed women. "The worst-case scenario is what Teri suggested this afternoon. We'll show up Thursday at the borrowed office and hope some of our patients show up too."

No charts, no financial records, no appointment schedules, just a frightened, angry and depressed staff was all he was left with. Bryson sent them all home and promised to call them the next morning with more instructions about starting to see patients again. He assured them again that their jobs were secure and that their paychecks would continue, though in the back of his mind he didn't know how he would pull that off for long. He hoped there would be patients to see and babies to deliver and that the scheduled surgery patients would show up at the pre-op room over the next few weeks. The biggest question that was beginning to form in his mind was whether he had the ambition it was going to take to successfully start all over again. Sleeping in that morning had felt like a novelty that he could get used to.

He and Marisa walked hand-in-hand back to his car. She had completed all the assigned tasks on her list and had given a sympathetic ear to the concerns the office staff had expressed.

The weary couple drove home in silence. Leftovers were eaten with little fuss and Marisa went off to soak away the pervasive smell of smoke from her hair, skin and clothes.

\*\*\*

Lying in the hot bathtub surrounded with jasmine-scented bubbles, Marisa tried to relax. Something kept nagging in the back of her mind that she wanted to tell Bryson but it didn't surface until later after they had gone to bed. Bryson had gone for a vigorous swim and had a bedtime glass of milk with homemade peanut butter cookies thawed out from the freezer.

They were both tucked in bed and nearly asleep when she remembered. She sat up and shook him. "Bryson, wake up! Didn't you tell me that you mailed the check for the office overhead insurance policy?"

He rubbed his eyes and then answered her question. "It was sent a week ago. I'm sure that it is too late to stop payment on the check." He rolled over to his other side to shade his eyes from the lamp she had turned on. "Please stop worrying about the money. I was just kidding about taking your clothes back to Nordstrom's."

"That's not it at all. Bryson, are you awake? I just remembered something else," she continued. "You have forgotten what the insurance agent said to us when he came by to review that new policy. You had received a call from the hospital in the middle of the conversation with the man. I don't think you even heard what he said. Bryson, we have insurance to cover the fire loss!"

He had started to pull one of his five pillows over his head when she grabbed it away from him. He turned back toward her, and squinting in the light, told her that he knew there was coverage for the office loss of equipment, furniture and to replace the charts.

"Listen to me, Bryson. The new insurance policy had a very specific paragraph, which said that in case of total loss of the office practice, the full value of the policy would be paid. I remember that he was very specific about that. It was his big selling point for us to change from the old policy. That value was set at one point five million dollars! One and a half million dollars," she repeated.

By now Bryson was fully awake and sitting on the edge of the bed. This awakening was just like he had experienced for most of the middle of the night deliveries he had performed—wake up from a dead sleep and pay attention to a problem. He turned on his nightstand lamp and walked into the bathroom. He returned with droplets of cold water on his face and hands. He took a seat in the lounge chair beside Marisa's side of the bed.

"Explain what you are talking about," he said. "I thought that one and a half million was just for additional liability coverage. You know, in case somebody slipped and fell or got their hand smashed in a closing door or something."

"Bryson, be serious for a minute. The policy will cover up to one and a half million dollars of loss of practice income. What if your practice just disappears because the patients go to someone else while you rebuild the office building? What if you show that the fire destroyed your business and you could only save it by starting over? It would be a total loss and we could claim the whole policy."

"That sounds like a big stretch of a long pipe dream. You know how those insurance jerks drag out everything and how they fight the little guy until he gives up. Even if the policy says what the guy told you, they will fight our claim to a bitter end."

"So let them fight it. If we get something out of it, they'll be the ones who are bitter and out the money in the end."

Marisa got out of bed and knelt beside his chair, taking his hands and holding them up to her cheek. "Bryson, you have worked too hard to start over again. We both have. We need to think about living our life, not just your patients' lives. Our family is almost raised and we need to spend more time together—just the two of us."

Marisa felt tears trailing down her cheeks. Bryson bent over and kissed the top of her head then stood up, helping her to her feet. He held her close and said, "Maybe you're right. Maybe we need to think ahead about our future together."

# Chapter Two

# COLLAPSE

The following morning began abruptly for Bryson with a call from Labor and Delivery. He had a gravida-four patient (three previous babies) in labor with her cervix already seven centimeters dilated. There was no time for a shave, a shower or even a bowl of cereal. He threw on a rumpled set of scrub pants and top that he had tossed in his hamper two days before. His car was fast and handled well, which helped get him quickly out of the neighborhood and onto the divided highway.

Luckily, it was early enough in the morning that there were no school buses or other significant traffic delays. By the time he reached the hospital, the nurses were holding the coded security door to the delivery room wide open for him and yelling for him to run. And so he did.

Once in the delivery room, he could see that the patient's long legs were already up in the stirrups and the baby's head was crowning. He grabbed the size-eight sterile surgical gloves off of the instrument table and tugged them on. There was no time to put on his gown or to slip a paper drape under her bottom. The woman had been as patient as she could be—panting to ease the pain—but with her next contraction she could resist no longer and gave a gigantic push.

Bryson caught the eight and a half pound screaming newborn girl in a graceful motion that reflected his skill and years of experience. He knew getting there in the nick of time had been just plain luck—mixed with speeding in gross excess of the posted limits and running two red lights. The new mother had giant beads of sweat dripping down her face, but was grinning from ear to ear. She had her new baby, who appeared healthy. That was all she cared about.

By the time Bryson finished delivering the placenta, carefully placing a few stitches in delicate places and posing for pictures with the Mom, baby and proud Dad, his heart rate was slowly returning to normal and the sweat-soaked back and armpits of his scrub top were starting to dry. He gave his patient a tender pat on the arm, resisting the embrace she acted like she wanted; he was just too sweaty.

Before he could leave Labor and Delivery, he had to complete the patient's medical chart on the new paperless medical record computer. The program had just been put into place the previous month; filling it out ate up more time than delivering a baby. It was a little over an hour before he was able to break free from the chart room and return to his illegally parked car. When he had stood up to leave the computer desk, he felt a little dizzy. As fast as it had come on, however, it was gone. Walking up to his car, he saw that the hospital security guard had already given him a warning ticket. He wadded up the carbon copy and sailed it into a nearby storm drain. Just one more burr under his saddle.

"This job is killing me," he said to the steering wheel as he settled back into the car's leather seat. He started to reach for the keyless starter but then sat back in the seat. Another wave of dizziness floated over him, this time with a feeling of nausea. He took a couple of deep breaths and thought that maybe he was too tired to drive back home to clean up and change clothes. He still had to make rounds on his in-hospital patients before he started seeing his scheduled office patients. He decided he would go over to his office and shower and shave. He always kept a full shave kit and change of clothes at his office just for times like this.

"Oh yeah, I don't have an office," he said to the steering wheel. Then the dizziness hit him again, but this time he felt something weird in his chest. *Maybe I'm just hungry, he thought. I should have eaten something in the cafeteria before I did that ridiculous computer medical record.*

He looked at himself in the car's vanity mirror and realized that he hadn't even taken time to brush his unruly hair. His beard was a scary, twenty-plus-hour, gray-speckled mess that had already started to itch. He looked down at his scrub pants and the front of his scrub tops. He could only shake his head in disgust at the splatters of blood and amniotic fluid he had trailed unknowingly out of the delivery room.

"That picture of me with the baby could be hung up in a post office along with the mass murders and Islamic terrorists," he said out loud to his reflection. *Thank goodness I chewed a piece of Dentyne gum on the drive here*, he added to himself.

He began again to reach for the button to start the engine when he took an involuntary staccato inhalation followed by a deep sigh. His shoulder belt felt tighter than normal, so he reached with his right hand for the adjustment button on the door pillar and slid it first up and then down, but even loosening the nylon belt didn't help the discomfort. He swallowed a couple of times and took two intentional deep breaths. He was feeling nauseated again . . . probably just hunger. Reaching a third time for the starter button, he felt another wave of nausea followed by profuse perspiration over his entire body. He retched up a small amount of bile and spit it into a rag he kept under the car seat.

✳✳✳

Maybe it was Bryson Bender's lucky day—though some would disagree—but the tapping on his car window stopped him from starting his car's engine and driving off.

"Bender, open the window."

The tapping grew louder until Bryson pressed the down button, lowering the tinted driver side window, exposing the face of his neighbor and golf-buddy, Jake Stern, one of the hospital's senior cardiologists.

"Hey, Bryson, I'm sorry to hear about your office burning. What the heck are you going to do with all your patients?"

Bryson looked up at Stern and tried to speak when another strong wave of nausea hit him, accompanied this time by what felt like an elephant stepping onto the middle of his chest.

"Hey! Are you okay? Bryson, you look like crap."

✳✳✳

Bryson had read the articles and heard many of the stories of near death with its out-of-body experiences. He had manned his share of defibrillator paddles in the early years of his medical training while rotating through the ERs and ICUs. Never, however, had he ever considered that he might someday be the body lying on an emergency room table while doctors and nurses talked as though he were a piece of wood or a raw leg of lamb that chefs couldn't decide which way to slice and prepare.

It had taken Dr. Stern less than a minute to recognize what was happening to Bryson and to get him out of the car onto the ground. Thirty seconds later—pumping on Bender's chest with one hand—Stern dialed the ER on his cell with the other, telling them to forget an ambulance but instead to run with a gurney and crash cart to the Labor and Delivery parking lot.

Bryson could remember everything that happened since he had awakened that morning, including the manic drive to the hospital, the baby's delivery and even the seat belt cutting into his left shoulder, then there was a long blank. His mind kept replaying Dr. Stern's voice yelling at someone, but what he couldn't figure out was why his chest hurt so much and why he was lying in the ER without a shirt on when he should have been in his office seeing patients. For some weird reason, he couldn't talk to the people hovering over him. He knew many of their faces and even recognized some of the voices, but when they asked him questions, he couldn't seem to get out the answers.

"Do you have any allergies? Do you have a history of heart disease or stroke?"

They gave up asking him the questions and directed questions to someone else. "Have you notified his wife?" the familiar voices asked. "Start another IV in his right arm and give him an amp of streptokinase. Did you stick an aspirin under his tongue? What does the last ECG strip look like? Where is the cath lab team? His ECG looks okay for now. Maybe the neurosurgeon wants him before you start the Heparin."

The voices kept popping up from this direction or that and the light was so bright. Bryson closed his eyes. *Why aren't you guys asking me the questions, and why can't you hear me? Why don't my ears stop ringing?* He opened his eyes again and watched as a nurse—he was sure her name was Karen—approached his arm with a syringe. He saw her put the needle end into her mouth to pull off the plastic needle cap and then, without even wiping the IV tubing injection port, she stuck the needle into the line and emptied the syringe content into it. Into his arm! Into his vein! *What the heck are you doing? That was not sterile technique. Don't you realize that I know better . . . better . . . better . . .*

✳✳✳

No one has ever really measured the exact length of a dream, but when Bryson awoke from what he thought was his bad dream, he would swear that it had lasted only minutes. He awoke in a brightly lit room with blue floral curtains that looked vaguely familiar to him. The television news anchor was talking about Mideast debates and some worthless dribble about a teenage Hollywood blonde. It was a little bit like home, he thought, until that is, he tried to move his arm and felt the IV tubing tugging on his left hand. Then he felt the splitting headache and his chest felt like the time his oldest son's pony had kicked him in the shin. He was blinking his eyes, trying to focus on the TV screen when he realized that the set was mounted on the far wall. Maybe he had fallen asleep in one of the on-call rooms. But what was with the hand and the IV tubing?

"Welcome back, Dr. Bender," the woman at his side softly greeted, putting one, long slender hand on his shoulder and brushing back a stray lock of his hair from his forehead with the other. "Your wife just walked down the hall to stretch her legs and get a magazine from the waiting room. We thought you would sleep a little longer."

Bryson knew this woman, a nurse, even one of his patients. But he couldn't bring her name to mind. It would come to him. He tried to speak, but his throat suddenly burned with a scratchy fire that he immediately recognized as thirst. At least something was working.

The nurse seemed to sense his frustration and placed a flexible straw between his lips. He sucked at it, but little happened at first. Then he felt the cold water flow over part of his tongue and trickle down his throat. He also noticed a trickle running down the side of his neck onto his chest—he couldn't feel his lower lip. His eyes darted toward the woman's as he heard her tell him not to worry.

"Everyone spills a little of the first drink of water after surgery," she said in a voice that was soft and kind.

It was really annoying him that he couldn't remember her name. He reached for his aching chest with his free hand, groping for an incision or whatever it was that was causing his pain, only to find multiple sticky ECG leads with their attached wires tugging on the hairs of his chest.

"I'm sorry, Dr. Bender. I didn't mean that you had real surgery. You had a cardiac catheterization and little tiny tubes put in your heart's arteries. Maybe your chest hurts from the resuscitation. They said that Dr. Stern and the ER nurses pounded pretty hard on you. They didn't have to shock you though. That's a good thing."

Suddenly Bryson knew her name. Kay Jensen, the nurse/patient who compulsively said, "That's a good thing" after every sentence. It was the most annoying cliché in the world. Or was, "What can I say?" more annoying? He couldn't decide.

"Why can't I concentrate?" He screamed, but again no words came forth.

"The recovery nurse told me that those little tubes or pipes the doctors put in your heart vessels were really hard to put in but that it will really help you. They call that heart angioplasty. That's a really good thing to have done for you—don't you think?"

"I think he knows what an angioplasty is," Marisa said from the doorway. For hours she had put up with the sweet nurse explaining things to her in fourth-grade language. "Thank goodness you're awake, Bryson." She nudged the nurse out of the way and kissed her husband on the forehead. "Do you remember anything? I know that the last time you were given Versed, you lost track of a whole day."

Bryson tried to tell her about his bad dream, but no words would come. He stared up at his beautiful wife and hoped she wouldn't be too worried about him or be upset with him because he didn't answer. Then he fell asleep.

***

It took a few more hours but he finally started to remember again. Little by little the bits and pieces of his previous hours—or was it days—started to come together. He could remember driving to the hospital for the baby's delivery and he remembered sitting in the car, not able to reach the start button. Then he remembered the dizziness, pain and nausea. He had a vague memory of Stern's roughness as he dragged him out of the car, and he clearly remembered the breech of sterile technique committed by the ER nurse. That was about it for the memories. Marisa had to explain to him three, maybe four times what the cardiac catheterization had shown and how many stents had been placed in his coronary arteries.

Two days later he was sitting up on the edge of the bed while his long-time friend, neurologist Dave Hadden, patiently explained that Bryson's heart attack had the secondary effect of producing a small clot, which had in turn produced a tiny stroke. The clot got stuck in an artery in his brain, blocking the free flow of blood to some of the brain cells, which had then affected his speech and the right corner of his face. There was some weakness of his left arm and leg.

"You have got to be kidding me," were the first intelligible words he was able to speak. The words were garbled and the volume went up and down, but he was finally speaking. Everyone in the room smiled and glanced at each other.

"I work out four times a week. I'm only ten pounds over ideal weight. I even take Advil every day for my knees. This shouldn't be happening to me."

As he said the words, all of which were true, he slowly realized that those in the room could barely understand his garbled speech. What he had done in the past to stay fit was now irrelevant. It had happened. He was now a statistic. He was one of the young sick guys who, when averaged in with the ninety-year-old men with strokes and heart attacks, produced a reasonable mean age of death. It wasn't his diet, or genetics, or lack of exercise that had done this to him. It was his lifestyle: his medical practice with its frantic unpredictable hours, carrying the burden of people's lives and potential lawsuits, and now the office fire with all the uncertainties. They had all culminated in a degree of stress, which had pushed his body's tolerance to the limit.

Not because he was a good doctor but because he was a horrible patient, was he allowed to go home on the fourth day. As his stroke symptoms vanished, his orneriness was increasing to the point that the nurses were begging his doctors to let him go home. A home health care plan was set up with visiting nurses.

Checking out of the hospital seemed to take longer than the entire medical event. When Bryson looked at the bill he nearly had another stroke. Four days at twenty-five thousand dollars a day. What a deal! That was more than he would get for delivering the next fifty babies, if he could ever go back to work. The thought crossed his mind that if he had died the bill would have been a heck of a lot less.

Bryson asked his wife to drive slowly as they approached the neighborhood. His front yard and the house itself had never looked so good. It was a bright, sunshiny spring day and the afternoon sun was casting just enough shadow across the driveway to enhance the beauty of his place. He couldn't remember the last time he had stood out on his street and looked at the elevation of his house with its many different roof lines and the intricate patterns and the color around the eaves. Marisa and he had tried eight different color swatches of paint on the stucco in order to get the color just right. Now, he questioned whether he had ever noticed which one they picked out. It was amazing how a rush every day to the office and hospital could sidetrack and even erase life's seemingly important decisions and events.

Marisa had been like a junkyard guard dog, keeping visitors away from Bryson's hospital room. Almost no one had been allowed to visit. She had phoned the kids at their scattered locations around the county to reassure them that their dad would be fine and that they were not to rush home. Friends and family had all been kept at bay. Even Teri, his secretary, was asked to handle the problems of the burned office and relocating patients the best she could but not to come by the hospital. Marisa knew that her husband would hate their friends and family to see him in his disabled condition.

"Hospitals are for medical care, not for social encounters," had always been Bryson's firm belief. He was pleased that she had honored that philosophy. Visits at home in a few days would be a different thing altogether.

Getting from the car to the house had exhausted him. When he came through the front door, leaning on Marisa as he slowly walked, he was overwhelmed with the fragrance of flowers. He looked up to see arrangements scattered around the room, each with a small get-well card or note attached.

"Who died?" he asked Marisa and Madeline, his youngest daughter.

Madeline and Marisa looked at each other and smiled. Their man was home. The spark was back in the plug. Now, hopefully, it could start a new fire.

"I'm starving. Hospital food is for the pigeons that hang out on the windowsills," he said.

He sat in his favorite blue leather recliner and read the get-well cards and notes on the flowers. Madeline insisted that she carry each arrangement into the family room for him to inspect before she would give him the card to read. He loved the special attention he was getting. He made a couple of comments, loud enough to be heard in the kitchen, about how great the aroma of the soon-to-be-served dinner was, but by the time Marisa had finished preparing his favorite beef enchilada dinner and helped him up to the table, Bryson was half-asleep and was ready for bed.

He lost track of time the next several days. When he awoke one morning he lay still in bed, listening to the sounds coming from the other parts of the house and from the birds in the backyard. He wiggled his extremities and manipulated his face and jaw muscles to see how he was healing. He then began talking out loud, saying the Pledge of Allegiance and repeating the words of a few songs he knew. He spared himself pain and discouragement by not singing the words. His speech had improved, and though he felt definite weakness in his entire body, his arms and legs felt strong. He sat up in the bed and reached for the glass of water on his end table. Gingerly taking a sip, he let out a little cheer. He could even hold water in his mouth without it cascading down his cheek. It had been ten days since the heart attack and stroke. Two weeks since the fire.

"Get up and get dressed, you lazybones," Marisa said as she opened the curtains, letting in the morning sun. "Brian is coming by with some papers for you to sign and to discuss your office insurance policy. He said he got a call from the agent yesterday. Also, Dr. Southwick, your upstairs neighbor, needs to see you. He will be here at eleven."

She came over to the bedside and leaned over him, giving him a kiss on the forehead, and then she left him alone in the room, shouting instructions as she disappeared down the hall. "Don't forget to brush your teeth. Your breath could take paint off an engine block."

Bryson grasped the wooden pole of the poster bed and tried to stand up only to fall sideways back onto the bed. His chest still hurt like heck—someone from the hospital finally admitted that an onlooker to his resuscitation had heard his ribs crack. He lay there half-on and half-off the bed, considering whether to call Marisa. He was lying in an awkward position, but he didn't try to move for a few minutes. Was he going to wait for someone to help him out of bed every morning for the rest of his life? Going back to the operating room and Labor and Delivery—not to mention his burned-out office—seemed an impossible task if he couldn't even get out of bed by himself. He watched the numbers on the alarm clock flip over a few times. That was all it took. He wasn't going to let the minutes and days of his life slip away with nothing to show for them.

He took a deep breath and rocked his body back and forth until he had the momentum to sit forward with his feet on the thick carpet. His heart responded to the effort with a rapid pounding, but no deep pain. He could almost feel his blood jetting through the four tiny new stents in his coronary arteries. He took hold of the nightstand, and with less effort than he expected, was standing on his feet. He was afraid to let go of the table for fear he would be dizzy, but did so anyway. Hey, he was stable, and without further hesitation, was on his way into the bathroom. He could take care of himself.

*** 

"Here's the skinny," Brian said, sliding a yellow legal-size notepad across the table to Bryson and Marisa. "The insurance company is waiting for the assessment from the fire department, but they will start issuing checks monthly to cover your office overhead. If it is determined that your practice is a total loss, they will pay a lump sum for the residual of the policy. That could take a year to determine. But don't hold your breath." Brian was the eternal pessimist.

"What about the disability insurance?" Marisa asked. Bryson had paid disability insurance premiums for medical illnesses or injuries for over twenty years.

"I called and got a hold of a man named Pete. He is sending you the claim forms. Are you going to be disabled?" Brian asked. "Lots of people go back to work after a heart attack or stroke."

Like any non-physician, when it came to really knowing anything helpful about medicine, he relied on what he had read in the paper or seen on the news.

"Your disability policy will probably require you to try to go back to work and then determine what percentage of disability you have. Maybe they will require you to retrain in some other specialty if you can't do your primary job. The days of the old disability payoffs are gone."

Bryson knew all of this, but also knew that his policy, the one he purchased over twenty years ago, gave him full coverage for any degree of disability.

Marisa seemed distressed by Brian's assessment. "Why did we even pay for that piece of crap policy if it's so bad?"

Bryson looked at her and laughed. Their life had been so stable and planned with every minute of every day, prescribed like some sort of anti-awareness medicine, that he found Marisa's sudden concern for money and its continuing flow to be the first funny thing he had witnessed in weeks. Of course, he was going to set her and their attorney straight on the realities of his policy, but maybe it would be good for everybody to worry a little.

***

Bryson had been sitting at the dining room table way too long. When he tried to stand, his legs didn't want to cooperate. "Crap," he muttered under his breath, not wanting

Marisa to have to come running to render help. Before she could return from the entry hall, he had dragged himself up and had made it to his leather rocker-recliner. He collapsed into the chair and let it rock back and forth on its own until it came to rest. He had no sooner reached for the remote control when he heard new voices in the hallway.

"Don't get up," came the familiar voice of his long-time office neighbor, Dr. Southwick. Bryson was surprised; he couldn't remember Southwick ever being in his home. They hadn't conversed since the day of the fire.

"Like I could jump right up if I wanted to," Bryson fussed. "Come in and sit down."

Southwick pulled a dining room chair over close to Bryson's recliner and sat down. Marisa poked her head in the room and whispered a goodbye. The two men just sat there for a couple of minutes staring out a large plate-glass window that looked out onto the pool, the manicured grass, the rows of flowers and the green cactus-strewn hills beyond. Three or four buzzards circled high in the distance. The house sat at the edge of the national forest, which in this part of the country was desert land, not the tall pines most associated with national forests.

"That is an amazing view. How often do you see wildlife?" Though the two men had seen one another almost daily in the halls of the hospital and office building and had often eaten lunch at the same cafeteria table, Southwick knew very little about the Bender family or their home.

"Coyotes and fox are regulars. Occasionally, we'll see javelina families wander by to stop at the fountain in front for a drink." Bryson was working hard at forming the words and not spraying saliva on his lap.

"Sounds like your speech is coming back quickly. My brother had an episode that sounds a lot like yours. It took some work, but he was back to normal within three months. When he asked me for advice, I told him to get up and start walking and singing to himself. It worked."

Bryson turned his head toward Southwick, raising his eyebrows in question, but then thinking about it for a moment, he nodded. "I'll give it a try. Thanks."

"I have some information about the office fire I wanted to share with you." He let the words hang for a moment then continued. "Also, I have a proposal. If you don't mind, I'll just run through it."

Bryson didn't try to answer, but instead nodded his approval.

"A patient of mine—I did a total hip on him last year—anyway, he works in city hall. He called me this week, out of the blue, to tell me that the fire investigation team was talking in their lunch break room, bragging about how the city and county were both going to cite the hospital for multiple violations of the city fire code. They were especially hot under the collar because some hospital maintenance guys had left two open five-gallon buckets of some type of flammable solvent in a back room of one of the offices. My patient milked one of the investigators later and found that the room was my back room where the old X-ray machine was being dismantled. The guy claimed that it was the cause of the building's fire. Somehow, the flammable solvent leaked or was spilled and ran down between the walls into your office. An unknown spark, maybe from your water heater or something, ignited it, causing the fire. My insurance company let me know that they are involved in their own investigation. I would imagine yours is, too."

Southwick looked at Bryson and paused. Then he went on, "I don't know about you, Bender, but that fire has probably destroyed my practice along with my office. I'm too old and tired to try to rebuild a patient base necessary to support a staff and still have something left over to take home. I get a migraine just thinking about starting over again. I haven't talked to an attorney about it yet, but I have been pondering the possibility of suing the hospital for not taking care of the old X-ray machine months ago when they were told to. They are also at fault for letting those idiots leave flammable solvents lying around in my office. And look at you! There isn't a sane person on earth who wouldn't agree that the stress of the fire led to your heart attack and stroke. It would be a slam dunk for you to sue the imbeciles."

Bryson found the story plausible, but knew the dead-end street most litigation goes down after weeks and months of accusation, depositions, filings and counter-filings. He could barely think about the rehab and physical therapy he faced in the coming weeks, let alone the task of trying to sue some huge corporation. He almost said no at the outset, but didn't want to damper Southwick's enthusiasm.

"Why don't you approach one of the better litigation law firms downtown and see what they think." Bryson paused for a moment to make sure his mouth wasn't acting ahead of his reasoning. Southwick seemed to understand the somewhat slurred sentence. "I'll go halves with you up to a thousand bucks to buy a seasoned attorney's opinion. If he thinks we have a reasonable case that can be settled quickly, then I would probably be interested. As you can see, I'm not much help at the moment."

Southwick smiled for the first time since he had walked through the Benders' front entry.

The men discussed a few details. Although Bryson said little, he could feel aching in his face and jaw muscles from the effort of enunciating the words. He nodded in agreement from time to time, but was getting tired and hinted with his body language that the conversation needed to end.

"I'll get the best law firm in the state interested or we won't even bother thinking about it," Southwick promised as he stood and leaned over to shake Bryson's hand. "You get well now. I'll keep you up to date. Start walking and try that singing. Like I said, it worked for my brother. His wife was about to throw him out though; his voice sounds like a cross between the rip of a rag and the strip of a gear." Southwick laughed at his own joke and waved goodbye.

\*\*\*

Spinners was the newest and classiest full-service gym imaginable. Just walking into the lobby one would think he had missed a turn and found the Ritz-Carlton instead. The rows after rows of spinning bikes faced windows overlooking a sea of treadmills and elliptical machines. There were flat screen TVs on nearly every machine and wall surface in the building. Outside the juice bar was a sea of shiny new free weights. A high-tech ventilation system kept the place smelling like an ocean breeze. Best of all were the steam showers, saunas and whirlpool baths. Four different temperatured baths were agitating in front of his eyes . . . "scalding hot, perfectly hot, wonderfully warm and Arctic ice cold." How could life get any better?

Bryson didn't even hear the sales manager explain the membership contract. He was already thinking about how great the steam bath and whirlpools would feel on his knees after a workout on the elliptical trainer. He pulled his American Express card out of his wallet and scratched his name on the X.

"When do you want to start, Mr. Bender?" the attendant asked.

"Hey, I'd start right now, but I don't have any workout clothes."

"Not a problem. We have a full line of Nike apparel in the shop behind the juice bar."

Twenty minutes and six hundred bucks later, Bryson had changed into his new togs and was trying to figure out the intricate programming instructions on the video screen of the shiny new Life Fitness elliptical machine.

"Just step up and start peddling, and I'll talk you through the menu," came a voice off to his left side. He turned his head to see a tall man in his early sixties standing on the next elliptical machine.

"That would be great, if you don't mind. It's my first day here."

"I'm working on bad knees. My name is Matt."

"It was ticker problems for me," Bryson said, intentionally not mentioning his stroke. He extended his hand and exchanged names with his new workout partner. He had taken Doctor Southwick's advice but found it too hot and boring to go for long walks.

Forty minutes later, the two men were sitting across from one another in a steam-filled room, waiting for their heart rates to settle down to a comfortable eighty beats per minute. Bryson's workout had been surprisingly easy for him with the exception that about every ninety seconds he would have a flashback to the crushing chest pain he had experienced less than four weeks before. The actual rib pain had subsided but there was still a rainbow of bruised skin over his sternum.

"How long ago did you have heart problems? Or do you mind talking about it?" Matt asked.

"I won't bore you with the long version. Four weeks ago I was working my butt off delivering babies, and then I had my heart attack. They put a few stents in my coronary arteries, sent me home to sleep off the anesthesia and then told me to join a gym. This is my first week here."

"Would you mind speaking up a bit; the steam jet is messing with my hearing."

"It's my voice," said Bryson. I had a tiny stroke when my heart stopped beating and it screwed up my speech. I'm sure you noticed. Thanks for being so polite."

"Hey, it's not a problem."

"What do you do for a living, Matt? It is Matt, right?"

"I'm with an insurance company. I've been there for a long time—too long, actually. I've been toying with the idea of quitting, taking my pension and finding something else to do and see. When the kids I sold their first car insurance policies to started collecting on their life insurance policies, I started thinking that it's time to quit—before my wife collects on mine."

Bryson laughed but knew that he had entertained the same thoughts.

"Now with my bum knees, I have an excuse to take a leave of absence from work and decide if I might like retirement."

Bryson looked at the scars on Matt's knee and thought about the small scar in his groin where the heart catheter had been introduced into his right femoral artery.

"Retirement sounds like a great idea to me right now, too. My problem is that I don't know whether I can afford it or not. I have a daughter who wants to go to an Ivy League school that will cost more for one year than my entire education did. One minute my attorneys tell me I'll be a multi-millionaire, and the next phone call I get they warn me of technicalities that could put me back in the delivery room till the day I die. Whoa, I'm getting overheated; time for the cold plunge."

The two men shook hands later as they left Spinners, agreeing on a time to work out again. Heading out of the parking lot, Bryson was driving behind a car that had a bumper sticker with a subtle advertisement for an insurance company. The company name looked familiar, Secured Future of America. That was the same company that Bryson had bought his new office insurance from just days before the fire. Then he saw Matt look at him in the rearview mirror and wave. *That's a very strange coincidence*, Bryson thought as he waved back.

✳✳✳

Marisa pulled into the garage soon after Bryson. The three separate garages with their own doors added a classy touch to the Tuscan villa. He had been trying to work up the strength to get out of the car and was startled when the garage door next to his driver's window started to rise. Marisa had been at the high school helping Madeline fill out her scholarship application for state universities. Madeline had wanted to go to Duke or one of the Ivy League schools on the East Coast and had received acceptances from every one of them. The problem was the cost. The other four Bender kids had gone to in-state universities and worked summer jobs. Both of the older girls had married and their husbands had good jobs. The caboose of the family was going to require much more. She was exceptionally bright and unequally spoiled.

Scholarships were hard to come by, and Bryson suspected that when the big-name schools found out Madeline's dad was a doctor, they would scratch her from the list. When he had added up the cost for four years at Duke or Yale, Bryson had broken out in a cold sweat. He had suggested that the East Coast was too far from home for an innocent eighteen-year-old female. He had insisted that she at least apply for one or both of the in-state universities. The cost difference over four years would be two hundred thousand dollars.

Madeline had not taken the news quietly, but when the fire and the heart attack rocked the family's life, she picked up the applications for local schools.

"How was your workout?" Marisa said with a smile as she took Bryson's gym bag from him and gave him a kiss. She slipped her arm around his waist and walked to the kitchen door. She had taken on a more laid-back demeanor the last couple of weeks, letting unplanned activities fill in the gaps of her busy days without stressing her. Perhaps the shock of the office fire and then the reality check of her husband's mortality had made her put the frivolities of their life on a back burner.

"The workout was fine. I watched an old episode of M*A*S*H while I did the elliptical. Maybe I should have stayed in the Army and become a trauma surgeon." They both laughed and then she stopped him in front of the door to the kitchen and kissed him with a more than usual heat of passion.

"What's this all about?" he murmured between kisses.

"I just want you to know that I'm glad you are here. I've been so worried about you, but I've been afraid to admit it to myself or to you."

He took her hand and opened the door. He led her down the hallway, passing the kitchen.

"Don't even think about it," Marisa said gently, pulling her hand away. "Your doctor specifically said to limit your exercise. You've had your workout for today." She gave him a playful squeeze and a laugh then left him standing in the hallway.

Bryson had learned long ago that most things usually work out for the best.

Moments later, Madeline burst through the front door with two girlfriends in tow.

"Mom, Dad, guess what? Come and see what I've got."

Marisa called out from the kitchen, and soon the four women and Bryson were sitting around the kitchen table and staring at a brown business envelope. The return address was written inside a crest, which Bryson couldn't read upside down.

"I give up," he said, cherishing the grin on her face. "Did you get the job at Wal-Mart?"

"No, Dad. What I got is an invitation to attend Duke University. With, I would like to add, a waver of tuition for the first year." She slid the letter out of the envelope and handed it to Bryson and Marisa. "Isn't it fantastic?" she said dancing around the room. "Now, I don't even have to mail in those stupid applications to the U of A and to ASU."

Unwilling to put a damper on his youngest daughter's happiness, he smiled and laughed with the others. He would figure out a way to pay for the rest of her expenses to go away to school.

# Chapter Three

# BUREAUCRACY

Little Johnny Southwick had never been one to let other kids kick sand in his face. As an adult he had taken a tactful approach to confrontations, but when diplomacy failed, he wasn't one to shrink from a rumble. When he met in the hospital administrator's office to discuss how the hospital could help him rescue his orthopedic practice from its charred pyre, he faced the blank face of Mr. Henry Heiner, the hospital CEO, a corporate veteran. The two men faced off across a large walnut desk. It wasn't their first confrontation. John had been the Chief of the Orthopedic Department for several terms and would often come to this room to argue the needs of his physicians. That had been a position he was used to assuming. This was an altogether different matter.

Henry Heiner was known to have worked his way up the corporate ladder by always having the interest of the hospital foremost in his mind, right behind the interest of Henry Heiner. He always dressed with impeccable style; his shoes were polished to a military sheen. He had no friends among the hospital's physicians, in fact, most of the hospital employees avoided eye contact with him. The board of directors of the multi-hospital chain, however, loved him. Over the past ten years he had brought their bottom line from red to green.

The hospital's board, fronted by Heiner, had a zero-fault policy. Heiner had been told by his board of directors to admit no fault in the cause of the office building fire. Many of the other doctors with offices in the burned building had been happy to be allowed out of their leases and to be rid of their worn furniture in a no-fault agreement with their insurance carriers. Many had quickly moved on to new digs or left town. Then there were the ones with collateral damage, like Bryson Bender and John Southwick.

John, unlike most of the other doctors, knew who was at fault. Heiner had known about the leaky X-ray machine for months and had even previously agreed that the machine was a fire hazard. It was also Heiner who insisted that hospital employees have access to Dr. Southwick's office. John had suggested a professional crew be used to remove the complicated two-thousand-pound apparatus. Today, however, Mr. Heiner had no memory of the machine being a problem and even went so far as to claim that the machine hadn't been removed earlier because Dr. Southwick's staff wouldn't let the dismantlers into the office.

A folder labeled "Office Complex Fire—CONFIDENTIAL" rested beneath Heiner's elbow. Heiner glanced at the folder during the meeting, but never removed his arm, nor did he open the folder.

Big John Southwick was getting nowhere with the corporate gatekeeper and was about to leave in disgust when Heiner's phone rang. Heiner answered it with an expression of concern. "Excuse me, Doctor, but I must take this call," he said, rotating his leather chair away from Southwick.

Call it foolishness or call it brilliance, but as the muffled conversation dragged on, John reached out and with a surgeon's deftness, snatched the folder off of the desk. With a single motion, he removed the contents and replaced the red-lettered folder back on the desk. Next, he rolled the stack of papers into a bundle while at the same time unzipping the fly of his loose-fitting pants. With only a faux cough to cover any sound, he slipped the papers into the front of his pants and zipped up.

"Sorry about that, Doctor," Heiner said, turning his chair back around to face John. "I'm glad we had this little chat," he said, rising to extend his hand. "Good luck to you. As you know, your hospital privileges are still in place, so we hope you will bring all of your future patients to our facility for their surgery and rehabilitation."

John stayed seated in his chair. He worried that the stolen or borrowed papers might slide down his pant leg if he stood.

"Henry, would you mind if I use your telephone for a private call? I'm going to miss my broker in New York if I wait another five minutes. I've got to arrange to pay my past-due bills from the office since my receipts all burned."

"Take all the time you need," Heiner said, picking up the folder from his desk and placing it inside the glass cupboard of the credenza positioned against the wall. He slid the phone toward John and walked out of the room.

Southwick slid the stack of papers down his leg and tucked the rolled papers into a calf-length sock, fitting it around his ankle like a paper cast. Thank goodness he always wore the extra-length, anti-embolus socks. He picked up the receiver, illuminating the light on the phone, waited a few seconds and then hung it up. As he walked into Heiner's outer office there was no sign of the administrator.

He waved at a few of his colleagues in the hallway but made no indication that he had time to chat. Twice he had stopped to readjust the papers in his stocking.

Inside his pickup truck, Southwick breathed easier. He stashed the papers in the truck's console. He had used the truck as a tax dodge. Six years ago, he bought a small farm and added three horses, two goats and a fat hog that he had intended to butcher. So far, Southwick had not had the heart to kill the massive animal that he had affectionately named Dispose-all.

***

The telephone beside the Benders' bed rang. Bryson lifted the phone from its cradle before the second ring. Over the past thirty years of middle-of-the-night calls, Bryson had tried to minimize the times Marisa was awakened by the phone.

"This is Dr. Bender," he said in a sleepy voice.

"Wake up and get to the hospital before you miss this delivery," the voice said, startling Bryson. "Just kidding, this is Southwick. I saw your wife going out your driveway and she said to wake you up. You are getting too used to long afternoon naps. I'm out in front of your house with some papers you'll want to see."

Bryson shook off the fog of sleep and sat on the edge of the bed, getting his bearings. Afternoon naps were a new experience for him. He had always worked the entire day, usually doing some type of surgery over the noon hour. A mid-afternoon nap would have been wonderful on the days following those thousands of deliveries in the middle of the night. Now that he had received doctor's orders to take them, naps were somewhat disturbing. Not only didn't he wake up as readily, he was also having strange dreams.

He stared at the phone and wondered whether the phone had actually rung. Years ago, after an unusually exhausting day, he had once awakened in the middle of the night, believing that he had received a call from the hospital about a patient who was ready to deliver her baby. He had gotten out of bed, dressed and driven to the hospital. When he entered Labor and Delivery at three in the morning, he was told that there were no patients in labor, not his or anyone else's. The nursing staff assured him that they had not called.

The ringing front doorbell startled him to full consciousness.

"Come on in the kitchen," Bryson told the aging orthopedic surgeon. "How about a Coke?"

"How about a glass of champagne?" Southwick said in an upbeat tone.

"Sorry, there's no alcohol in the house. Is the news that good?"

"You can be the judge of that, but to me it looks far too good to be true."

"You know the danger of that statement, don't you? If it's too good to be true?" Bryson said, as he pulled a couple of glasses from the cupboard, filled them with ice and retrieved a partially empty two-liter bottle of Diet Coke.

"Help yourself. We only serve the good stuff to company," Bryson joked.

Southwick spread the contents of a large business envelope on the table and the men sat down to digest the information. The frosty glasses of soda were soon forgotten. The first two pages laid out an interchange between the maintenance company that the hospital employed and the administrator, Mr. Henry Heiner. Page three, dated four days before the office building fire, warned the administrator that the removal of the X-ray machine from the office of Dr. Southwick was something they had never attempted because it would require cutting torches and a special solvent that was flammable and toxic. The copy of the email Heiner sent back to the manager of the maintenance company stated that he didn't care how they removed the machine. "Just get it out of there by the weekend."

Page four's reply was sent the Friday afternoon before the fire, telling Mr. Heiner that solvent had been used in large volumes to clean the drainage pans of the developing machine; and a five-gallon container of the liquid had been tipped over without anyone noticing it, and that the resulting fumes had caused the office staff of Dr. Southwick and possibly additional offices to evacuate the building. The men working on the machine had also left the building because of the fumes. They had not taken their equipment with them but would go back later when the air cleared and try to cut the last couple of pipes and floor bolts holding the machine in place.

On the pages that followed, there were legal volleys of accusations and recriminations between the owner of the maintenance company, his attorney, Heiner, the CEO of the hospital's parent corporation and its attorneys. In several of the statements and memos, Heiner and the maintenance company blamed one another for the fire. Most incriminating was the CEO's memo stating that the machine should have been removed during the week Dr. Southwick had been on vacation three months prior, as Southwick had suggested, and that everyone needed to remain tightlipped about the solvent being spilled.

"Our insurance company will pay for the physical damage. The tenants can worry about their own problems regarding any loss of records and time out of the office. Most, if not all, of the physicians have office insurance," the note stated.

As if to make it worse for the hospital, on a separate sheet of paper stamped confidential, was a note from the fire marshal telling the hospital that an empty five-gallon can of cleaning solvent had been discovered in the ashes of the fire and that Dr. Southwick had no explanation as to the origin. "Did the hospital, the landlord of the building, know anything regarding its presence?"

Heiner had fired back an email stating that he "hadn't the slightest idea how the container got into the building. Surely it must be the doctor's mistake."

Dr. Southwick stood up and started pacing around the kitchen. "There is a mistake, all right! Heiner lied to the fire marshal, which is the same as lying to the police. I went over this with the attorney we just retained. He thinks it is not just a smoking gun, but the guillotine, for the hospital. Incidentally, you owe me two hundred bucks."

"So, what amount of damage do we ask the hospital for?" Bryson asked, trying to assimilate the news and exactly what it would mean to him.

"Our new attorney said to calculate our loss of income, just like one would calculate the sale of any small business. Three years' gross income was a suggestion. I think I will demand five million. That doesn't include the money for the sharks. The attorney called a friend of a friend and found out that the hospital carries fifty-million dollars in insurance liability coverage. I'm going for its throat."

Bryson stared out the window and took a couple of deep breaths. He had never earned a million dollars in one year or even three years for that matter. Maybe he should have been an orthopedist.

"Tell me this," Bryson said. "If the hospital and Heiner hid the truth and are found guilty of a felony, say willful negligence or something like that, wouldn't that negate their liability insurance company's responsibility to pay?" Bryson was now staring at Southwick. "And it probably would tie everything up in court for years. I think that if we want to get anything out of this experience besides bleeding ulcers we should ask for a reasonable settlement then take some money and run for it."

Southwick looked at him as if he had grown a cycloptic eye. "Listen, Bender, this is my only chance to survive the next twenty years. I owe money on everything and still have three young kids to educate. My practice has evaporated. My patients have disappeared like roaches when the lights come on. Besides, I have fought with the administration for twenty-five long years. For once I want to win."

"How are you going to explain taking the papers from Heiner's desk?"

"Easy. I copied them in the presence of a notary who will swear that the copies are real. Then I went back to the hospital and dropped them off in the mailroom with Heiner's name on them. He will get the originals back tomorrow and will just have to guess how they ended up in the mailroom. I've planned this all out this morning. I know it will work. Two hundred bucks, please."

Bryson looked up to see Southwick holding out his hand like a street beggar. The man no longer looked like the seasoned professional, but a crazed fanatic, desperate for a mega-dollar closure that Bryson could not imagine ever happening.

Bryson got up from the table and excused himself to retrieve his wallet. He felt dizzy and confused. He had never sued anyone and hated the guys who did. "Malpractice attorneys are the pond scum of the world," his professors had always said. Bryson knew lots of attorneys and liked most of them. He just didn't like the idea of living from day to day wondering whether some lawsuit would make him rich or not.

In the bedroom he found his wallet and looked under his driver's license where he always tucked a couple of big bills and walked back to the kitchen. "Here is your money, John. I want to talk this lawsuit business over with Marisa and my own attorney and maybe do a little research on my own. Why don't you have your attorney put my name on the paperwork as a John Doe for the time being? I just need to get my health back before I pick a fight with somebody. I really appreciate your time and the risk you have taken and I will back you up every step of the way. Just give me a few weeks."

Southwick looked puzzled, as if he didn't know whether he had been misunderstood, fired, dismissed or all three. He accepted the two hundred dollars and started to speak, but Bryson held out his hand like a traffic cop. Southwick nodded and turned and walked away.

Alone again, Bryson collapsed into the white plantation rocker on his front porch. If he never saw Southwick again, it would be all right. If he never saw the hospital or the inside of an operating room again, it would be just fine too.

Bryson was finished practicing a profession that had become too taxing and too unappreciated and no longer fun. He had made up his mind. Sitting there on the porch, he rocked back and forth in the chair, breathing the fresh spring air and listening to a pair of doves cooing in a nearby tree. Strange, he thought. He didn't remember ever taking the time to sit in this rocker ever since the day twenty-some years ago when he had untied it from the roof of the old Oldsmobile station wagon and carried it up to the porch. Where had the years gone? As his mind wandered, it wasn't long before he felt some pangs of hunger. At first, a warm chocolate chip cookie sounded good, but then he remembered another taste: chicken fried steak.

# Chapter Four

# SURPRISE

Everybody likes a surprise. Presents, not just on birthdays or Christmas; tax refund checks that the accountant under-calculated; news of healthy grandbabies born to healthy moms; even those unwanted surprise birthday parties that one insists he or she doesn't want but deep inside hopes someone will plan anyway.

The Benders' surprise was so unexpected that after the cheering and crying was over they still could not believe it wasn't a dream. They had gone to the mall to find some new pants for Bryson. He refused to put on any of the pants he had worn to the office for many years and had even gone so far as to stuff them into garbage bags to take to the Salvation Army. "Let someone else wear them," he insisted, leaving his closet's pants rack empty except for a couple pair of Sunday slacks and several pair of faded jeans.

The cell phone in Marisa's purse chirped away as she struggled to find the correct pocket in her purse. She caught it just before it went to voicemail.

"This is Marisa. Yes, he is right here."

She handed the phone to Bryson, who had walked ahead of her and had to turn back.

"Who is it?" he asked, slightly irritated at the intrusion on one of his rare ventures into the Monster Mall.

"Someone from Trans Advantage Insurance. The name sounds familiar."

"This is Dr. Bender."

"Doc? This is Matt Jamison, you know, from Spinners."

"Hey Matt, how are you doing? I missed you yesterday."

"I had to work late. As a matter of fact, I was working on your policy information. That's how I got your wife's phone number."

Bryson stopped walking and leaned against a pillar at the side of the entrance to the mall. "Which policy are you talking about?"

"It's your disability policy. The one you took out . . . it looks like in 1981. I came across your name in the file and reviewed it . . . that's my job. Anyway, you were telling me about your health problems and so I took the liberty of perusing the thing. This is a fantastic policy."

"I guess in all the craziness of the last month I forgot all about it. I don't even remember if I paid this year's premium." Bryson waved at Marisa, coaxing her to come over to him. He motioned for something to write on and a pen.

"You paid it a year ago. It is due again any day but when you are not able to work the premium is waived. What you need to do is let me get the paperwork to you and get it turned in. I see that there is only a sixty-day waiting period, which means it should start paying out within the month." Matt's voice sounded excited to be announcing a payout rather than discussing premiums. "I can drop the papers off to you at your house or to the gym."

"Yeah, sure. Just bring them to the gym if you don't mind?"

"That will work out fine. I'll fill out as much as I can. You will need to get some medical records and an updated evaluation from your doctors. It's a hassle but it could pan out to be worth your time."

Bryson's heart was starting to pound and his knees felt a bit weak. He nodded toward a cement bench, and Marisa took his elbow to help him, not that she would be of any use if his legs gave out.

"Matt, could you hang on for a second?" Bryson settled onto the bench and took a deep breath. "Sorry. Tell me something. What exactly is the benefit of the policy you are talking about? It's been a while since I had time to review it."

By this time Bryson was holding the phone away from his

ear, and Marisa was cheek-to-cheek with him, trying to hear both sides of the conversation.

"It pays ten thousand dollars a month plus it has an annual cost-of-living increase," Matt said in a matter of fact voice, as though he handed out buckets full of money every day.

"How long does that continue?" Marisa asked, then blushed as she realized she was barging in on the conversation.

"It will pay out monthly as long as you can't perform one hundred percent of your ordinary occupation until age sixty-five. Since you paid with personal funds, the benefit is also tax free."

Bryson held the phone away from his ear and stared at it as though the tooth fairy was going to fly right out of the mouthpiece.

Marisa put her hand over her mouth and started to giggle. She walked away.

"Doc, are you there? Doc?"

"I'm here, Matt. Tell me where you are and I'll come by for the paperwork right now. I haven't anything better to do and I need to get out and about for a while."

Bryson snapped the cell phone shut and looked at his wife. Simultaneously, they broke out in smiles that were nearly painful to their unexercised facial muscles. Neither of them spoke. Marisa held out her hand to help her stunned husband to his feet. He nodded toward the parking lot. The pants shopping could wait.

✳✳✳

The paperwork from Matt had been straightforward. The prospect of getting a huge return on the effort made it painless. The only problem was that they did not have a copy of the original policy. The agent who had written the insurance had retired years ago and moved to Alaska. The realization of their lack of attention to detail recently started the two worrying. What about the rest of the insurance? They hoped Matt could find back-up copies. What else had they been paying premiums on for years? Homeowners and life insurance policies were somewhere around the house, or was it somewhere around their old house? Or had they burned up in the office fire?

Late in the afternoon the two of them sat at their kitchen table and tried to make a list of all of their insurance policies. Bryson had always handled the bills and for years had taken the household bills to the office to pay. Everything, including the past year's checkbook stubs, the receipts and all of the insurance policies had burned up along with Bryson's office records and patients' charts.

Their memory produced a list that was short and had lots of blank spaces where names of companies or agents or amounts belonged. Bryson knew he had a couple of disability policies but the details escaped him. Since his stroke, some of his memory was just plain gone. He had to pause at times even to remember his extended family's names. How could he be expected to remember the family finances?

"Bryson, what good are all those thousands of dollars we've spent for insurance premiums if we can't find the rest of the policies? We won't get a thing," Marisa commented in a flat voice.

"Call Teri," he said in frustration. "She stuffed all the envelopes and mailed everything that has ever left my office for the last fifteen years; maybe she can sort out some of it."

He picked up his camera and walked out to the front yard to take some pictures of his neighborhood, the place he had taken for granted and ignored for the last twenty years.

\*\*\*

Often fear is like a rainstorm. One can watch it approaching on the horizon, anticipating the energy within. And then one can feel its fury when it arrives; yet if one is patient, the storm and the fear will pass with time, usually in a very short time, and then life resumes its normalcy.

The Benders' fear, like a passing summer storm, was short lived. Not only did Teri remember most of the insurance policies and their respective agents and companies, but she had kept at home a copy of an emergency liquidation plan Bryson had written some ten years prior. Within the couple of days, Marisa with Teri's help had called or written to all the insurance companies and had received confirmation of the various policies' coverage or lack thereof.

Less than eight weeks after the fire and Bryson's subsequent heart attack, the first check arrived.

"I can't believe it!" Marisa shouted. The insurance money would stop the hemorrhage from the family checking account.

Within the next week, the couple had more good news with the confirmation from Matt that Bryson would receive full disability.

The big remaining question was what the hospital liability would be for the fire, if any. Though Bryson hadn't heard directly from Southwick, there were rumors among the office staff that the hospital's insurance company was talking about a cash settlement to the affected doctors.

*** 

"So Dad, when are you going back to work?" Madeline asked. They were sitting around the dining room table enjoying a Sunday dinner of prime rib with all of the accompanying wonders of gustatory delight one would expect in a five-star restaurant. The mixed green salad with blue cheese crumbles, pecans, extra virgin olive oil and just a whiff of balsamic vinegar had started the dinner right. The meat was cooked to perfection. The braised asparagus with its cheddar glaze—steamed to Goldilocks tenderness. The dessert, homemade coconut cream pie, was Bryson's favorite.

Madeline's question didn't really put a damper on the meal but it did route his mindset back to reality.

"What if I don't ever go back to work?" Bryson posed the question back to his youngest, and maybe smartest, daughter.

"Dad, you may be old, but you're not dead. What about all the patients who depend on you, and what is Mom going to do with you around the house day and night? I remember you saying once that you would never retire, that you would go crazy. Besides, how can you afford to live for all the years ahead?"

"That's why I'm sending you to that fancy college, so you can support me in my old age," he said, laughing.

Marisa rose from the table and passed behind her daughter on her way to the kitchen. She put a hand on Madeline's shoulder. "Your dad has a plan and has made smart decisions with our money. We will be just fine."

"Okay Dad, just don't become like the country club bums you tell us about. You can't play golf and sit around watching TV all day."

Bryson laughed again, this time even louder. His little girl, still in high school, had suddenly reversed the child-parent role and was giving him a dose of his own medicine.

Madeline started clearing the table. "Seriously, Dad, you have been busy every day of your life. What are you going to do with all of your time?"

*** 

The question of whether one dreams in color or black and white has been bantered around for centuries. Whether one can dream smells or aromas is even more subjective. Bryson would swear on any stack of Holy Bibles, Korans, Talmuds,

Dead Sea Scrolls, Gray's Anatomy or his mother's receipt books that he could smell food in his dreams.

Bryson jerked his head off of the pillow, pulled himself into a sitting position and yelled down the hallway to Marisa. "What are you cooking for breakfast?" It was barely daylight, a Monday morning, nine weeks since his Ob/Gyn practice went up in smoke.

Marisa was never one to react to noise during the night; there had been just too many medical calls over the years. Rather than answering the absurd question, she simply rolled over on her stomach and buried her head in one of Bryson's extra pillows. They were always on her side of the bed anyway.

"Sorry, sweetheart," he said realizing that she was not down the hallway cooking breakfast but instead right next to him, doing her best to snuggle back into a cozy position. "I must have been dreaming. I could have sworn that you were frying chicken fried steak with gravy and mashed potatoes. I could smell it. I could even hear it sizzling in the pan. Can you believe that?"

Marisa made an unintelligible moaning sound and pulled the pillow tighter over her head. She wasn't coming out soon.

The smell of the frying beef with its pepper seasoning and crispy edges would not leave Bryson's mind. It was almost as disabling as having a song stuck on replay in the brain.

By eight that morning, Bryson was desperate to get the image out of his mind and had decided that the only way was to get in his car and drive out to the edge of the city to find a truck stop. He thought he knew just what he was looking for . . . the perfect truck stop with the perfect chicken fried steak.

Trying to explain his motivation to anyone else was not even worth the effort.

Marisa had no plans for the day, so Bryson's first priority was to suggest something.

"Did you ever get the presents for those baby showers you missed when I was in the hospital?"

Marisa glanced up over the edge of the newspaper, giving him a look of suspicion. "What in the world would make you remember baby shower gifts from two months ago? Did you forget to take your blood thinner or something?"

"What about the wedding gift for the Larsen girl? I remember you said that you needed to find them something special," Bryson said, trying to act nonchalant.

Marisa closed the pages of the newspaper, folded it and stood up. "Why don't you go for a drive," she said, putting her arm around his waist and leaning her head on his shoulder. "It would do you good. Why don't you drive out to the new auto mall and kick some tires and take a new Mustang or that new Camaro for a test drive?"

"I don't want to leave you here all alone with nothing to do all day."

"Bryson dear, listen closely. For the last thirty years you have gone off to work every day and have not given a second thought to leaving me alone. Why would you think that starting today, I suddenly need someone to keep me busy?"

***

It felt great to be behind the wheel again. He strapped in and adjusted the driver's seat then tuned in his favorite talk show on the radio and backed out of the driveway.

Bryson pulled onto the main road and got into a line of traffic. He couldn't believe how much traffic there was at ten in the morning. Didn't these people have jobs to go to and families to take care of?

He was six miles out of town on the highway headed toward the mountains when he saw the first truck stop restaurant. The problem was that there just weren't any trucks. He pulled up to the pump and looked around. His fuel gauge was on full, so he opted out of topping off the tank and drove around to a parking spot near the entrance door. A hand-painted sign across the entrance announced that he was at "WILL-UM'S CAFÉ."

The sign in the window promised homemade blueberry pie. Unlit neon signs hanging from every window pitched several brands of intoxicants. When he swung the door open, he was met with a blast of cold air and the smell of Lysol disinfectant. The tables and chairs were wicker with some kind of fabric-padded seats that were stuck to the base of the chairs with an accumulation of spilled catsup, syrup and booze.

There wasn't another soul eating in the place, but he pulled up a chair anyway. The menu was written on a chalk-board on the wall with little lines of green chalk stars beside the cheeseburger and the fish-and-chip selections. No place on the menu was there anything close to chicken fried steak. At the top of the board was a listing for a Trucker's Breakfast with eggs, pancakes, hash browns and sausage. His mouth started to water. He had skipped breakfast and had wolfed down two oatmeal cookies and a Diet Pepsi instead.

"What'll it be, mister?"

The woman behind the voice was skeletal skinny and had more perforations than a bullet-riddled Louisiana stop sign. Worse still were the tattoos. They had obviously been applied when the woman was many pounds heavier. Even the Minnie Mouse on her overexposed shoulder was skinny.

His appetite was waning.

"I'll tell you what. I just remembered an appointment."

The swinging door didn't even come close to hitting him on the way out.

Next, he stopped at the Ford dealer and kicked tires per his wife's instructions. He even asked for a test drive in the new British racing green Mustang GT with a white stripe down the middle, only to be told that the car was already sold and was on display only. By noon he had worked out at Spinners and was back at the house. An empty house.

Marisa had gone to lunch with her sisters according to the note on the kitchen counter. He searched through the pantry and fridge and came up with a box of Ritz crackers, a couple slices of cheese and some strawberry jam. He opened another can of Diet Pepsi and sat down at the patio table.

He looked down at his lunch and took note. He was snacking on the same exact food that he had eaten the past thirty years in the Outpatient Surgi-Center. He took a swig of his drink and realized that it was lukewarm. "Oh yeah! Just like old times."

***

Bryson was in the bedroom when Marisa arrived home. He was on his hands and knees wearing only an old blue swim-suit whose waistband had lost its elasticity. His dresser drawer's contents were strewn across the bed. He was care-fully folding and aligning his socks and handkerchiefs in the middle drawer. The casual reading books on the wall of shelves were now neatly organized as to the height and color of the jackets. He had cleaned off his desk, read and sorted all the recent mail, and had even surveyed the stack of magazines on the coffee table in the family room, dis-carding all but Marisa's Martha Stewart and Family Circle.

"Are you okay?" Marisa asked, sitting down on the edge of the bed.

He continued fussing with the socks, holding the dark ones up to the light to separate the black ones from the dark navy ones and then carefully rolling the pairs together and placing them in their newly relegated por-tions of the drawer. "Just a couple more pairs then I can help you unload the groceries from the car or whatever you need."

Marisa was not a psychology major in college, but in the course of getting her B.A. in education, she had taken enough mind study courses to recognize aberrant behavior. Her husband's behavior had been anything but normal the last two months.

"I need you to do something for me," she said, offering him both of her hands to help him stand up from his kneeling position. "I need you to unload, but not anything from the car."

She led him to her side of the bed, and when he started to form a question, put a finger gently on his lips. Turning toward the overstuffed chair beside the bed, she quickly unbuttoned her rose-colored silk blouse, removed it and laid it out on the arm of the chair. Likewise, she unzipped the black slacks and folded them carefully and placed them on the arm of the chair.

"Could you help me with this hook?" she asked, turning her back toward him. No sooner than he had complied, freeing her of the last of her clothes, did she turn around and playfully push him backward onto the bed.

"Is the doctor available? It's time for our appointment."

She smothered his every attempt at talking with kisses. Later, both breathless, she was lying on his arm, just like they had done for so many years. Then her real agenda began as she started to ask him questions.

At first they were simple ones about his morning and about a few of the friends they had seen or heard from recently.

With gentle touches and rubs and tiny pecks on his cheek, she got Bryson to relax and start talking. They talked about all the weird places they had been forced to spend the night. They talked about the kids and the future grandkids, two of which had been recently announced. Bryson started to talk about money, but Marisa would have none of it.

As the sun was casting shadows through the window shades, Marisa asked her most poignant question. "What do you really want to do with the rest of your life? It is our life, you know. Not mine or yours. It is our life. We have enough money to get by and we have all the education either of us needs. I know you are feeling stifled sitting here at home. Watching you doing little or nothing with your time has made me realize how trivial most of my own daily activities really are. Let's find something memorable to do for a few months. Then by the time those grandchildren arrive, we will be ready to settle down and enjoy them. Right now you are like a corralled racehorse. Maybe if we get you out of here and let you run for a while, we will both be able to return to the barn. I love you, Bryson. I know how hard the last few months have been on you. Think of something you would love. Take your time, but find something and let's go for it."

She leaned over and kissed him and then slid off the bed and disappeared into the bathroom.

His mind sorted through a world of possibilities, each one holding little attraction. Then he started to focus. He needed facts. He needed courage. He needed advice. He needed two hundred thousand extra dollars, and he needed Marisa to agree with his plan. But would she?

# Chapter Five

# THE TRUCK

Bryson's laptop announced its readiness, grabbing his attention. First he checked his active bank accounts and then went to the travel sites. He liked many of them but had found that there were some that lauded two-star flophouses with broken-down mattresses as four-star resorts. He brought up a USA map and, making an imaginary route across the country, he started to calculate the best non-freeway roads and the acceptable hotels. Bryson estimated the cost of driving cross-country but taking time along the way as he traveled.

Next, he went to websites and began to accumulate all he could about large diesel trucks. It didn't take long before he found the first really good advertisement for a new Peter-bilt eighteen wheeler, which he printed. He studied the specifications and the payloads. He looked at interactive pictures of the cabins on the better trucks and found them to be like small motor homes complete with mini-kitchens, hidden toilets and beds long enough for a full-size man to stretch out on. The colors of the trucks were beautiful and the interiors were real leather. He was just starting to figure out the bottom line when Madeline rushed out of the patio door.

Dinner was ready and she had more college information to share. He saved his online information and tried not to think about it again that evening as they talked and planned for Madeline's graduation.

His youngest was really going away to school. Far away. Clear across the country. As Madeline and Marisa talked about airplane tickets, luggage and bedspreads, Bryson's mind raced through the possibility of hitting the road with North Carolina and Duke University being his first stop.

"What do you think, Dad?"

"What if we save the money on plane tickets and Mom and I drive you back to school?" Bryson asked, presenting an idea that shocked his daughter and aggravated his wife.

"Why would we take five or six days to drive clear across the country when she can get on the plane and be there in four hours?" Marisa asked in a voice that left no question regarding her opinion of the idea. "Surely it will cost a lot more in gas and food and hotel rooms than it would for a plane ticket. Besides, I'm not sure that our car is up to a round trip of six thousand miles."

"Madeline, just think of how much fun it would be with just the three of us together. No phones ringing or friends dropping in. We could talk and sightsee along the way. Maybe go north through some of the national parks. When we get there, Mom and I could help you settle into the dorm and decorate your room. We did it for the other kids. Just because it's further away is no reason to discriminate." Bryson laughed.

"Dad, I'll have a lot of luggage to take and it will really be crowded, don't you think?" Madeline's tone was almost more condescending than conciliatory.

It was at that precise moment that Bryson made his big decision. He was going to become a cross-country truck driver. He would haul his daughter and all of her stuff along with his wife in the spacious cab of a new Peterbilt eighteen wheeler semi. It was a brilliant plan. Not only would they go in style with the best truck money could buy, but it would be spacious and comfortable, and best of all, he could possibly even get paid for hauling a load of whatever trucks hauled, something to make the trip a business event, not just a family experience. He would start truck shopping in earnest the very next day.

Would he have to get a truck driver's license? How would he line up trucking jobs? He wondered, would he have to load or unload the truck himself? Maybe Madeline and Marisa would give him a hand loading the thing . . .

"Bryson! Bryson, are you all right?" Marisa was shaking his arm. "Are you going to take this phone call or not?"

He looked up to see Madeline standing beside him holding out the phone and his wife sitting next to him, staring at him as though he had sprouted a third eye. He couldn't remember the phone ringing.

"Who is it?" he asked in a slightly defensive voice.

Bryson arose from the table, and carrying the portable phone at his side, walked out onto the patio. The screen door closed behind him.

"Hello, this is Dr. Bender."

"Hey Doc, it's Matt. Hey, I hope I'm not interrupting anything."

"Oh hi, Matt. No, we had just finished dinner and were ready to clear the table. What's up?"

"Listen, I know this is none of my business, but all of us insurance guys have our own little grapevine of info. Anyway, this afternoon two of the office girls stuck their heads in my office and asked if I had heard anything about the doctor who got arrested. It turns out that one of the doctors whose office burned up . . . is this sounding familiar?"

"Not really," Bryson answered.

"The cops showed up at the doctor's house with warrant to search the house and then arrested the guy, charging him with stealing hospital documents and with suspicion of arson. They are saying he burned down your office building."

"Did you get his name?" Bryson asked, pacing back and forth on the patio. Tiny beads of sweat were springing from every pore on his face.

"I think she said Southward or Southwind, something like that. I'm pretty sure she said he is a bone cruncher. Do you know the guy?"

Bryson could barely speak. He collapsed into a chaise lounge, his mind racing and his pulse throbbing at his temples. Matt's secretary had to have the story screwed up.

"Doc, are you there?"

"Yes, I'm here. When did this arrest thing happen? Did she say?"

"Can you believe those maniac cops hit his house at dawn this morning, just like a bunch of Nazi Gestapo agents? One of the girls in my office knew the man and said he was a good old boy, kind of grumpy but a good doctor. Do you know the guy?"

Bryson paused again before answering and then said, "Yes, I think his office was the one above mine. We've known each other ever since I started practice here years ago."

"Well, I've got to go but I'll do more checking in the morning. Sorry again for calling so late. Say, did you get the second check for your disability yet? I got a copy through the office email so I know it's been sent."

"No, I haven't seen it yet but I didn't check the mail today. Thanks, and if you hear anything more, give me a call."

He sat on the patio, listening to the spring crickets trying to get their tunes going. His head was spinning and his mind was racing. What had Southwick done now? Had the man completely wigged out or was the whole thing part of the hospital administration's cover-up?

Madeline broke his train of rumination when she opened the door and asked if he was done using the phone. As he handed her the phone, she bent over and gave him a kiss on the forehead.

"Thanks, Dad, for all you do for all of us. Thank you so much for making it possible for me to go away to an awesome school."

The door opened again and as Madeline went into the house, Marisa came out and sat down next to Bryson.

"Is everything okay? You aren't looking well," she said.

He paused for a minute and then answered her question with an explanation of Matt's call. She listened with no sign of surprise. Bryson went on talking, venting his anxiety that he might get dragged into the situation and that the lawsuit Southwick proposed could come back to haunt the Benders.

Marisa stroked his arm. "Everything is going to work out just fine, honey. I know it will. Let's go and get ready for bed then we can watch a TV show and relax. Madeline is going out with her friends to a night baseball game. The house will be quiet. Tomorrow we can get the facts and decide how to deal with it."

She stood and offered her hand, and then withdrawing it, added, "Bryson, I almost forgot to mention, there is no way that all three of us are going to drive cross-country for five or six days to take Madeline to Duke. The two of us talked it over while you were on the phone. She and I are going to fly there and get her settled in, then you can join me and we can see some of the sights. Maybe a week at Hilton Head or Williamsburg would do us both good. Among the three of us, we can bring six large suitcases plus carry-ons. That will be all the things she needs to get her started. Incidentally, the thing she didn't get a chance to tell you before you got on the phone was that she is going to North Carolina in time to start summer school. We will need to leave the first week in June."

*\*\**

Bryson first thought he saw the truck in a dream, but then realized that he had dozed off while sitting in the Mega Mall parking lot waiting for Marisa. The truck was not an apparition but a really big eighteen wheeler rolling into an open space of the parking lot less than fifty feet away. It was candy-apple red and the abundance of chrome on it reflected enough sunlight that to see it clearly, he had to reach for his sunglasses, which he had thrown on the dashboard.

Marisa and Madeline had left him in the car while they ran in to find one more suitcase for her trip. He didn't understand the rush. There were still a few weeks of school left before graduation, but the girls couldn't wait to get every last loose end tied up in a strangle knot. Airplane tickets had been purchased and hotel reservations were made near campus.

A blast from the truck's air horn startled Bryson. Intently watching to see the fabulous truck in motion, Bryson got out of his car and leaned on the bumper. The truck was a Peterbilt, all right. Its large, red-and-silver, oval insignia on the grill left no doubt. It was a streamlined beauty with a sleeping shell behind the cab the size of a small travel trailer. Bryson could not remember ever seeing a truck that was so sleek and yet so huge. He could hear the turbo-diesel engine rumbling with low sensuous throaty sounds—they could actually be felt—not the clatter of the old diesel tractors and trucks he remembered as a kid.

Just when he expected to see the truck pull away, the driver opened the cab door, climbed down the steps to ground level and walked toward Bryson.

"Morning," the man said. He was dressed, not in the low hanging jeans and loose-necked T-shirt of the archtypical trucker guy, but in a long-sleeve, blue-and-white striped button-down collar shirt and a pair of tan slacks with sharp creases. He wasn't even wearing boots but instead had on a pair of penny loafers.

"Good morning. That is one beautiful truck you have there," Bryson said. "I thought it was a 747 landing when you first pulled in the parking lot."

"Yes, I wish it was mine. It belongs to a bank . . . don't they all? I just picked it up at the dealers and have to drive it to Fresno for the new owner. It is pretty nice."

"What exactly is that monster?" Bryson asked, prying for more information.

"It's called a Premium Length High Roof Sleeper 387 Peterbilt. How's that for a mouthful? It's their top of the line with the newest fuel-efficient, turbo-diesel engine and the latest in navigation and weather electronics. The thing has more switches and cameras than a space shuttle."

"What are the seats like?"

"Come take a look for yourself. My wife is in the mall picking up a few things for our trip. She'll be a while. How about you?"

"Wife and youngest daughter . . . suitcases for the trip to college. I'd love to take a look inside your truck, or do you call it your rig?"

The man laughed and offered his hand. "Winston is my name. And yours?"

"Bryson, with a Y. Tell me, Winston, do you drive trucks for a living?"

"I used to, but now I own a truck driver's school. I have a few offices scattered around the country, but this is my home."

Winston pushed the button on his FOB, unlocking the cab door with a chirp. He climbed into the cab then disappeared. He stuck his head back out the massive door and motioned for Bryson to follow.

Bryson struggled to get a handhold on the vertical chrome side rail and to lift his leg high enough to get safe footing on the step. Groaning, he managed to pull himself up enough to reach the next step. It felt like he was climbing a ladder. He swung his body into the seat, needing to take a deep breath before he could settle into the driver's seat.

"Wow! This thing sure sits up high."

His entire body felt sucked down into the soft contour seat and he could smell the new leather. The seat seemed as big as his recliner at home.

"This seat is wonderful. How do you stay awake? This thing's cozier than my bed."

Winston had moved into the cabin section in the back and motioned for Bryson to join him. There were two over-sized bunks, each with its own tiny flat screen TV and DVD player. Other cool features included a small fridge, a microwave oven, a row of shelves with cubbyholes and a bank of drawers. There were directional reading lights, and in the corner, a miniature john. Bryson took it all in and then slid over to the passenger's seat. It was even softer and more comfortable than the driver's.

"Amazing, this thing is truly amazing," Bryson said. "What can you haul with this thing?"

"Anything you want," Winston said with a chuckle.

"How do you line up jobs? You know, find things to haul and coordinate the trips so you don't travel loaded one way and then come home empty?"

"It's all done through freight agents or brokers. Most planning is handled by the private companies and overseen by the unions. If you are lucky enough to own your own rig, then you find an agent and he lines up the jobs. It's easier than you would think. The money is good right now in spite of fuel prices. The railroads are maxed out and so ships and trucks are the only alternative."

"How can a rookie get started? I'm a retired doctor, but my family tells me that I'm not dead yet and this looks like something that would appeal to me."

"First things first. You have to have a truck and a special license. I could help you with both of those things. Then the rest of the arrangements sort of fall into place."

There was a sudden tapping on the passenger door. Bryson looked down to see a petite blonde woman looking up in surprise at the face of a stranger.

"I think your wife is finished shopping."

The men visited a few minutes more and exchanged business cards with Bryson, explaining that his office address and phone numbers were no longer the same. He scratched in his home number and cell, unsure that they were even legible. He waved farewell and then stood in awe as the truck fired up its engine and smoothly pulled out of the parking lot.

Oh, but for the want of a camera. This was the truck for him. This was the machine he wanted to drive back and forth across the country. This would be the freedom he had longed for. This would be home away from home and a moneymaker to boot. He was so excited that he nearly bumped into the girls as he rushed into the mall to find them. The two of them were lugging very large boxes. More luggage, no doubt.

* * *

"Gosh, Dad, you would think you had seen an albino giraffe wandering the parking lot," Madeline exclaimed after several nonstop minutes of Bryson's exuberant monologue about the truck.

"He's all right, honey; he's just been cooped up in the house too long. Give him a couple of weeks and he'll have forgotten all about it, just like the Ferrari and the Porsche Speedster that he just had to have years ago. It's one of the things guys just do."

The girls laughed as Bryson settled into his own world of thought. They just didn't get it. If they had been able to crawl into those seats and feel the grain of the leather and smell the aroma of newness, and all those awesome electronic features . . . well, Marisa was going to love it. She just needed the chance to find out.

# Chapter Six

# REVENGE

John Southwick wasn't thinking about trucks. He was thinking of finding a gun and killing the hospital administrator. Henry Heiner had gone way over the line. Not only had the man reported the missing file contents to the police, but he had dreamed up a story about how the good doctor Southwick had come to him in anguish, saying that he had set the fire in desperation to collect on his insurance.

Southwick was finally back at home after the shock of having his house invaded, being roused out of bed and manhandled into handcuffs, all in the dawning hours of the morning. Then there was the humiliation of only being allowed to put on pants and house slippers. What animals those policemen had been. As they ransacked his house from top to bottom, one would think they had found Jimmy Hoffa's body when they waved the documents from the hospital in his face and then dragged him to a squad car while his neighbors looked on. The booking, arraignment and bond hearing had been like Twilight Zone nightmares, each more humiliating than the first.

His attorney didn't do criminal law—of course—so Southwick had to wait in an interrogation room for an extra couple of hours while another attorney finished his Sunday morning golf match. At least they didn't throw him in the lockup with the Saturday night drunks. It had cost twenty-thousand dollars for a bond just to tide him over until he could get to the bank on Monday. He would lose ten percent in the transaction. What a sleazy business.

The first thing he wanted to do when he got home late in the afternoon was to take a long shower and then call Heiner. He was so mad that he left the shower running and went to the phone first. His attorney warned him not to talk to anyone about the incident, but he couldn't contain his anger. A young teen answered the telephone at Heiner's house and reported that his dad wasn't home. Southwick almost tore into the kid but got a grip on his anger at the last second and hung up the phone. He undressed and went to the shower to wash off the disgusting feeling of the police station, only to find that the hot water had run out.

He walked through his trashed house, trying to straighten and reorganize the searched cupboards and closets. Thank goodness his wife and kids had taken a plane to Dallas to stay with her mother for a few days. He was starved and attacked leftovers in the fridge and then tried the shower again. Sitting at his kitchen counter, he felt alone and helpless, as the adrenaline of the day wore off, leaving only a worried wreck. The room grew dark around him without his even noticing until he felt thirsty and stumbled on a bar stool in the dark. The physical pain was enough to jolt him out of his funk. He turned on the lights and found Bryson Bender's home phone number. He dialed only to get a voice mailbox.

***

Bryson heard the phone ring far down the hall. Marisa had turned off the phone in their room. She wasn't just trying to spare Bryson late-night phone calls; she was through listening to them herself. Thirty years of never knowing whether she could sleep all night without interruption was long enough.

Bryson felt over on Marisa's side of the bed, which was empty. Moments later he heard her whisper his name and ask if he was awake enough to talk.

"It's your friend, Dr. Southwick. He sounds really upset. I think you had better take the call."

By the time John Southwick had unloaded his story of rousting and arrest and intimidation, Bryson was pacing the room with elevated pulse, blood pressure and fear. According to Southwick, several of the doctors in the office building were under suspicion of setting the building on fire and Bryson had been mentioned as a coconspirator in the theft of the hospital's documents from Heiner's office. The man on the other end of the phone didn't sound like the John Southwick Bryson knew. He was sounding like a raving lunatic. The problem was that much of what Southwick said sounded plausible enough that Bryson was developing his own state of acute paranoia.

Bryson heard Marisa go into the study and pick up the extension phone. She would never have done such a thing a few months ago but lately had become much more protective of him.

"You need to stay as far away from that guy as possible," she said after the call.

"What if they say I helped Southwick steal the papers in order to substantiate a lawsuit?"

"The whole thing is crap and you know it. The hospital knows they are liable for the fire and now they are putting pressure on him so he will go away. So all of the doctors will go away. Bryson, you need to forget this thing and let us get on with our life. We are going to get through the next few weeks, graduation and all, and then take Madeline to school. After that you need a long vacation. We all do. Maybe you should even learn more about that truck you are always talking about."

For Bryson, Marisa's last sentence was the go-ahead he needed. It was like she had just waved the green flag at the Indianapolis 500.

Marisa was asleep within seconds after turning out the lights.

Bryson lay awake formulating plans. Not just silly daydreams but real plans. He was going to get up on Monday morning and go shopping, and it wouldn't be at Nordstrom's.

# Chapter Seven

# SHOPPING

Bryson awoke early and ate his usual breakfast of hot chocolate, a cookie or two and a Diet Pepsi. He read the paper, showered and dressed and then waited for eight o'clock, the earliest he imagined any truck businesses would open. He had a list of big truck dealers, which he had printed, and was about to leave the house when Marisa joined him and offered a suggestion.

"I suppose you are going out to kick some big tires. Maybe it would be a good idea to have your cousin ride along. Jack is probably just as bored as you are. He called twice last week to see if you were well enough to go to the Cabello's grand opening. He claimed it is the ultimate in the outdoor sportsman's shopping paradise. I did remind him that you would rather stick needles in your eyes than go bass fishing."

Jack Glen was Bryson's first cousin and a retired farmer who had spent forty years of his life raising potatoes and beans. He was a big, strong, fair-skinned Scandinavian who had earned his living by the sweat of his brow. Jack and his wife had raised six kids and ten thousand head of fat beef cattle. Two years ago, when his last son went off to Chicago to sell wheat and pork belly futures, Jack sold the farm to a corporation who was using the land to raise hops for the ever-increasing number of beer drinkers of America. He moved to the desert with money in the bank and time on his hands and absolutely no interest in golf.

"Jack probably knows more about trucks than you do about ovaries," Marisa said. "Who knows? Maybe he can tell you enough bad things about those trucks to get the fixation out of your mind."

***

Jack was eager to drop what he was doing and ride out to the end of town where the real men of the road hung out. His wife, Jenny, was a pretty brunette who looked and acted ten years younger than her real age. She had a zest for life mixed with a healthy cynicism that she had acquired over the years surviving the duties of a farmer's wife: cooking, cleaning, raising kids and doing the chores, which often included feeding the livestock and nurturing her husband during tough years.

They had seen the price of potatoes, soybeans and beef go up and down like a roller coaster, while every year the cost of fuel for the tractors and clothes for the family had gone up. They had been one of the lucky farmers. They had kept their marriage strong, their four kids in school and had sold the farm when the market was stable. Tired of the cold weather, they had packed up and moved to the desert.

Jenny had easily settled into a life of the suburban housewife, micro-managing her grown kids' lives and trying to keep her husband busy. She had signed them both up for a gym and had acquired a new wardrobe. She played tennis twice a week and had joined Marisa's book club. Jack, on the other hand, was struggling with retirement. Before Bryson could end the call, Jack already had on his faded John Deere hat.

***

Along Interstate 8, there were no less than ten new and used commercial truck dealers. Mack, Kenworth, International, Volvo, Peterbilt and even Mercedes had representative dealers. The men stopped at all of them. They had crawled in and out of trucks until their knees and shoulders ached. They had filled their bellies with free soft drinks and mini-candy bars while the salesmen rounded up pounds of glossy sales brochures. By the end of the afternoon, the cousins were exhausted but happy. Bryson had for sure found his favorite. He knew he could never settle for anything other than the Peterbilt 387 he had seen that day at the mall.

Back at home, he told Marisa, "Let it just be said that we went, we looked, and we came home confused with bad headaches and with a severe case of sticker shock. I did, however, find the truck of my dreams."

"One hundred and ninety-thousand dollars for a truck? You have got to be kidding me! That's enough to pay off the boys' dental school loans or to put Madeline all the way through four years at Duke. Don't they have used trucks available?"

"Don't worry, I didn't sign anything. Besides, nothing we looked at will fit in our garage."

This got a laugh out of Marisa and he followed her lead with a hearty laugh of his own, which made his head hurt even more. He headed to the kitchen medicine cupboard to grab his usual four Advil.

"You can't take those," she reminded him. "No Advil with your blood thinners!"

"No wonder sick people get hooked on hard drugs. I've got a super-bad headache and nothing else is going to work. What's for supper?"

***

They had just started dinner when the knock came at the door. Marisa had massaged the back of Bryson's neck until his headache had started to fade and then had prepared his favorite homemade lasagna at his majesty's request.

Answering the door, Marisa gasped when she saw the two men standing on her front porch. One wore a plaid sport coat and dark slacks. The other man wore a blue police officer's uniform. She began instantly thinking that they were the bearers of some horrible news.

Kids, grandkids, where were they right now?

She couldn't remember ever having had policemen come to her door.

Each of the men introduced themselves in a polite and almost timid manner then presented identification badges. The man in civilian clothes produced a piece of paper from his coat pocket and handed it to Marisa who immediately handed it to Bryson, as if it were a hot potato.

"Dr. Bender, I am embarrassed to do this. You probably don't remember me but you delivered my three kids. My wife loves you. Anyway, this is a search warrant. It only covers your home office or study. It should only take a second."

"What is this about?" Bryson asked, trying to stay calm and yet in command.

"The county attorney was told that you might have some papers that a Dr. John Southwick allegedly stole from the hospital. I'm sure he is wrong and I tried to talk them out of doing this tonight, but there is a hearing tomorrow and Mr. Marshall insists that we do it tonight. He's a jerk and I don't even care if you quote me."

Bryson looked at the paper and then took his reading glasses out of his pocket and studied the warrant, as though he knew what he was reading. He carefully folded it and returned it to the detective.

"My study is this way, down the hall. Don't be embarrassed about having to do your job." He looked over his shoulder as they walked. "Your wife's name is Kathy, right? Those three boys of yours are a handful. She brought them with her on her last visit so we could take a picture together. Tell her I would love a copy."

Bryson turned on the light switch and stepped aside, gesturing for the two men to enter his study. Hesitantly, they stepped inside the room and glanced around at the stacks of medical journals and old textbooks. There were neat stacks of papers on the shelves, desk and computer countertop. Some obvious IRS tax forms were arranged in the center of the desk with another pair of reading glasses lying nearby.

"This should just take a second," the proud dad said in a voice loud enough for Marisa to hear clear down the hall.

"That is all we needed to see," the detective said less than a minute later. He had glanced at the desk and quickly opened and closed a single drawer before nodding toward the door for his uniformed partner to start moving. "We came, we looked, and we left. That should satisfy Marshall."

At the door both men apologized to Bryson and Marisa then left with a promise that the photo of the three boys with their mom's doctor would be mailed to Dr. Bender.

"How about some cold lasagna?" Marisa said, walking back into the kitchen. She scraped their plates full of food into the sink and put the serving dish with its leftover contents back into the oven.

"Let's see, a couple of weeks ago you were saying how boring it was going to be to be retired. Right? Well, at the pace we are keeping, when would you ever have had any time to work? What with fires, insurance forms, graduation, college decisions and giant trucks. Let's not forget strokes, heart attacks, rehab and police invasions." She paused while she stuck her head in the fridge to retrieve lettuce and tomato for a new salad. Then she went on. "It is a wonderful thing that God saved up all these fun trials and surprising annoyances for us until you completed your medical practice; otherwise, your patients would have had to lay in the hospital with their legs crossed until you found the time to drop by and deliver them."

This entire kitchen scene played out while Bryson leaned against the granite countertop. He was grinning at her the whole time and trying to suppress a laugh. The entire day had been full of new experiences for him and now his beautiful wife was venting in a form of comic relief he hadn't seen since John Candy and *Laugh-In* went off the air.

"We could just skip dinner and go straight to bed," Bryson jested with raised eyebrows but faint expectations.

"And miss your special Italian dinner? Not a chance, buster. You are going to eat until this is all gone and then you are going to call your attorney."

***

Attorneys, accountants and actuaries: the triple A's of bloodsucking. If Bryson could have gone back in time and never paid an attorney or an accountant or an actuary, he would have saved enough to put Madeline and her three best friends through college. Thus, it was with reluctance that he dialed Brian's number and glanced at the clock, knowing that his attorney friend would also be looking at the clock, probably making a note of the time for billing.

Bryson and Brian—what a team they had made back in graduate school. Point guard to center, like Stockton to Malone. They had won the All-Church League and even considered the All-City Three-on-Three Hoops contest. That was before Bryson had had his finger broken by a flipped-out, pregnant drug addict who didn't want a pelvic exam but failed to mention it to the nurse or chief resident. When Bryson tried to check the woman's cervical dilation, she just grabbed his gloved hand and with all of her might, backed up by over two hundred pounds of solid fat, twisted Bryson's little finger until it snapped with a sickening pop that could be heard by everyone in the room.

"Bryson, are you really still alive? I guess the rumor of your demise was greatly exaggerated. Why do I get the feeling that this is going to be my lucky day?"

Bryson could picture the lean, semi-retired attorney sitting in his tufted leather chair with his feet up on the desk, watching the hands of the clock move "click, click" as dollars moved like freight train cars into his bank account.

"Hey Brian, thanks for the flowers you sent to the hospital. They probably looked a lot better at the cemetery the day before. You could have at least taken off the note that said, *From Cousin Bubba. May Aunt Henrietta rest in peace.*"

"Geez, Bender, I didn't know having a stroke would make you grow a sense of humor and imagination, or are you still on pain meds? And just for the record, I didn't send flowers because I remembered that you have always said you would rather have a good meal than a pot of wilting flowers. So when would you and Marisa like to join us at Fleming's?"

The friends caught up on kids and wives and then Bryson explained what he could about the search warrant and his relationship with Dr. Southwick. Brian promised to make some calls and in less than ten minutes, by his clock, the phones were back in their cradles.

# Chapter Eight

## THE GUN

The next three days went by painfully slow. Marisa had more tennis and Madeline had school activities from dawn until way after dusk. Bryson spent his time cleaning out the garage and scrubbing its floor. He sorted everything he owned. He even started going through old boxes of personal letters and pictures.

There was no new word from his attorney, the county attorney or anyone else of consequence. His eyes were hurting from the dust in the old storage boxes, so he pushed them aside for the day and decided to go for a swim. He had lost enough weight that his favorite suit was barely hanging on his hips, and after diving into the pool, the suit required a substantial hitching up. It only took a couple of laps before his heart was thumping and his breathing labored. He sat on the pool step, enjoying the peace of his little part of the planet, taking slow, deep breaths.

As he sat there in the pool, he studied the intricate design around the eves of his gazebo and the rock-lined flower beds around his swimming pool and yard. It reminded him about the time he had gone to the local nursery to buy bedding plants for a window box at their first apartment. He had come away empty-handed because the charge for the flowers was six dollars and he only had four and a quarter in his pocket. It was three years later before he had his first Visa card. "Forget those good old, flat-broke days," he told himself and switched mental gears to wondering about Marisa's plan for dinner.

Then he heard the sirens.

It sounded like there was more than one vehicle and they were definitely getting closer. He stepped out of the pool and walked toward the side of the house where he could look through the gate toward the driveway. Over the top of his back fence he could see an unfamiliar white sedan parked crossways in his driveway. The sirens were still getting closer, but no police or fire trucks were visible.

Bryson reached up and undid the latch on the side gate, swinging it just wide enough to look through. He had only a quick glimpse of a man dressed in a business suit rushing toward him before he felt the stinging pain in his right shoulder, jerking his body away from the gate. His instant thought was that his bare shoulder had been stung by a wasp, but then his brain processed the firecracker-like sound that preceded the searing pain. Could he have just been shot? He looked up and saw the face of the man standing less than thirty feet away, screaming at Bryson. It was a face he recognized, but in his distress, he couldn't put a name to it.

Bryson looked at his bare shoulder again, hoping it was a wasp sting. Instead he saw the crimson jet coming from a neat hole into his right deltoid muscle. He grasped his shoulder with his left hand only to see blood erupt through the spaces between his fingers. Looking at the man who was now twenty feet away, he saw the man's arm extend again. The disheveled looking figure was definitely holding a gun and was screaming something at Bryson about papers and fires and Southwick and police fools.

✽✽✽

The involuntary buckling of Bryson's knees probably saved his life. A second gunshot went straight through the middle of the Benders' wooden gate, a little less than five feet above the ground. As he fell to the ground, the bullet zinged through the gate past his ear, nicking it just enough that he could instantly feel a new burning pain; later calculations hinted that, had he still been standing, it would have pierced the middle of his chest. He felt a warm trickle of blood from his ear. Interestingly, the pain in his shoulder was replaced with stinging pain all over his face. The second bullet had splintered the wooden fence, spraying slivers into his face.

Bryson heard shouting and sounds of a scuffle just on the other side of the gate. Then he heard the third shot but couldn't get up to investigate. He crawled up against the side of the house and grabbed onto an ivy-wrapped trellis. He held still and finally caught his breath. He could hear more shouting and then more sirens. Pulling himself to his feet with his left arm, he moved toward the back door, leaving a trail of blood.

"Halt," was the first distinct word he recognized. This he did, but only after diving behind his built-in barbeque grill.

"I'm the police. Are you okay?" The voice echoed through the backyard. "You can come out. We've got the shooter in front of the house. Are you armed?"

Bryson peeked around the corner of the stone base and saw a large man dressed in blue and wearing a baseball cap with a block letter logo. He, too, was holding a gun but placed it in its holster while Bryson slowly dragged himself into the open. He was a mass of blood and gore.

"Holy crap! You're wounded," the officer said. "Stay right there while I call the paramedics."

And so here he was on another trip to the hospital in an ambulance. The chaos of the emergency room followed, with its frantic voices, and later he listened to the worried voice of his wife through the sliding fabric curtains. Luckily, the pain meds hit his brain shortly after the first jolts of a new pain, caused by the young doctor probing his shoulder wound with a Kelly clamp. Brains can do weird things. The next thing Bryson thought to himself was, *Who was the Kelly clamp named after? Gene Kelly? Jack Kelly? Or should they have made the clamp green and named it Kelly Green?* Then the pain was gone.

*\*\*\**

Marisa was stroking Bryson's cheek and humming the chorus to *Take it Easy* when he woke up. She started slowly talking to him, bringing him up to speed on the last few hours of his life, starting with where they were and how he got there.

"I'm awake enough," he mumbled. "Give me the whole story. I remember walking to the gate and hearing sirens."

Marisa passed him a sip of water and then started her second-hand version of the shooting.

"You know the hospital administrator, Mr. Heiner?"

Bryson nodded, wishing she would get on with it.

"Apparently, when the police didn't find the papers they were looking for at our house or at your friend Dr. Southwick's, they searched Mr. Heiner's house and car and found the papers, or at least copies of them, in the glove box. Don't ask me why they looked there. I've never seen them do that on TV. Anyway, they confronted Mr. Heiner about the papers, which apparently hinted that it was the hospital employees who may have started the office fire. When Mr. Heiner found out that the county attorney was going to drop the charges against Doctor Southwick, he left his office in a huff. About an hour later, Mr. Heiner barged into Dr. Southwick's house and shot him . . . I believe in the abdomen or upper leg."

Bryson tried to sit up in the bed, but Marisa motioned for him to be still and listen. Then she went on. "Southwick is here in the recovery room. He is much more serious than you, but the doctors said he is stable. When Heiner left Southwick's house, I guess thinking he was dead, he decided to attack you as well. He drove over to our house. On the way he ran through a red light. A policeman saw him and tried to pull him over, but he wouldn't stop. Before he got to our house, someone had called 911 about Dr. Southwick, so there was a whole string of police cars chasing him. None of them saw what he did to you but they heard the shots and finally tackled him. He shot himself in the leg in the scuffle. They took him to the county hospital and no one has heard anything about him since then."

She gave Bryson another sip and continued explaining. "The surgeon, Dr. Deyden's new partner, told me that the bullet went into, but not out of, your shoulder. They got the bleeding stopped but couldn't remove the bullet at first because it is too close to the main nerve and artery. They had a vascular surgeon . . . I can't remember his name . . . come in to take the thing out. They said since the bullet was small that there is little damage except for the hole. Your shoulder should heal up just fine. Your face, however, is another thing. It looks like you were dragged through a pile of old railroad ties. I think I can still see splinters. They were from the bullet hitting the wooden gate. Incidentally, your ear looks like a cow or sheep that had its ear notched for identification."

"Thanks a lot," Bryson said, reaching to feel the bandage on his ear.

"They took a half pound of splinters out of your face and chest. I guess you didn't have on a shirt?"

"I was swimming," he said in defense.

"Well, I guess it's a good thing this happened in the daylight, so you at least had on swim trunks." She gave him a little told-you-so smirk. "Anyway, the police said he shot you and Southwick with a 32 something . . . whatever that means. I guess a 33 or 44 or 55 would have been worse. I've called all the kids and told them you will be all right. You'll probably be the lead story on the ten o'clock news. I didn't want the kids hearing it from their friends. I told them not to put the hospital number on their speed dials just yet. We'd give you one more chance to stay out of trouble."

Bryson lay in the bed, staring up at the ceiling trying to remember anything more, but the anesthesia had done its job. Soon he was drifting off again. He could hear the sizzling and smell the aroma of the meat frying. The griddle was enormous, at least the size of the pool table. There must have been two hundred pieces of tender breaded beef cooking far across the room. He was starving, and even though he risked burning his fingers, he tried to sneak one of the chicken fried steaks from the griddle, but every step he took closer, the griddle and all of that meat just moved further away. "But I'm so hungry. Can't I just have one piece? You have so many, and they will burn if you cook them too long. Please!"

\*\*\*

"Please what, Daddy?" Madeline's voice jolted him awake. She was standing at his hospital bedside, holding a clean shirt for him. "Haven't they fed you anything? You kept saying you were hungry."

"Food would be a good thing," he mumbled.

"You sure are hard to wake up lately. Mom said for you to put on this shirt and just keep on your scrub pants. She's downstairs signing you out. We're stopping at Pei Wei on the way home to get you some takeout."

Bryson looked out the window to a night sky. "What time is it? Matter of fact, what day is it?"

"It's still Friday, Dad. You know I did have a date tonight. That jerk who shot you could have at least done it on a weekday." She leaned over the bed and gave Bryson a big kiss. "Just kidding, Daddy. I'm so happy that you're going to be okay and get to come home tonight. Let me help you up."

And so, for the second time since his office had burned to the ground, Bryson was pushed in a wheelchair through the corridors and lobby of the hospital where he had practiced medicine for thirty years. He rolled by the administration area where he noticed yellow crime-scene tape across the door of his would-be assassin. As they rolled into the hospital's portico, he looked across the parking lot to the empty space where his large, handsome office building once stood. For just a second he thought he could still see his office door with his brass nameplate. Then he blinked and the door and the building were gone. A construction fence around the charred rubble was the only thing standing.

***

High school graduation was a lot different when Bryson and Marisa graduated. There were, of course, the robes and the all-night parties and the teary goodbyes with promises to keep in touch, but there were none of the modern trappings of digital video recordings, same-day airplane trips to Disneyland and back in time to meet the limo for an early gourmet dinner before the graduation ceremony, followed by the progressive all-night parties where enough food would be wasted to feed a battalion of marines. The presents some of the coddled graduates received were even more outrageous. Cars, boats, jet skis and quad ATVs.

And then there was poor Madeline.

"I thought the new luggage was her graduation present," Bryson protested. "And now you are giving her a thousand-dollar watch? I don't remember talking about that one. What did we give the boys?"

"You know good and well. You gave them each a shotgun and a new set of golf clubs. I think you even had them fitted for the clubs. As I recall, they were twelve hundred dollars a set and you would never tell me how much the guns cost. Why are you so worried about money all of a sudden?"

That was a very good question with a very clear answer. He had too much time, not enough money and time to think about them both.

In the ten days since the shooting, Bryson had not been able to go to the athletic club nor had he been able to swim. "The wounds have to stay dry," he was told. It was the least he had exercised in years. In spite of his precautions, he had acquired a mild infection in the wound. His good arm, the left one, had an intravenous port through which Marisa gave him antibiotics three times a day. His right arm was in a sling most of the time and he was just starting to be able to dry himself off after a shower. The only good news was that he was starting to eat right-handed again. To say he was frustrated with himself and everyone else was an understatement. Marisa was running thin on patience as well.

He had been spending the days and many long nights sitting in front of a computer screen, learning about the world. He looked on Google Earth at his ancestral towns and cities. He found a tiny town in Illinois, whose city hall his great-grandfather Bender had supposedly helped build. A sudden wave of nostalgia traveled through his brain and hit him like a chocolate cream pie in the face. His idea of owning a big truck and searching for the world's best chicken fried steak wasn't so stupid after all. He didn't have one clue about what the real North America was like. He had seen much of the world but little of the USA. He had been in less than fifteen of the fifty states. The truck thing might really work.

***

Graduation night was pleasant with clear, warm weather and lots of decked-out families parading through the parking lot toward the stadium. Madeline had never looked more beautiful in her cap and gown and too-high high heels. Marisa wore a new summer dress that made her look like a frisky young soccer mom, not a grandmother graduating her youngest of five. Bryson had left his sling at home and worn a lightweight sports coat to conceal the dressing he still had to wear over his shoulder wound.

Just as one would predict, the first one of their acquaintances they bumped into clamped his left hand on

Bryson's injured shoulder while he vigorously shook Bryson's unoffered hand. Tears came to his eyes as Marisa turned the man away from Bryson with a question and a tug of his sleeve.

"I don't think I can do this," Bryson said to Marisa. "Save me a place on the South thirty-yard line and I'll come from the car after the National Anthem is played."

Not even waiting for her to answer, he turned and headed back toward his car. He had to struggle to pull the keys out of his jacket pocket where Marisa had dropped them. She had been driving. He hadn't tried driving since the shooting. He sat in the car and thought about how he might drive a big truck with his injured arm. Like the answer to a prayer, there was a knock at the window.

"Bryson, why are you sitting in the car?" His cousin, Jack Glen, was standing beside the car dressed in jeans and a pearl button shirt, holding a flashlight.

"Hi Jack, what are you doing? Looking for cars to break into?"

"The principal lives next door to us and asked me to help with the parking and then to wander around to keep the perverts away and to make the hooky-playing dads like you go back to the ceremony."

Bryson got out of the car as the two men laughed. They leaned against the car and talked about their kids and all the graduations past.

"Say, I guess the shooting put your truck idea on the back burner."

"Actually, it took it off the stove altogether for a while but now I'm thinking about it again. I didn't really get serious about it after we looked that day; the money is still an issue with my wife. It seems like it might be a hard sell to get the bank to loan money to somebody who is out of work and technically disabled. There are a couple other possibilities in the mill, so I'm still hoping."

"How's your arm doing?"

"That's the other problem. I need to take the truck driving training course to get my upgraded license but my shoulder still hurts like heck."

The men talked a while longer and then music flooded the air again and Bryson started feeling guilty for not being in the graduation audience.

"Say, Jack, I just had a thought. Would you consider looking at trucks with me again one of these days soon? If I can figure out the financing and my doctor says it's okay, I may just get serious about the truck again. Do you still like the Peterbilt best?"

"It's all about brand loyalty, but that midnight-blue 387 the dealer showed us on the Internet was pretty awesome. Where was that exact model you loved?"

"Montana." Bryson paused, remembering the several pictures taken from different angles of the blue truck. "It was awesome, wasn't it? Well, who knows, maybe I'll give you a call Monday and we can take one just like it for a test drive. I'll let you know. You do still have your trucker's license, don't you?"

"That's an affirmatory, big buddy," Jack answered in a mock trucker's voice.

✳✳✳

The line of graduating seniors went on for what seemed like forever. Madeline was easy to pick out standing in the group of her peers. She was tall and beautiful. She wore a pink ribbon in her blonde hair. The single ponytail that she had pulled to the side to accommodate the mortar board made her blue eyes reflect the stadium lights. Bryson was a proud dad. It was the Z's turn to go first this year, so the Benders had a long while to wait.

Bryson got restless again and took a walk out to the side of the bleachers. Standing around the grassy area were a few smokers feeding their addiction. Bryson moved away from them to a place where he could still see Madeline.

A vise grip on his shoulder made him jump. He turned his head and was surprised to see John Southwick standing next to him.

"Sorry Bender, I guess that was your bad shoulder."

"Something tells me that you knew darn well that it was," he answered, turning to face the man on crutches. "And which one of your legs do I get to kick?"

Both men were silent and turned to watch the procession of students. There were the usual troublemakers on the field who threw their hats immediately after receiving their diplomas, or ran into the stands screaming.

"I didn't know you had anyone graduating," Bryson commented, breaking the silence between the men.

"I don't. I came because my wife said you would be here and she forbids me going to your house again. She is embarrassed and feels that I am the only reason that you got shot. But I need to talk to you."

Bryson looked at the man and shook his head. "How did two guys who were working hard, minding our own business just two months ago, end up here, unemployed, crippled and suspects in felony arson?"

"That is what I need to discuss. The cops have dropped all charges against me and were never going to charge you in the first place. They arrested Heiner and are throwing the book at him. He has been fired by the hospital board. You probably knew that too. The real news is that my attorney, who incidentally never accepted your money as a client . . . I gave the two hundred bucks to your wife. Anyway, my attorney has been talking to the hospital's legal boys. They are trying to stick fingers in the leaking dike, but are finally admitting that they want to talk to both of us. My attorney thinks that if we're willing to be reasonable, we can expect a quick settlement."

"I can't believe that they will cave in without a big fight. Besides, I don't even have an attorney," said Bryson.

The men's discussion was interrupted by an ambulance driving through the parking lot. Probably some excited mom fainted when she realized her baby was turning into an adult, or one of the students had started his or her celebrating too early. Bryson didn't have anything to add, but agreed to visit with Southwick the following week and hustled back into the stands just in time to watch his baby girl accept her diploma.

He didn't tell Marisa about the possible money settlement from the hospital until late that night. The two were lying in bed talking about the graduation events. They couldn't sleep, being too anxious about their daughter staying out for the all-night graduation party.

"I talked to Dr. Southwick tonight. He has been talking to an attorney. What would be your feelings about accepting say, a million dollars from the hospital for burning my office building?"

"No way," she said, surprising Bryson. "Their administrators caused your office to burn down, in turn causing you to have a heart attack and a stroke, not to mention that they sent the police to search our home. Then, as if that wasn't enough, the head man comes to our house and shoots you. There is no way I'm going to let you settle for a paltry million and we're not sharing it with a lawyer, especially some stranger. If we get money, we can get Brian to handle the paperwork. We'll take him out to dinner for his trouble."

She rolled off of his left arm and sat up in the bed, facing him. Light coming from the back bedroom windows behind her cast a halo of light around her long, flowing hair. Her silky nightgown was slipping off her right shoulder as she gave an animated argument for fighting for every possible penny. Bryson couldn't remember when he had respected or loved her more.

"I know that you are too beat down to deal with it, Bryson. I have Madeline's graduation behind me now, and once I can get her settled back at school, then I can get involved, and I will fight this thing until we win." The adrenaline was surging through her and a surge of endorphins were adding to the mix. He couldn't help thinking how fortunate he was to have her in his life. She leaned over to him, and for the second time that night, made him thrilled to be her husband.

# Chapter Nine

# BONANZA

Marisa Bender, "would-be champion of the fight for just compensation," never had the chance to fight. Early on Tuesday, the morning following Madeline's graduation, the three of them were eating breakfast on the patio. The birds were singing. The croissants and homemade raspberry jam tasted delicious. Then the phone rang.

"Dr. Bender? My name is David Flatt. I represent Western American Medical. We own the hospital where you work."

"Worked is closer to the truth, Mr. Flatt. I'm all too familiar with your company," Bryson answered.

"I would like to meet with you and your wife for just a few minutes today. Would that be a possibility?"

"I think that's out of the question," Marisa answered from the extension phone, which she had picked up the second she heard the hospital mentioned.

"If you will give me just a minute of your time, I might alleviate your anxieties and the possible need to pay a lot of money to an attorney."

"What is it exactly that you want to discuss?" Marisa asked, taking the lead of the conversation.

"I can be at your front door in twenty minutes, and an hour from now, I promise, you will be happy you took the time. If later in the day is better, we could meet then instead."

Marisa's eyes met Bryson's, and he gave a slight shrug, leaving the decision to his wife. She frowned at the phone and then agreed to meet the man at their house, but not for an hour.

They finished their breakfast, not clueing Madeline in on what was happening. She was sent off to pack a couple of boxes for shipping to school. The two of them went to get dressed. Bryson even shaved, something he had taken to doing randomly. They talked a bit about keeping calm and pokerfaced when they met the hospital representative. They sat in the family room, trying to stay calm, and concentrated on the network morning news.

David Flatt rang the doorbell at exactly nine-thirty. Gentlemanly looking, mid-fifties, of average height with slight graying around his temples, he wore the most expensive gray pinstripe suit Bryson had ever seen. The shoes were classic black oxfords. He carried a tan leather briefcase, the exact style Bryson had been given by Marisa the day he started medical school nearly forty years before.

The three of them made formal introductions and then they settled in the living room. Marisa had opened the shutters, filling the room with pleasant indirect light.

"I didn't tell you my position with Western Americana Medical because I didn't want you to slam the door on me, so to speak," Flatt began. "I am the chief counsel for the company and have been so for the last twelve years. I live in San Francisco. As you probably know, we have over fifty large hospitals in our Western group and own another two hundred physician office buildings. Needless to say, we are one of the biggest players in the health care field."

Bryson and Marisa listened without comment.

"I have reviewed the entire case file of your office building's fire and studied its probable cause. I have secondhand reports of your heart attack and subsequent small stroke, not that any stroke should be considered small. I have followed, on an almost-hourly basis, the bizarre events involving our previous hospital administrator, and of course, the unfortunate shooting of both you and Dr. Southwick."

"I still don't . . . " Bryson started to interrupt but was stopped mid-sentence by his wife's dagger-eyed glance.

"I will be the first to admit that in all the years I have

been involved in the health care industry, I have never been more saddened or embarrassed for my company than I have these last eight weeks. This is not the way our Americana does business, as reflected by our previous history. Presenting your file to the board of directors, we all felt like an airline company with a perfect flight record only to have a plane crash because of a lightning strike or sleepy pilot."

Bryson and Marisa sat pensively listening to what they supposed would be a lame attempt to apologize through some meager compensation.

Bryson leaned forward and said, "A drunken pilot is probably a better analogy."

"I couldn't agree more," Flatt said with a humble nod of his head.

*This could get interesting*, Bryson wanted to whisper in his wife's ear.

"Dr. Bender, my auditing department has looked at the record of your patient admissions over the last ten years, and plugging that into our national model, we have a pretty close idea of the income your office has generated. We realize that your personal physician has recommended full disability for you because of the stress of an Ob/Gyn practice, and we have been told that you have already started receiving compensation."

"And just how is it that you have been able to plug your nose into our personal lives so easily?" Marisa asked. "And by the way, your airline analogy is flawed. Instead of lightning or sleepy, you should have said the plane crashed because of a drug-crazed psychotic pilot." She stood from her chair and began pacing her living room.

"Let the gentleman speak his peace," Bryson said in a gentle tone.

"Just one more piece of information that you need to know," Mr. Flatt continued in a tone that suggested he was as uncomfortable as they were. "Three months ago, Dr.

Bender, you bought an office overhead policy from a company that Western Americana owns." He turned to the pacing Marisa and said, "Yes, Mrs. Bender, we also own some insurance companies." He paused to see if she was going to raise another protest. "That is how we have been able to survive the managed care assault.

"In your policy is a tiny clause that was strictly a marketing idea. The clause states that if your practice is lost because of fire, you could receive up to one point five million dollars compensation. Unfortunately for the client and fortunately for the insurance company, in another small clause it clarifies that the payout is only up to fifty percent of your gross overhead and is only paid out monthly up to age sixty-five, blah, blah, blah. Forget about the details."

Marisa had stopped looking at the man and was standing in front of the open picture window. Bryson's face was getting slightly warm and he had moved to the front edge of the club chair he was sitting in. He looked at Marisa and saw from his angle that her eyebrows were at high mast.

"Perhaps you could get to the point a little more quickly," Bryson suggested in a tone that hinted future homicide.

"Sorry for dragging this out. My company has authorized me to offer you a one-time lump settlement for the following: You will sign off on all legal and criminal action against Americana and against our previous employee, Mr. Heiner—by the way, they had to amputate one of his toes— I guess he literally shot himself in the foot. You will also accept the bottom line settlement as payment in full from the office overhead insurance policy. In short, you will agree to end all claims against our company and to free us of any future obligations. I have the papers all drawn up and there is a notary public waiting for us in my car."

"And?" Marisa said, clearly out of patience. "You are obviously having a jolly good time dragging out this explanation."

"In return for the above," Flatt continued, looking at the papers on his lap instead of at Marisa or Bryson, "considering all the problems, pain and suffering you have endured and the distress your five children have suffered in mental anguish, we are very aware that they have potential claims against us as well."

"How do you know about our children?" Marisa demanded.

"Madam, your children are a matter of public record. In any event, we have prepared and are ready today to hand over to you, in the form of cashier's checks, the following— by the way, the IRS laws are very clear that insurance payouts in legal settlements are not taxable."

"Would you please get to the point," Bryson said. He was now worrying about Marisa, whose face was beet red.

"For each of your five children, here is a check for two hundred thousand dollars. That's two hundred thousand for each of them." He extracted a plain manila envelope from his briefcase and sorted out the five checks.

Marisa and Bryson's jaws went slack. She turned to face him and stumbled to a seat on the blue wingback chair.

"For the two of you . . . and please believe me when I say that I went to bat for you because I think you have been completely victimized . . . the company is willing to pay you six million dollars. I have the cashier's check right here." He withdrew a perforated sheet of paper from his folder and held it out to them with two hands as his head bowed in Japanese-like offering.

The sentence rolled across the room like a blanket of silent fog. Both Marisa and Bryson sank back into their chairs and swallowed. Not a word was spoken for several seconds, then Flatt cleared his throat and suggested that they talk it over for a minute.

"If you don't mind, I will go out and let the young woman in my car know that we are almost finished. Please just pop your head out the door when you are ready for me—or us—as the case may be." He left his briefcase on the floor and left the room.

Bryson and Marisa's discussion lasted a total of four minutes. They looked over the summary face sheet of the contract and studied the six checks.

"This has nothing to do with your other disability policy, right?" Marisa confirmed.

"Right, the companies have nothing to do with each other. I'll still get the other check each month for the next three and a half years," Bryson confirmed.

"I need a drink of water, and then I vote that we accept," Marisa said in a choked-up voice.

"Me too," was all Bryson needed to say.

When Mr. Flatt returned, he offered to let Bryson call his own attorney to look over the documents, but in their eagerness to get on with the deal, both Bryson and Marisa waved off the offer and settled down around the dining room table to sign the raft of papers. An attractive young woman had joined them to witness and notarize the official signing of the documents.

Madeline had stuck her head in the door a couple of times to pretend to have important clothes-packing questions but had the good sense to realize that something major was occurring.

By ten-thirty the hospital corporation's attorney and his notary had packed up their cases and headed for the door.

The room was silent as the company car crunched the gravel and accelerated out of the driveway. Marisa silently cleared four water glasses from the dining room table as Bryson gathered up their copies of the legal work. He carried them into his study and laid them in the middle of the desk next to a stack of bills waiting to be paid. For most of his married life, the day he sat down each month to pay the bills had been the worst day of the month. Perhaps that would change.

When he walked back into the kitchen, he found his wife and his daughter wrapped in an embrace with tears in their eyes. The six checks were spread out on the counter and Madeline's eyes were fixed on the one with her name. Bryson put his arms around both women.

# Chapter Ten

# EIGHTEEN WHEELER

An old sage once said, "It is very difficult to endure lowering one's position in life, but oh so very easy to elevate it."

The day after the confirmation of the insurance funds clearing the bank account, Bryson picked up Jack Glen and again went shopping.

Marisa and Madeline were off to the travel agency to pick up their tickets for the flight to North Carolina. While they were waiting, they looked at some travel posters on the walls. Marisa quickly called her husband then made a spur-of-the-moment executive decision. Madeline concurred wholeheartedly. She made reservations and purchased tickets for the entire family to meet at an expensive rustic lodge near Jackson Hole, Wyoming for an emergency family reunion. No one had asked why they had chosen Jackson Hole. The glorious mountain scene on the posters had done its job.

Marisa and Bryson hadn't told the other kids about the money. Now, Marisa called each of her older four children and instructed them that they needed to make whatever arrangements were necessary to be in Jackson Hole in eight days. It would be worth the effort, she promised. Each of the four young families had fiscal challenges and personal worries, trying to raise young families in an ever-changing and very expensive world.

At first, each of the four married kids had excuses and balked at the idea, but when their dad's questionable health card was played, they each suspected some sort of "bad news" and agreed to show up.

\*\*\*

"No one has to lift a finger for the whole three-day weekend," their mom promised. "We will eat out for every meal."

They had heard that promise before, but after the first or second two-hundred-dollar meal check, Dad had always suggested doughnuts, cold cereal, cold cuts and pizza. They couldn't believe that history wouldn't repeat itself.

The Peterbilt dealer had several models and colors of the trucks but not the color Bryson wanted. It had to be a Peterbilt 387 in nautical blue with light tan leather interior.

Bryson and Jack had finished their second round of complimentary soda when the manager returned waving a sheaf of computer printouts.

"I found exactly what you want, Dr. Bender. The only problem is that, just like I told you a few weeks ago, it is in Bozeman, Montana. It's the same truck we discussed, and it hasn't been sold, which is surprising. Do you remember the truck?"

Bryson nodded and smiled as he took the copy of the spec sheet and read over it.

"The truck was apparently built for a movie star-wannabe cattle rancher and delivered a couple of months ago to the dealer in Bozeman, but it seems the guy's wife ran off with a Canadian cameraman, so the actor canceled his order and left the deposit on the table. That can be a good deal for you because the dealer is eager to get the thing off of his inventory and he's already made a tidy profit on the rig. This truck has everything in it you could ever order, including two flat screen TVs. All the electronics and mechanical options are premium, including the biggest Caterpillar engine they can put in a truck. I can send a driver up there and have the truck here in ten days, pending financing approval of course. Another option is for us to arrange a hauling job for you in the Bozeman area. You could fly up there and pick it up yourself. You would need a driver of course," he added, nodding at Bryson's right arm, which still hung lifeless in its sling.

Bryson asked the salesmen for a few minutes to talk it over with Jack, and they were left alone in a small office with the door closed. Bryson looked across the desk at Cousin Jack. "How would you like to take a little trip with me, all expenses paid and round-trip tickets for your wife to meet us at Hilton Head? We could pick up the truck and load somewhere in the Northwest and deliver it to the East Coast. Marisa is flying back to North Carolina with Madeline anyway. The four of us can meet there and have a great vacation."

It took Jack less than ten minutes to talk Jenny into some minor plan changes. Her plate for the summer had been pretty bare; the idea of a free week on a beach on the Atlantic coast sounded wonderful.

The paperwork took what seemed like hours. When they finally walked out of the dealership in mid-afternoon, Bryson was the proud owner of a nautical blue Peterbilt 387. His recently enriched bank account was down by $188,745.00 but he was the happiest man on the planet.

Bryson's slow, boring days were over. He had work to do. He called Winston, the owner of the truck driver's school, and made the arrangements to take a private driving class. Over the next six days, he would rush through a truck driver's course.

His shoulder was getting stronger but still ached by the end of each day. The last scab from the bullet wound peeled off three weeks after the shooting. He came home from driver's school to Marisa's wonderful dinners and then fell asleep in the recliner, long before the local news aired.

Marisa had completely taken over the organization of the upcoming trips as well as the household money matters. Bryson never opened another piece of mail. Their lifelong worries about money were a thing of the past.

***

"What are you going to do with this monster?" Madeline asked her dad. She was holding up a glossy eight-by-ten photo of his new truck. "I hope you aren't going to park this thing out in front of the house. It's almost as big as our garage. I'll bet Mr. Larsen isn't going to like you blocking his view of that blonde lady who sunbathes on her front lawn."

This drew a laugh from the dinner group of her friends seated around the kitchen table.

It wasn't the first time he had heard the ribbing. Bryson's friends and several of his extended family members had posed the same kinds of questions. What was he going to haul? Where would he be hauling it to? How was he going to load and unload a massive truck? Would he make enough to even pay for the fuel?

Bryson didn't get into medical school by being stupid and irrational. By the Wyoming reunion date, he had it all figured out. He had contacted a trucking agent suggested by the Bozeman truck dealer. The agent had put him in touch with a company that transported vintage and exotics cars and had set him up for a cross-country trip. He would pick up his first load in Reno, Nevada and deliver it to a classic automobile auction near Miami, Florida. An enclosed auto-trailer would be provided by the car company. The pickup date was just two days after the family's upcoming Jackson Hole reunion.

Jack and Jenny had cleared their schedules. Bryson had passed his rapid emersion truck driving course and had the appropriate licenses and insurance. With Jack's tutelage, they would be all set to hit the road. Bryson planned to go to Bozeman straight from the family get-together in Jackson Hole. Jack would fly to Bozeman from Phoenix. The men would meet their wives two weeks later in North

Carolina or Florida, depending on whether the girls wanted to ride in the truck or not. Bryson just knew that they would. The one thing Bryson couldn't figure out was how Marisa had known to make the family reunion plan in Jackson Hole—a half hour flight from Bozeman.

"Woman's intuition," was all she would say.

# Chapter Eleven
# WHEELER DEALERS

"This is Fritz."

"Hey Fritz, this is Chubby Brown over in Bozeman. I think I have the rookie driver you've been searching for." The Bozeman truck dealer had a Cheshire cat grin on his face as he held the telephone to his mouth. He had previously met Fritz at a sleazy casino on the outskirts of Reno to take delivery on a 600 SL AMG Mercedes, which Fritz had advertised online. The price had been a steal for the Bozeman truck dealer. Little did he know that for Fritz it had been free.

They had talked about cars and trucks and women. At the time, Fritz had asked Brown if he could hook him up with a six-car enclosed auto trailer and someone to move cars from Seattle to his newly acquired site in Reno. Fritz recently asked for help finding a truck and driver to move cars from Reno to Florida.

"Some retired doctor from Arizona just sent me a fax contract for a new Peterbilt. He is so eager to get a load to haul to the East Coast that he might pay you for the privilege of pulling it. Not!" Brown laughed. "I told him about your needing a good, safe driver to haul fancy cars to Florida and he jumped all over it. He is picking up the truck next Monday and can be in Reno on Wednesday morning. This guy is for sure a rookie, but has some other guy with experience helping him. They have no affiliation with the union or a regular booking agent, so no one will be watching their back. Just what you wanted—right?"

Fritz Krefeld hung up his phone and rubbed his hands together as he walked into his warehouse. He threw a breaker box switch and turned on the lights. In front of him lay six of the most beautiful cars he had ever seen, let alone owned. They were the cream of the crop. It had taken him months to get them all together in one building and show-ready for the upcoming sale. He had thought about waiting for the Concourse de Elegance at Pebble Beach, or even waiting for the new Barrett Jackson sale in Vegas in October, but then it got complicated.

In the safe in his warehouse office lay thirteen brown-paper-wrapped bundles. Each was about the size of a five-hundred-sheet pack of copy paper. One of the bundles appeared slightly different from the others. It was marked with a large red X. Even more important than the bundles was a small, red, leather pouch. It was nearly as heavy as one of the paper bundles and made a strange muted sound as the metal objects inside made contact. Fritz hefted the pouch and had an idea—he always had an idea. He went to his desk for a pair of utility scissors and a roll of packing tape. He found a thick, empty cardboard box on a dusty shelf. Knocking off the dust, he took it back into the office and laid it on his desk. With a sharp box cutter in hand, he began carefully cutting the shape and pattern he had in mind for the coins' new hiding place.

✳✳✳

Fritz was a newcomer to Reno. He had grown up in a small town in West Germany, close to the famous Nuremberg rink. The rink was a test track for Europe's exotic car dealers and the site of numerous auto races. He grew up to the screaming sound of high revving, speeding cars circling the nearby racecourse. He had his own secret hole in the race-track fence and it was a daily experience for him to sneak through onto the forbidden property to watch the cars. Formula Ones, Indy cars, Ferraris, Mercedes, Porsches, Lamborghinis and Aston Martins all were familiar sights. The pictures he took of the secret prototypes adorned his tiny bedroom. By the time he was twelve, he had stolen a

Zeiss camera and had made a small business of selling his secret "vorboten fotos" to a local newspaperman and later to automobile magazines, including Auto Week and Motor Trend. The manufacturers couldn't figure how quality pictures of their supposedly secret early prototype models were showing up in the media.

When Fritz was fifteen, his father's work brought the family to Vancouver, Canada. Once living in a foreign land with a different language to learn, Fritz was immediately labeled an outsider. Though he learned English well, his accent prevailed. By the time he could speak and write like a local, he was behind in school and in most social settings. He was never able to get his grades up high enough to get into college. He did, however, master the computer and turned to it to educate himself all about life, money and most importantly, his childhood passion, cars. Next, he went to the street for his continuing education.

Fritz soon learned where the rich people lived. Thus, he was able to locate and observe the best and most expensive cars coming and going from their driveways or garages. Walking a dog he had picked up from the pound, he was surprised at how negligent many of the owners of these vehicles were. Often he saw the owners leave cars unlocked with the keys in the ignition. The wives or girlfriends were the worst.

By the age of twenty-one, he had created a small car theft business that eventually established him as the go-to man for anyone in British Columbia wanting an exotic car for a fraction of the normal price. At the tender age of twenty-four, he found himself sitting in a stark, freezing-cold Canadian jail cell awaiting transfer to a prison in Calgary.

He had been ordered by a judge to serve a five-year stint with free room and board. The mistake Fritz had made was to lift a Bentley Continental from the owner of a small, but successful, insurance company. He then resold the car to a local stockbroker who, that very same day, called his friendly broker to purchase insurance on the same car. Two plus two equaled a jail term for the young car thief.

His cellmate in the Vancouver jail was an older man who had immigrated to Canada from Austria. Fredrick Landsberg had made a fortune as an artist of sorts. He could forge anything that one could write or draw on paper and was very good at it. His favorites were historical letters and documents for which naive collectors paid enormous amounts of hard-earned money just for the bragging rights of owing an Adolf Hitler shopping list, or a memo pad kissed by Princess Diana. He had also learned the art of engraving metal, which he had turned into one of any government's worst fears: the capability of producing a near-perfect bank note.

Fredrick had taken a liking to Fritz, who reminded him of his own son. While waiting for two months in the Vancouver jail, he had begged, borrowed and stolen enough materials to make himself and Fritz a complete set of identification papers. They both became instant citizens of the United States of America.

During the transfer to the Calgary prison, a dozen counterfeit Canadian hundred-dollar bills had purchased five minutes of a guard's inattention and a spare handcuff key. Fredrick and Fritz calmly walked down an employees' corridor and out of the train station free men. No one had even questioned the blue jumpsuits they were wearing with the word PRISONER printed on the back. People who looked at them must have thought of it like an FBI ball cap—a new fashion statement.

Once across the border into the U.S., the men temporarily parted ways. Arriving in Seattle later in the week, the two met up again and found a small apartment in the Belmont area. Fritz remembered having read that it was a town where there were lots of wealthy Microsoft employees. Stealing the locals' identities would prove to be easy.

Fritz thought it humorous that the smartest computer

geeks in the world were also some of the most apathetic people toward protecting their own identity. All it took was a person's social security number. With those nine numbers, Fritz and Fredrick could go online to drain a bank account, reassign the ownership of a house or car and even scramble a man's work computer, creating distraction and nightmares for the poor sucker.

Fritz had sworn off stealing cars after he was arrested in Canada, but his first Friday night in Belmont, his feet were tired of walking. An idling Porsche Turbo in the Belmont Mall parking lot was more than he could resist. Within two days, the car was carrying new windshield VIN numbers and even had a bogus service record backed up by a computer sales printout from a Tacoma Porsche dealer. Fritz drove the car for four months, building a service record at a dealership in Everett where he was becoming a familiar fixture. It was there where he met the golden contact.

Bill Vance was an original employee of the Microsoft team and had taken more than an average share of stock in lieu of salary in the early days. Now he was forced into making frequent sales of his stock option holdings, which created an enormous tax burden. The poor man was required to take home four to five million dollars a quarter in stock earnings. What to do with it? Fritz, hearing the sad story while waiting for their cars to be serviced one morning, had the perfect answer. He feigned sympathy for the man, then presented his suggestion.

"Why don't you start a car collection and then donate it at a generous markup to a worthy charity, thus blessing the lives of others and giving yourself a sweet tax break? I can help you find the cars, and when you have fifteen or twenty, I can offer a generous appraisal. Then you simply donate them at the end of the tax year, saving yourself millions in taxes. I've done it for several wealthy families," Fritz lied. "It's a wonderful way to help others and still look out for your own interest."

To Mr. Vance, Fritz's offer seemed too good to be true. Within a few months, Fritz had acquired ten of the nicest cars on the planet, including a 1967 Ferrari 275 GTB and a 1972 Ferrari California Cabriolet appraised at six million dollars. He found a 1958 frame up restoration Mercedes 300 SL with working gull wing doors, two rare Lamborghinis and a forty-year-old Aston Martin identical to the "007 James Bond Goldfinger" car. They were offered to Mr. Vance as part of the package. The cheapest car of the bunch was a Porsche Carrera GT with serial number 00021. The software mogul had gladly parted with the large sums of money. Vance had shown up once to inspect the cars and was so pleased that he had Fritz find and buy an eleventh car for himself, a Ferrari Enzo, in a one-of-a-kind neon orange color. Fritz charged a modest one hundred thousand dollar commission on that million-dollar purchase.

Once the purchase of all the cars was accomplished, to the tune of fourteen million dollars, Fritz contacted a local tax exempt foundation and offered to donate the cars in Mr. and Mrs. Vance's name. The cars could then be auctioned off at the annual black tie dinner, the proceeds going to the foundation's many charities. Vance would take a generous tax write-off in excess of twenty-five million dollars. The cars were to be delivered to the foundation in time for their Good Friday Gala. Fritz agreed to store the cars for Mr. Vance until the auction. That was the last Vance ever saw of the handsome Fritz and his ten very expensive cars.

Fredrick the forger had also been a busy man, creating a brand-new set of ownership papers for the cars with a slight change in the type of cars delivered to the charity. It wasn't until the Wednesday prior to the gala that the ex-Microsoft executive received an upsetting letter thanking him for donating his four cars (not the ten originally promised) and asking about the most valuable one, the 1976 Bicentennial Corvette. Could they perhaps get an updated registration, since a previous owner had shown up with the police, claiming that the Corvette had been stolen in front of his house three months prior, and the man wanted his car returned? When the police were asked to investigate the crime, they broke into the storage warehouse where Mr. Vance swore his exotic cars were stored. They found a 1989 Olds Cutlass with no wheels or engine but with a rental contract taped to the hood of the car. It confirmed the cash payment for six months of rent on the warehouse. It was signed by a Mr. Thomas Jefferson.

None of the original ten cars could be found. The police and the IRS would eventually wonder if they ever existed. Likewise, none of the supposed stolen cars could be traced to the kind, young automobile broker, Thomas Jefferson.

Fritz secretly transported the ten classic cars to a small warehouse at the back of an Audi-Aston Martin dealership in downtown Reno, Nevada. The warehouse had no association with the car dealer in front, but gained credibility by proximity. The stolen cars all had a new identity, just like their new owner. Fritz sold four of the lesser valued cars to a poker player who was on a roll in a World Poker Championship and had fallen in love with the '99 Lamborghini but couldn't decide to leave the other three either. Flush with cash, Fritz ordered a new enclosed transport trailer, which would hold and hide six cars. The rest of the money he loaned to his old friend Fredrick for a half-share in his newly purchased printing and engraving business. Fritz also purchased a tiny Reno metal foundry. Fredrick and Fritz were now in the engraving and printing business. They even bought a big new neon sign to place on the front of the building: "GREAT REPRODUCTIONS."

With lots of free time on his hands and plenty of money under the mattress—both real and counterfeit—Fritz had taken up a new hobby. He had seen an article in National Geographic Magazine about ancient Persian and Babylonian coins, which were stolen from the Baghdad Museum in 2001. The article told how the coins were priceless and that many buyers were trying to track them down. As Fritz studied further, he found that one of the most precious sets of seven coins was for sale on eBay. The bid at the time was for three hundred thousand dollars, but the seller had the bid limit set far higher. The sellers were foolish enough to include high quality photographs in their offerings along with photographs of the other missing coins. The exact dimensions and the assay of the gold alloys were also stated. It was a forger's dream. Fredrick and Fritz went to work studying metallurgy. The world wanted ancient coins and now they were going to get them. A couple of quick gold jewelry grabs and they would have everything they needed. Just like the printed money, swapping bad paper for good wouldn't be a big problem.

There was, however, one new problem for Fritz.

Fredrick's only son, Clause, had shown up one night at their apartment. He was about Fritz's age but taller and stronger and wore his blond hair pulled back in a ponytail. He, like Fredrick, spoke with a slight accent, but unlike his frail father, was built like his childhood hero, the body builder, Mr. Universe and now governor of California. The father was very pleased to see his only son. It had been years since he had come to visit in Canada. Now reunited, the father was quick to include his son in the business of printing and engraving. Fritz was outwardly agreeable but deeply jealous. More than anything, he was panicked. This new partner was dumber than a nickel slot machine jockey, yet stronger than a bull. It soon became apparent to Fritz that Clause believed every problem in life could be solved with brute force. Including, taking over Fritz' share of the business.

The first thing Fritz did was to make secret plans to move his precious cars. They were not a part of his partnership with Fredrick. He looked for the most distant place he could find where high rollers were abundant. The next thing he did was to go to work on the Babylonian coins. Fredrick would soon have the blanks engraved and Fritz was learning quickly how to cast and age the precious replicas.

He remembered the hick truck salesman from Montana whom he had fleeced with the stolen Mercedes. Fritz had jacked up the price by merely sticking some AMG decals and emblems on the stock-equipped car. He gave the jerk a call, putting out the word that he had to move some cars and needed a novice driver.

# Chapter Twelve

# REUNION

The mother and daughter team had everything they needed for their trips: E-tickets for the plane flights, rental cars for all the kids in Jackson Hole and a Hertz full-size SUV waiting to handle Madeline's plentiful luggage in North Carolina. The family get-together in Jackson Hole was going to be very short, but lots of fun. It seemed all the families had commitments, which would only allow them to be gone for a long weekend. The oldest son, Sawyer, had to buy his two days off pediatric call.

Shadow Lake Lodge was one of earth's windows into heaven. Marisa was told that early June is by far the best time to see Jackson and Yellowstone. No place on earth has more wildflowers or bigger mosquitoes, but the bugs don't usually hatch until July.

Unfortunately, the spring rains can come late, and on the Bender family's weekend in Jackson Hole, they did just that. Not only did it rain, but by Friday evening when the stragglers arrived at the lodge, there was two inches of slush on the ground. Lots of activities had been planned for Saturday and Sunday, but the storm settled in, and by noon on Saturday, the little kids were driving the childless couples crazy.

Early in the afternoon a reluctant daughter was elected spokeswoman for the four married Bender kids. She approached Bryson as he rolled around on the great-room floor with his toddler grandkids, receiving painful blows to his sore shoulder in the process.

"Dad, I know something is going on. You and Mom are planning some kind of extra-special dinner tonight. Madeline is a tight-lipped, spoiled brat. She knows something but won't share a word. We have all been talking. Anyway, we just got the weather report and the Jackson Hole airport is closed and probably won't be open again until Monday. How about we have the secret dinner early and then we can all get the kids to bed and play card games like we used to do? In the morning, I think we are all going to drive to Idaho Falls and catch early flights home. Let's do this get-together again in the fall, when it is supposed to be dry here, or better still, let's do it in Newport or Hawaii."

The new plan made sense, but it took a little of Marisa's wind from her sails. Ultimately, she conceded. The early evening dinner was excellent but chaotic, plus there was a pall of hidden gloom in the room. The older kids all thought that the dinner meeting was to announce bad news, perhaps an illness.

Instead of bad news, each family was given a box of Godiva chocolates with a large Madeline-made greeting card. When they opened the cards to find their checks, they were stunned. Explaining about the money was fun for Marisa. When good old Dad announced that he had spent a nearly equal amount on his new eighteen wheeler, they almost died. The card games and early bedtimes were forgotten.

Family togetherness and joyful conversations ruled late into the night. Who says you can't buy happiness?

The rain continued. By Sunday at noon the lodge had cleared out and even Madeline and Marisa had packed their bags and were ready to leave. It had been a wonderful but short thirty-six hours together. The four married families were still in shock from the huge checks. Hugs and kisses were exchanged and then they went their separate ways.

Around noon, Bryson saw Madeline and Marisa off at the Jackson Hole airport, which had reopened just in time for their flight back home to Phoenix and then on to Duke. Bryson returned to the lodge to gather up his traveling clothes. Looking around the large, empty, great room with its massive fireplace made him sad. Only a few embers remained from last night's roaring fire. His footsteps echoed down the hallway to the bedrooms where laughs and cries of joy had filled the air just hours before. Parting had been tough. He loved his kids, but they had to get on with their own lives, and he and Marisa with theirs.

# Chapter Thirteen

# BIG BLUE

Jenny took her "trucker boy" Jack to the airport and bid him farewell. If all went as planned, they would meet in North Carolina in about two weeks. Jenny was so excited thinking about a long vacation clear across the country. Doing it all first-class was a dream. Jenny was a practical gal. She grew up in a middle-class family and worked part-time to get through college. She had often dreamed of world travel, but marrying her high school sweetheart had meant years pinching pennies on the farm. She had a handful of successful kids to show for all her hard work but not many stamps in her passport.

The Benders' invitation to join them and to leave their money at home sounded wonderful. Jenny liked both Marisa and Bryson and spending time with them would be great. Her kids were all off on their own, married with lots of children, pets, lesson schedules, soccer practices and homework. They had little time in their lives for her. She had found living in the desert a huge change from the farm. There she had been a pillar of the community with social engagements and church activities to fill her day. Now that Jack had sold the farm, the days were long and predictable.

She was thrilled to see Jack excited about driving the truck with his cousin. Maybe it would turn into a regular activity, which would be a lot better than his recent no activity. She was ready for a change and some fun. This trip could be the start of a new kind of adventure in life. At least, she might have some new stories to tell the kids and her friends back in Idaho.

\*\*\*

Bryson faced a three-hour drive to Bozeman where he and Jack agreed to meet Sunday night. As Bryson repacked his bag, he threw in some things that he would never have taken if he had gone with the girls.

Against his basic nature, he had let Jack take him to Cabello's and had bought an eight-inch-blade hunting knife, a pair of high-power Nikon binoculars and a .38-caliber revolver, which he had hidden in Marisa's check-on luggage. Jack had been raised around guns, but this would be the first handgun Bryson had owned since he first started having to take overnight calls as a medical student. He had bought a used pistol for Marisa to keep in the nightstand drawer. She had refused to even practice-firing it. Two years later, when their first baby had started crawling, Marisa had insisted that the gun leave the house.

Now, looking at the new pistol he wondered aloud, "Why did I ever buy this thing? I'll never use it in a thousand years."

✳✳✳

Bryson's drive through Yellowstone Park and Jack's flight to Bozeman coincided with a fabulous early summer sunset. They left Bryson's rental at the airport and took a cab to the Best Western motel. They found a brightly lit café nearby and ate a greasy cheeseburger and homemade cherry pie for dinner. There was no chicken fried steak on the menu.

They turned in for what was supposed to be a long night's rest but their sleep was often interrupted. First it was late-arriving guests, then big diesel trucks gearing down to stop and start again at the nearby intersection. The next-door neighbors had a lovers' quarrel after midnight and then Jack started to snore. Bryson never really went back to sleep.

✳✳✳

The Peterbilt dealer, Chubby Brown, picked Jack and Bryson up at the motel at eight sharp in an expensive Mercedes. They had already eaten a pancake and sausage breakfast at Denny's. The salesman was a young, energetic fellow dressed in pointed-toe boots and tight Wrangler jeans. He boasted of being the fourth generation of Browns to sell big-rig trucks in Montana. The man talked constantly on the drive from the motel to the outskirts of town where the dealership was located.

Bryson's big blue Peterbilt truck was waiting out on a neatly mown patch of grass in front of the dealership. The bright morning sunshine was capturing the tiny morning dewdrops, making the truck sparkle like an enormous wet sapphire. It seemed so much bigger than the pictures they had emailed to Bryson. The three men walked full circle around the machine, silently admiring it, and then the moment of christening came. Mr. Brown handed Bryson a thumb-sized black FOB. With a squeeze of Bryson's fingers, a loud chirp sang out from beneath the hood of the truck and the door lock mechanisms clicked open. Bryson reached up and opened the driver's side door. With his left hand, he awkwardly pulled himself up into the driver's seat, sinking into the soft contours of the tufted leather chair with its fresh, rich, new leather aroma. As he looked around the cabin, the truck's interior seemed much larger than the similar model he had looked at back home. He was so happy and comfortable that he didn't want to ever move.

Brown insisted on giving the men a detailed orientation to the myriad of dials, knobs, switches and gauges. The paperwork had all been completed thru FedEx and the bank's money transfers were confirmed.

"You can skip most of the explanations," Bryson told Brown. "We'll read the manuals as we drive to Reno."

Bryon and Jack shook hands with Chubby, the smiling drugstore cowboy, and threw their bags into the sleeping cabin. They buckled into their seats, and with a blast from the air horn, off they went.

Bryson insisted on Jack driving the big blue monster out of the city limits of Bozeman. He had slept on his right shoulder the last couple of hours, causing more morning pain than usual. They could trade places once they reached the open road where there wouldn't be as much gear shifting. Maybe his Advil would kick in by then. Bryson was as excited as the day he delivered his first baby, but he was also just as nervous. They stopped at a highway service yard on the outskirts of town and traded places without even getting out of the truck.

They were off again. Bryson was trying hard to contain his excitement as Jack talked him through the first combination of gears, propelling them down the narrow roads toward the mountain pass to the west. He couldn't believe how high up off the highway they were sitting. Oh, how wonderful was the smell of the new leather and shininess of the paint. Even the new linens on the oversized bunk beds smelled great. Everything was better than Bryson had dreamed.

Once they were familiar with the basics, Jack got out the owner's manual and started orienting them to the satellite connected navigation and weather reporting systems. The traffic was light and the weather promised to be a beautiful day.

They had driven about fifty miles on the state highway when the pain in Bryson's shoulder became too much to handle; he pulled off the road at a tiny rest stop to trade places. They each bought a Pepsi from a beat-up vending machine and reminded each other to stop at a grocery store in the next town to stock their tiny fridge.

Jack took over the driving and Bryson dove into the thick owner's manual. He was reading and studying the myriad of instrumentation when something totally unexpected happened. He was stricken with a massive wave of nausea.

He spared ruining the inside new-leather smell of the truck, but just barely. By the time Jack slowed the truck and found a safe place to pull off the road, Bryson was hanging outside the door, standing on the running board and wishing he would die. He finally got to terra firma and lay down in the weeds alongside the road, watching the big, puffy clouds overhead spin like tops.

"I guess I forgot to tell you about the swaying motion of the cab. It's because we sit up so high off the road," Jack explained, leaning over his stricken friend and laughing in sympathy. "Don't worry, you'll get used to it by tomorrow."

Jack helped Bryson to his feet and offered to stop and buy him some Dramamine. Bryson shook his head and staggered up into the sleeper cabin. "I'll try out that special mattress instead." He added more Advil to the last swallow of Pepsi and stretched out on the feather-soft bed. Within moments the swaying motion had rocked him to sleep. Two hours later, Bryson was wide awake and getting antsy to take the wheel again.

"How about stopping for lunch and then we'll switch," Jack suggested. "You left breakfast behind. Marisa warned me to keep you well fed."

As they approached a little town, the neophyte trucker started seeing roadside signs for restaurants. Suddenly, there right in front of his eyes stood the roadside café of Bryson's dreams.

"That's it, that's it! Stop the truck right here."

Jack quickly began decelerating. With a roar of downshifting, engine-braking and the whine of new brake pads on new disks, the bright blue monster turned off into the dusty parking lot.

Bryson still felt a little lightheaded but couldn't resist the opportunity to eat a meal in an honest-to-goodness truck stop café. His empty stomach's growling helped perk his interest.

The men climbed down from the cab for the third time that morning and stretched their legs. Jack's bum knee was hurting but he wasn't going to say a word. He had been having the time of his life and at Bryson's expense. A big lunch followed by a nap sounded terrific. The old farmer's rule of a short nap after lunch had always worked for Jack. There were only four trucks in the café's parking lot but it was a little early for a lunch crowd. The screen door leading into the dark emerald green building was barely hanging on its hinges. As the men walked inside, the door slapped the frame behind them, assuring those inside that only very fast flies would make it through the door.

The air inside was warm and stale and was mingled with the lingering smell of bacon, maple syrup and stale beer. Green upholstered booths lined two walls and four Formica-top tables were positioned in the middle. Chrome napkin holders and disposable paper salt and pepper shakers adorned the red tables. In the far corner was a Gibson jukebox with the lights on and a Johnny Cash song gyrating from its speakers. Bryson had a flashback of stopping at just such a place when he was a kid.

He was disappointed to see a Coca-Cola soft drink dispenser next to the kitchen door, complete with paper cups and ice maker. It seemed far too modern for the setting he had fixed in his mind. He was even more disappointed to see a shelf of aging Twinkies, Snowballs and Hostess Cupcakes in sparse supply standing where he had expected to see a circular glass homemade pie display case.

There were two middle-age men sitting in a corner booth. Two other younger guys sat on round, chrome-based bar stools, leaning on a beat-up green Formica countertop. On the back side of the counter were the remnants of a soda fountain with two broken-handled dispensers. A large etched glass mirror hung on the back wall. It was cock-eyed by a couple of degrees and had scattered black spaces where the silver on the back had worn off. The neon lights in the room buzzed with an annoying din. All four of the patrons turned to look at Jack and Bryson. None of them smiled.

The two newcomers took a seat at one of the tables, nodding a greeting to the men at the nearby counter. Both of them wore stained jeans and sweatshirts with the sleeves cut out. Their arms displayed scattered tattoos of various color and quality. The men in the booth had on Western-cut shirts with snap buttons. They were a good ten years older than the two at the counter but just as rough-cut looking. Their cowboy hats hung from long hooks on a chrome pole attached to the booth. They had matching beards and the closer Jack and Bryson looked at them the more they looked like twins. Their shirts even matched.

"Nice-looking truck you got out there," one of the brothers said. "Our triplet brother rolled one just like it 'bout a year ago. Them Peterbilts don't seem to like crosswinds."

"I hope he was all right," Bryson answered in a cheerful tone, glad to be actually talking to a real trucker.

"The cab collapsed on him like a cheap Coors can. We had to have a special coffin made. It was nearly five feet wide and only four inches tall. Poor guy's head looked like a deflated basketball."

"That's horrible," said Jack. "Crosswinds? That's a big problem, eh?"

The brothers looked at each other and then started to snicker. One even covered his mouth to try to hold it back before he gave up and they both started pounding the table and laughing.

"We had you guys going there, didn't we?"

Embarrassed and a little aggravated, Bryson feigned a complementary chuckle then picked up a sticky menu and started reading. Jack's face was already buried in the menu.

A loose, hand-printed page stuck in the menu with a paper clip announced a special of fried beef liver with onions, bacon bits and pork-and-beans. The mere thought of it almost made Bryson gag. Gratefully, he found a description for what sounded like chicken fried steak, but it came with fries. No potatoes or gravy were mentioned. He tried to find something that sounded good, but most of the entrees reminded him of his recent bout with motion sickness.

"Howdy boys," came a voice from behind followed by the sound of swinging doors leading from the kitchen.

All six men turned their attention to a gray-haired woman whose girth was so great that she had to squeeze behind the check-out counter to retrieve an order pad. She was wearing a faded, sleeveless muumuu just like Bryson had seen some of his morbidly obese patients wear. Her wrists were covered with dozens of silver bracelets, which jangled as she waddled over to the table to write down their order. There were so many rings on her fingers and thumbs that Bryson was amazed that she could hold the pencil.

"What can I get for you boys? Betcha you two worked up a mighty appetite driving that new blue rig."

Bryson found it a bit strange that everyone in the room knew what they were driving even though the windows in the café were tiny and covered with lace curtains and flyspecks.

"My name is Gladys. The cheeseburgers are fresh and the liver comes from my nephew's 4-H steer that bloated yesterday. It was still steaming when Tad brought it in this morning. It don't get no fresher than that."

Jack ordered a cheeseburger and fries. Bryson was still just slightly queasy and nothing greasy sounded good. He had grown up eating liver and fried onions buried in catsup and had always enjoyed the smell, but not the taste. He wasn't about to eat the liver of the beef that had died in a field that morning.

"Do you have any yogurt or maybe an apple Danish?"

Immediate laughter erupted from all four of the other men and from Gladys. Even Jack was having difficulty suppressing a smile.

"I'm sorry, honey, but we just ran out of our wide selection of yogurt. We're also out of tofu and pussy willow flavored water in those little pink bottles. That stuff sells like hotcakes around here."

The men in the room were laughing and pounding the tables. Jack gave up restraining himself and joined in the laugh.

"I still have some pancake batter I was fixing to throw out but there's enough for a short stack? I get the feeling the rest of our menu doesn't turn your crank." She glanced at the men in the booth and grinned.

Bryson nodded in agreement and ordered a Diet Coke to wash down the pancakes and the bile. Jack asked for a bottle of Heinz 57 from the counter.

The meals were eventually served and quickly eaten. The other truckers had left and Bryson thought he heard all the trucks leave. He was wrong. There, sitting on the running board of his new truck, was the ugliest and meanest looking of the four drivers. He was tall and muscular with tattoos on both arms and half a pound of metal studs piercing his earlobes. He was wearing a leather Harley hat with its stubby little useless brim and smoking a cigarette, holding it cupped in his hand like Bryson had seen pot smokers do. He didn't stand up, but instead crossed his leg, giving the distinct body language that he had no intention of moving. His dusty black boots had pointed metal studs around the toes. Bryson turned around for backup, but Jack had gone into the freestanding men's room at the other end of the parking lot.

"I'm wanting to take your shiny new truck here for a little test drive," the creepy-looking man said in a loud, demanding voice from across the way. He held out his hand for the keys.

Bryson could smell the cigarette now and it wasn't a Marlboro. The idiot's body odor was dank and offensive even in the open air as he squatted on the spot Bryson or Jack would have to cross to enter the truck's cab.

"Would you please move?" Bryson said in a firm but polite voice.

"Gimme the keys and I'll show you rookies how to double clutch this thing so it purrs like a kitten."

Bryson's pores opened and tiny beads of sweat burst out on every centimeter of his skin. He could feel his blood pressure raising and his heart pounding in his chest. He could also feel the pain in his shoulder as his neck muscles tightening in anger. He spoke to the man, trying to reason with the guy, but he wasn't making any headway. The man had both fists clenched and was almost screaming his demand for the keys to the big blue truck. That's when Jack yelled from across the parking lot.

"I think something is wrong with your engine!" Jack shouted, motioning toward the older black semi. It was attached to a trailer loaded with bales of hay. The engine had been running the entire time the man was in the café, as was normal with the older type of diesel engines.

Smoke was coming out from under the front of the older truck. Bryson's nemesis jumped to his feet, throwing his reefer to the ground. He ran across the parking lot toward his smoking truck. Jack crossed paths with him midway and by the time the idiot found the source of the smoke, Bryson and Jack had scrambled into their truck and were pulling onto the highway.

"What happened back there?" Bryson asked, not even stopping to think about the fact that he was in the driver's seat and they were rolling sixty-five miles per hour down the road.

"A cardboard box full of broken tumbleweeds somehow made its way under his truck and that's when the spontaneous combustion must have occurred," Jack replied with a sarcastic edge to his voice.

Bryson was now staring bug-eyed at Jack. "You're kidding me, right?"

"Hey, you and I are in no condition to fight some thirty-year-old pothead. If he hit either one of us once, we would be dead! Watch the road!"

And so he did. From the truck stop café to the first turn onto the Interstate, heading toward Reno, had been just long enough for Bryson to cut his teeth on driving the big truck. Jack read instructions from the owner's manual and Bryson scanned the dashboard with its array of gauges and dials and toggle switches. The hardest thing for Bryson to master was the transmission. Every change of gears reminded him that his shoulder still wasn't normal. Once on the Interstate, it was smooth sailing in the luxury of their leather-lined cab with little shifting required. As the sun's angle changed, it caused a glare on the bug-splattered windshield. They were approaching the outskirts of Elko, Nevada and it was time for fuel and a windshield scrubbing.

They pulled off the freeway into the sprawling parking lot of the biggest truck stop Bryson had ever imagined. He had passed mega-truck stops but had never stopped at one. There was row after row of fuel pumps and a drive-through automatic truck wash as big as a gymnasium. Semi-tractors of every kind and color were lined up with their trailers in neat rows. It reminded him of the pictures he had seen of B-29 bombers on the runways of Saipan and Tinian, loaded and ready for takeoff for the bombing of Tokyo.

Bryson carefully guided "Big Blue"—the apparent nickname for his truck—alongside one of the fuel pumps. Not having a trailer attached made it pretty easy. Tomorrow would be a different challenge. The place seemed friendly and inviting, unlike the dusty roadside dive where they had eaten lunch and nearly gotten mugged.

What a great feeling Bryson had as he climbed down from the cab and realized that he had just driven over three hundred miles behind the wheel of his very own eighteen wheeler. Every bone and joint in his body ached but he still felt great. He had the trucking world by the tail. And then he tried to refuel his truck.

Jack had made a dash to the head, leaving Bryson standing alone by the fuel pump. Somehow, the pump just didn't look right. There was no place to slide a credit card like all the gas pumps he had used for years. There was just one big toggle switch. Who kept track of the charges? Shrugging his shoulders, he picked up the heavy nozzle whose hose was almost as big as his wrist and turned to place it in the truck's filler spout only to remember that he hadn't removed the cap. He had probably put gas in his cars a thousand times yet he felt inadequate trying to put diesel fuel in his new truck for the first time. He had already made a noticeable mistake. He hung the nozzle back on its hook—it took both hands to do it—and turned his attention toward removing the cap. The cap was polished chrome and the diameter of a small Frisbee. He tried to unscrew it with one hand but quickly resorted to two. That's when he heard the nozzle and hose behind him hit the ground with a sickening thud. He jumped back as fuel sprayed from the wide nozzle, soaking his pants' legs and shoes and creating a widening pool of smelly diesel fuel.

Several attendants appeared out of nowhere, shutting off the pump and scattering an absorbent on the several gallons of spilled fuel. Although other truckers walked by and looked at the mess, none of them said a word. No one was unkind to Bryson about the accident and one roly-poly attendant admitted that the same thing had happened to him once—when he was twelve.

Jack made a late appearance having run into an old farming friend in the truck stop's store. He took over the fueling and sent Bryson to the showers.

He had started out the day so excited that he had barely slept but now had already made a fool of himself at the fuel pump. His energy and spirits were sapped. He leaned his head back against the shower wall and sighed. Words of his dad came to his mind like a living voice: "Son, be careful what you wish for."

✻✻✻

It was after ten at night when Jack pulled Big Blue into the Exotic Moto's parking lot. Sitting at the back of the two-acre lot was a shiny, chromed auto-transport trailer. It was awaiting the arrival of Bryson and Big Blue. The twelve-wheeled transporter was solid chrome and polished to a jeweler's sheen. There was no lettering on the trailer. It was only identified by a series of numbers painted across the bottom of one of the rear doors. It looked like a Rolls-Royce version of most of the truck trailers Bryson and Jack had followed all afternoon.

The weary men climbed down from the cab of the truck to get a closer look. They hadn't walked twenty feet when they were met by a no-nonsense security guard. He wore a generic uniform complete with sewn-on patches advertising his authority. He was leading a young, strong, hundred-pound Rottweiler.

"Where is the paperwork?" the guard asked in a strictly business-like tone.

"We don't have anything except an email telling us the time and location of pick-up and delivery," Bryson explained. "Our booking agent has a copy of the contract. I think this is the trailer we'ree supposed to pick up. The numbers look correct."

Jack suggested that they could wait until morning. That was fine with the guard. He walked away, leaving the men to fend for themselves. Bryson looked around the parking lot and decided the truck was already parked in the most level place he could see, so he set the brakes and shut the truck down.

It took a while for the two men to get settled in for the night's sleep. What had previously seemed to be a spacious sleeper cabin was shrinking with each step of getting ready for bed. There was no need to flip coins for who was to get the upper or lower bunk. Jack was a good four inches shorter than Bryson and the top bunk was the shorter of the two. By the time Bryson finally stretched out on the narrow mattress, he could already hear Jack snoring.

Bryson leaned over the bunk's side and shuffled through his backpack until he found his cell phone. In all the day's excitement, he had forgotten to call Marisa. He figured Jack was too far gone to be disturbed by a phone conversation, so he punched in Marisa's number. Her phone was already ringing when he realized that they were separated by three time zones.

"Hello," Marisa answered in a sleepy voice on the phone's fourth ring. "Bryson, is that you?"

"Hi, sweetheart, just wanted to let you know that we are safely in Reno. Sorry it's so late. Are you okay? Marisa, are you there?"

After a moment, Bryson could hear his wife's deep rhythmic breathing followed by the silly little snore she claimed she didn't have. He smiled to himself and shut off the phone. She was safe and so was he. His empty stomach growled in hunger but he was too tired to care.

✳✳✳

Marisa, Madeline and Jenny had enjoyed a flawless trip to North Carolina. Their connections were easy and the accommodations comfortable. Marisa had reserved a Suburban to meet them at the airport. Madeline's new luggage was moved to her dorm on Duke's main campus without as much as a scratch. She kept just an overnight bag with her when they went to the hotel.

Their breakfast at the Hyatt had been delightful. Marisa had eaten her favorite, Belgium waffles with strawberries and whipped cream. Madeline had really loved the eggs Benedict. Jenny was not a breakfast eater and had opted for an extra hour of sleep.

"And Dad, did you know that you can have lobster tails for breakfast? They are so good! Just joking."

All of this chatty news was being supplied over his cell phone by his daughter while Bryson and Jack ate stale powdered doughnuts and drank lukewarm sodas. The mini-fridge in the truck had never started to cool, thus spoiling the milk, ham and cheese they had saved for just such a breakfast occasion. Jack had finally found the hidden plug. When he plugged it in, the light inside the tiny fridge came on. The perishables had been thrown out.

"Dad, I told you Mom can't take the phone right now. She's already late for her appointment."

"What appointment?" Bryson asked, a bit irritated.

"She's down at the hotel's spa having a massage and her nails done."

Bryson switched the phone to his left hand because his right shoulder was throbbing from sleeping all night on his side in the narrow bed. In the process of moving the phone, he felt a momentary tingling in his right arm and flexed his hand to improve blood flow.

"Dad, are you there?"

"I'm listening, sweetheart. What are your plans for the day? Don't you have to register for school or finish unpacking?"

"No Dad, I already registered online and we're waiting for my roommate to check in to decide on which colors to use to decorate the room. Mom and I are just going to hang out at the pool and maybe go to see a movie after dinner.

Jenny is booked for a tour of the local Civil War sites. How about you and Uncle Jack?"

Jack at that moment was waving for Bryson to come and have a look at what was being driven out of the Exotic Moto warehouse.

"Sorry, sweetheart, I have to go load the trailer. Give Mom a kiss for me."

Madeline's answer was drowned out by the sweet sound of an Italian V-12 engine.

# Chapter Fourteen

# THE EXOTICS

As the driver revved the engine and then released the clutch, the bright red Ferrari 275 GTB began slowly rumbling its way toward the transport trailer's ramp. A couple of additional rumbling revs sent it climbing into the trailer. As he listened and watched, Bryson's heart skipped a beat. The hair on the back of his neck stood on end like it sometimes did when the National Anthem was played at a ball game. The music this automobile made was amazing. He hadn't heard anything quite so wonderful since the first cry of his youngest daughter.

"What else are they going to load on board?" Jack asked the man standing next to him. "I haven't kept up with the price of cars but I would guess that that Ferrari is worth more than our truck."

Fritz Krefeld, the apparent owner of the automobiles, turned his head and looked at Jack and at Bryson, who had just joined them. A wide grin spread across his suntanned face. He was a tall, lean, young man with short auburn hair. He wore wraparound sunglasses pushed up on his head and carried a clipboard. In an accent that was slightly European, he said, "I don't know what your truck is worth but that particular car went through the Barrett-Jackson auction in Scottsdale last January for three and a half million dollars. I'm expecting to get over five million at the Miami auction. How much did you say your truck is worth?" The man laughed at his own question. Bryson's heart rate increased twenty beats per minute.

Over the next hour, the truck was carefully loaded with another Ferrari, a California something, a vintage "James Bond" Aston Martin, a Mercedes 300SL with clamshell-like doors and two Lamborghinis. The last two cars sat so low to the ground that Bryson doubted he would be able to crawl into one of them to drive it, let alone be able to get out afterward.

The owner of Exotic Moto was pacing back and forth behind the truck the whole time, giving instructions to his single employee, an equally tall man with a long mane of light blond hair. Once all six cars were on board, extra attention was paid as the two men crawled around on the floor and tightened each of the tie-down chains securing the cars in place. The cars were loaded such that three cars were on the floor of the trailer while the other three were suspended overhead on a second tier, their tires on an open ramp.

When Bryson first saw this he was concerned that oil or dirt would drip down from the upper cars onto the ones below. His worries were soon put to rest when he noticed that the undercarriage of the upper cars were as cleaned and polished as the hoods. There was room to move up, down and between the cars but the fit was tight.

Fritz and his helper, who was never introduced to Bryson or Jack, took one last long appraising look at the cars and their tie-downs then closed the trailer's rear doors. A two-and-a-half-foot long lever, hinged at the top and bottom of the back doors, was swung into place, securely latching the doors. A huge padlock was then snapped into place on the shiny locking lever. With a show of finality, the padlock's brass keys were slipped into Fritz's tight front pocket.

"You won't need to open the rear doors. The person accepting the cars in Florida will have his own set of keys," Fritz said. "Go ahead and back up your truck," he said, nodding toward Bryson and the blue Peterbilt. "Just be careful. The insurance value of the eight cars inside is over sixteen million dollars. Wrecked or damaged cars are worthless to me."

Jack looked at Bryson and said, "Go ahead, Dr. Bender; after all, it's your truck."

Bryson swallowed hard and started to protest, but Jack was already walking the other way. D-day had arrived for Dr. Bryson Bender, obstetrician and truck driver. It was time to fish or cut bait. Put your money on the table or get out of the game. How many other clichés could he think of to arrive at the realization that his trucking dreams were becoming a frightening reality?

He walked to the driver's side of the truck with trembling knees. Climbing into the cab, he realized that his hands were sweating. He didn't even notice the pain in his shoulder. As he eased himself into the deep leather driver's seat, he could feel his pulse thumping in his neck. He took several slow, deep breaths to minimize the twinge of chest pain he was starting to feel. He would be fine. Then like the electric jolt from a frayed wire, the realization hit him that he had never backed up the truck. Sure he had backed up pickups, and had often backed his boat down the ramps at the local lakes, but backing up this truck to that trailer full of mega-dollar cars, while the owner of the trailer's contents watched? This was definitely insane.

He started the engine and adjusted the mirrors only to see Fritz in one mirror and Jack and the white-haired guy in the other. All three were waving him back toward the extended trailer hitch assembly. He stared down at the gearshift knob and suddenly realized that he wasn't sure where reverse was located. It took two embarrassing attempts but he finally got the truck in gear—reverse gear.

Luckily the thing hadn't stalled. He eased the clutch out and gave the accelerator a little tap. The truck nearly jumped off the ground.

Bryson could see Fritz waving frantically for the truck to slow down.

Once the truck was in motion, Bryson's instincts kicked in, allowing him to control the angle of approach and his speed. He turned the wheel just enough to align the two masses of steel. The ninety feet between tractor and trailer shrank to inches in an instant and then Bryson applied the brakes, stopping the truck just as the trailer hitch locking mechanism snapped into place. Too late to be of any use, he remembered that the truck had a back-up camera. He looked at the screen but only saw the silver image of the trailer, mere feet from his cab.

Fritz handed Bryson a manila envelope and said, "Here's the invoice for the truck stops, a copy of your payment check and the cell phone number of the guy taking delivery in Florida. When you deliver the trailer, you can be paid in cash if you prefer or he will give you the actual check. You've got plenty of time to get there. Just make sure that the trailer is always hooked to your truck. These cars have got to be in Miami in one week. Earlier is better. Late is unacceptable. Don't get stopped by the cops for some dumb traffic violation. They will want to look inside the trailer and you won't have a key. If you really get into trouble, call me." Fritz scribbled some numbers on a piece of paper and handed it up to Bryson.

Bryson took the envelope and shook Fritz's hand. Another threshold crossed. He was actually being paid to drive his fancy new truck. He started to question not having a key to the inside of the trailer but Fritz was already halfway across the parking lot, and Jack was climbing into the passenger's side of the cab, saying something about breakfast. Bryson took another deep breath, pulled the gearshift lever into first gear, and they were off.

The onboard computer was mounted in a clearly visible position imbedded into the dashboard of the truck. The instruction manual was intimidating but the device itself was pretty easy to use. Within fifteen minutes of fiddling with the thing Jack had their route out of Reno plotted and had already calculated the total mileage to Miami if they took the quickest route. They had absolutely no intention of doing that.

Jack had spent days before the trip planning how to best see the sights along the way. He was a war history aficionado and whether the war was with Indians, Yankees, Germans, Japanese, Mafia gangsters, New Mexico aliens or anyone else for that matter, Jack had an interest and some knowledge of its history. Bryson just wanted to safely drive the truck and eat as many chicken fried steaks as he could find along the way.

About two miles out of Reno the men stopped at a huge truck stop to stock up, refuel and stretch their legs for the hours of driving ahead. The place was nearly deserted, so they didn't have to wait. They filled up the fuel tank—no spills this time—and stocked the mini-fridge. It was now staying cold and working much better since they had plugged it in. Neither of the men were hungry so they settled for juice and coffee. The next stop they had in mind was outside Carson City. There was a great story of a fight between the cattlemen and silver miners there, the spoils of silver and gold going to the man with the fastest draw.

The morning sun gave a pleasant glare off the truck's windshield as they cruised up the freeway ramp to join the lines of fast-moving cars and trucks heading east and then turning south on the freeway toward Carson City, Winnemucca and eventually Las Vegas. Jack was typing instructions into the navigation system and watching for the freeway signs while Bryson managed to stay in the correct lane and keep pace with the commuter traffic. He was making fairly good time when the morning's commute came to an abrupt standstill.

For years he had watched from his car in amused silence as young women in small cars drove on the freeway to work while putting on their makeup, doing their hair and drinking their breakfasts. A cute blonde in a Toyota Corolla was applying her eyeliner with one hand while she steered the car with her knees and held her coffee cup in the other. A car to her right cut in front of her, causing her to slam on her brakes. Her coffee flew toward the windshield and the tiny car veered directly into the side of the car in front of Bryson. He had no choice but to lock up the brakes, causing the enclosed trailer full of cars to fishtail to the right and bump against a pickup truck and a motorcycle. When the squealing tires and their clouds of blue smoke had quieted and the smoke cleared, a chorus of horns sounded. Traffic had stopped behind them, creating three blocked lanes.

Jack and Bryson scampered down from the truck's cab to evaluate the welfare of the accident victims. The poor blonde girl was soaked in coffee and smeared with eyeliner but otherwise fine. Her car had minor damage. The other car was not seriously damaged either. The pickup and motorcyclist were shaken but not seriously injured.

Bryson's attention turned to his trailer and its priceless mechanical passengers. The padlock on the trailer's rear doors was of Fort Knox vintage. Bryson was in a cold sweat worrying that the cars inside the trailer had been shifted and damaged. The three on the upper level gave him his most concern as their tie-downs were less solid. He was about to panic and call Fritz to inform him that they had made it less than fifty miles and had been in a wreck. Then the ambulance and Highway Patrol arrived. A large crowd of rubberneckers had gathered and one of the rather sleazy-looking guys stepped forward and offered to help.

"I'll bet you need to get inside and take a look, don't you?" the grizzly bearded man said. "You got twenty bucks on you?" the man said, picking up the padlock and squinting at it with one eye from just a few inches away.

"What do you have in mind?" Jack asked the man.

At this point, Bryson saw a highway patrol car roll up. The officer adjusted his hat and gun belt as he approached the truck.

"I said have you got twenty bucks on you?" the loser repeated.

"Will you talk to him, Jack?" Bryson pleaded in a soft voice, glancing toward the tall officer.

The dirtbag looked at Bryson with raised eyebrows. "Weren't you driving?"

Bryson glared at him.

"I don't know what you have in the truck, mister, but if it has broken loose and shifted the weight enough, you could just topple over on the next steep turn or big gust of wind. For a hundred bucks I can open the lock and you'll be able to lock it afterward. If I cut it with bolt cutters the guy who has the key is going to be mad . . . right?"

"I thought you wanted twenty bucks."

"That was before the cop showed and your buddy lied to him about who was driving."

"Stay right here; I need a minute." Bryson walked over to Jack and the patrolman and listened in on the conversation. The patrolman was all about getting the mess cleared and the traffic moving.

Bryson turned away and took some bills out of his wallet, turned back to the homeless-appearing man and slid two twenties into his hand. "That's all the cash I've got. Open the lock."

The man grinned, exposing a mouth full of rotten teeth. On the far side of the road was his battered Nissan mini-truck. He reached into the back of the truck and appeared with an enormous pair of bolt cutters. Bryson looked closely at the truck and saw the faded lettering on the door announcing "Billy's Locksmith."

Bryson tried to intercept the man before he reached the truck's rear doors but was too late. With one swift motion, Billy swung the red steel bolt cutter into place with the menacing blades over the tempered steel loop of the lock. Bryson heard a loud metallic snap and saw the lock fall to the ground.

Bryson was furious. "You said you could open it without cutting it!"

"That was for a hundred bucks. Cheapskates get the twenty-dollar snip job."

Without another word, the man turned and disappeared into the crowd of cars.

Bryson and Jack opened the back door of the truck. Bryson boosted Jack up into the trailer then scrambled in himself. They crawled around on hands and knees, tugging and rattling chains and wheel blocks until they were convinced that the six cars were secure and undamaged. The chains securing the cars had become loose but the cars were fine.

The patrolmen soon had the traffic moving around the big blue truck and involved cars. Surprising everyone, the senior highway patrolman walked up to Jack and handed him a card.

"I'm going to let you boys get on down the road. It's obvious that you were not at fault. Call me at four sharp and we'll do the report over the phone. I have another wreck with injuries up the road three miles to check out right now."

\*\*\*

The Peterbilt ran smoothly with no indication of having just been in a fender bender. Soon Jack had the machine up to speed. No one spoke until they were several miles down the road and then they glanced at one another and started to laugh, venting the pent-up anxiety of the incident.

The road from Reno to Las Vegas is one of the fastest traveled roads in the country. On a clear day it isn't unusual to clock cars at one hundred and ten miles per hour and the truckers drive nearly as fast. The highway patrol in Nevada consider fast driving illegal only if it's the last week of the month and the county is short of funds for their payroll.

Bryson had heard stories of people averaging over a hundred miles per hour on cross-state trips.

Jack was getting tired but still clipping along at a rapid eighty miles per hour when he caught a glimpse in his mirror of a stream of trucks approaching. As they passed Big Blue, Bryson counted eight trucks all drafting off of the lead semi.

"They have got to be going over a hundred miles an hour," Jack said, glancing at his speedometer and applying a little more pressure to the accelerator pedal. "I can't keep up that pace. I'm getting a migraine; how about if you take over?"

"There's a small town coming up. You probably need some good food under your belt. Let's get some lunch and look for a padlock for the trailer. We can eat and shop and then I'll drive while you sleep off your headache."

Jack started slowing the truck on the outskirts of the little ranching town and followed the signs and the turns winding his way toward downtown. He could see the dome of the courthouse and then a friendly Ace hardware store. They parked the big rig, locked it up and headed into the store.

Bryson was directed to the lock section by a perky young redhead. She was tall, intelligent appearing and very inquisitive. He found the biggest lock in the store. He had two extra keys made and headed out the door toward the truck. Once the lock was in place, Bryson was ready to go but couldn't find Jack. He went back into the store and found Jack chatting with a clerk.

"We've got to go take a look at this young lady's family ranch," Jack said to Bryson.

"It was the scene of one of the biggest shootouts in Western history. Tombstone was a food fight compared to the slaughter out here," the redhead clerk added.

"What is there left to see?" Bryson asked, curious about the place, yet eager to get on down the road.

"You'll have to see for yourself, but I'll bet you haven't had lunch, and my aunt runs a bed-and-breakfast on the place. The cooking is the best in Nevada. She has one item on the menu each day. I think today she is fixing steak. You like steak with mashed potatoes and gravy? She calls it chicken fried steak, but trust me, it has nothing to do with chickens."

# Chapter Fifteen

## ALMOST RIGHT

The little dirt road ended up being three miles long, peppered with potholes. Eventually they crossed a cattle guard and then passed under a twenty-foot-high entrance gate that had a burnt wooden sign hanging from it bearing only the simple brand in an exaggerated size that read "P7." The ranch house and surrounding corrals and barns had been well kept and appeared to still be working cattle. Off to the side of the main house was a small outbuilding with a row of windows and a screen door. Hanging near the corner of the long wooden porch was a large triangular steel dinner bell suspended from the end of a thick rope knotted with an authentic hangman's noose.

The two men sat in the truck for a minute until the last of the dense cloud of dust the truck had stirred up floated off into the breeze. Bryson could smell the cooking as soon as he stepped down from the truck. He was ready to eat.

The old bunkhouse had slept up to forty ranch hands in its hayday. Wild mustang horses and Texas longhorn cattle had been the original livestock of the P7 but that had evolved over the years to registered Herefords and racing quarter horses. The restaurant conversion had taken place in the early eighties with long tables and benches made of pine now polished glass-smooth by years of use. Only a scattering of pickups and cars were in the parking lot but the tables inside were crowded. The customers were elbow to elbow at the long tables. Everyone was busy eating, not talking.

Jack and Bryson were waved to a bench by a thin gray-haired woman wearing a long denim skirt and a red plaid apron.

"Gentlemen," she said in a cultured voice more reminiscent of Maine than Nevada. "What could I offer you to drink? I hope you are aware that there is no choice as to the entrée."

"Diet Pepsi sounds good," answered Bryson, excited about the steaming plates of food at the table across from him.

Jack tried to pump the woman for history information but she waved him off and left to get their drinks. She returned with a laminated newspaper front page from the Silver City paper dated 1883. It described a range war between miners and ranch hands that lasted three days and left over one hundred dead and wounded. Bryson was trying to listen to Jack read, but once the plates of food came sliding down the long table, he lost interest in the past.

Bryson thought he had arrived in Nirvana. The oversized plate waiting in front of him produced a plume of steam that rose to the low ceiling. An uninteresting side of mixed vegetables was nearly crowded off the plate by a beautiful breaded piece of meat cooked to a perfect golden brown. It was nestled between two piles of fluffy, white mashed potatoes, each with a deep reservoir full of thick creamy gravy, which was nearly as white as the potatoes. His tall glass of Diet Pepsi was filled with soft crushed ice, the coolness of which had glazed the outside of the glass with tiny beads of condensation. Bryson added a few shakes of freshly ground pepper to the meat and potatoes then took a deep breath. Could it be? Was this going to be the meal he had craved for what seemed like an eternity? He picked up his fork and knife—not that he would need a knife to cut the tender, juicy selection of choice beef.

"Hey, mister, is that your truck out there by the loading chute?"

Bryson looked up, irritated at the distraction. The first

generous bite of meat, dripping with hot gravy, was perched on the end of his fork. "Yes, it's mine."

"You ought to go check it out then. Some dude just opened the back trailer door. What kind of cars are those in there anyway?"

Bryson and Jack stared at each other for a full second and then dropped their forks and jumped to their feet, nearly toppling the wooden benches.

"Somebody call the police!" Bryson yelled while dashing through the door.

Dodging a couple of newly arrived cars, the men made it to the truck just in time to see two wimpy-looking guys with long, straggly braids and multiple tasteless tattoos, pulling the trailer's drive-up ramp out of its recessed slot. These idiots were trying to steal a car.

There was a brisk wind blowing, kicking up a bit of dust, which lessened visibility. Jack and Bryson stopped behind a pickup truck and whispered to each other and then separated. Jack picked up a handful of powdered parking lot dirt and approached directly, while Bryson circled around the pickup and then crawled under his truck, yanking a tire iron from its holder.

"Nice-looking car you got there," Jack said. He was just a couple feet from the nearest loser.

The would-be thieves whirled around to face him, dropping the heavy metal ramp, the corner of which landed on the shorter thief's toes. He yelped and reached down to grab his foot just as Jack threw a handful of the sand and pulverized dirt into his face. The bigger of the two started to yank a weapon out of his pocket, cursing Jack as he struggled to retrieve it. Just as the idiot revealed his short-handle knife, Bryson brought the huge steel tire iron down with a whipping motion against the man's wrist, producing a sickening crack, like the sound of a dry tree branch snapping underfoot.

Both thieves were on their knees, moaning with pain; one, rubbing his eyes and the other trying to move his arm.

Jack yelled at the two losers to stay on the ground or risk getting their heads beamed with the tire iron.

It took a while, but a sheriff finally arrived and hand-cuffed the thieves to a metal fence pole.

"I ought to arrest all four of you," the corpulent officer warned. "We don't cotton to vigilante activities in this neck of the woods."

Bryson, feeling arrogant for having subdued the two would-be car thieves, almost asked the cop where the cotton or the woods were. For as far as the eye could see, there were only rolling hills and sagebrush.

Jack found the padlock lying in the powdery dirt open with a key still stuck in the tumblers—an Ace hardware key.

"Excuse me, Sheriff, when you book those two, you might ask them about their accomplice. She works at the Ace hardware store and has red, curly hair."

"Y'all means Mindy?" the deputy said. "She ain't no ac-complice; she's the Sheriff's daughter."

### ✳✳✳

Bryson was again behind the wheel and flowing along with the rest of the light traffic. It amazed him how fast he had grown accustomed to driving Big Blue with its long, shiny trailer full of million-dollar cars.

Jack had crawled in the back for a nap and Bryson was in-tent on tuning in a Diamondback baseball game from a Las Vegas station that kept fading in and out.

A gust of wind caught a clump of tumbleweeds from behind a long stretch of barbed wire fence. The seven-foot diameter of thick weeds blew up over the fence, flying in from the right on a collision course with Bryson.

Bryson's first inclination when he saw the mass coming at him was to swerve the wheel, but he held on and let the truck's bumper and grill demolish the tumbling weeds. The next gust was full of small hailstones and sleet. The force and surprise of the bombardment nearly caused Bryson to lose control of the truck. Reaching for the wiper switch, he realized in an instant that he didn't know where it was. More waves of sleet and raisin-sized hailstones pelted the truck's windshield, nearly obliterating visibility. He fiercely gripped the wheel with his right hand while fumbling blindly with the instruments, trying in vain to find the wiper switch. The truck began swerving side to side, requiring both hands on the wheel to regain control.

"What's up?" Jack asked, popping his head out from the curtain separating the sleeping area from the main cabin. He didn't need an answer to assess the ferocity of the storm. Within seconds he crawled into the passenger's seat and found and switched on the wipers. By now the sleet and hail had turned to giant snowflakes. The lines on the roadway ahead were obliterated and the tracks of the preceding traffic were no longer visible. Bryson slowed the truck to under forty-five miles per hour, and with their eyes glued to the road, they were able to stay in the middle of the pavement.

Nearly as quickly as it had struck, the storm that had blasted them for nearly an hour disappeared and bright late afternoon sunshine glared into the cab. Bryson saw the signs indicating a rest area ahead and started gearing down. Not a drop of rain had affected the dusty parking lot where the truck and exhausted drivers slowed to a stop.

Bryson walked away from the truck toward a restroom building, massaging his throbbing right shoulder as he walked. Once inside, he turned toward the mirrors over the sinks and stared at the old man facing him. Not only did he look ten years older than he had six months ago, but he felt as though he was losing his confidence. Thank the Lord that he didn't have to go into an operating room right now and perform an emergency C-section. At this moment, he barely felt capable of unzipping his pants. For several minutes he stood leaning forward with both hands on the grimy sinks. Slowly, a wave of new energy seeped into his bones and muscles and the throbbing in his shoulder diminished.

"Hey Buddy, are you okay?" A stranger had come into the restroom and having finished his pit stop, needed to use one of the sinks.

"Yes, sorry," Bryson said, and moved to the side.

"You sure you're all right? If you don't mind my saying, you look like crap."

"Thanks for your concern. It's just been a crazy day. I'm going to be fine."

Outside, Jack was watching the truck and awaiting his turn when Bryson walked out, drying his hands on his pants.

"Sorry I took so long. I guess I needed to look in the mirror and see who was really in these clothes."

Bryson walked out to the truck. Remembering that he was supposed to do a walk-around each time they stopped, he slowly walked around the truck, inspecting each of the eighteen tires and wheels and checking the brake lines and the tailgate. He smiled at the jumble of twisted barbed wire, securing the latch on the rear door of the trailer. Jack hadn't trusted the lock with its many keys so he had wound the latch with old barbed wire. Here in front of him was a two hundred thousand dollar Peterbilt tractor rig pulling a custom trailer loaded with fifteen million dollars' worth of cars and the best they could do for securing the load was a couple of feet of rusty barbed wire?

He walked over to a boulder at the edge of the parking lot and sat down. He looked again at the back of the trailer and laughed out loud.

\*\*\*

The reflection off the night sky from the light of Las Vegas is like the unique taste of a homegrown tomato. It's hard to describe. The sign said it was still fifty miles to the town yet the lights would have one believe Vegas was just over the next hill. By the time they could see the twinkling lights and the outline of the strip, both Bryson and Jack were running on empty. They had traded off driving twice since the storm. They had topped off the tanks and bought a new lock at a Flying J, north of the city, and much to Jack's delight, had decided to spend the night at the Bellagio Hotel.

Bryson had gone online with his Blackberry and found a last-minute special for two rooms for two hundred bucks apiece. When Bryson suggested that his shoulder needed some Jacuzzi time and his stomach needed a good steak, Jack had been more than willing to agree. Bryson had also placed a call to the owner of the cars to give the guy a progress report but was told by a woman who answered the phone that Fritz had left for Italy and would be gone for two weeks. If they had an emergency they were to send an email. *Forget it*, Bryson thought. *I'll call the guy again when we get to Florida.*

As they pulled off of the freeway near the hotel, the lights of the Las Vegas Strip were dazzling. The back parking lot of the vast hotel complex had plenty of room for the truck and the quarter-mile walk into the lobby let them stretch their legs.

The brightly colored Murano glass chandeliers were a welcome contrast to the gloomy sixty-watt bulbs at the Bozeman Best Western. Both men carried only backpacks, and wearing dusty jeans and work boots, stood in stark contrast to the haute culture of the women loitering in the lobby and casino. Money was, however, money and when Bryson pulled out his Platinum American Express card, the snobby registration clerk gave a slight raised eyebrow of approval and handed over the room keys.

By the time Bryson got to the room and threw on his swimsuit, Jack had already filled the tub and had called to tell Bryson to go on without him. They agreed to meet at the steakhouse downstairs in an hour. Bryson put on his white robe and tried to squeeze his feet into the terry cloth slippers provided in the room; they were a tight fit. Looking at himself in the mirror, he chuckled at the image. His hair was tousled, he had a day-and-a-half growth of stubble and now he had on a robe that might have been big enough for Marisa and dainty slippers adorned with gold filigree crests. He looked like Klinger, the cross-dressing sergeant from M*A*S*H. Undeterred, he rode the elevator to the pool level, daring anyone to make eye contact with him.

The swimming pool complex was one of the most luxurious in the world, with acres of water and multiple spas, cabanas and surrounding gardens. The one big problem was that it was closing for the night. Why in the world would they build a multimillion-dollar pool and then be too cheap to pay a lifeguard to hang around until later in the evening? Bryson gave the attendant ten bucks to look the other way and slipped past the barrier rope. He found a Jacuzzi pool and stepped down into the wonderful cocoon of hot, churning water.

It was a struggle to stay awake as the hot water gently massaged his aching joints and muscles, relaxing his body and soul. His wounded shoulder felt like a sponge soaking in the heat and moisture. His sense of thirst finally told him it was time to get out. He wished he had remembered to bring along a bottle of cold water. Feeling a little bit dizzy, it took a Herculean effort for him to climb the steps out of the spa and to stagger to the edge of the main swimming pool. He dove into the frigid water, feeling the rush of tingling over his entire body. Several deep breaths and life was fantastic again.

The steaks were thick, juicy and cooked to perfection. Both men were rejuvenated and starving. The cold to-go meal at the P7 ranch house was a digestive bad memory. The men watched the parade of Americana walk by as they ate their meals. Las Vegas was America's new melting pot. What happened in Las Vegas stayed in Las Vegas, especially the homeless, the broken-down drunks, and the gambling table's losers.

It didn't take long until the two men had seen and eaten enough and were headed for their rooms and the luxury of smooth, soft sheets and a mattress designed by angels. Best of all, the beds were not moving.

# Chapter Sixteen

# THE TAINTED DESERT

The men met at the truck at daybreak. Bryson, eager to go, took the first shift at the wheel. They drank juice and ate croissants out of paper sacks from the hotel bistro. The goal was to beat the early commuters.

They listened to the morning news on the satellite radio until their news addictions were fulfilled and then tuned in to a soft rock station. Once on the main highway they started to fly. Kingman, Flagstaff, Gallup and the vastness of New Mexico lay ahead. In most places, the highway stretched out in front of them like a long, black, silk ribbon.

Checking the time to be sure he wouldn't awaken Marisa, Bryson dialed her cell phone to say good morning. It had been a whole day since they had spoken and he wanted to catch her up on all of his adventures. The phone rang several times before it went to voicemail. This was a little unsettling as he was spoiled by her always taking his call no matter who she had been talking to. He tried it again with the same result.

"Try the hotel," Jack suggested. "Better still, let me try, while you keep us on the road. The guy behind us thinks you had too much to drink last night."

Bryson felt a twinge of anxiety with its slight surge of adrenalin as his mind ran through the possible scenarios of Marisa not answering her phone. Beads of perspiration dampened his forehead. His stomach began to feel a noticeable cramping. He tried to concentrate on the driving but couldn't help straining to hear the conversation as Jack spoke, first with information and then with the front desk of the Hyatt in Durham.

"Good news and bad news," Jack said, closing his cell phone. There is a message from our girls that they checked out but there is a second message for both of us. Apparently, there isn't enough to do in North Carolina, so as soon as they got Madeline settled into the room, the three girls checked out of the hotel and flew off to New York City to see some plays and do some shopping. I knew it was a mistake to let my wife out of the kitchen, and with shoes on no less." He looked at Bryson with a mock frown.

"So what's the good news?" Bryson asked, instantly feeling his shoulders relax and his heart rate go down.

"That was the good news," Jack responded with a smirk.

"Then what is the bad news?" Bryson asked, starting to feel another surge of physical uneasiness.

"This one I'll have to quote. According to the hotel desk clerk, the note said, 'I'm in love with my American Express card. I didn't leave home without it.' It was signed, 'Marisa Bender, Consumer Expert.'"

Bryson laughed out loud. "She told me she would get even for my buying this truck."

*** 

For most people driving cross-country along America's Interstate Highway system, there lies ahead a long, tedious process interrupted only by stops for fuel and food. One might equate it to painting a ten-mile-long picket fence using just a paintbrush. It's slow-going with little visible progress and excitement only when the paint bucket needs refilling.

For Bryson and Jack, nothing could have been further from the truth. When one was driving the other would be busy adjusting the GPS or the radio stations, or studying the numerous history books Jack had brought along. "Interstate 40 from Kingman, Arizona to Oklahoma City followed the old Route 66," Jack explained.

The scenery was magnificent and the historical facts were endless. Tales of ancient Incas and Aztec Indians mingled with the legends of Cortes and his search for the Seven Cities of Gold filled the truck's cabin as Jack purged his memory bank for names and dates and anecdotal stories. This road they were driving on was built on the route of the famous Southern Pacific Railroad where such names as Sitting Bull, Geronimo and Howard Johnson Hotels had become household words. The hotels were built at each of the train refueling stops so that the passengers would have a place to eat and rest.

They read about the famous range wars between the sheep men and the cattle barons that occurred along this route when the first railroad cars to come down the tracks brought hundreds of thousands of sheep and cattle.

"The cattlemen claimed that the sheep ate the grass down too close to the ground, while the sheep men claimed that the cattle, especially the bulls, would attack the docile sheep by kicking or goring them. To help fund the railroad, the government had sold parcels of land in 640-acre sections and alternated it with federal land in a checkerboard fashion. Both sheep and cattle investors had purchased the railroad land," Bryson read out loud.

"To this day, there are still alternating private and federal sections of rangeland bordering the freeway and railroad lines for fifty miles on each side of the tracks," Jack told Bryson. "There are also still ancestors of the two most contentious sheep and cattle families, the Grahams and the Tuchsberrys, who to this day are always looking for ways to get even for the hundreds of murders the other family's ancestors committed."

This was the trucking Bryson had been lusting for. Straight, fast driving, on smooth highways, in an awesome machine accompanied by an intelligent friend. The morning flew by.

# Chapter Seventeen

## SNAKE

Big Blue started running low on fuel just west of Flagstaff, just past the turnoff to the Grand Canyon. Bryson was finding that the distance between two places on a paper map and the real distance were quite different. He watched the roadside signs for the perfect place to refuel and soon thought he had found it. He pulled off the highway onto an access road and decelerated to a stop at a modern style truck stop.

Even though the seats in Big Blue were amazingly comfortable, both men had become stiff after sitting for such a long stretch. Climbing down from the cab and stretching was a welcome feeling like taking off ski boots at the end of a good day on the slopes.

They agreed to not leave the truck unguarded while at the pumps so Jack headed for the comfort station and Bryson started the refueling process. Bryson was again reminded of the truckers' policy of doing a walk-around each time the fuel tank was filled. With the tank full, Bryson began the inspection.

As Bryson walked around his truck thumping the tires, the wind was blowing hard and coming in irregular gusts. Without warning, just as he was getting to the last set of four tires at the back of the trailer, the wind lifted Bryson's golf cap right off his head and took it for a ride. The hat was one of his favorites and he wasn't about to let it fly away without a good chase. It tumbled and skipped for a good hundred yards before getting wedged inside a stack of old fence posts at the far end of the parking area.

When he caught up to it, he put his foot on the brim and leaned down to reach for it. That's when he heard the loud gunshot. Instantly, his hand felt the sting of the shattered slivers of wood. He jumped, spinning around to find the source of the gunshot.

"You are a lucky man, mister." The voice was soft and low and paced like the flow of cold molasses. "I been watching that snake for the last forty minutes, trying to give it a chance to head back into the forest, but it had its mind set on seeing the world and kept trying to skitter onto the asphalt. It's a black timber rattler, one of the less common varieties in these parts, but also one of the most deadly."

Bryson stood frozen in a state of shock. He stared between the long, crooked poles where the reptile convulsed and died. Out of breath and slightly dizzy, Bryson welcomed the man's firm grip on his arm. He bent down and snatched his hat from the pile of logs and turned to face the stranger.

He was a weathered old man with chestnut-colored skin, anthracite-black hair and gray eyes. His facial skin was deeply wrinkled, creating squint-like creases lateral to his eyes. He wore a dusty, brown, wide-brimmed, felt hat with a turquoise studded hatband. The hat, like the man, appeared ancient. Faded blue Levis hung loose around his narrow hips. His boots had worn away any polished finish years ago and his red-plaid, pearl-button shirt with its cowboy-cut yoke was threadbare around the collar and long sleeves. A few long, gray whiskers trailed from the man's chin, giving him a Charlie Chan appearance, but the heavy turquoise and silver squash blossom necklace around his neck left no doubt about his heritage.

"Thanks for saving me from that snake. I guess it could have bitten me," Bryson said. He looked up and down his arms to see if the tiny stinging areas from the splinters had caused any bleeding. "You're pretty good with that gun."

"It's a necessity of survival. Black timber rattlers do give a nasty bite. The venom this time of year is more powerful than a cobra's."

Bryson heard Jack's voice and both men turned toward the truck.

"What's going on?" Jack hollered as he briskly approached the two men. He was carrying a small grocery sack full of snacks and staring at the gun in the stranger's hand.

Jack stopped dead in his tracks. "Bryson, are you okay? You left the fuel nozzle still in the tank."

"This gentleman just saved me from a deadly snakebite," Bryson explained, pointing to the snake. "The wind caught my hat so I ran after it and that's when the snake showed up."

"My name is Frank Bearwater," the man interrupted, offering his calloused hand to Jack and Bryson. There was a strong smell of alcohol on his breath.

Bryson and Jack both shook the man's hand then Jack walked over toward the snake.

"Stay away from that thing!" Frank shouted. "Those things can bite a long time after you think they're dead. Their spirits take a long time to find someplace else to reside."

Bryson and Jack both took a couple of quick steps backward. The man's voice had been much harsher than was necessary. The two looked at each other and turned toward the truck.

"Hey, you guys are headed to the east, right?" The man started after them in a hobbling gait. "How about giving me a ride as far as Winslow? It's about two hours down the road. I really need to get there by tonight." The pistol was still in the weathered old man's hand.

"I don't think that will work," Jack said, nudging Bryson toward the truck.

"You owe me, you know. That snake could have killed you. I just need a ride for a hundred miles or so. I'm not asking for anything complicated. I know you've got plenty of room. I'll sit on the floor if you think my clothes will dirty your seats."

Bearwater had caught up with them by now in spite of his apparent limp and wrinkled age.

Bryson was embarrassed for having refused the old man and nodded to Jack that they needed to huddle.

"Not a good idea," Jack said. He wrinkled his eyebrows and gave a shrug then walked away toward their truck without another comment. It was the first apparent disagreement he and Bryson had incurred.

Jack said he would finish the refueling and walk-around. Bryson went off to the restrooms and the Indian used the pay phone to make a call.

***

The road ahead was wide open and a slight tailwind pushed the truck along. They had been driving for a little over an hour. Jack was sound asleep in the back sleeper cabin when Bearwater slid the pistol out of his backpack, and holding it in his lap, insisted that Bryson pull off the road at the next exit. Bryson glanced at the GPS and immediately knew that there was only a county road leading off the freeway into the hills to the north. Although the man didn't point the gun in any menacing manner, Bryson felt threatened, and with Jack asleep in the back, he felt vulnerable as well. At first he considered arguing but just looking at the gun made his healed shoulder ache. He shifted down and started to slow the truck. It was then that he first noticed a truck behind him, which had also began to slow rather than pass him. It had its turn signal on as well.

"I thought you wanted to go to Winslow?" Bryson asked the old man. "It's still twenty miles ahead."

The old man gave a hard stare. "Just do what you are told and you can be on your way in fifteen minutes. We don't have any beef with you or your grumpy friend, but we have a job to do and you stopping this truck will make it easy for everyone."

Bryson couldn't believe what was happening. But after watching the truck behind him put on his turn signal, the events of the last hour with the timely shooting of the snake, the friendly introduction and the plea for a ride in the truck all fit together like pieces of a puzzle. He realized that they had been had. He wasn't sure what it meant at the moment, but the isolated road didn't give him hope for anything good. He could hear Jack snoring in the sleeper cab.

The barrel of the gun went back into Bearwater's bag, but the old man's hand was still on the grip. Bryson brought the truck to a stop on the dusty, graveled side road. Only a few hundred yards away to the south lay the abandoned tracks of the first railroad to cross the Southwest. It was the same railroad that had been robbed by Mexicans and white bandits hundreds of times in the days of the Wild West. It suddenly became apparent that the thievery was about to happen again. The other truck was pulling an empty car transport trailer. It drove down the road past them, its wake enveloping Bryson's new truck with a thick layer of powdery dust. About a quarter mile away, it drove out onto the flat desert terrain, made a full one hundred eighty degree turn and headed back toward them. The truck pulled up even with Big Blue and stopped. Bryson studied the empty auto-transport trailer attached to the old truck.

"What is it you want?" Bryson asked the old man.

"We want the cars. They belong to some guy from Seattle who paid a lot of money for them and he wants them back."

Bryson was stupefied. The incongruity of this ancient-looking Indian man wanting Italian sports cars was almost laughable.

"And what are you going to do with Ferraris out here? Get to the trading post bars faster than on your mules?" Bryson said, unable to resist the sarcasm.

The old man's reaction was slow and meaningful. He took the gun out of the backpack again, pointed it back into the sleeper cabin, and in a matter-of-fact voice said, "You will apologize for your rudeness or I will shoot your friend."

When Bryson hesitated, Bearwater tilted the gun toward the roof of the truck, but at the last second, pointed it out of the open window and pulled the trigger. The noise in the confined space was deafening. Jack's face poked through the curtains to find the barrel of a pistol inches from his nose.

"I'm sorry! I'm sorry!" Bryson exclaimed.

The smell of cordite from the expelled bullet was heavy in the cab as the three men climbed down from the truck. The driver of the other truck was already standing on the ground. He also held a pistol and looked even older than Bearwater. His salt-and-pepper hair was braided into a tight, two-foot-long rope, which hung over his shirt collar. He wore an Arizona Diamondback cap, which shaded his squinted eyes. The gun he held was bigger than anything Bryson had ever seen but also was obviously rusty. Bryson doubted that it even worked.

"Open the back of the van. I don't want to hurt anybody," the old man ordered. He flicked the long barrel in the direction of the back of the trailer and waited for Bryson to start moving.

Jack followed Bryson around to the back of the enclosed trailer.

Bryson fumbled with the keys to the shiny new padlock, his hands shaking. When he couldn't get the newly ground key to work, the old man pushed him away and yanked the keys out of his hand. Bearwater held the gun at his side as his partner struggled with the lock.

Jack stood off to one side and looked both confused and nervous.

The lock popped open and the two old men swung the trailer doors open wide. A cascade of recently acquired dust from the access road was hanging on the door's ledges. It fell from the huge doors and, caught by the wind, flew straight into the older Indian's eyes. He let out a holler and turned away from the doors, rubbing his eyes and dropping the rusted gun. When Bearwater turned to help, Bryson, using reflexes he didn't know he still had, grabbed a broken cedar tree branch from the ground. Swinging it like a base-ball bat, he struck Bearwater in his lower arm. The gun flew from his hand as he yelped in pain. Jack, who at the moment was standing back from the swinging doors, gave one of the doors a mighty shove, causing it to crash into Braided Hair's shoulder and head.

The fight was over in seconds. Two seventy-year-old geezers conquered in battle by two citified sixty-year-olds—all four of them panting for breath. Bryson picked up the long-barrel gun then kicked the rusty one into the dirt yards away. Jack went back up into the truck to get his cell phone to call the police. He made a 911 call then realized that his call for help was in vain. His phone's screen showed that there was no signal.

"What in the world are you two old goats thinking? And how did you know there were cars in the trailer?" Bryson shook his fist at the men.

"Just shoot us and get it over with," Bearwater said. "We'll both die in jail anyway. Hell, we were just trying to make a few bucks."

"By hijacking a truck? Are you both crazy? Were you going to kill us too?"

"Heck no," Braided Hair said. "Don't you ever go to the movies? Indians are afraid of dead people. Some guy back at a truck stop in Kingman said you would be stopping along the Interstate some place. He said you stole his cars in Seattle and that if we could figure a way to get the cars out of your trailer and to Holbrook, he'd give us each a thousand bucks. We've been following you since Kingman."

Baffled by the response, Bryson lowered the gun and asked, "What about the snake? How did you know it would be there?"

"That's our old trick we been pulling for years. We got a whole cage full of them kingsnakes at our cabin. The owners at the truck stops pay us twenty bucks every time we trick some city slicker into believing he almost got bit by a snake."

Bryson and Jack looked at each other and just shook their heads. Waiting for some highway patrol to wander down the road could take hours. Putting the two old idiots in jail would be a crime. They probably were right; they would die in jail. Jack closed the trailer door and replaced the padlock.

"Let's just get out of here," Bryson finally said to Jack. "You two tell me one thing and I won't call the police. Who hired you and how were you going to get in contact with him?"

"We never saw the guy before. He came into the truck stop last night and gave us three hundred for fuel and told us to drive to Kingman and wait for a new blue Peterbilt with a chrome trailer, then to follow it until it stopped. We was supposed to take the cars and drive to a rest stop west of Holbrook then wait for him to find us. We didn't intend to hurt you two, just scare you and take your truck keys when we left. Honest."

"Which cars were you supposed to take? Your trailer will only hold five."

"He said a red Ferrari was the most important, but I just figured we'd take the first five we could get our hands on. How many cars you got in there, anyway?"

Bryson ignored the question. "So you were going to abandon us out here in this windswept wasteland with no keys? Why I outta shoot both you fellers and leave you for the coyotes," Bryson said in a John Wayne accent.

Jack was already climbing into the driver's seat. He was firing up the big diesel engine when Bryson told the two men to walk out into the desert away from the dirt road.

"I'll throw your truck keys out the window up where the pavement starts. Maybe that will give you time to realize how stupid your plan was. Next time you need liquor money, try selling newspapers at the intersections," Bryson yelled at the two as he picked up the second gun and retrieved the keys. Once inside the truck, he looked at Jack, who was laughing at him.

"I couldn't think of anything else to say. Just get us out of here."

The last thing they heard from the two Indians was Bearwater yelling, "We don't want the money for booze. We buy REIT debentures and pork belly straddles, you idiots! We could have cut you in on the deal."

Bryson threw the truck keys out on the dirt road just where the pavement started. A mile or so later, he flung both pistols out of the truck window into the roadside weeds and sagebrush. Neither of them could stop glancing in the rearview mirrors for several miles. They didn't talk, just sat ruminating over the nutty experience.

Finally, with the lights of Holbrook on the horizon, Bryson spoke. "Should we stop and talk to the police and look for the guy who paid them? It's just a tiny town. We need to find out who is telling everyone that we have cars in the back."

"Are you out of your mind?" Jack answered. "Who in their right mind is going to believe our story? I vote that we just keep on driving until your adrenalin dissipates. Incidentally, Bryson, if you agree to pick up any more intoxicated Indians or anybody else for that matter, I'm going to lock you in the back with the cars and drive to the nearest airport. Go crawl in the back and take a nap. I'll wake you when we get to Gallup. We can look for your chicken fried steak for supper."

# Chapter Eighteen

# THE FLATLANDS

When the phone rang at five forty-five the next morning, Bryson was dead to the world. Marisa, on other hand, was full of vitality and enthusiasm and wanted to chat with her husband.

"You won't believe how much better *The Lion King* was here on Broadway than the traveling troupe we saw in Phoenix. Madeline even wanted a CD and a shirt this time. After the play we went to the best steakhouse and honestly, I have never seen a filet that thick. Bryson, I went in a men's store to look for something for my brother for his birthday and found a white dress shirt that cost seven hundred dollars . . . no, I didn't buy it. Can you believe it, seven hundred dollars for a shirt?"

She paused, as if waiting for some kind of response, but didn't get one, so she went on. "And Bryson, did I mention the food? Remember the cheesecake we had at Lindey's? You know, by the ice rink at Rockefeller Plaza?"

"I'm glad you're having a good time. Sorry I sound a little sleepy, but it's still kind of early here."

Bryson glanced at the clock for the third time and finally sat at the edge of the bed. He was exhausted when they got into Albuquerque late the night before. He was feeling it even more now. Every muscle in his body ached. Every joint was stiff and even his teeth hurt. Bryson had driven from Gallup and the last hour Jack had crawled in the back and gone to sleep again. When they finally arrived at the La Quinta motel, Jack had told Bryson to go on inside. He was sleeping in the truck. They had agreed after the parking lot night in Reno not to both sleep in the truck at the same time.

Listening to his wife talk about the great food in New York made Bryson remember the four tacos he had eaten for dinner. They had looked for a diner to get a decent hot meal but all they found were the typical roadside fast-food franchises. The acid was still in his throat.

"How was your day yesterday?" Marisa asked. "You don't sound like yourself."

"It was okay. Just a long, straight road and lots of other trucks, all of which want to travel a mile or two per hour faster or slower than we do, so we're constantly having to speed up or get passed and then slow down for slower cars or trucks ahead of us. It's frustrating." Then noting his own negativity, added, "but it's still lots of fun. Listen Marisa, I am also so glad that you had the wisdom to refuse to come in the truck with me. I really did want you to come but now I realize what it would have been like for you and Madeline."

Bryson started to lie back down on the stiff, rough pillow-case when the knock came on the door and he dragged himself off of the bed to answer it. Jack was standing outside, holding his travel case and shaving kit. He looked about as bad as Bryson felt but did have a smile on his face.

"Good morning, Sunshine," he said. "You look like the floor of a milking barn. Why don't you go back to bed while I shower and tank up the truck?"

\*\*\*

After a shower and a Grand Slam at Denny's, chased down with a large Pepsi, Bryson was as good as new. Jack had reviewed the historical sites that lay ahead the next thousand miles. There wasn't much. He went back into the truck stop store and bought a Clive Cussler novel on CD. At least they would have some distraction from the boring highway ahead.

The morning sun glared in their eyes as they pulled onto Interstate 40. It promised to be a bright, sunshiny day. It was day four behind the wheel of Big Blue and though lots had happened, they hadn't logged many miles to show for it. They needed to make up some time. The wide-open plains of America's heartland lay straight ahead and the truck was purring like a twelve-thousand-pound kitten. Big Blue was everything Bryson had hoped for in a truck. Even the other truck drivers who passed him gave envious second looks. He loved honking the horn when kids in passing cars gave the signal to pull the handle dangling from the ceiling of the truck. The joys and frustrations the two men had experienced already were enough to write a book. He hoped that for the next few days he wouldn't have enough to write a sequel.

✳✳✳

The heat build-up in a black rubber tire rolling down a black asphalt highway on a calm summer day can be extreme. Big Blue's front tire's nylon fibers failed and the tire blew out just before they were planning to stop for lunch. They had left New Mexico and were on smooth Texas asphalt traveling at eighty miles per hour when an invisible gorilla took hold of the steering wheel and started yanking it back and forth. Of the eighteen tires on a big rig truck, the worst one to blow out is the left front, pulling the truck to the left into oncoming traffic. Luckily it was Bryson's right front tire that blew. It sounded like a cannon being fired. Both men jumped as the violent explosive noise entered the cabin, interrupting the Eagles singing.

The truck lurched to the right, heading off the paved surface toward a deep bar pit. "Don't overcorrect. Don't overcorrect," were words of counsel that sprang into Bryson's head. Pulling hard but not jerking against the force of the wheel rim cutting into the soft shoulder of the highway,

Bryson braked the truck and then held it steady—not too much right or left. With shreds of rubber slapping against the wheel well, and with an occasional flap of black rubber zinging past the passenger window, the noise was ear-shattering. When the truck finally came to a halt, it was at a dangerously tilted angle, half on and half off the pavement. The only sound they could hear was the pounding of their hearts slamming blood into the tiny vessels around their eardrums.

The men sat looking at one another. In spite of the air-conditioned cab, beads of sweat trickled down their foreheads.

Cars passing on the left rocked the cab with their slipstreams of air. Inspecting the damage, Jack and Bryson found that the front right edge of the truck rested less than a yard from an embankment, which fell away from the edge of the pavement at over thirty degrees. The highway itself was making a gentle left turn. Had they not stopped for another fifty feet, they would have been doomed to fly off the road, rolling and cartwheeling as their momentum carried them into a scattered expanse of boulders. The tire was long gone; the largest remaining piece was dinner plate size, the rest of the tire having been scattered over the highway. The huge magnesium rim looked like a product of weapons testing. Whole chunks of metal were missing. It had cut a groove into the hot asphalt tracking back three hundred yards.

"Now, what?" Jack asked. He had not been a part of any of the discussions regarding warranty and emergency roadside service.

"I have a number in the service book to call," Bryson answered. He had taken several deep breaths and was back in full control. "I'll give the Peterbilt hotline a call and see if they can get in touch with someone who can replace the tire and wheel. Maybe we'll get lucky."

Bryson wasn't on the phone long before he looked at Jack and asked, "Have you ever changed a truck tire?"

"No I haven't, nor do I ever intend to do so. I have heard the story over and over about the guy who tried to change a big truck tire and the wheel rim exploded apart in the process, flying across the room and taking his head with it. Couldn't you get a hold of anyone?"

"There is a truck on the way but it will take an hour and I thought we could get a head start on the job. I guess we'll just wait."

And they did. It was two hours and many phone calls later when the men, sitting in the shade of a ten-foot-tall boulder, spotted an old rusted-out Dodge tow truck pass by, slowly heading in the other direction. It went down the road and then turned and pulled around to the front of the truck. It then backed up to within a couple of feet of Big Blue. A teenager in greasy coveralls got out of the cab, slamming the door twice before it would stay closed. He walked around the front of Big Blue and inspected the destroyed wheel.

Without so much as a glance up or down the road to locate the truck's driver, the skinny kid went to the back of his truck and unfastened a long hydraulic tow bar, which he then slid under the front bumper of Big Blue. In a matter of seconds, he had the entire front end of the semi off the ground. From where Bryson and Jack were watching, it was looking as though the kid was going to leave, pulling Big Blue behind. As the two trucks started inching forward, Bryson jumped to his feet.

Bryson and Jack took off toward the truck yelling.

"Wait just a dang minute!" Bryson screamed, worrying that the driver was already too far away to hear. The two old men ran toward the trucks—if you could call a controlled fast hobble a run. After a couple more shouts, the kid looked back in the mirror at them then stopped.

Bryson and Jack were winded and gasping when they reached the trucks. They both bent over in the classic tripod position of chronic lung patients: hands on knees, head stretched forward, mouths agape, trying to catch their breath.

"Why were you leaving?" Bryson demanded between breaths.

"Don't get yer panties in a bundle," the kid answered. "There's a pullout about a quarter mile up that hill where we're gunna wait fur my boss. I radioed him with the tire and rim size and he'll meet us here in 'bout an hour. You can ride in yer truck or ride with me." The Texas twang in the young man's voice was so profound it made Willie Nelson's accent sound British.

Bryson could already feel the bright sun burning the top of his head and face. He needed to get out of the sun but wasn't going to trust their fate to the unmonitored will of the driver. He decided to get in the tow truck cab with the driver. Jack shimmied up onto the passenger's side step of the Peterbilt's running board, which was lifted an additional foot off the ground and on an angle. Just as he got the door open, the kid in the tow truck popped the clutch jerking the truck forward. Jack grabbed for a handrail, but with sweaty hands, couldn't get a good grip.

Falling straight toward the ground, when one trips, seems instantaneous. The ancient scientists and philosophers taught that gravity's force was merely the properties, which originally came from the earth, returning to the earth. The reality is that whatever gravity is, it can just reach up its invisible hand and jerk you to the ground. Falling from a considerable height, however, can be a seemingly slow-motion, dreamlike event. Bryson looked back out of the dusty rearview mirror of the old rusty tow truck and watched helplessly as his partner fell backwards, windmilling his arms in a futile effort to regain his balance.

Bryson couldn't hear Jack hit the ground, but it had to have been a sickening sound. Screaming at the driver to stop, Bryson was out of the truck's little cab in a heartbeat and at Jack's side before the forward motion of the trucks ceased. Jack had landed far enough off of the hard pavement that when his head finally hit the ground, it was on dirt and gravel, giving a merciful cushion to the landing. The thirty-degree embankment was just a couple of feet away from the prone Jack, forcing Bryson to kneel partially under the giant wheels of the truck as he examined his injured friend.

"Don't move your head or neck," Bryson commanded, his early years of emergency room moonlighting experience kicking in.

The command wasn't necessary. Jack was out cold. Bryson quickly unbuttoned and removed his own shirt, and folding it carefully, slid it under Jack's head. Pulse, respirations, and a general check of arms and legs assured Bryson that no visible injuries were present. Bryson yelled at the bewildered tow truck driver to get some water and a towel out of the cab of Big Blue, only to find the idiot in the process of lowering and unhitching the truck.

Bryson's shout at the kid was just what Jack needed. He abruptly opened his eyes and sat straight up, nearly knocking Bryson off balance. Bryson was torn between attending to Jack and stopping the tow truck from leaving. Once Jack appeared alert and free from any neurological damage, Bryson pushed himself to his feet and confronted the kid.

"I got to get out of here. I can't waste the day waiting while y'all play nursemaid. You gotta call somebody else."

This was a statement Bryson wasn't prepared for and wasn't going to accept. He walked to the cab of the tow truck and took the key out of the ignition. Then he returned to the front of his truck where Jack was now on his knees, mopping the back of his scraped head with Bryson's shirt.

"What the hell is going on?" Jack asked, shaking his dirt-covered hands and rotating his head in a wide circle to test out its mobility.

Bryson led Jack to the shady side of the truck and had him sit on the running board while he argued his case with the unreasonable tow truck driver.

Before a resolution was reached, the kid's boss pulled up in a pristine service truck with a newly mounted tire in the back.

Money talks and losers walk. Within a half hour the service center's owner had a new rim and tire on the truck. He accepted Bryson's American Express card with a smile and informed the boy that he was to drive the old tow truck back to the service center and clean out his locker.

"I didn't mean to get the kid fired," Bryson said, feeling sorry for the idiot, "but he could have killed my friend. Why did he insist on moving the truck down the road?"

"I think he was going to meet someone there. Just after you made your initial call, a guy who had been loitering around the service center became very interested in your call for help and said something to Arvin that I didn't hear. But I did hear the words, 'Italian sports cars.' I don't think Arvin knows that there is an Italy, let alone cars from there, but he has heard of hundred dollar bills."

When Bryson finally crawled up into the Peterbilt's driver's seat, he looked at his friend. Jack was lying in the sleeper cabin bed with an ice pack on the back of his head.

"How are you doing?" Bryson asked. "It shouldn't take more than an hour before we can get you to the hospital."

"I've already seen the doctor," Jack answered. "Let's just get some miles behind us. I'm going to be fine. Let's get a move on. By the way, what are you fixing for lunch?"

And so they did get a move on. Bryson insisted that Jack remain in the back and get some sleep. They stopped for fuel and cheeseburgers fifty miles east. Later, as they were crossing the panhandle of Texas, Jack—still hungry—made cold cut sandwiches from the stock of food in the little fridge.

**\*\*\***

Driving by himself for the next eight hours left Bryson with time to think. Who was that tow truck kid conspiring with? Why so many weird events over the last four days? What was next? Along with a bit of paranoia can often come nostalgia and self-pity.

As he drove the truck down that seemingly endless strip of asphalt, Bryson's mind wandered back to his years in practice.

Did anyone really appreciate the long years he had spent to acquire his training and the right to practice? The four years of college, then four long, expensive years of medical school and the four years as an Ob/Gyn resident. Why hadn't he become a real estate developer?

A fast-rolling Freightliner's horn startled Bryson back into the present. The huge red truck was just inches away from the side of Big Blue; a quick glance taught Bryson that he had drifted across the center line. Jack's head popped out from between the blue-and-white checked curtains separating the sleeper cabin from the driver's cab.

"Are you okay?" he asked, looking for reassurance that Bryson wasn't falling asleep.

"I'm doing great! How is your head?"

"My headache is gone, but I feel so sleepy that I would be afraid to try relieving you behind the wheel. How much further is it to the next big town?"

"It's only thirty miles to Oklahoma City. From there we need to head south toward Shreveport. I'm going to need some help getting around the Oklahoma City traffic if you feel up to it. After you find us a route to follow, how about calling ahead and getting us a couple of rooms?"

**\*\*\***

There were two requirements for any of Bryson's overnight hotel stays. The first and most important was that the establishment had a swimming pool, and if possible, a Jacuzzi that was clean and hot. The second was the availability of at least four pillows on a soft bed. Unfortunately, what he required and what he got were not necessarily the same thing. By the time Big Blue arrived at the motel four hours later, the swimming pool and spa were closed and the extra pillows were all the type probably made of shredded tractor tires. Holiday Inn Express just barely met Bryson's criteria, but after driving most of the day, he was beyond caring.

Bryson started running the water in the bathtub and made a dash back to the truck to double-check the locks and alarm system. As he came around the front of the truck, he thought he saw someone slip into a shadow at the back wheel well. He stopped and listened but didn't hear any footsteps in the gravel. Maybe fatigue was taking over. He circumnavigated the truck but saw nothing more. Except for the sounds of traffic on the adjacent freeway, he could hear nothing suspicious. Remembering the running tub water, he hustled back into the room. The light under the door from Jack's room was out, so he dropped the idea of telling him about the phantom in the parking lot.

Parting the blinds on the tiny window, Bryson could see a portion of the parking lot but only the front end of his Peterbilt. *Forget it*, he told himself, and headed into the bathroom.

Sinking into the hot water of the economy-sized tub felt fantastic. There was nothing like clean, hot water to settle the nerves and calm the soul. Unfortunately, by the time Bryson's entire body had settled into the contour of the tub, most of the water had escaped down the overflow drain. He tried to turn on the water with his foot to refill and reheat the tub but the valve was too tight and the corrosion on the handle scratched his big toe, creating a tiny laceration. He considered trying to sit up and pull on the faucet knob with his hand but gave up and lay there letting his mind wander instead.

He thought about each of his kids and wondered what

they were doing. He had made a practice of calling each of them once a week but since the fire and shooting they had called home so often that his calls had seemed redundant. They were all doing well anyway and it often seemed as though he was interrupting their evening when he called. He thought about Marisa and Madeline and wondered what their day had been like but had missed the window of time to call without waking them.

Finally, he thought about the six cars in the back of his truck and all the disjointed attempts to steal one or all of them. Something weird was going on. He made up his mind to try again to call Fritz, the owner of the dealership. The whole thing was getting stranger by the day. His mind then drifted into a fog interrupted by a sudden jerk of his muscles, jarring him back to consciousness.

With some difficulty he crawled out of what was left of the shallow, tepid bathwater and staggered to the bed. He was dripping water but was too tired to bother with a towel. He glimpsed out of the window one last time but saw nothing in the parking lot.

✳✳✳

The morning Texas sun was bright and hot. The increasing humidity as they traveled from the Western deserts toward the great Gulf of Mexico added to the guarantee of some discomfort as Bryson and Jack left the air-conditioned comfort of the motel. The men had slept in longer than anticipated and barely made it in time to get the last scraps of the free buffet breakfast. The food had been picked over and the morning newspapers scattered and soiled.

Jack teased Bryson about his complaining over the lack of good doughnuts for breakfast. "First you want to find the perfect breaded surprise with wallpaper paste gravy and now it's the world's most delicious doughnut. You are a hard man to please. How does Marisa put up with you?"

"I would have been happy this morning with just one doughnut that hadn't had the frosting picked away by little kids."

The men both laughed as they rounded the parking lot corner only to come upon a group of high school band geeks staring into the back of the shiny auto transport trailer. Its rear doors were swung wide open. The teens, dressed in what appeared to be some sort of marching band outfits, stood gape-mouthed, admiring the glistening front end of the outward-facing black Lamborghini. One of the girls dressed in baggy, black-silk, striped tuxedo pants, shiny black military dress shoes and a very tight pink halter top, was climbing into the trailer using the car's front bumper as a handhold.

"Hey, get down from there!" Bryson yelled, startling the girl and scattering the crowd.

"Butt out," came the voice of a tubby boy with peach fuzz on his chin and bulbous lips that could only belong to a tuba player. "She just wants to get a couple of pictures sitting on the car."

Jack extended his hand to assist the girl down, but she folded her arms across her chest and refused to get down. Her expression was a mixture of obstinance and pleading.

"I just want one picture with me on the car to show my boyfriend. He's a jock and always tells me that band people never have any fun."

In spite of the shock of the trailer doors being open, Bryson and Jack looked at each other and shrugged.

"Why not?" Bryson said. "But please just lean on it; don't sit on it."

This was the wrong thing to agree to. Immediately there was a lineup of kids waiting their turns to have a photo-op. While Jack supervised the kids, Bryson tried to figure out how the lock had been removed and if anything was missing from the trailer or the cab of the truck. The other question was why the intrusion alarm hadn't gone off.

"I saw two old Indian guys walk away from the back of the truck when we all came out from the motel," one of the girls volunteered. "They were carrying a big tool that looked like a giant fingernail clipper. When they saw us they both got into a pickup. That's when Amy saw the open door and peeked in. Are those all your cars?"

Bryson saw his padlock lying in the dusty gravel close to the wheel of a nearby Suburban, which was hand-painted with pep rally slogans on its sides. He picked up the lock and inspected the neat cut across the supposedly bullet-proof latch. He handed it to Jack and shook his head.

"We might just as well paint a sign on the back of the trailer announcing exotic cars inside and leave the back end open each night."

"The least we can do is buy some new locks at Costco. I noticed that they sell them in packages of four. It might save us trips to the hardware stores."

When the teenagers were finished with their picture taking, Bryson swung the rear doors closed and asked one of the passing motel workers where a hardware store or Costco was located. Jack jumped into the driver's seat and started the huge diesel engine to warm it up while Bryson performed a walk-around, inspecting the pneumatic brake lines and thumping each tire with a heavy rod to estimate the tire pressure. He looked under the truck for any surprises and then gave Jack the thumbs up.

When the way was clear, Bryson climbed into the right seat and they were off. The first thing Bryson did was open the glove box and retrieve his pistol. He wiped it down with the oil rag it was wrapped in and checked the cylinders. It was loaded and needed only the release of the safety to be ready to fire.

A Home Depot was open early for the building tradesmen and the parking lot was spacious. Jack made a wide circle with the truck and parked in a place with a straight shot outbound. Bryson headed for the store and the lock section.

\*\*\*

Jack could see the food and smell the aroma of hot coffee at a small snack trailer not fifty feet away from where he was parked. He tried to resist but in the end decided a breakfast hot dog would taste good. He set the brakes on Big Blue and leaving the engine running, climbed down, locking the doors with his extra FOB key. There was a small line waiting to be served as he took his place. At first he thought his imagination was running wild, but then squinting against the glare of the sun, he saw the familiar men.

The two old Indian codgers who had tried to rob them in Arizona were sitting in a battered Ford pickup looking at the big blue truck with binoculars. Jack ducked out of their line of sight and circled around behind the trailer. He worked his way around a row of wheelbarrows and slipped into the entrance of the store. He found Bryson tucking his wallet into his pocket, having already swiped his credit card for the purchase.

"Did we forget something?" Bryson asked.

Jack didn't answer but instead picked up a razor-bladed carpet knife off the impulsive buyers rack and threw a ten-dollar bill on the counter, not bothering to get his receipt or change. He grabbed Bryson by the arm and headed for the entrance door instead of the exit. An employee hollered at them, but Jack waved the guy off.

"You won't believe who is shadowing us in the parking lot." Not giving Bryson time to answer he said, "Dumb and Dumber . . . the Apache versions . . . are sitting out there waiting for your new locks so they will have something to cut with their bolt cutters."

"You have got to be kidding!"

"I wish I was kidding." Jack glanced at the "snake killer" man, Bearwater, who was slumped down, as if trying to be inconspicuous in the passenger's seat of a truck that had seen better days. "If you will go to the truck and start pulling away, I'm going to circle behind them and check their tire pressure." Jack gave Bryson a smirky grin and held up the skill knife.

Bryson said he didn't like this division of labor and took the knife.

Keeping up appearances, Jack walked back to the truck and took time to go to the back of the trailer and install the new padlock on the rear doors.

Next, Jack unlocked the door and climbed into the cab, revved up the engine, released the air brakes and started pulling out toward the road. Through the passenger's side mirror he caught a glimpse of Bryson approaching the back of the old pickup in a near crab-like crawl. That was when Jack remembered that the old Indian might have retrieved the gun Bryson had thrown into the desert.

In a move not burdened by forethought or planning, Jack swung the wheel of Big Blue, making a wide circle around the parking lot. He then headed the truck back toward the store and straight toward the driver's side of the Indian's pickup truck. He honked the horn four or five long pulls, startling the people in the coffee line and getting full attention from the two old men in the pickup. Their eyes widened as the grill and bumper of the huge truck rapidly approached. With a screech of the brakes, Jack stopped the Peterbilt less than six inches from the driver's door. The men inside sat stunned and motionless.

Sitting up high in the truck, Jack could see what the old idiots couldn't. While the Indians held a frantic conversation, Bryson used the newly purchased knife and, in spite of his rusty surgical skills, performed an air-ectomy on two of the pickup's four tires. Jack gave the horn a couple more blasts, causing the Indians to jump, and then he began backing away.

By the time Jack got the truck straightened out and was heading for the parking lot exit, Bryson had jumped onto the running board, pulled the door open and climbed in.

The pickup tried to follow, but went less than fifty feet before it came to a halt in a cloud of blue smoke.

*** 

By the time the Peterbilt pulled onto the Interstate, Bryson had his phone out and had placed another call to the Reno car dealer, Fritz. Unlike previous tries, this one produced a live voice that sounded like the owner but the connection was so poor that trying to explain anything about the attempts to steal the cars in the trailer was not getting through to the guy. The last thing Bryson could understand before the connection was disrupted was that the cars had to be in Miami on time and that Bryson was at least a day behind schedule.

Bryson snapped the phone shut. "Something we don't understand is going on. We keep thinking that somebody wants to steal the cars, but maybe it's something inside of the cars they want. Every time they get the back door of the trailer open . . . what's that now, four times? Every time, the cars aren't really bothered. It just doesn't make any sense." Bryson settled deep into the leather passenger seat and stared out the window, trying to review all the nonsense of the last few days.

"I'll tell you what I think. I think we should call the cops and let them in on all this stuff and maybe they'll get those two Indian idiots off our case," Jack said.

"Incidentally, weren't we supposed to fill up before we headed out this morning? We're about out of fuel and I'm starved," he added.

Bryson pointed to an intersection sign and said, "I saw a sign a ways back for a restaurant on that highway. It said that they had the best cherry pie in the world. The world is a big place. Let's see if they're lying."

The big dual stack mufflers gave out a deep, throaty rumble as Jack geared down through the numbers of Big Blue's transmission. The truck slowed to seventy, then fifty and then to a crawl at thirty-five as they took the turn onto a Louisiana state route.

"There it is," commented Jack, pointing toward a large old antebellum home surrounded by gigantic magnolia trees and fields of cotton. A small hand-carved signed announced the entrance to Edith's Kitchen.

"I don't see many cars, but maybe it's early for lunch," Bryson said with more than a hint of skepticism in his tone.

He slowed the truck and pulled off the asphalt road into a parking lot of crushed oyster shells. Once the truck was stopped, the men sat in silence and took in the scene of a restaurant that was years ahead of its time—back in 1850, that is. The white building was brick and stone and had a cedar shake roof. The windows all had outside storm shutters with clever patterns cut into the wood. There were eight dormer windows on the second story and a rooster weather vane attached to one of the many red brick chimneys. The house itself was surrounded by a stunted forest of flowering shrubs and bushes. Bryson and Jack were mesmerized by the scene, but weren't sure about stopping to eat until a gigantic truck with an even more gigantic oil drilling rig mounted on its back pulled slowly into the parking lot. It stopped in a shaded area and when the four doors of the crew cab flew open, six men, all dressed in coveralls and wearing hard hats, marched briskly toward the old house. Bryson noticed a trail of dust from yet another truck approaching from the other direction and nodded toward it.

"This looks like the place to be," Jack said.

Both men crawled down from their respective sides of Big Blue. They were moving slowly as joints popped and ground and stiff muscles sent out their pleas for medication. Bryson heeded the warning and took a couple of seconds to stretch his back and arms.

When the door of Edith's opened, the wonderful smells of home cooking escaped. The clatter of dishes and the voices from the back echoed through the cavernous dining room. Only three tables were occupied, all by men in work clothes. The tables and chairs were plain but solid wood. There were only six choices of entrées. To Jack's amusement and Bryson's delight, one was chicken fried steak.

The place was filling up fast, and Bryson was afraid that they hadn't been noticed when they arrived and would lose their place in the lineup for orders. He was feeling the pressure to eat and get back on the road. He knew that when they got close to the Mississippi River country, Jack had an arm's length list of Civil War sites to visit.

More men were arriving with each passing minute. He had his eye on the swinging kitchen door, letting his hunger power his anxiety about being overlooked. Finally, a very pretty twentyish young woman came out from the kitchen, balancing a stack of steaming plates. She glanced his way and gave a wink then scattered the plates like a blackjack dealer throwing out aces. Before they had time to blink, she was at their table with tall glasses of ice water.

"Let me guess," she said. "Since we're only cooking one entree today, I bet you young boys both want the pickled pigs' feet with grits and fried okra, right? Just kidding, fellows!" she said and giggled. "Some days the only laughs I get are when I try funning somebody. My name is Nelly." Her long blonde hair was pulled back into a double ponytail and her apron was red and white plaid over a red V-neck T-shirt. She was wearing skintight black jeans and New Balance running shoes, the same high-end style that Bryson used at his gym. Her only jewelry was a large silver signet ring on her right middle finger with the initial N outlined in rubies.

"That was definitely a good joke," Bryson said, smiling. "Could we get our order in now? We're kind of in a hurry." He was glancing at the other tables, which were getting fuller by the minute. A couple of other waitresses were now in the large room with pads in hand, taking orders.

"Why sure, honey, you jest tell little Nelly here what y'all want and I'll get your order faster than an Okie yeller jacket stinging a Yankee."

Bryson glanced at the order pad still in her apron pocket and then up at the face staring down at him. She had her hands on her hips by now and her eyebrows were raised.

"I don't need to write your order down if that's what you were thinking." The hillbilly accent was gone and so was the smile. "Though I'll bet you won't believe it, I graduated from Wellesley. I can remember every order I've taken here in my mother's place since I was fourteen. I'll bet I can remember one cheeseburger and one chicken fried steak with two Diet Cokes. Ya think?"

Bryson started to apologize, but she put her index finger softly on his lips stopping his comment.

"That is just what you boys want. Right?"

The lip thing was a bit beyond flirtatious and her guessing their orders was downright spooky.

Jack and Bryson nodded and then watched as she sauntered off swinging her hips and nodding and waving at the regulars as she headed toward the kitchen. The two men stared at one another and didn't say a word.

The orders were flowing out of the kitchen as though on a conveyor belt. Several men who had arrived after Bryson and Jack were already eating.

"Maybe those guys called in their orders ahead of time," Jack finally said, sensing Bryson's anxious fidgeting.

"They look like they know a good meal when they find it. I'm way starved. I think we've found the right place to eat."

He had barely finished his sentence when there was a shadow over their table and Nelly's presence was noticed, standing like a statue, holding steaming oval plates, one overflowing with gravy and the other with crispy French fries. It had been less than five minutes since the perky waitress had left the table.

"May I?" She waited for the men to remove their elbows from the table to make room for the plates. Somewhere hidden from their view she had mysteriously carried two twenty-four ounce glasses full of crushed ice, lemon and diet colas. All were placed gently on the table.

"Since you boys are new here I'll give you a word of warning. My dear mother watches every order of chicken fried steak that she prepares. No, don't bother looking around for the camera, just trust me. You can add as much pepper, mustard, catsup or even A-1 . . . if your taste buds are that bad. But please, do not and I mean do not, shake salt on that steak or gravy. I've known her to come out here and bludgeon a customer to near death with a long-handle skillet for insulting her by adding salt to her perfect recipe. Any other dish is okay to ruin any way you want, but do not salt the chicken fried steak." She whirled away and was across the room in a flash.

Bryson looked down at his plate of food. Jack had already dug into his burger and fries and downed half of his drink. The piece of breaded meat on Bryson's enormous plate completely covered its surface. Mashed potatoes lay on top of a third of the meat, and gravy smothered nearly every inch of both the meat and the potatoes. There were no vegetables. No sprig of parsley. No color at all except the tan milky gravy and the walnut color of the breaded and pan fried meat. Could this be the one? The perfect example of what he had dreamed about? The Holy Grail of food?

The first forkful of the meat hit his mouth, awakening his taste buds and his soul like the beginning strains of the Philadelphia Philharmonic playing the National Anthem. He could feel the piloerection of each of the hair follicles on his arms and the back of his neck. Was this too wonderful to be true? He sank back into his chair and took a deep breath and chewed.

"Bryson are you okay? Look, you have goosebumps on your arms," Jack said with a half-full mouth of food and a dribble of mustard on the edge of his double chin. "Hey, did you know that in Guam the locals call that chicken skin?"

Bryson, not wanting to be rude, but also not wanting to get into a conversation about regional misuses of language, was fixated on eating and continued to chew and savor his meal. Cut, savor, chew, swallow. Over and over, then suddenly his plate was empty. He looked around the room to see if anyone except Jack was watching, and then using his index finger like a spatula, he wiped the few remaining streaks of gravy onto his finger and carefully licked them away. That pleasure was repeated six or eight times before his plate appeared to have been washed clean.

When he looked up again, Jack was leaning back in his chair, arms folded behind his head, and doing everything he could to keep from laughing out loud.

"It was really that good, huh?"

"You should have tasted it, Jack. It was created in heaven. It was the best thing I have ever put in my mouth . . . Well, maybe the second best thing. You really should have tasted it."

"I would have gladly had a bite had the opportunity arisen. I would have allowed you a bite of my hamburger too. It tasted great!"

Bryson finally caught on and apologized for not offering Jack a taste.

Jack's own plate was also squeaky clean. Their mirth was interrupted by the whisking away of their plates only to be replaced with dinner sized plates holding three separate thick slices of homemade pie and a double scoop of rock-hard vanilla ice cream.

"I see neither of you liked your meal, so I brought you dessert," said Nelly, giving them a sly grin. "Don't even think of refusing or telling me some lame 'I'm full or I'm on a diet lie.' We only have three flavors of pie today so you get all three: cherry, apple and pecan."

They both looked at their plates with the anticipation of trying to eat more food while already full.

"Go ahead, have a bite. I want to make sure it's not going to waste."

Both men dug in, trying bites of the three types and quickly digging back in for more. The whole time Nelly stood beside the table, arms crossed, watching them eat.

Jack looked up at her, dabbing caramel away from his mouth. "That is the most fantastic pecan pie I have ever tasted."

"Why don't you Yankees learn to talk?" she said. "It's pecan pie, not peck-on pie," she enunciated. "Try saying pee, like . . . you know, and then can, like into a can. Pee-can. It's not that hard."

Both men were laughing out loud by the time she had finished her grammar lesson. Those at tables around them were also enjoying the conversation.

When Nelly was finished, she magically produced a bill and two individually wrapped, homemade hand-dipped chocolates and placed them equidistant between the men.

"It's twenty dollars even. We don't take to no complicated higher math here," she said dropping back into her faux-Southern accent, and then she was gone.

Bryson considered going back into the kitchen to compliment the creator of the divine meal, but Jack tugged on his shirtsleeve, nodding to the four men who were waiting for their table. Bryson peeled off a twenty and then a ten and left them under the edge of the Coke glass.

The chicken fried steak was everything his Uncle Bill had said it would be and more. What a lucky find, a gourmet restaurant in the middle of the armpit of Louisiana. He laughed out loud as he thought about the saucy Nelly and her scolding of Jack for mispronouncing pecan. The chicken fried steak's flavor and texture and the entire scene would be imprinted on his memory, never to be forgotten.

# Chapter Nineteen

## THREATS

Seven hundred and ninety miles away, Marisa and Madeline were sitting in a hotel room eating stale Tostito chips and sipping on warm bottled water. They were trying to stay interested in a remake of a Jane Austin romance classic, but Madeline kept interrupting to ask her mom what the characters had just said. The heavy British accents of the actors and actresses required a tuned ear.

Jenny loved New York but had become restless hanging around the hotel and campus of Duke. She had gone for several long walks, and even tried the school's lovely art museum, but sitting around waiting wasn't one of her strong points. She had decided on the spur of the moment to take a shuttle flight to Atlanta to visit a cousin. "I'll be back when the boys roll into town in their toy truck."

The phone on the nightstand rang. Madeline held out the phone for her mother. "It's some guy who says he owns Daddy's truck trailer and something about him being late. The guy sounds really mad."

At first Marisa didn't even reach for the phone. A wave of fear jolted through her. Had there been an accident? She took the phone, and inhaling slowly, began to speak. "Can I help you?"

"Are you the Doc's wife?" the voice interrogated. He had a strange accent and his rudeness was preempted by what Marisa recognized as stress.

"Who is this calling?"

"Lady, you need to call your husband and tell him to get a move on. He is over a day behind schedule delivering my trailer to Miami. I have to have the cars there on time. I've told him that, but he keeps stopping and playing along the way. Maybe you can help."

"I have no idea what in the world you are talking about, and if you dare to call me again, I will not hesitate calling the police."

She handed the phone back to Madeline to hang it up. She immediately got off the bed and went to her purse to get her cell phone. Her hands were shaking and she was getting tiny tears in her eyes. She turned away from her daughter, not wanting to frighten her.

"Is Dad okay?"

"He is fine, sweetheart. That was just some creepy guy. Why don't you get ready and we'll go out to dinner? We shouldn't be eating this junk food. I'm going to call Dad."

Marisa tapped Bryson's number into her cell phone and walked to the opposite corner of the room to face the window. It looked like a beautiful summer evening outside. The blossoms and new leaves had a nearly neon color in the evening light. Marisa had a memory flash of looking at a similar scene just a few months ago when their life had been simple and routine. Bryson had been going to work every day and the kids and grandkids were busy with their own lives. She was living her own life as well: tennis, women's club, church responsibilities and plenty of leisure time to call and visit friends and family.

"Hello, are you there?"

Bryson's voice brought her back to the present.

"Bryson, where are you?"

"I'm in the middle of a convoy," he answered in a joking tone.

"Seriously, where are you?"

"We're outside of Monroe, Louisiana. They have had a lot of rain here the last couple of months. You wouldn't believe how green this place is. Remember when we went for the Ayerst meeting and it was brown . . . "

"Bryson, stop talking and listen to me," she interrupted. "I just got a nasty call on our room phone here at the hotel. The jerk said to tell you that you were behind schedule and that you needed to hurry. Why are you taking so long?"

"I'll call the guy and tell him to leave you alone. I have no idea how he got the number. I don't want you to worry. We've had some minor problems but will travel faster and stop less often. If the guy . . . his name is Fritz, calls again, just hang up," he said.

After the phone call, Marisa and Madeline finished getting dressed for dinner. They were going to just get a hamburger, but Marisa decided to take out her frustration on her American Express card, so they went to Ruth Chris instead. Maybe they would even split a lobster tail and have the crème brûlée. Oh what comfort foods could provide.

***

Bryson tried to focus on the road, but he couldn't shake the thought that the Reno car dealer or Fritz—or whoever—had actually called his wife, getting her involved. For a moment he even considered driving to the next major city and catching a plane to Durham to talk to Marisa and alleviate her fears. The time zone difference was narrowing. *Oh, forget it*, he told himself. He explained the call to Jack, who pulled out his Blackberry and started crunching numbers. Maybe they could cut some miles and time off the trip. The list of Civil War battle sites to visit was quickly being forgotten.

It took nearly half an hour of going back and forth between the Garmin GPS and the Blackberry before Jack had a new and less scenic route planned. The men both had wanted to see New Orleans and to savor some of the famous cuisine. Abandoning that route, they elected to stay to the north and to postpone the sightseeing and food grazing for the return trip. They had been content to trade off driving when convenient; now they decided to drive straight through the night. The party was over.

They had made it nearly to Meridian, Mississippi when a red warning light on the instrument panel started flashing. Jack was driving and Bryson was changing clothes in the sleeper cab. They had both taken quick showers at the last truck stop but hadn't taken a change of clothes into the showers with them. There was seldom any place to hang things and the floors were in a constant state of soaking wet.

His arm was throbbing so he scarfed four Advil in anticipation of his next turn at the wheel. He had stopped his prescription anticoagulants two days ago, feeling that he needed more joint pain relief but couldn't risk driving with narcotics in his bloodstream.

"Hey Bryson, we have a problem!" shouted Jack.

Bryson parted the curtain and looked at the dashboard where there was the obvious red flashing light. He got out the owner's manual and in the dimming light of sunset, searched for an answer to the flashing light. He found it buried in the middle of the telephone-book-sized manual under the brake lines.

"We better stop at the first place we find that has good lighting. It looks like one of the coupling lines for the air brakes could be losing pressure. You know this stuff better than I do, Jack. When we stop, you can take a look."

It was only a few nervous miles down the highway before they came to the Flying T, a new modern truck stop. Bryson took his foot off the accelerator pedal and started to apply the brake. As he did, another light began flashing and a loud warning bell began to ring, but the truck didn't slow down.

The brake pedal still had some resistance, but the forward momentum of the thirty-thousand pounds of moving truck didn't respond. Jack quickly downshifted into a lower gear, forcing the engine's massive cylinder compression to act as brakes. He downshifted over and over, until he was in second gear and Big Blue was rolling forward at just a snail's pace. He guided the truck off the highway onto the frontage road. When he finally got into a position near the brightly lit service bay of the truck stop, he pulled the truck down into first gear, let out the clutch and killed the engine. With a jerky rattle and rumble, the Peterbilt came to a stop.

The two men looked at each other and sighed. They crawled down to the asphalt from the massive cab. Bryson slipped on his shirt and then handed Jack one of their four-battery xenon flashlights. They turned on the intensely bright lights and set out examining the truck. It took a few minutes, but when they found the problem area, the cause was obvious. Deep between the eight rear wheels of the tractor part of the truck, caked in mud and road grime, was a spreading moist area the size of a cantaloupe: brake lubricating fluid was dripping down a stalactite of grease onto the pavement. On close inspection, the problem appeared to be nothing more than a loose fitting. The solution would be simple: tighten it with a pair of pliers and replace the lubricant fluid.

Jack went back to the cab for a pair of pliers while Bryson looked for any additional problems. He was on all fours when he thought he heard Jack's approaching footsteps, so he continued his search. His anxiety level escalated, however, when he found a place on the long metal brake line where it had been recently rubbed clean. He called out to Jack to come see, but received no answer. The footsteps he was hearing faded away only to be replaced by others. This time they were Jack's.

"I think we're in luck," said Jack, as he approached. "I glanced in the owner's manual and it said to check this exact fitting every three thousand miles. Apparently, coming loose is a regular problem. These pliers should do the trick. It's a good thing that we packed those extra cans of lubricant."

"I think it might have had some help," said Bryson. "Take a look at this cleaned-off area. Say, was there someone walking around the truck just now?"

"I haven't seen a living soul in this end of the lot since we pulled in. There are a few people fueling up trucks over by the pumps, but the service place here is abandoned for the night."

"I could have sworn I heard footsteps. And look at this line. Someone has wiped the grime off of it since we went through the rain and mud clear back in Nevada. It's as though they were looking for a splice or joint in the line."

"Let's fix this thing, then we'll both look around to see who or what is out there."

Bryson saw Jack slap the side of his jacket pocket when he said "look around" and figured out that he hadn't retrieved just the pliers when he went to the cab.

The connecting joint was quickly tightened and the rest of the undercarriage inspected. The men came out from under the trailer and stretched as they were finally able to stand up straight. Bryson's knees were throbbing and dirty from kneeling on the pavement wearing his thin cotton scrubs. "Look! There he is," said Bryson, staring across the parking lot at the battered Ford pickup with what looked like their old Indian acquaintance standing at its side, staring back at them through a pair of binoculars.

"How the heck did he get his tires fixed and catch up with us so easily?" Jack questioned. "And where is his buddy?"

"Give me the gun," Bryson said. "I've had it with those idiots." Realizing how abrupt he had been, he changed his tone and added, "Please put in the brake fluid and then bring our truck around by theirs. I'm going to go have a talk with our stalkers."

Reluctantly, Jack pulled the pistol from his pocket and, checking the safety, handed it, barrel down, to his cousin. It had always been that way with Bryson. Once he made up his mind, there was no point in arguing with him. It would only cause a fight, which Bryson would win in the end anyway. Jack held tight to the gun handle for a short second, just to get Bryson to look up.

"Do one thing for both of us," Jack offered. "Don't shoot them here in Mississippi. I've heard that the prisons here are the worst in the Western hemisphere. If you're going to shoot something, shoot their radiator."

And that is exactly what Bryson did, but not before he snuck up on the spying man and yanked the binoculars out of his hand. The other goofball was slumped down in the cab, pretending to be asleep. This one had a new face, taller and younger, not who they had faced on the high plateau country of Arizona. Bryson held the gun on both men and tried to get some information, but Bearwater just whined and complained until Bryson was sick of listening to him.

Jack had pulled the big truck up close by, blocking the view between the Indian's truck and the fuel pumps and store. He watched the men argue for a minute and finally hit the air horn, startling all three of the men standing in front of Big Blue's blazing headlights.

"You idiots have had plenty of chances to leave us alone!" Bryson screamed. "And you, whoever you are," Bryson indicated to the new stranger, "you've taken up with the wrong person. This old geezer is a total idiot. The smartest thing you will ever do is to walk away from this sociopath and never look back."

Bryson stomped around to the front of the old pickup, and motioning for Jack to pull the air horn lever again, raised the gun and fired two shots into the grill of the old pickup truck. As the sound of the horn died away, the Indian and sidekick were cowering alongside their wounded truck, which was giving its last breath as a hissing sound, the hot radiator water pouring onto the black asphalt.

Bryson walked around to the passenger's side of the truck and climbed into the seat. Jack released the now properly functioning brakes, and Big Blue surged toward the superhighway entrance. Glancing in the mirror, Bryson noticed that Bearwater's new companion had removed his hat, releasing a mop of long, nearly white hair. He was already holding a cell phone to his ear.

"What do these guys want?" Bryson asked in frustration. "I think it is time that we get a thorough look at the cars inside the trailer. There must be something else they're after."

"And why the rush to get the cars to Miami in the first place?" Jack added. "That guy Fritz said there was a car show there, but I've looked and looked on the Internet, and I can't find a car show in all of Florida this whole month."

Both men were silent for several minutes and then they spoke at the same time. "Drugs."

"It's got to be drugs," Bryson said. "Who else could afford to send a trailer with millions of dollars' worth of cars across the country with a novice truck driver? Those guys don't care about the cars. It's got to be about what's *in* the cars."

***

Marisa and Madeline had eaten a gluttonous meal and had then worn off the calories walking around a Galleria mall. By the time they returned to the room it was late and they were exhausted.

The following morning, Marisa opened the curtains.

"Time to rise and shine, Maddie. Today is the day you have been waiting for. Move-in day at the dorm. We need to pack you up and clean up this messy room so you don't leave anything behind. The dorm doors open at ten."

"What's the big rush? The meeting for dorm rules isn't until two."

"I woke up this morning thinking that I need to fly to Orlando and meet your dad. That way I can ride the last few hours with him into Miami and maybe force him to get some rest. I could tell from his voice that he's tired and overstressed."

"What about Jenny?"

"She can fly down to Miami from Atlanta and meet us there. It will be good for you to get a head start on spending time with the girls in your dorm. Your dad said that Jack had hinted at wanting to do some fishing down in the Florida Keys, so maybe the four of us will spend a few days there before we head back."

"What's Daddy going to do with the truck? Can't he just sell it and fly home?"

"That's a great idea. Next time you talk to him, why don't you raise that question? If I were to do it he might just drive his big blue truck off into the sunset."

As they packed, Marisa repeated some of her concerns about leaving her daughter alone on the far side of the country. The warnings Marisa hoped Bryson would extend to their daughter were obviously not going to be delivered by good old Dad. Wasn't it just like life, to change one's carefully laid plans abruptly and without warning? Their fairy-tale idea of meeting in North Carolina and saying goodbye to Madeline together was just like all the dinners and movies and weekend getaways of the past that medical emergencies and impatient unborn babies had cancelled.

Marisa sat down on the edge of the bed, and using her cell phone with its bulging directory of most-used numbers, found the Delta Airlines number and called to make a reservation for the afternoon flight to Orlando.

Later in the morning, they hugged and kissed and then parted, Madeline with tears of joy and excitement for her future in her eyes, Marisa with tears of sadness and a sense of loss as one of the biggest mileposts of her life flashed by. Her baby had flown out of the nest.

# Chapter Twenty

# HIJACKED

The sun came up fast in the eastern sky as the big blue Peterbilt passed into the same time zone as the Bender women. In disobedience to the national safety standards, Bryson and Jack had not stopped for over twenty hours. With the exceptions of the occasional weigh-in inspection station, fuel, fast food and the shooting of a clunky Ford pickup, the driver's seat had never been empty.

They were in the middle of a deep forest of southern Alabama headed for Pensacola, Florida. Although the fuel gauge showed just under half full, they could barely see out of the windshield. They had been killing trillions of bugs with the windshield and headlights.

The combination of bright sunlight and the dried earthly remains of several swamps' worth of bugs was too irritating for Bryson. Fuel was getting lower and his stomach was complaining about too many sodas and doughnuts. He started the process of slowing the truck and signaling to turn off the freeway. Jack popped his head out from behind the curtain to see what was happening.

"Time to clean the bug massacre off of the windshield and get some real food," Jack said, catching a glimpse of his sleepy-eyed cousin in the mirror.

"We need to take the time to go through the trailer. How was the nap?" Bryson asked as he slipped the transmission into third and headed up an access road to a well-advertised yet hidden truck stop.

Once the forest opened up, the men saw a small parking lot and a row of only twelve pumps. The buildings and pumps looked to be of an older era, but there was lots of traffic so Bryson felt comfortable stopping.

Bryson asked Jack to start the fueling process while he

had a look in the back. Opening the trailer doors for the first time in two days created a cascade of dust and grit. Climbing into the trailer was painful. His joints, especially his shoulder, were stiff and sore from sitting in the truck for so long.

Being careful not to wipe his hands on the cars' surfaces where the dust would act like fine sandpaper, Bryson squeezed alongside and in between the six cars. It was a tight fit, but he was able to easily see around, in and under five of the masterpieces of Italian, German and British craftsmanship. The sixth car, the one at the very front on the lower level, was a forty-two-year-old Ferrari 275 GTB. It sat so low to the floor of the trailer that Bryson couldn't fit his body between the bumpers of the Lamborghini in back, to look underneath the Ferrari. As it turned out, he didn't need to see beneath any of the cars because the reflection of the sun from the windows of the other five created a condensed area of bright light in the empty rear luggage space of the GTB.

Where in its earlier days there would have sat a handmade set of leather luggage manufactured explicitly for the 275 GTB, there was something else. Stacked in the compact space were multiple brown-paper-wrapped packages about the size of flat shoe boxes. They were tied up with packing string. The packages, nearly twenty in number, appeared to have been covered with what looked to Bryson like an old handwoven Indian blanket, which had apparently slipped off the packages as they were tussled to and fro with the motion of the trailer. One of the packages near the side of the sack had a torn edge. Bryson shined his flashlight through the window and was certain that what he saw was the very corner of a one hundred dollar bill. Beneath the bill, in the tightly wrapped packages, he thought there must be more of the same. He wiggled around to the door of the car and tried the latch but it was locked. Working his way back toward the opening of the trailer, the combination of high humidity, the blazing morning sun and his sudden anxiety at the prospect of all that money hidden in his truck, soaked him like a sauna.

He climbed down from the trailer and looked around for Jack but couldn't see him.

Afraid to leave the area by the truck, he started to close the doors when around the corner of the truck came a whistling Jack, trying to balance two steaming Styrofoam cups and a bag of cinnamon rolls. Bryson stopped him at the driver's side of the cab, and taking one of the cups, told him about his find in the back of the Ferrari.

"I want to see," Jack insisted, already heading toward the back and trading the cinnamon rolls for Bryson's long-handle flashlight.

Just as they reached the back of the truck, a full-figured gal with long gray hair pulled into a ponytail, yelled at them across the parking area. She was waving a piece of paper and yelling something about the credit card not going through.

"I'll take care of it," Bryson said, laying the sack and the cup on the truck's bumper. He gave Jack a leg up into the trailer and then turned to follow the woman. Once inside, the woman ignored Bryson while she took cash from a woman with a screaming baby. She then turned to him and explained that the charge had not gone through and could she borrow the card again.

Bryson took his wallet from his pocket to give her the credit card and then watched as she handwrote the number onto a triple-copy charge slip. He couldn't remember the last time he had seen this method used—maybe ten years. He hoped the diesel fuel just pumped into his truck wasn't that old. Eager to return to the truck, yet needing to visit the restroom, he yielded to nature's call.

*** 

Jack was just about to look into the back window of the 275 GTB when something inconceivable happened. The giant back doors on the auto trailer swung closed with a tremendous boom. Instantly, the inside of the trailer became pitch black. Jack was stunned. He fumbled, trying to turn on the flashlight, and finally found its switch. Then he heard the truck's engine rumble to life, and to his aghast, he felt the truck start to move. He knew it was not Bryson driving.

Jack started to move toward the back of the trailer but was having trouble keeping his balance in the moving cage. Inching alongside the low-profile cars, there was nothing to hold onto, and with the first unanticipated turn of the truck, Jack was thrown off balance. First, he stood straight up, smacking his head on the suspended steel wheel rack of the upper cars. Then he fell backward, landing on the hood of the Lamborghini, sliding to the ground between it and the back of the Ferrari. His head hit the metal floor of the trailer with a thud, and the flashlight flew from his grasp, landing on the far side of the cars. He tried to stand up, but another turn of the truck threw him crashing onto his knees. He steadied himself, grasping onto both cars. He thought of yelling but knew it would be useless. He could feel the warm blood trickle from his head down the back of his neck but didn't dare let go of the cars to feel the wound. He was dizzy. Maybe he would just lie down for a minute and see if it would go away. His last conscious thought was to find the flashlight and get a look at the money . . . maybe go back to the cabin to get some Advil . . . then . . .

✳✳✳

Bryson walked out of the restroom, shaking excess water from his hands and silently cursing negligent attendants everywhere for not keeping the paper towel dispensers full. He was walking toward Big Blue and squinting in the bright sunlight. He felt in his pocket for his sunglasses but guessed he had left them on the floor of the trailer. Then he stopped walking. Something just wasn't right. Thinking he must have turned in the wrong direction, he turned back toward the office and again stopped abruptly. There on the ground he saw the sack full of doughnuts and the two spilled coffee cups.

Hadn't he helped Jack crawl into the trailer? There couldn't have been time for Jack to crawl to the front of the trailer, check out the cache of money and return to the cab of the truck and drive away; and why would he?

Bryson scanned the parking area for any sign of his truck and through pure luck caught a glimpse of the blue cab moving through a distant stand of pine trees in the opposite direction of the freeway. It was moving slowly down a small county road that went south. And again, why was it moving at all?

Bryson ran in his hobbling gait toward the back of the truck stop parking area, trying desperately to follow the line of sight of his truck. He thought he could still hear its turbo diesel engine, but the trees obscured his view. When he stopped running, he had to bend down with his hands on his knees to catch his breath. What was happening? His truck had just been stolen; and where was Jack? He reached for his cell phone to call 911 but found the holster empty. He was positive he had been wearing it when he went to the office to pay the fuel bill with his credit card.

He looked around for anyone who might help him but saw no one except a car full of teenagers with inflated inner tubes tied on the roof and a blue-haired woman struggling to put gasoline in her Buick with the diesel hose. He ran toward the office but had to stop again halfway there to catch his breath. He was starting to feel pain and pressure in his chest. Sweat was streaming from every pore. Short of breath, he slowed his pace and finally made it to the office. The heavyset clerk, who had just taken his credit card numbers, looked up from her magazine as if surprised to see Bryson again, then she smiled.

"I'm sure glad you came back. This is what you're looking for, right?" She reached behind the counter and held up his cell phone.

Bryson took the phone from her and sat down on a plastic chair next to an ATM machine. He ignored the woman's stare and dialed 911, trying at the same time to take deep breaths and ignore the increasing pressure in his chest.

The 911 operator answered immediately. She was polite and efficient, and within a couple of minutes had Bryson connected to the local sheriff's office. He listened to Bryson's story and then tried to placate Bryson by saying, "I'm sure your friend just decided to take a little spin and will be back in a jiffy."

Bryson explained the situation and added that they had already experienced several attempts to break into the trailer. He held back the story of the packages of money.

"Well, Dr. Bender. I and one of my boys will be out there at the truck stop in ten minutes. In the meantime, I'm gunna get on the radio and see if somebody has seen your buddy driving round in that truck. What color did you all say it was?"

\*\*\*

The sheriff arrived nearly half an hour after Bryson first made the call. The siren could be heard far off in the distance as the big white and blue Ford sedan drew closer. It pulled into the parking lot with full siren and more flashing lights and radio antennas than he had ever seen on a vehicle.

Just like in the movies, the police car approached Bryson fast then slammed on the brakes, coming to a sliding stop ten feet past the last set of pumps. Both front doors flew open and the occupants stepped out, stretched and then carefully applied their ridiculous flat-brimmed hats to their shiny bald heads. They looked like twins, except one was older and had a bigger beer belly.

The two lawmen approached Bryson, confirming that it was he who phoned in the truck theft. They made brief introductions then asked for his ID. Before he could even get out any clarification of the situation, the sheriff held up his hand like a British traffic bobby demanding a lorry to stop.

"I might have found your truck," he said, arms slowly crossed over an immense protruding abdomen.

He was no more than five-foot-five and was in the process of bursting each of the seams in his shirt and pants. The other hefty officer was an inch or so taller than his boss. Looking nervous, almost frightened, he stood with his hand on his hips, his right hand just inches below his gun handle.

"That's great," said Bryson, breathing a huge sigh of relief. "Where did you find my truck?"

"It's not some place you would be familiar with," the sheriff said. "My boy and I'll need to go have a look. What I want you to do is sit under that shade tree and fill out these papers. We'll be back in no time at all."

Bryson stepped out of the way of the car as it drove off, lights ablaze, sirens screeching and tires spinning. He had been oblivious of the many semi trucks as they had come and gone during the previous forty or so minutes, but now had an idea. He approached a big red Kenworth, which was pulling a double trailer loaded with logs. Both the tractor and trailer had more rust than paint. The driver was in the process of fueling his truck and talking on a cell phone simultaneously. Bryson stood a couple of yards away and motioned to the guy that he had a question. Three long minutes later, the guy hung up.

"Sorry about that. What can I do for you?"

"Have you got a radio that works, you know a CB?"

"I sure do, but you're just as welcome to use my cellular. I got one of them unlimited minute plans," he said, handing his phone toward Bryson.

Bryson took two deep breaths and began an explanation of the situation. Maybe if the man got on the radio and put out a broadcast on the CB someone might have seen the big blue Peterbilt.

The log hauler looked at Bryson. "What you a hauling in that trailer? Diamonds or rubies?"

"Just some cars to a car show in Miami," Bryson said, trying to get the guy to focus on finding Jack and the truck.

It took the guy time to finish his fueling but then he climbed into the cab and picked up the mike to send out a message. Bryson thought the man had switched into a foreign language as he spoke into the microphone.

*** 

Jack was awakened not by motion or noise but by the silence. He had no idea how long he had been out and at first had to rack his brain to even remember where he was. His head was throbbing, and when he reached back to localize the pain, he felt a slimy mat of hair and congealed blood. He felt around in the dark for the flashlight but only came up with a sliver in his finger from the wooden slats on the trailer floor. He tried to sit up but couldn't get a grasp on anything to pull against. The car next to him was too close to maneuver his wide shoulders. He needed help. He filled his lungs and was ready to let out a lusty call for help when the trailer door swung open and light poured in through the back.

"Get your skinny butt up in there and find them packages. You're little enough to fit 'tween them cars," a mean deep voice outside the trailer commanded.

The gravity of the situation hit Jack like the sting of a scorpion. The truck had been hijacked and he was trapped inside and about to be discovered. Bryson wasn't there to help him. Jack quickly figured that if he just laid there he would be found hurt or worse.

Some loud arguing outside the trailer ensued, giving Jack a couple minutes to hide. The clearance beneath an Italian exotic was less than four inches. Jack's head alone was at least eight—if hat sizes had anything to do with it. Crawling under one of the cars was hopeless; however, where the front wheels of the GTB Ferrari were resting the trailer floor was elevated about a foot. It might just work.

Wiggling like a wounded lizard Jack worked his way toward the side and then the front of the trailer. When he was in front of the right rear tire of the GTB he felt the space between car and trailer floor increasing. He wiggled faster, and at the same time, heard the panting and shuffling of feet as someone worked their way toward the front of the enclosed trailer. The light suddenly became brighter as the man shined his flashlight toward the front.

*I'm a dead man*, thought Jack, as the bright light lit up his left boot. Just as quickly as it came, however, it flashed away in another direction. Jack pulled his legs quietly inward beneath the car and tried to breathe evenly and silently.

"Get in here, quick. We got trouble," the voice of the person standing less than six inches from Jack's face called out.

"What's the problem?" The voice from the trailer entrance was harsh.

"I think I can see some packages in the back of this here Cam'ro, but I can't find no door handle."

Jack took a deep breath and let it out slowly.

"It ain't no Cam'ro, you retard. Look for a button or a tiny latch on the side of the door. Can ya see it?"

"I sure hate to mess up this car."

"Break the damn window and get them packages out here b'fore I come back there and use that tire iron on your face."

The explosive crash came suddenly, startling Jack. He was sure he had jerked his legs out from under the car and heard his own flashlight rolling on the floor of the van afterward. The thief didn't notice.

"It's some kind of safety glass, Elmer. It crumbles in little pieces and won't break apart."

Jack heard loud grunting and mumbling and could feel motion as Elmer pulled himself up into the trailer and struggled toward the front.

"Gimme that thing, you idiot."

The car above Jack rocked as the bigger man pried away at the rear window of the Ferrari. Cubes of glass tinkled down around Jack until the sheet of plastic laminate between the layers of glass gave way and the window was apparently rolled out of the way.

"Holy crap! Is that what I think it is?" the smaller idiot asked.

"Don't you mind what's in them packages. You just pack 'em out to my pickup and keep your eyes where they should be. Since we had so much trouble, I'm gonna give you two hundred bucks 'stead of a hundred. You better remember to keep your trap shut though, or I'll come around and shut it for you."

The men took two loads each but dropped one of the packages. This was followed by a string of cursing.

"You damn fool, you busted the wrapper. You make sure you pick up every last one of them bills."

Jack's legs and arms were cramping and his head had started to bleed again. He caught a glimpse of his flashlight just as the trailer doors were slammed shut. He lay there listening, expecting the truck to start but heard only the slamming of a car or small truck door. He waited what seemed like hours before he started wiggling out from under the Ferrari. The glass pieces on the trailer floor cut and stung his hands and belly as he freed himself from his hiding place. "Now what?" he said out loud.

He forced himself to his feet, leaning on the cars as he moved. He scooped up his light and shuffled toward the back of the trailer. With his flashlight he was able to see okay, but his fear was that the van doors would be locked from the outside. He stopped several times to listen for any kind of sound outside. He thought he heard the car leave but wasn't sure. Then he heard a crow making a fuss, so he doubted there was anyone outside. Once at the back doors, he gave them a shove and was rewarded with movement. Slowly opening one door he peeked out. He could see no one. Opening the door more he found that the truck and trailer were parked on a narrow farm trail lined with old-stand pine trees. He had no clue where he was and wasn't even sure of directions since the sun was at its zenith.

He slowly crawled down to the ground. He was dizzy and thirsty and his head was still oozing. He shouldn't have taken so much Advil the last eight days. He started heading for the cab of the truck then turned back and closed the trailer doors. Bryson was going to be furious. Tree branches along the narrow trail had scratched the sides of Big Blue, leaving nasty, deep lines in the custom paint. Jack crawled up to open the cab door but found it locked. Inside, he could see that someone had ransacked the cab. His cell phone was lying on the floor with its battery alongside it. He worked his way around to the passenger's side of the truck and tried the door. It, too, was locked.

Jack was at a loss. Feeling a wave of nausea, he leaned into the bushes and threw up then sat down beside the truck. He tore off the bottom of his shirttail and made a headband to stop the constant ooze of blood.

When they had stopped in Nevada for the first time to buy a new padlock for the trailer doors, he had seen Bryson buy a magnetic key box. Jack had grabbed a Mountain Dew and taken the lock outside to put it on the trailer door while Bryson finished the purchase, but what had he done with the key box?

Crawling on hands and knees through the weeds, Jack searched the undercarriage of the truck for the small metal case with the hope that it would contain an extra door and ignition key. Sure enough, attached to an "I" beam of the truck's frame was the small gray metal box with a sliding lid, carefully secured in place with duct tape. Using a broken stick, Jack tore away the tape and opened the box. Into the grass and dirt fell two shiny brass keys.

A new rush of adrenaline gave him the energy to crawl out from under the truck and head for the cab. The key slid smoothly into the ignition chase and turned, lighting up the dashboard. Big Blue's engine turned over quickly, belching black smoke from the dual stacks. It settled into a smooth rumble, and to Jack's relief, the air-conditioning flooded the hot, humid cab with cold air.

He retrieved his cell phone from the floor and replaced the battery. He held down the tiny red button and held his breath at the same time. With agonizing delay, the phone came to life. He was torn between calling Bryson and concentrating on driving and getting out of the forest or farm or wherever he was. He glanced at the time and realized that it had been over an hour since he had last seen Bryson. He had no clue where he was but then thought of the GPS.

He was nervous that the hillbilly guys would return but had to take the time to locate his position. The GPS hadn't failed him before and came through in just a matter of seconds showing Jack his location. He typed in the coordinates and was relieved to see that he was less than five miles from the truck stop. He punched Bryson's cell number into his phone and again held his breath.

✳✳✳

Bryson was trying to overcome his panic. Drinking a second caffeine-loaded RC Cola hadn't helped his nerves or his blood pressure. The sheriff returned after twenty minutes only to report that his lead was a dead end. He had offered Bryson a ride into town, but Bryson had insisted on staying at the truck stop just in case Jack returned. Now, thirty minutes later, he was having second thoughts. He began thinking that he should go to town and rent a car and start looking for the truck himself. The sheriff promised to put out a bulletin on the truck, but Bryson couldn't remember the license plate number, so the sheriff had backpedaled, saying that with only the physical description to go by there was no way they would find it.

Bryson was sitting in a broken chair when his cell phone started vibrating.

"Jack, is that you?"

"Bryson, man, am I ever glad to hear your voice," Jack said, his relief lost in the crackle of phone interference.

"Where the heck are you?" Bryson asked, trying to hide his frustration.

"I'm heading toward you and should be at the truck stop in eight or ten minutes."

"Where have you been? I've called the police and called your cell a hundred times. Why the heck did you leave? There is a police APB looking for you and the truck," he said, fudging a little white lie.

"I can't believe you're mad at me. How could you fathom that I had been stupid enough to drive off and not even call to let you know what was going on? I'll explain everything when I get there. Just find some wet paper towels and be ready to leave when I get there," Jack said, starting to warn Bryson but was cut off by Bryson first.

"The sheriff is calling. I better take his call. Just get here as fast as you can."

✳✳✳

Jack stared at his now dead cell phone. He was injured, dizzy and now felt accused. He drove onto the highway and headed toward the truck stop. He was driving fast and getting more upset every minute. He was the one who was hijacked and injured. Bryson had probably sat in the shade and eaten the cinnamon rolls while he was waiting.

Less than a mile from the Flying T, Jack thought he heard a siren. Looking in the rearview mirrors, he saw a decked out Dodge pickup with flashing lights coming up fast on his tail. He hit the brakes but then realized there was no place to pull off the narrow highway. He slowed down to forty miles per hour and continued toward the entrance of the truck stop, now visible ahead.

The sheriff's truck turned on a second set of sirens and the driver inside was waving frantically for Jack to pull over and stop but Jack had made up his mind to go on. He turned into the truck stop parking area, scanning the large lot for his best route to the office. He was sure the sheriff was right behind him but was startled when a second police car, a Ford sedan, it too with lights ablaze, screeched to a halt straight in front of Jack's intended path. Jack stood on the breaks to little avail. The momentum of the truck and trailer were not something to stop on a dime. With the tires smoking and the weight of the trailer still pushing forward, Jack guessed the cop car would soon be crushed. With less than a yard to spare, all eighteen tires grabbed pavement and the truck came to a bouncing stop.

Before the blue tire smoke had cleared, four fat angry-looking policemen with hats askew and guns drawn were surrounding the cab of the truck. Each of them was waving a huge pistol and screaming for Jack to put his hands up and get out of the truck. Jack could see Bryson running with a hobble toward the melee.

Moving very slowly, Jack shut off the engine and raised his right hand in the air.

✻✻✻

Bryson was screaming at the police to put down their guns, but they were not listening to a stranger's hysterical warning. Their adrenaline levels were the highest they had been for months. They were angry, at whom no one really could say, but they were ready for action. All they needed was the slightest excuse to open fire on the Yankee sitting in the cab with half a shirt wrapped around his head like some Arab.

Bryson screamed so loud into one of the deputy's ears, insisting that he put down the gun and that the truck driver was his friend, that the officer turned toward Bryson and pointed his gun two inches from his nose. This episode was going from bad to worse.

The scene in the parking lot suddenly seemed frozen in time. Jack was motionless, sitting half in and half out of the cab. Bryson, now looking down a gun barrel for the third time in so many months, refused to raise his hands but stared silently at the adolescent-appearing deputy holding the loaded revolver. The other three deputies were likewise motionless, all pointing their guns. The only noise was the sound of newly arriving trucks pulling in for fuel. Even the crows feasting at a nearby garbage dumpster were silent.

Then it fell. The portion of Jack's shirt, which he had torn off and wrapped around his head to stem the bleeding, slipped away from the clotted mass of hair and dirt and fell from his head. A feeble twisting breeze caught the bloodied rag and lifted it into the open air. The breeze carried it straight toward the deputy holding the gun on Bryson. As though it had eyes, the bloody rag settled downward, ultimately coming to rest on the barrel of the deputy's outstretched revolver.

All twelve eyes were drawn to the surreal sight of the gun with a bloody white flag of truce draped over its barrel. Ten of the eyes then focused on Jack's bloody head where the dried clot had created streaks of crimson extending down both sides of his face like sideburns. A fresh trickle of blood hung over his right eyebrow ready to drip onto the ground below. Then he fell forward, and his entire body crumpled to the ground.

The deputies looked at one another and holstered their pistols. One gained enough composure to press the button on his collar-mounted communicator and asked the dis-patcher to send an ambulance. Then the roles reversed.

Bryson started giving the orders. Within minutes they had Jack lying on a blanket in the shade of the auto-trailer. He was awake and somewhat lucid. Cool, moist towels mopped the blood and sweat from his brow, and using the scissors of a Swiss Army knife, Bryson trimmed the matted hair away from the laceration on Jack's skull, exposing a three-inch long, but shallow separation of skin. A first aid kit supplied courtesy of the sheriff's department had anti-septic and gauze four-by-fours. Bryson cleaned and dressed the wound. He was giving Jack sips of cold water when the ambulance and the sheriff pulled into the parking lot. Jack had been filling Bryson in on the events of the last couple of hours.

As the paramedics broke through the growing crowd of onlookers, Bryson was helping Jack to his feet.

"Hold it right there, good buddy," came the voice of the sheriff. He had conferred with one of his deputies and was now taking charge of the scene.

"You boys put cuffs on that man," the sheriff ordered two of the youngster deputies.

"Sheriff, you damn idiot. These are the victims, not the criminals." The husky voice came from a woman, the cashier at the office. "Where have you been the last two hours, anyway? This poor man is hurt and the other one who you already met is a doctor. He owns the truck."

Bryson, totally perturbed and exhausted by the whole af-fair, ignored all of them and led Jack around to the passen-ger's side of the truck. As the audience stared at him, he opened the door and boosted Jack up into the passenger's seat. He then shut the door and walked around to the driv-er's side of Big Blue, again ignoring the confused crowd, which had grown to a mob of about twenty.

"I'm taking my friend to the hospital in another county. All I have seen here is incompetence and stupidity. If you try to stop me, I will sue each of your deputies for assault, battery and reckless endangerment. By the way, you might want to wipe the scrambled egg off the front of your shirt, Sheriff. It makes you look even more like an idiot."

He took a couple of steps toward the cashier whose name he never learned and bent down and gave her a peck on the cheek. He then climbed into the shiny blue cab, closed the door and started the engine.

There was still the patrol car, its lights flashing and doors wide open, parked immediately in front of the Peterbilt. Bryson put the truck in gear and nudged it toward the squad car in a couple of jerky motions. A deputy looked at his boss, who shrugged, so he ran to the patrol car and backed it out of Bryson's way.

Bryson hit the air horn long and loud and popped the clutch on the truck, scattering the remaining onlookers and deputies. He headed for the Interstate entrance and didn't look back.

Bryson was dying to find out the details of what had happened to Jack but saw that Jack had closed his eyes and leaned the power seat back as far as it would go. He was breathing deeply and was quickly asleep. In all the confusion, Bryson didn't even know if the rear trailer door was closed, let alone locked.

✳✳✳

Forty-five minutes later, Jack was in a wheelchair being pushed by a gorgeous blonde candy striper toward the emergency room of a modern little hospital just inside the Florida border. Jack's nap and a Coke had brought him back to full alertness. He had insisted on changing his filthy shirt and even trying to comb his hair before he would agree to enter the hospital. He admitted that his head was still throbbing; otherwise he wouldn't have agreed to be seen.

The cute girl had left the men behind a blue curtain with a clipboard full of forms to fill out. While Bryson did a cursory "doctor's version" of filling in the ridiculous number of inane questions, Jack explained what had happened from the time he crawled into the back of the auto trailer until he was back in the driver's seat and pulling into the country truck stop.

Bryson had placed a new padlock on the trailer door when they arrived at the hospital but hadn't taken the time to look into the trailer.

"So they shattered the Ferrari window and took the money?" Bryson wanted to be clear. "It looked like a lot of packages. How did they haul it all out?"

Jack looked up at Bryson from his low-sitting vantage point. "I don't know and I don't care. The money isn't ours, and you and I are alive and maybe even safe. I just want something for my headache and a hot shower. Maybe you could find us a Dairy Queen when we're done here. I would love a chocolate shake."

They agreed that the wound on Jack's head needed stitches. Bryson snuck into the OR doctor's dressing room and took a quick shower. He found clean scrub clothes for himself and Jack and made a mental promise to mail them back to Magnolia Memorial Hospital when they got to Miami. He grabbed a plastic bag for his dirty clothes and headed to the truck. He figured he had half an hour to kill while Jack got stitched up and decided to inspect the van.

First he dumped his bag of laundry in the truck and retrieved his pistol and a flashlight from the glove box. He looked around the hospital parking lot to make sure he was alone then unlocked the back of the auto trailer and swung the doors wide open. The inside of the van was a mess. The hijackers had tracked mud, leaves, pine needles and broken branches in on the floor. Shards of broken glass had worked their way from the front near the 275 GTB with its shattered rear window, all the way to the back doors. As Bryson slowly inched his way forward he saw a pool of dried blood, probably Jack's, on the floor between two front cars. There were bloody handprints on the three floor-level cars. They had to be smudges Jack left as he had struggled to his feet and worked his way back to the open doors. Bryson felt a sad empathy for his friend and a wave of guilt at the anger he had earlier felt when he supposed he was abandoned back at the truck stop with no idea where Jack had gone with Big Blue.

Scattered around between the Ferrari and the Lamborghini were several brand-new hundred dollar bills. When Bryson shined his flashlight through the shattered rear window of the Ferrari, he saw several intact paper bundles wedged under the old Indian blanket. The hijackers must have taken what they could grab in a hurry and left the rest behind. The sight made Bryson break out in his third or forth massive sweat since morning. If the police or FBI showed up now, he and Jack would have hell to pay before they could explain how they came to be in possession of the cars and the money and why they had fled the scene at the truck stop.

He debated what he should do about the bundles of money. Small gusts of hot June wind were scattering more loose hundred dollar bills around the trailer. Once he started picking them up from around and under the three floor-level cars, he had a fistful of the crisp bills. He stuffed them into the one back scrub pant pocket and went back to the GTB where he carefully reached in through the shattered window and lifted out the five tightly wrapped bundles.

Of course Murphy's Law would raise its ugly head. As he withdrew his arm with the last package, he scraped his right arm on the serrated edge of glass, neatly slicing three long furrows for eight inches along the inside of his forearm. There was no particular pain at first, and sweat was dripping down his arms anyway, so it wasn't until he was standing in the open trailer doorway that he noticed the blood covering his arm, hand and the five packages as well as the side of the green scrubs.

He paused, then glanced up to make sure he was still alone. There, not fifteen feet from Bryson, was an elderly couple getting out of their dusty white Buick. The man was struggling, trying to remove a gift box from the backseat. The tall, silver-haired woman was standing still and staring straight at Bryson. Wrinkling her brow, she squinted at Bryson's arm and the now bloody bundles. She flipped down the clip on sunglasses attached to her bifocals to get a better look. Bryson quickly stepped back into the shaded part of the trailer and waited for her to leave.

"I suppose you should get that arm looked at by the doctor." The woman's high-pitched voice came from right in front of him. He stepped out of the shadow to see her now standing three feet from the van door.

"Are the doctors here any good?" Bryson asked, without thinking.

"My son-in-law is the doctor on call today and I can assure you that there isn't one any better in the entire county. It is his birthday today and we are going to eat lunch with him in the cafeteria. You should take the time to have a good meal while you are here and eat a generous serving of vegetables. I know that they take credit cards at the hospital cafeteria. I doubt that Mabel will be able to make change for a hundred dollar bill." She tilted her head toward his foot.

Bryson, already in a state of near shock, looked down to see one of the crisp hundred dollar bills stuck to the front of his shoe. His arm continued to slowly drip from the fresh lacerations.

"Come dear, this man must have things to do." The woman's husband had caught up to her and was struggling under the weight of the package he carried.

"Don't you dare procrastinate the treatment of that cut," the woman chided as she turned to leave. "I'll tell them inside that you will be right in. We would appreciate it if you came now so Duffy can treat your cut and then we will have our birthday luncheon."

Bryson reached down and tugged the stray hundred dollar bill from his shoe . . . the sticky blood was a really good adhesive. He climbed down from the truck and took the bundles to the cab, where he found a small cardboard box and stashed them with the loose bills. He then stuck the box in a cubby under his pile of dirty clothes.

Bryson noticed a garden hose at the edge of the hospital building and rather than going inside as instructed by his new medical consultant, he washed the blood off of his arm and shoes and let the hose run on his face for a minute to help cool him off. He held a clean handkerchief on the lacerations and was just finishing up when the doors opened and the same candy striper pushed Jack out the door.

Jack's head was wrapped in a full bandage. They must have used ten yards of gauze to create the soft white lid on his crown.

"Holy schmolly," the girl said when she saw Bryson. "You better come inside and get a dressing on that cut on your arm."

"I'll be just fine. Would you mind pushing my friend over to the side of that big blue truck?"

Jack didn't say a word but just stared at Bryson, who had his hair slicked back with water from the garden hose. The scrubs he was wearing were soaked. Jack smiled.

She helped Jack up into the truck and gave him some valuable last-minute instructions. "Don't run the garden hose on your head bandage like your friend. And make sure you take Tylenol every six hours for your headache."

Bryson shut the passenger door and was going around to the driver's side when the girl grabbed him by the sleeve of the damp scrub top and whispered, "There was a call from the police a few minutes ago asking if any truck drivers had been in to get treated for a cut on the head. I told them that we haven't seen a single solitary person today. Did I do good?" She smiled, giving him a questioning look.

"That was very nice of you," Bryson answered. "We are fine now thanks to you and the good doctor, but we need to get going. The police just want to ask us some questions and that would put us way behind schedule. Thanks for being so thoughtful."

"You take good care of your friend and don't worry. I won't tell anybody that you were here and I won't tell them that you borrowed the hospital's scrub clothes either." Then with a big smile she leaned over the empty wheelchair and gave Bryson a peck on his cheek. Before he could react, she had wheeled the chair to the curb and was across the parking lot and nearly up to the automatic ER doors.

"Thanks," he shouted, but she didn't turn or wave or anything.

***

Back onto the Interstate where they would follow the asphalt ribbon to Miami, Jack turned to Bryson and asked, "What did you say to that young woman to earn a kiss?" He was holding the side of his head and laughing.

"She's the one who deserved a kiss." Bryson told Jack about the girl covering up their being there at the hospital to avoid the police. He went on to tell him about the scattered hundred dollar bills, the five bundles and the nosey old lady who insisted that they eat vegetables in the hospital cafeteria.

Jack had received fifteen stitches in his head laceration. The large amount of Xylocaine used to numb it had slowed his thinking. Before Bryson could finish the part about the hundred-dollar bill stuck to his shoe, Jack had leaned his seat back as far as it would go and was snoring. Bryson nudged him and suggested he go to the bed in the sleeper cabin.

Before they had left the hospital parking lot, Bryson had retrieved the pistol from behind the Lamborghini's wheel and secured the back doors of the trailer with one of the new padlocks.

Where had the day gone? It was already one in the afternoon. They had planned on making it to Miami by sundown. Now with Jack probably unable to trade off driving, Bryson was faced with driving alone into the night. He was starving and thirsty and couldn't reach the snack fridge from his driver's seat without stopping the truck. He blindly reached back with his right hand and rummaged around on the floor, hoping to find a bag of chips or a loose apple. The best he could come up with was a half full bottle of Jack's lukewarm Coke. He secured it between his thighs and twisted off the lid, hoping for at least a little poof of carbon, but the drink was as flat as Lake Bonneville. He had a swallow anyway, and after the first disgusting aftertaste, he chugged the whole thing, thinking that it was at least fluids and a tad of caffeine. He looked at the GPS and advanced the cursor toward Orlando, then pressed the set button. His course lit up and it was relatively straight Interstate highway all the way there. He could do this.

✳✳✳

Marisa had waited all afternoon for a call from Bryson and had even held her cell phone in her lap so she wouldn't miss the call while she returned the rental car to the airport. She had tried his number over and over but only reached his voicemail. She left messages and even text messaged him, which she was sure he wouldn't figure out how to retrieve. Frustrated, she decided to make the plans for the four of them herself.

She called Jenny, who had just arrived at the luxurious hotel in Miami. Jenny hadn't been able to reach Jack either. The wives decided to go ahead with plan A. Marisa would meet the men in Orlando and ride with them to Miami where they would all reunite. Jenny had gone on to Miami, politely refusing to ride in the truck.

Marisa was hurrying toward Gate 23 at the Raleigh/Durham airport when a tall blond man tugged on her sleeve and said, "Excuse me, but you must have dropped this." He then handed her a rumpled envelope. She accepted it and shoved it into her purse with the other clutter.

She had misread the boarding time for her flight and arrived at the gate to find a state of last-minute confusion. They nearly closed the door on her. She was one of the last people on the plane and was rushed to her seat by a curt flight attendant.

Only when she settled into her seat and was searching for a Kleenex, did she remember the note. She looked at the tan-colored envelope, knowing she hadn't dropped it herself and almost stuck it in the back pocket of the seat in front of her. Then she saw the name written in tiny scrawl.

Bender Trucking.

She hastily opened the envelope and found a neatly folded piece of paper addressed to her. Startled, she read the note:

> If your man does not get my cars to Miami on time you both will pay the price. I am watching your girl and will not be nice to her if I don't get my cars to Miami on time.

Marisa felt like she was going crazy—like a snake or spider was crawling on her and she had to get away from it. Had the plane not been already moving, she would have bolted for the door. She was trapped in an airplane, miles away from her husband and daughter. She had no idea what was going on with Bryson and Jack, and now, she and Madeline had been threatened by total strangers for reasons that seemed completely absurd.

Someone knew who she was and what she looked like.

They also knew a lot about her daughter. She felt desperate and useless. She had to do something besides sit and look out the window and watch the ground fall away.

Everyone around her was doing his or her own thing: reading, sleeping, snacking or just staring into space. There were no flight attendants in sight, so she retrieved her cell phone from her purse and turned it on. She ducked toward the window and tried Bryson's number again. This time it rang. Four times it rang and then she heard his voice.

"Bryson, are you there?"

"Marisa? Where are you?"

"Excuse me, madam, but you can't use the cell phone on the airplane."

Marisa turned and looked up to see the serious-looking flight attendant scowling at her.

"It's an emergency!" Marisa told the woman. "I've got to talk to my husband." She turned back toward the window. "Bryson, are you there?"

"It is against the law to talk on that phone when we are flying. Are you stupid?" the uniformed attendant said.

Ignoring her, Marisa tried to complete a sentence, but the nasty attendant reached over Marisa's shoulder and snatched the cell phone out of her hand, twisting Marisa's wrist and cutting her own hand on Marisa's diamond ring.

"Look what you did!" she screamed at Marisa, holding her bleeding hand out for everyone to see. "I'm going to have you arrested when the plane lands. You have risked the lives of everyone on board so you could make your obsessive little phone call." She waved her bleeding hand again and then huffed her way to the front of the plane.

Marisa buried her face in her hands and sobbed. Not one to often cry, she surprised herself that she felt so sad and hopeless. Marisa felt a hand on her shoulder and looked up.

The man in the aisle seat leaned across the seat and patted Marisa's arm again.

"I don't mean to intrude, but you look like you could use some help."

Marisa wiped her nose with a tissue and slowly shook her head.

"Listen, that woman was way out of line. Talking on a cell phone isn't going to make the plane crash. I know about these things. I'm a federal law enforcement officer." When Marisa looked sideways at him, he continued, "I can show you my credentials if you'd like." He started to reach into his left rear pocket. She shook her head, indicating that digging for his wallet wasn't necessary.

"Tell me what the problem is and perhaps I can be of help."

Marisa again dabbed at her nose and then turned slightly to face the stranger. She reached down to the floor and pulled a small bottle of Fiji water out of her purse, and with her eyes studying the man, took a long swallow.

"My husband and his cousin are driving a truck across the country hauling some kind of exotic cars." She paused again to wipe her nose. "I'm supposed to meet him in Miami tonight. Yesterday a man called me at my hotel . . . I was in North Carolina . . . My daughter is starting school at Duke . . . Anyway, the man is threatening to hurt me and my daughter if my husband doesn't get the cars there on time. Just now someone gave me a note saying they were going to hurt my daughter if the cars get there late."

"So where is your husband now?"

"That's just it. I don't know. I haven't been able to talk to him for nearly two days."

With this load off her shoulders she broke down crying again, unable to talk for nearly a minute. She took a deep breath and continued. "He was behind schedule and was going to drive all night, but he has been ill. He should not be driving so much. I just now got him to answer his phone when the lady took my cell phone away. I'm so worried about my husband and my daughter that I can't even think."

"Well, at least you know now that he is all right," the man said.

"Or maybe he's lying in a hospital bed," Marisa whined, thinking the worst and starting to sob again.

The man placed his hand on her arm. "I'll bet he is just fine and that he is almost there. As soon as we land in Orlando, you can use my phone to call him and find out exactly what is going on. When we deplane, I'll talk to the pilot and explain the situation and get you your phone back. Trust me, they are not going to do anything to you. The flight attendant was totally out of line."

Marisa looked at the man's face. She wanted to give him a hug or maybe she just needed to be hugged. In either case she restrained herself and settled back in the seat of the plane.

\*\*\*

"Where are we?" Jack asked from behind the blue and white fabric curtain separating the sleeper cabin from the front seat of Big Blue. Though the voice was obviously Jack's, the energy and enthusiasm Bryson was so used to hearing was missing.

"We're just getting into the Gainesville area. I've got to make a pit stop. We're out of fuel."

Jack dressed in the clean scrub clothes Bryson had borrowed from Magnolia Memorial. Bryson was still in his borrowed scrubs as well. Though the blood had dried on the sleeve and on his arm, he could still feel the glass cuts sting every time he moved.

"How is your head feeling?"

Jack adjusted the sun visor mirror then laughed. "I've had better days. Have you heard from either of the wives? They are never going to believe our story. I'm not sure I'll believe it myself when it's over."

"Matter of fact, Marisa called about two hours ago but just said my name a couple of times and then hung up. I tried her several times since but can't get anything but her voicemail. I called Madeline but the same thing happened. Maybe they went to a movie. I left messages. You want to try Jenny?"

Bryson had pulled into a massive truck stop and edged the truck up alongside a long row of fuel pumps. He handed his phone to Jack as he opened the door. Jack, who was up and moving, decided that he better make a beeline for the restroom while Bryson started the fuel.

Fifteen minutes later with full fuel tanks and stretched muscles and joints, they were all set to head out on what they hoped would be their last leg of the delivery.

"Did you get a hold of Jenny?" Bryson asked, noticing his cell phone lying on the console. He was back behind the wheel again, not feeling comfortable having Jack drive. The idea of Jack driving a big rig on the busy Florida Interstate with his head wrapped in ten yards of gauze was too much to even consider.

"Oh crap, I forgot to make the call. I'll do it right now." Jack picked up the phone, squinting at the screen. "Say, it looks like you have a message on the phone. It's an area code I don't recognize. Want me to check it?"

"Sure. I've got my hands full right now," Bryson said. A feeder highway had just joined the freeway they were on and the traffic had nearly doubled. "On second thought, I could use some help with navigation for a few minutes."

Another half an hour passed before Jack picked up Bryson's phone and touched the voicemail connect button. He listened carefully to the message and then pressed the replay button and pressed the phone against Bryson's ear.

Marisa sounded winded, like she had been running, then he decided that she was whispering but that there was a loud background noise. When he finally concentrated on the message, a wave of panic swept over his entire body. What the two of them finally agreed they had heard: Marisa was in Orlando; she didn't have her own cell phone at the moment, but hoped she would get it back from the airline; someone had threatened to hurt her and Madeline unless Bryson gets the truckload of cars to Miami by midnight. Then the message abruptly ended.

Bryson stared at the phone and then looked at Jack. "Did you get that?" he asked.

"I heard it, but I don't get it. What is she doing in Orlando?"

"Try that number she called from," Bryson said, then waited while Jack fumbled with his reading glasses and then tapped in the phone number that the caller ID had listed. Finally, after the sixth ring, a man's voice answered.

No, Marisa wasn't at the number, but the man answering said that he had loaned his phone to an attractive woman who had temporarily had her phone taken away by the airlines. He thought that the phone was returned to her. The last time he saw her she had been requested to fill out some paperwork at the airport security office. He thought she was fine, but he knew that she had been very upset and extremely eager to speak with her husband.

As Jack related the call, Bryson looked ahead on the highway for a place to safely pull off, and after about a mile gave up, turned on the emergency flashers and slowed to a crawl, incurring the wrath of numerous following trucks and cars. Pulling up onto the shoulder of the road, he locked up the brakes and slid to a halt, spilling what was left of his soda. Jack handed him his cell phone.

Bryson's shaky fingers required three tries to successfully dial Marisa's number.

After waiting a number of seconds, he heard the phone ring and Marisa's cheerful voice, reciting the familiar greeting that she wasn't available but that if one would leave a number she would call back.

He nearly smashed his phone onto the steering wheel, but took a couple of deep breaths instead and redialed with the same result. This time however, he did leave a message, telling her to call him immediately and advising her to stay at the Orlando airport terminal. He was changing his route and would pick her up there. Jack looked at Bryson dumbfounded. His computer-like mind quickly did the math.

"If we divert over to the Orlando airport it's going to add at least two hours to the trip," Jack said.

"I can't just leave her there. We can still get to Miami that way, and we'll miss the rush hour traffic, so that should make up some time," Bryson said.

A shrill, short blast of a siren interrupted the moment. Both men looked out their respective rearview mirrors to see a highway patrol cruiser behind them with its lights flashing. Bryson's first reflex was to pull the truck back into traffic and leave the cops behind but Jack put his hand on the gearshift knob and shook his head at Bryson. Bryson leaned back in the driver's seat and took deep breaths waiting for the patrolman to approach.

"I hope you put the gun back in its hiding place," Jack said.

Bryson watched a short but muscular patrolman get out of his car. He was holding a clipboard and disappeared behind the truck, apparently checking the plates. He then approached the passenger's side of the truck. He waved at Jack and motioned him to roll down the window.

"Are you gentleman having some kind of trouble?"

Pulling a tall tale out of the recesses of his imagination, Bryson answered.

"A big gator started onto the highway and the car in front of us panicked and slammed on his brakes. My friend here hit his head on the dash and accidentally spilled his drink on the console. I thought we better stop and check to make sure everything was okay." Bryson held up a wet rag dripping with brown liquid.

"What happened to your head?" the patrolman asked Jack.

"Brain surgery," Bryson answered for Jack. "Hitting his head on the dashboard doesn't help in the recovery."

The patrolman looked around inside, holding on the assist rail and tugging his aviator-style sunglasses from his face. "Why are you men wearing hospital scrubs?" He then looked at Jack and his bandaged head. "Where is your co-driver? This guy can't possibly drive in his condition."

"My buddy here can drive just fine. He is almost healed up. It's just that he has to wear the bandages to keep the flies from buzzing around the incision."

There was a momentary silence, then the patrolman's radio speaker squawked a loud, incomprehensible message. The officer stepped back down to the ground to answer the radio call.

After several tense minutes and several squawks from the collar speaker, the patrolman pulled himself back up on the truck and again filled the open window with his hat-clad head.

"Today is your lucky day, boys. I just got a call about a real emergency and have to leave right now. I don't know what you really have going on here but will write this little encounter up as one of the better bullcrap stories I've heard all year, and believe me, I hear some whoppers. You gentlemen can go on your way but do try driving safely and be very careful pulling back onto the highway. You never know, there are bound to be other truckers who are even stranger than the two of you."

Bryson watched until the police car had pulled up a quarter mile then crossed the median and headed north. He was about to put the truck in gear when he was startled by the ring of his cell phone.

"Bryson? Are you there? It's Marisa!"

# Chapter Twenty-One

## RENDEZVOUS

The husband and wife sorted out the whys and wherefores and missed communications. Someone was threatening them and using their daughter as leverage. After hearing about the threats, Bryson knew that he had to go to Orlando to pick up his wife regardless of the time lost.

"Sweetheart, remember that great little steakhouse along the highway near the entrance to Disneyworld?" Bryson asked, trying very hard to sound calm and in control. "Do you remember the name of it? I think it was Trevor's."

"I remember it. It's next to the Hyatt."

"Marisa, listen carefully. Jack has the GPS on in front of me. We can be there in about two hours. If you meet us there we won't have to drive all the way to the airport. Take a cab to the restaurant and get a table. Have something to eat and you could even get something to go for the two of us. Call me when you get there. We can pick you up and not lose any time."

"Oh, Bryson! What about Madeline?" He could hear her break down over the phone and almost started crying himself.

"Call her and tell her to stay with her friends . . . not to let them out of her sight. These guys want the cars and what's inside, and then they will leave us alone. There's a lot more to the story that I'll tell you about later. Can you do what I just said? Go to the steakhouse and wait? Are you sure you are okay?"

"I'm okay. You drive safely and I'll have some food waiting for you. Tell Jack that Jenny is already in Miami at the Four Seasons waiting for us. No one had called to threaten her as of this morning but she had two hang-up calls that she thought were weird. I will call her now and tell her what's happening."

"Good idea."

"Where exactly are you supposed to deliver the cars?"

"We don't even know. The guy who loaded them in Reno said that he would call us but thus far we haven't heard anything. I guess he will call. He has a GPS transponder on the truck so he knows where we are. Get directions to the Four Seasons for us and as soon as we unload the cars, we can meet Jenny and get on with our lives."

"Bryson, what are you going to do with your stupid truck?" Marisa asked, as if she didn't want to break the connection with her husband.

"My truck is going to stay in the family. Don't worry about it right now. Just get to the restaurant and get food for us and we'll see you in less than two hours. I've got to hang up now. Love you."

Bryson placed the phone on the console and mashed down on the accelerator. His anxiety was quickly changing to anger. Why were these idiots threatening his family? Why didn't they just let him do his job and be done with them?

✳✳✳

Marisa looked at her phone and thought about Bryson's call. She was sitting in a corner of an expansive arrival area at the airport where the majority of travelers were young families with tired but excited children on their way for a week of fun at Disneyland, Epcot Center and Busch Gardens. Many of the families had grandparents with them. These could have been her and her grandkids. Why had she been so stupid as to go along with Bryson's lamebrain idea of buying a truck and driving it across the country? Were they both becoming senile?

232 Steven I. Dahl, M.D.

She was on the verge of calling Madeline when she saw the missed call notice on her phone. She looked at the number and nearly dialed it, when she realized that the area code was different from her home or North Carolina where Madeline was. She walked over to the information counter in the main airport terminal and asked a woman at the desk for a phone book. Looking up the area code, she was surprised to see that it was from Nevada. She hadn't had caller ID at the hotel so didn't know the origin of the last threatening call. This new information frightened her enough that she was going to call Bryson again but then she saw another notice on her phone. She looked it up quickly and found it to be a Miami area code. This distracted her enough that she focused again on meeting Bryson. Besides, her phone battery was dying and she had rush hour traffic to deal with. She put the phone in her purse and ran out the door to catch a cab.

✲✲✲

The late afternoon traffic was building up quickly. With all the confusion the two had not yet had the time to fully discuss the hijacking and the findings in the cars. When they came to a construction site and had to make a complete stop to wait for a flagman to give them the go-ahead, Bryson unfastened his seat belt and reached in the cubby under the sleeper bed. He pulled out one of the bundles and a fistful of crumpled hundred dollar bills and set them on Jack's lap.

"These and five bundles are what were left in the back of the Ferrari. I cut my arm reaching for it. The loose bills were flying around the inside of the trailer."

Jack picked up one of the bills and examined it closely. He held the bill up to the light and pulled on the edges, testing for strength. He poured some of the melted ice water from his Coke on the bill and tugged on it some more.

Rolling down the road again, Bryson watched Jack out of the corner of his eye and finally asked what he was doing.

"I haven't a clue," Jack said. "This bill looks pretty normal to me. I want to compare it with the real thing. Hand me your wallet."

"It's in the glove box. There should be several hundreds."

"I can't see any difference between the two." Jack tore away the edge of the paper wrapping on the package and took out one of the wrapped bills to compare it to the other two. "The bills in the bundle look brand new. That's the only thing that I can see that would distinguish them. If anything, I would guess yours is a counterfeit; it's all dirty and somebody wrote Happy Birthday on the edge."

Both men laughed, but deep inside they were wound up tight.

"How many bills are in the package, would you guess?"

"These things are wrapped tight. There has to be four or five hundred in this bundle. How many loose bills are stuffed back there?"

Bryson thought for a minute and then guessed. "At least twenty or thirty, but there are still a lot more loose bills in the car and scattered around inside the trailer."

"So, that's somewhere around five or six hundred thousand that they left behind. You saw the stack under the blanket. How many packs would you guess there were to start with?"

"Maybe twenty or twenty-five, but I just don't know for sure," Bryson concluded.

"It just doesn't make sense. Why would someone pile several million bucks in the back of a two-million-dollar car and then turn it over to a novice truck driver?"

"And why the bogus attempts to steal it or steal the cars along the way? If you were going to steal that much I would think about hiring professionals, not a bunch of idiots. And then to call attention to the truck's contents by threatening us about not being on time. None of it makes sense."

234 Steven I. Dahl, M.D.

Jack leaned back in the tall, well-padded passenger's seat and sighed. He put both hands on his head bandage and tried to shift it around to make it more comfortable. The pain meds were wearing off, and though he was feeling a little better, every jolt and abrupt motion brought on discomfort. "All I know for sure is that a long, hot soak in the Jacuzzi tub and a twelve-hour nap between soft, cool sheets at the Four Seasons is going to feel fantastic. Maybe I'll order a rib eye . . . medium rare and a double hot fudge sundae."

Bryson looked at him. "Don't forget that we still have to get there, deliver the cars, and then explain the broken window and missing money. Also we need to figure out what to do with the stuff sitting on your lap. By the way, put my real hundred-dollar bill back in the wallet. I may need it."

The traffic lightened up and they were seeing billboards advertising the bargain-priced dumpy hotels and greasy spoon diners lining the highway on the fringe of Orlando. Jack swallowed a handful of Advil and was studying the GPS when the cell phone rang.

Bryson was busy changing lanes to make the correct turn-off, so Jack took the call.

He guessed it would be Marisa but he was wrong.

"Is this Dr. Bender?" a male voice asked.

"This is his partner. He's busy driving." Jack turned off the radio and put the phone on speaker. "Who's calling?"

"You must be Jack. I'm Fritz's partner. You know, the man who loaded the cars in your truck in Reno, the tall blond guy. It looks like you have made good progress today," the man said.

"The plan for the cars has changed just a little," the caller went on. "We thought you would be coming straight from Tampa but I see you are in Orlando. Sorry, but you'll have to wait a few days to go to Fantasyland." The man laughed at his own joke. "Since you'll be on the East Coast anyway, I want you to deliver the cars to Boca Raton, so head that way immediately. When you get closer, I'll give you exact directions. Just head for Boca. At your speed, you should get there before ten tonight. Don't try to call me back and do not let anyone else in the back of the transporter van."

Before Jack or Bryson could say a word, the connection was broken. Jack snapped the little clamshell closed and waited for Bryson to comment.

"Why couldn't we have just picked up a truckload of Pampers or Rice Krispies? I can't wait to get rid of this trailer and all the problems."

"So, what do you think about the route? This place we're picking up Marisa is not too far out of the way. Actually, it's less than a mile off of the freeway, but there is a more southern route if she meets us ten miles south of Disney World."

"Things are confusing enough for everyone as it is. I don't want to put more worry on her mind. Let's stick with our plan. I'll just have to drive faster. You try to get a hold of Jenny. See if she can get us rooms at one of the good hotels in Boca Raton or Palm Beach. She can take a cab up from Miami and meet us at whatever hotel she finds. Matter of fact, ask her to try the Breakers first. The place is supposed to be fantastic. At this point, I don't care how much the rooms cost."

Bryson was driving faster than he had the entire trip. He was cutting in and out of traffic and abruptly changing lanes to the frustration of the cars around him, making Jack very nervous.

"Do you think these guys are going to let us off the hook for the broken window in the Ferrari and what about the missing money? Who does it belong to?" Jack asked.

"Once we know what Fritz wants and where he wants to meet us, we will decide together how to handle it. I'm starting to think that Fritz and the blond guy have different agendas."

"Maybe we should just notify the police or the FBI and let them take care of it," Jack suggested.

"Go ahead and call Jenny and see how she is doing and have her get us hotel rooms. I'll give Marisa time to get to the restaurant before I let her know about any change in plans."

Jack picked up the phone to follow through with his instructions.

Bryson thought for a minute and then said, "I think we need to do exactly what they tell us to do. Marisa will have a fit if she thinks we are doing anything that might endanger Madeline. If somebody is watching Madeline, and we call in the police, who knows what might happen? Why don't you use your phone in case Marisa tries to call back?"

Jack closed Bryson's phone and crawled into the sleeper cab to find his phone. "Where in the heck are you guys?" Jenny started in, not even saying hello. "I have been having a nervous breakdown waiting to hear from you. No one is answering their phones. Have you heard from Marisa?"

Jack started to talk but she cut in again telling him about the fun she had been having in Atlanta and her flight to Miami. She went on, not letting him interrupt, about how she had already checked into the room at the Four Seasons in Miami and had talked the manager into a room with a view of the bay.

It was good to hear Jenny's voice and the feel of her enthusiasm. Jack was reluctant to start in on all the crappy news he had to share. He couldn't tell her about a single good Civil War memorial they had visited. Telling her about his own battle would not be believable. Jenny was not one to sweat the small stuff, but big problems would put her into a frenzy.

"Did I mention going shopping? If not, I'll show you all the cool stuff I found when you get here. When are you going to be here?"

He hated to break her heart but had to tell her about the change in plans. He explained the situation and told her to enjoy her bath before she changed hotels. When he was done there was silence on the other end of the phone. For a long moment he thought she had hung up on him.

"I have a better idea," she said. "I'll have the concierge here make reservations at the hotel in Boca Raton and when you get there and get the Benders checked in, you can give me a call. Maybe I'll take a hotel limo up to meet you, or maybe I'll just stay here and you can come join me."

They left the plans at that. Jack looked at the silent phone in his hand and was content with not insisting she do things his way.

\*\*\*

Bryson was trapped by the heavy traffic. He had heard faint fragments of one side of Jack's conversation with his wife and had concluded that Jenny was probably not going to meet them in Boca Raton. He really didn't know her that well, and from what Marisa had inferred, he was going to have to put on lots of charm for them to become best of friends. He would do his best. Until then, he really needed Jack to travel with him. With all their travails they had become like brothers. Whatever Jenny's part of the deal required was fine for right now.

The traffic coming into Orlando proper was horrible. Bryson got stuck in a lane behind an oversized load. They crawled along so slowly that he started worrying that Marisa would give up on them.

"Jack. Would you mind calling Marisa again and telling her we are twenty minutes away?"

When no answer came, Bryson unfastened his seat belt and twisted around, parting the curtain. He could see Jack's feet up on the bed. When the truck ahead came to a complete stop, Bryson jumped out of his seat and quickly crawled into the back. Jack wasn't just asleep. He appeared to be unconscious.

Behind the truck and trailer horns were suddenly blaring, protesting his stopping in the middle of already bad traffic. He jumped back into the driver's seat and caught up with the truck ahead and then started scanning the GPS. He found the services menu and scrolled to hospitals and tapped in the list. Some of the names were familiar to him from articles and associates he had met over the years. It looked like the closest one was not far away but was a few blocks behind him.

Priorities are just what the word defines them to be at the moment—the things that must be done prior to anything else. Never had he had such a conflict about which was more important. Finally, he concluded that taking on one problem at a time was best.

He laid on the air horn, clearing traffic around Big Blue and cut across six lanes of freeway traffic where he took a bus only exit. Within less than three minutes he was pulling up the Emergency Room driveway, honking the air horn to warn a couple of pedestrians.

By the time Bryson had stopped the truck and set the brakes, five emergency room staff were outside. "Move the truck!" they shouted. Bryson's calm demeanor and ability to explain in medical terms what was needed settled the group down to work.

The medical team assisted Bryson in figuring out the best way to extricate the unconscious patient from the back of the truck's cabin. Once on the ER gurney, Jack was found to have good vital signs and was responding to verbal stimuli. He just kept drifting back off to sleep the moment the talking stopped. A neurologist was called and a STAT CAT scan of Jack's head was ordered. The ER doctor was very courteous to Bryson and waited until things were ordered and an IV in place with steroids running before he reminded Bryson that the truck needed to be moved.

"I'm pretty sure he has a slow leaking subdural hematoma," stated the physician. "The neurology guy we have here is excellent. If you wouldn't mind moving your truck and then waiting in the lounge, I'll get back to you as soon as we know anything."

"Thanks for your help. I have a major conflict. I left my wife down the road waiting for me to pick her up. She is pretty helpless on her own. Would it be too thoughtless for me to leave for a while and have you phone me when you get the CT and consult results? It appears you have everything under control here."

The ER doc looked at Bryson like he had horns and a tail, but agreed to take Bryson's cell phone number and call within the hour.

Outside he had to confront the security guard about his truck, ultimately just getting in and driving away. Five minutes later he was back on the freeway headed for Disney World's entrance road to meet Marisa. His carnal mind had even started thinking about the juicy steak he knew she would have waiting for him. He was starved.

✳✳✳

Marisa was sitting in the back of the filthiest taxicab she had ever imagined. The airport had a long queue to wait for cabs and as the nicer ones rolled up the people in the line ahead got in with smiles and warm welcomes. Her driver didn't even get out to open the trunk but just popped the trunk lid and waited for her to struggle with her own suitcase. She was dripping with sweat by the time she crawled into the backseat with her large travel bag and purse. When she told the man where she needed to go he scowled at her and told her, in a strongly accented English, that the restaurant called Trevor's was closed.

Now as the cab pulled into the parking lot of the familiar looking place, she could see that the grizzly-faced driver had been correct. She dragged her bags over to the darkened entrance and fished in her purse for her cell phone.

\*\*\*

Bryson's phone vibrated in his pocket just as he was trying to negotiate the massive coalescence of what seemed to be every freeway in central Florida. Ever since leaving the hospital he had been torn with guilt for leaving Jack, and yet Marisa needed him as well, and he was starving. He had a splitting headache and his right shoulder hurt him worse than it had for days. Even the laceration on his arm was causing problems, oozing through the bandage the ER nurse had put on it, smearing blood on the driver-side door and armrest.

He had no choice but to ignore his phone, which was vibrating away in his shirt pocket, and fight his way over into the far right lane to make the freeway exit.

Before he could even think about the phone again, he was off the exit ramp and onto the wide, tree-lined boulevard leading to the world's most famous amusement park. Both sides of the road were lined with hotels, restaurants and gas stations. Instinct jumped in and without even seeing a sign for the restaurant he turned on his blinker and pulled into the darkened parking lot of Trevor's Steaks and Chops. His phone was vibrating again. He was so shocked to see the darkened building instead of a thriving steakhouse that he nearly ran over a pallet stacked with travertine floor tiles. He stopped the truck and picked up the phone, feeling panic about Marisa, or could the call already be from the ER doctor with news about Jack?

Bryson set the brakes, and without thinking, shut off the engine. Silence filled the cabin. After hours and days of constant road and engine noise it was a welcome moment of peace. He fumbled around in one of the pigeonhole compartments in the console and came out with his scratched glasses. He was trying to bring up his missed calls on the phone menu when there was a sudden pounding noise on the passenger door. Bryson jumped in the seat, startled by the interruption. He stared at the dark window and then, like an apparition, saw his wife's face appear in the window.

"Unlock the door!" she yelled, pounding on the window with her right hand and hanging on to the assist rail with the other. Her appearance was such a surprise to him that it took him a minute to recover and find the locking switch on the door panel. When the door lock stem popped up from its recessed position, Marisa twisted the handle and pulled the door open. Bryson was fumbling with his seat belt to get free and come around the truck to help her but was too slow. Before he could even open his door, she was inside the cab and crawling across the passenger's seat into his arms. Her embrace was a fantastic relief. She was safe and they were together again.

As they kissed and held each other, the days and last few hours of tension and fear and uncertainty drained momentarily away and were replaced with tears of joy. They cherished the moment alone together, and then the reality of their present situation rolled over them like a rogue wave.

"Where is Jack?" Marisa asked, her head clutched against Bryson's throbbing shoulder.

As he began the explanation of the day's events, Marisa slowly moved away from him to a more comfortable position. Marisa had always been a patient listener. The closed restaurant and the events leading her there would hold for another time. The truck and its features, all new to Marisa, were likewise ignored.

Marisa's phone battery was dead, so she plugged it into Bryson's charger and used his phone to call Madeline. Bryson threw her luggage into the sleeping cabin and then

242 **Steven I. Dahl, M.D.**

put the truck in gear and began the task of getting the seventy-five-foot-long truck and trailer out of the small parking lot.

Their daughter answered on the first ring.

"Hi, Maddie. How are you doing?" Marisa's tone of voice and rhythm of speech gave away no clue as to the predicament the young girl's parents found themselves in. After listening for a couple of minutes, it sounded as though Madeline was having a great first day of college. The two chatted and visited for the next few minutes while Bryson fought his way through the heavy evening traffic back toward the hospital.

What to do about Jack and Jenny and the trailer full of cars was still an irresolvable issue in his mind. The basic facts remained. He had to get the cars to Boca Raton within the next five hours or face the possible consequences that the car owner's threat was real: real to himself and his wife, real to their daughter, and probably real to Jack and Jenny.

***

Marisa took a long look at her husband as he struggled with the traffic in an unfamiliar city. For the first time since she had climbed into the truck, she noticed the bandage on his arm and the bags beneath his eyes. Worried, exhausted, he looked like he might slump over the giant steering wheel at any moment. She had been the witness to hundreds of episodes where Bryson had been up all night in the delivery room or operating room and came home exhausted. She didn't recall any of those situations when he had looked as worn down as he did right now.

Marisa was experiencing her own share of fatigue and concern about the situation. She felt helpless and just a bit resentful.

"I hope you have enjoyed your road trip, Bryson," Marisa said as they drove back to the hospital. "It sounds like just what you were looking forward to—a long, casual, pressure-free cruise across the heartland of America in a giant Rolls-Royce. I hope you at least enjoyed a few of the delicious chicken fried steak dinners you had talked so much about."

He nodded. He wished he had the energy and time right now to share the great moments of the trip with her—the feeling of cruising down the open highway and the feeling in his very soul of the vastness of the country he loved so much. He wished she had been at that dinner table when he had eaten the finest chicken fried steak in the entire world. Most of all, he wished that the trip had gone as planned from the start and that Jack wasn't lying in a hospital bed and that Jenny wasn't two hundred miles away, angry at him and her husband. Suddenly, he wished he could just pull into a Wal-Mart parking lot, unhitch the trailer and drive off, not ever looking back.

"Bryson, watch out!" Marisa screamed as a pickup cruised through the red light of the intersection immediately in front of Big Blue. Bryson was startled back to full alertness but didn't have enough reflex time to even hit the brakes. The front bumper of the Peterbilt missed the back end of the pickup by less than a foot.

"Are you asleep?" Marisa screamed at him again as he failed to slow for the upcoming yellow light.

"I'm okay. Sorry about that. That guy should have stopped. I'm fine. I think that's the turn to the hospital," he said, motioning toward an opening in the highway median across from businesses where a large, five-story building stood. "Keep your eye open for a good place to park."

Two minutes later Marisa stood in a darkened parking lot seemingly miles from the hospital ER entrance, waving her hands as she guided Bryson into a tight parking area, taking up enough room for at least ten cars.

He asked her if she wanted to wait in the truck while he checked on Jack, but she wanted to freshen up and frowned at his offer that she could use the truck's mini facilities.

When Marisa joined him in the hall outside the ER, Bryson introduced her to the three doctors who filled them in on Jack's condition. He was awake and alert and had eaten a small snack and was mad as hell that his friend had abandoned him dressed in scrub clothes in a strange hospital in a strange city. They were expressing to Bryson their concerns about moving him tonight versus keeping him overnight. Were Bryson not a physician there would have been no conversation, but common courtesy and respect for fellow senior doctors was leading the three to agree that Jack would be in competent hands.

Jack's diagnosis was a "minor concussion." The loss of consciousness was probably drug- and fatigue-induced, not a subdural hematoma. The CT had been normal and so had his lab and vital signs. They had changed his dressing, reducing the size of it to a less than mummified look.

Checking someone out of a hospital could be a tedious and irritating process. For Bryson it was at the top of the list along with finalizing the purchase of a car or emptying the black and gray water on a motor home. Thus, as soon as the doctors gave the green light for Jack to leave, Bryson, still in hospital scrubs, simply found a wheelchair and pushed it to Jack's room. He loaded his friend into the chair and off they went toward the truck. The admission desk had a copy of Jack's insurance card and a swipe of Bryson's American Express card. That was good enough for Bryson. They were off, the paperwork be damned.

Jack was tucked into the bed in the sleeper cabin, and while Marisa returned the wheelchair to the ER entrance, Bryson typed the address of the Boca Raton Golf and Tennis Resort, their supposed rendezvous spot, into the GPS. The engine was idling a bit rough from standing cold but soon warmed up and they pulled out of the hospital parking lot.

"I'm starving," Bryson said to his wife. "When did you eat anything last?"

She didn't answer directly but mentioned, "I saw a Mc-Donald's sign just up the road. Just stop along the street and I'll run in." She rummaged through her purse and was having trouble when Bryson handed her a one hundred dollar bill. It was crumpled and had a rust-colored stain on the edge.

"Here, use this. I have a lot of them," Bryson said and grinned.

A Mercedes got caught midway in an intersection and had to pull around Big Blue and drive up the street to the next light. Marisa watched the man in the front seat shake his fist. An old man sat in the backseat quietly. He looked like the old Navajo.

*** 

Jenny took a long bath in the exotic gigantic tub. She had lit candles and put a wee bit too much bath gel in the water. A rim of bubbles lay along the edge of the stone-tiled floor. Though she had the idyllic room and even a floor-to-ceiling view of the ocean and bay with its shadows and now twinkling lights, she was unable to relax.

Never in all the years she and Jack had been together had she not done what he had asked of her. There may have been arguments about why or how or when things needed to be done, but she knew that if he asked her to do something it was because he couldn't do it himself, not because he wouldn't do it. With that thought nagging at the back of her mind, she finished her bath and toweled off in front of the window feeling a little thrill of exhibitionism—standing in the glass-walled bathroom twenty-five stories high, with the curtains open and the possibility of unseen eyes out there somewhere on the bay. Slowly, she fixed her hair and makeup. She started to put on her nightgown and then changed her mind and picked out an outfit of new clothes.

She sat on the edge of the luxurious bed and called the concierge. She ordered a town car for the drive to Palm Beach and then asked the woman to make her a reservation for two rooms at the Breakers. While she waited for the call back, she finished dressing and packed her bags. The knock at the door took her by surprise, but not nearly so as the shock she felt when she opened it to face a stranger dressed in casual slacks, a form-fitting crewneck shirt and loafers without socks. He was definitely not a bellman. He had a pleasant enough face and the trim body of an athlete— maybe a tennis player. He was tall and handsome with white-blond hair pulled back in a ponytail. When he spoke, it was with a slight northern European accent.

"Mrs. Glen?"

"Yes, can I help you?"

"I have some information about your husband and his partner. There is a problem."

Jenny turned and walked to the edge of the bed and sat down. She was so afraid of some horrible news, she could barely breathe.

"Has there been an accident?" she mumbled timidly, more to herself than to the stranger.

He followed her into the room and closed the door. "Actually, there was an accident of sorts, but the latest word is that your husband is okay. He and his partner were shaken up a bit but will be fine. There is, however, one problem with which you can be of great assistance."

Without any threatening tones or profanity, the man explained to Jenny how there had been a mistake made with the cargo her husband and the doctor were transporting. He was very forthcoming about the illegality of the cargo and that there was more than one interested party involved. He apologized in advance for any inconvenience he might have to impose on her, and then he picked up the phone and called for a porter. He warned her that any failure to comply with all of his instructions would be of great and painful consequences to her, her husband and the Benders.

She sat in silent shock.

"Not to be personal," he continued in a polite but firm tone, "but there won't be any facilities where we are going."

Jenny took a few minutes and then came out of the bathroom, dry-eyed, carrying her makeup case, which she placed in her new tan Coach handbag. She had thought about calling for help from the phone in the bathroom but was afraid that the man would catch her and punish her. Thus far, he had been polite and reasonable. She could tell from the look in his eyes that his demeanor could change rapidly.

The blond man didn't seem to care what she took. To her surprise he had even finished packing her suitcases for her and was standing them near the door, apparently for the bellboy to take down to their car. She was confused and angry all in the same moment.

"How can I meet my husband and Bryson if I have to go with you?" she complained.

He ignored her question as he opened the door and looked into the hallway.

"I'm not going to repeat myself about what will happen if you don't do exactly as I tell you. Do you understand?"

Now her attitude had changed from fear to resentment and anger. Who did this jerk think he was? If Jack were here, he would break the guy's nose and throw him out in the hall. Her daydreaming was interrupted by the blond guy grasping her by the upper arm and jerking her, half dragging her out into the hallway, leaving her suitcases behind.

"Hey!" she yelped, trying to pull away for the assailant, "You're hurting my arm."

He tightened his grip momentarily then let go.

"You're leaving my bags in the room? I need my suitcases. I just bought some of that stuff," she said, rubbing her arm.

He didn't answer but grabbed her wrist and dragged her down the hallway toward the elevator. There he leaned his mouth down next to her ear and told her to shut up and behave.

She was about to snap back at him when the door opened and a chubby teenage bellman came out of the elevator car pushing a luggage rack.

"We're the ones who called down for you. Would you mind putting the bags in the storage room until we get back from dinner?" he said to the teen.

The kid accepted the folded ten-dollar bill, and headed down the hall.

Jenny yanked her arm away from the abductor again then turned to face him squarely in front of the elevator entrance. "You are going to have to shoot me or kill me right here unless we get a few things straight," she hissed. "We are not leaving here without my luggage, and I am not getting in some car with you. Whatever you and your other parties are up to, I couldn't care less. Obviously, you consider me a part of your sick plan, but guess what? I'm not cooperating unless you get my luggage and unless I talk to my husband first."

The man was reaching up to put his hands around her throat when the bellboy came around the corner with her three bags.

"Say madam, I'm sure glad I caught up with you. There were several sacks under the bed that still had clothes in them. I folded them and put them in the larger suitcase. It had enough room. I hope that was okay."

Jenny turned to thank the boy, then snarled at the blond guy. "You were going to leave my new outfits under the bed? You're a bigger jerk than I thought."

The three of them got on the next elevator car, which already held two middle-aged couples dressed up for a night out on the town. The ladies wore low-slung dresses and lots of glittery jewelry, and the men looked uncomfortable in their salsa shirts. The women's perfume was on the heavy side and the bellboy started to sneeze. Over and over he sneezed until he lost his breath and started to wheeze. The elevator kept stopping at the lower floors where a few more people insisted on crowding in.

Jenny worked her way to the front by the buttons, separating herself from Blondie. On the next floor, a huge black man wedged his way onto the car. Here she saw her chance. She leaned up on tiptoes to reach the ear of Mr. Linebacker.

"You look like a football player."

"Why, yes. I play for the Miami Dolphins."

"Do you have a game this week?" Jenny asked, inching further away from Blondie.

"No," the man said and laughed. "It's the off-season right now, but I'm in training for the Olympic boxing tryouts."

"Would you please help me? That dirty-minded blond man in the yellow shirt is trying to kidnap me. He has already choked me and bruised my arm." She nodded down at her wrist, which was red and bleeding slightly from where her tennis bracelet had scraped her skin. "Please, please help me."

She looked at the blond man, and in a snide tone said out loud, "I told you to keep your hands off of me, you pervert. This man is going to protect me." Turning to the confused bellboy she said, "I'm not going with that nasty blond man. Please put my bags in the hotel's town car; it should be waiting in front."

The other people on the elevator car stared at the sudden drama, their heads turning left and right, left and right, like mid-court fans at a tennis match as the angry words and deadly glares were exchanged.

The elevator door opened and the shocked group scattered into the lobby with Jenny in the lead. Blondie tried to catch up with her but a vice-like grip clamped on his neck.

"Why don't we just let the little lady have a minute to herself," said the football player.

"Is there a problem here?" a guard asked the two.

The ruckus gave Jenny the moment she needed to escape. By the time the would-be abductor got to the hotel's portico area, there was no sign of Jenny or her bags. A long stream of taillights were visible disappearing onto the boulevard.

*** 

Big Blue was rolling along at eighty miles per hour. Bryson was stuffing his mouth with French fries and the remaining fragments of his Quarter-Pounder with Cheese, some of which had fallen onto his lap as he drove. Marisa was trying to read the map on the GPS but was getting sick from the constant rocking motion of the truck's elevated cab. She had been too upset to eat anything but had ordered a hot fudge sundae for an energy boost.

"Stop looking at the GPS and just watch for the highway signs," Bryson warned her, knowing her motion sensitivity. "We still have a long way to go and the signs will give us plenty of warning. Are you going to be okay?"

"Why does this truck rock so much? Is something wrong with it?"

"No, it's just that we're sitting up high and the wind moves the trailer and the cab around a little. You'll get used to it."

"Don't count on it," she said in an irritated tone. "Don't worry about me, just drive. When we get there, I'll get out and never have to get back in this thing again."

Bryson glanced over at her and smiled at her little joke only to realize that it was no joke but a crystal-clear line of resolve drawn deep in the proverbial sand. Bryson changed the subject by asking her to check on Jack.

*** 

Marisa unlatched her seat belt and crawled into the space between the driver and passenger seats. She parted the heavy curtains and fumbled with a bank of switches before she found the dome light in the sleeper cab. Jack was lying on his side facing the front. His eyes were wide open, looking at her. Though they had never been particularly close friends, the circumstances of the last few weeks had created a strong affinity.

"How are you doing, you poor guy?" She put a hand on his shoulder and lifted a drink cup out of its holder, moving the straw close to his mouth so he could drink.

"I'm fine. It's just that every time I try to sit up, the world starts spinning." He spoke so softly that she had to move her ear close to him. "Marisa," Jack whispered. "Bryson is doing a great job handling a very complicated situation. Don't be too hard on him. He has had to take care of some very weird situations with some very nasty people and still has a huge problem to solve tonight. Have you ever used a gun?"

The question sent an electrical jolt through Marisa's entire body.

"Why would you ask that?" she said, moving abruptly away from Jack.

He motioned for her to draw closer again and explained. "Bryson has to end this thing in less than an hour. He is going to need some backup and I don't know that I can give it to him. It may be up to you." He reached into one of the nearby cubbies and pulled out a folded oil rag, handing it to Marisa.

The rag and its contents were heavy and smelled strongly of some type of petroleum cleaner oil. She sensed immediately what was inside the folded cloth but was reticent to open the folds. Finally doing so, she saw the shiny metal and the shape of the revolver. Marisa had grown up in the West where everyone owned guns. Target practice was a common activity at family picnics. At first, she withdrew her hand from the gun, but then looking Jack in the eyes, reached out and lifted the heavy, cold pistol. Perhaps the weight of the responsibility was commensurate with the weight of the weapon itself.

"Are you two okay?" Bryson called back from the cab. "Marisa, can you help me up here? The traffic is going faster and the road signs are getting closer together and more confusing."

She returned the pistol to Jack with a reluctant nod of agreement to help, then crawled back up into her big leather seat and sat back. For some strange reason, she felt relaxed for the first time in what seemed like days. The seat was amazingly comfortable and the view of the highway ahead was unlike anything she had experienced. The cars were tiny and far below, and what she could see of the countryside in the dimming light was amazing.

"How are you doing, Bryson?" She asked, reaching over and resting her hand on his arm. He had both hands on the enormous steering wheel that seemed to fill his entire half of the truck's cab.

"I'm fine, sweetheart. I'm sorry this has turned into such a nightmare for you, and especially for Jack." He went on to relate parts of the story of how they both were injured and his hypothesis as to what was actually going on. Bryson told her about the attempts to open the trailer clear back in Nevada and again in Arizona and Texas and about the hijacking then finally about the money.

"Maybe it's stolen money or maybe it's counterfeit; I just don't know. The cars are worth millions if they're original. We were listening to a program on NPR one night that told of knock-off classic cars that can barely be distinguished from the originals. If that's the case maybe all we're hauling is a load of awesome-looking fakes full of somebody's fake money. Whatever the case, someone wants the cars delivered and someone else doesn't care about the cars but wants whatever else still remains in the trailer. We're definitely dealing with more than just a worried car owner. The only good thing so far is that we haven't run into any sign of drugs."

"Is that the exit you want?" Marisa pointed to a sign that read, "Boca Raton six miles."

"That's got to be the one," Bryson said, taking his foot off of the accelerator and signaling to get into the right lane. No sooner had he turned off on the exit than his cell phone rang.

# Chapter Twenty-Two

# THE EXCHANGE

Jenny had told her driver she would give him an extra twenty dollars if he would make the quickest possible time to Palm Beach. He had gone through no less than ten yellow lights on the way. Finally, he pulled into the long, circular approach to The Breakers resort. It had been just over an hour since they had left the hotel in Miami. She had looked out the rear window numerous times, trying to be reassured that no one was following her. When her driver pulled to a stop at the front entrance to the world-famous hotel, a traditionally clad and very cheerful bellman opened her door to greet her. Then her phone rang.

"I'm here," she said into the tiny pink cell phone, expecting Jack to be the one on the other end.

"Hi, Jenny, it's Marisa. Where is here?"

"I just arrived at the Breakers, just like I was ordered. Where are you? And where the heck are our husbands?"

Marisa started to explain but was interrupted.

"Listen, some creepy guy tried to kidnap me back at the hotel in Miami. I got away from him unscathed . . . it's a long story, but the guy said Jack and Bryson had been in some sort of accident. Do you know anything about it?"

"I don't know much of the story, but I'm in the truck now with Jack and Bryson. They are both all right, but very tired."

"How did you meet up with them? I thought you said you would meet me at the Four Seasons."

"Please listen to me. You are where you need to be. If everything goes according to plan, we will all be together in an hour or two. Go ahead and check in. Then stay where you are."

254

"What do you mean? I'm still in the car in front of the Breakers' lobby."

"I mean stay there at the hotel. Just a second . . . Bryson says to go check in for all of us, two adjacent rooms, and then stay in the room until we get there. Don't go out."

"What is going on? I'm getting kidnapped and now shut up in a room, not to mention having to leave that gorgeous room in Miami, and you won't tell me anything."

"Jenny, just please be patient for a couple of hours. Until just a few minutes ago I didn't know what was happening either but . . . "

"I'm done being patient," Jenny interrupted. "Where is Jack? Let me talk to my husband."

"Wait just a second," Marisa told her, putting her hand over the mouthpiece and leaning over to Bryson. "She is really mad and insists on talking to Jack. Somebody tried to kidnap her in Miami but she is at the Breakers now."

"See if he is alert enough to talk to her," Bryson said, nodding his head toward the back of the cabin.

Marisa crawled out of the huge seat again and parted the curtain. Jack was rolled over, his back to her and his face buried in a pillow.

"Jack? Jenny is on the phone and wants to talk to you."

He rolled onto his back and took the cell phone. He talked to her for less than a minute and then handed back the phone and rolled back toward the rear wall.

When Marisa spoke into the phone again the line was dead.

**✻✻✻**

Bryson was so exhausted his mind was starting to drift. When Marisa had alerted him that the Boca turn was coming up fast, it startled him. He slowed to a crawl and managed to pull off of the freeway onto the main city road.

Checking his mirrors, he noticed a silver Mercedes starting to pass him. It accelerated quickly and then cut sharply in front of his truck and slowed to normal traffic speed. He blinked his eyes to clear them, not believing what he was seeing. In the rear window of the Mercedes was a two-foot-long white sign that read simply "FOLLOW ME DOC B."

"Do you see that?" Bryson said, suddenly very alert.

"Now what are they going to do?" Marisa said. "Have us follow them to some secluded place and murder all of us? We should just pull into a big store parking lot and leave the truck and the trailer. We can walk into the store and call the police and then leave and never come back." She looked at Bryson for an answer.

"What about Madeline and Jenny, and what about Jack? He isn't in any shape to walk into Wal-Mart," Bryson answered in a soft, calculating tone. The apparent trap they found themselves in initially made Bryson want to throw up his hands and say he quit—but he couldn't. He wouldn't.

Within moments, his mind had cleared and he had devised a plan. He thought it through a second time and then shared it with Marisa. She agreed to help, crawling into the back and turning on the sleeper cabin lights, as Bryson had instructed.

*** 

Jack opened his eyes and slowly tried to sit up. His head was swimming, but he held his balance as Marisa discussed Bryson's strategy. Jack took a bottle of cold water and drank the whole thing, then bent down to put on his boots.

He knew the mechanics of the truck much better than Bryson, especially the hitching mechanism. During the time since they had picked up the new Peterbilt in Bozeman and driven it to Reno, Bryson had only crawled up on the hitch platform of the truck once. When they hooked Big

Blue up to the shiny chrome auto-trailer in Reno, Bryson had backed the truck while Jack attached the pneumatic brake and electrical lines connecting the semi-tractor to the trailer. They had not unhitched the trailer since then. For Bryson to succeed with his plan, he was going to have to have Jack's skill and knowledge and physical help.

While Marisa and Jack talked over the plan, Bryson continued to follow the silver Mercedes, keeping a distance at least two to three hundred yards behind. Jack threw back the curtain between the cab and the sleeper cabin and crawled into the passenger's seat. Marisa used Jack's cell phone to call Madeline.

\*\*\*

"Maddie? This is Mom."

"Hi Mom, you are never going to believe this cool . . . ."

"Don't talk for a minute, sweetheart, just listen. I know this is going to sound crazy, but I want you and your roommate to go down to the dorm recreation room and sit there with some of the other kids. Buy pizza for everyone or whatever it takes to keep a crowd there for an hour or two. Do not go anywhere alone. Do not stay in your room. Keep your phone on you and I'll call you back in less than an hour. Now do what I told you and please keep your phone line open. Got it?"

Marisa's next call was to the Duke Campus Security where she gave an anonymous tip to the police that a Peeping Tom was loitering around the freshman girls' dorm and asked that they keep an eye out for the person.

\*\*\*

Bryson's pulse was racing and every nerve ending in his body had ramped up to high alert. He felt like he was an actor in an adventure movie, driving the huge truck through winding streets of rich man's Florida, playing a speed game with the Mercedes. Every time the car would speed up, Bryson would slow down, intentionally slowing enough to have to stop for a red light, requiring the Mercedes to pull off the road and wait for Big Blue. He was stalling for time and it was working. Marisa told Bryson that Jack had downed a Mountain Dew and a Snickers; his dizziness was gone, and his strength returning.

Bryson had decided that, no matter what happened next, within the next hour he was going to get rid of the trailer one way or another. Jack had retrieved the truck owner's manual from the glove box and was reviewing the hydraulic, electrical and mechanical aspects of the hitching mechanism. The biggest problem was that detaching the tractor from the trailer could not be accomplished from inside the cab. Someone would have to get out of the truck and manipulate the hoses and electrical cables and rotate the mechanical lock on the actual hitch. They also had to lower the trailer's front metal parking wheels. For the plan to work, Bryson would have to remain behind the wheel.

The men talked over the plan with Marisa listening from between the seats where she was kneeling on a pillow she had thrown on the floor. Just when they had decided on the final details and how Jack could carry off his part of the plan, his head slumped against the side window.

"Jack, are you okay?" Marisa shouted but received no answer.

Bryson looked over and saw his cousin's limp neck and shoulders sinking deeper into the seat. He took his foot off of the accelerator. The rapid deceleration propelled Jack forward and he slid off of the seat into a heap on the floor.

"Bryson!" screamed Marisa. "You have got to stop the truck."

Jack lifted his head and began a struggle to get himself back up in the passenger's seat.

Bryson pulled into a bus stop area and was out of his

door, running around to the other side of the truck to help move Jack.

"Be careful with his head!" Marisa said in a loud and commanding voice. Tears were streaming down her face. She had snagged the front of her silk blouse on the headrest of the seat and tore off the top two buttons. Her diamond tennis bracelet had ripped a long abrasion on her arm, causing a trickle of blood to smear onto Jack's arm as well. Between the two of them, they positioned Jack back in the seat and strapped him in place with the seat belt.

Jack shook his head and looked around like he had just emerged from a deep pool of water. His first words were, "What did I do to deserve the two of you dog-piling on top of me? You'd think we just won the state basketball championship."

Marisa, her blouse hanging open, with her hair hanging over her face, and Bryson, who was trying to ignore the ripping pain in his shoulder, looked at one another. Then they laughed.

"What's so dang funny?" Jack asked. His head bandage, which until now had been a perfectly symmetrical crown of white gauze, was smeared with blood from Marisa's arm and tilted to a jaunty forty-degree angle.

"You look like an Egyptian version of Fred Astaire getting ready to sing and dance in the rain," said Bryson.

Marisa bent over the seat and gave Jack a kiss on the cheek. "Why don't I help you crawl into the back so you can lie down?"

"I'll stay right here, thank you. We still need to follow through with the plan," Jack responded in a stubborn tone. "But I sure could use another cold drink. That sissy yellow water did nothing for me."

Ignoring the honking horns of the cars behind his truck, as well as the flashing turn signal of the Mercedes waiting intrusively a hundred yards ahead, Bryson turned to Marisa and asked. "What would you like to drink?"

"Make mine a Diet Coke with lots of crushed ice." Some

wives would have questioned his timing, but Marisa had noticed the convenience store immediately across the four-lane road and knew that Bryson wasn't kidding.

"Don't leave without me," Bryson said as he circled around the front of the truck, pausing to check the oncoming traffic.

He walked in front of the light traffic, completely ignoring the presence of the Mercedes whose driver now was out of the car, staring back at Big Blue with its numerous flashing lights. Bryson confidently and slowly walked into the 7-Eleven. He took his time filling three Big Gulp cups with the three drinks of choice and then raked three candy bars from the shelf. The elderly attendant gave him a carrying tray and his change and commented. "That is a mighty big truck, mister. You know that very few trucks park in that spot. It's a bus stop."

"Really?" said Bryson, at first being a little sarcastic. Then he had a brainstorm. "Do you see that silver Mercedes in front of my truck? My wife thinks that it is the car from the kidnapping at a daycare center. She heard it on the radio. She said they kidnapped eighteen-month-old triplets. She is afraid for us to call it in but she said there is a reward. Would you mind calling 911 and telling the police? That car has a Nevada license plate. Maybe you can be the hero and earn a reward. It's probably worth a lot of money."

The skinny man looked at Bryson's bloodied scrub clothes, tousled hair, two-day old beard and bandaged arm. "I think you're full of crap, but I'll call it in just in case. I got a reward once back in seventy-seven. I found some lady's poodle and . . . "

Bryson was out the door without listening. He hurried across the street and climbed into the cab just as a black-and-white patrol car turned on its lights and pulled behind Big Blue. The drinks and candy bars were passed out and Bryson strapped in, keeping the cruiser in view the best he could. Trying to outrun a police car in the truck would be hopeless, and at this point, he was too exhausted to care much. The officer started to walk alongside the trailer, carrying his clipboard and a flashlight, but he suddenly stopped and tilted his head toward his collar radio mike. He looked up the road toward the parked Mercedes and then turned and ran toward his patrol car.

As the three guzzled their drinks and nibbled their snacks, they watched amused as the scene played out. Four black-and-white squad cars converged on the silver Mercedes as Bryson shared his brainstorm with Jack and Marisa. Not only did the police cars surround the silver sedan, front, back and side, but six or seven uniformed officers sprang from their cars, drawing their guns and hiding behind opened squad car doors while aiming their guns at the Mercedes. The lone male driver and the old, slow-moving passenger in the backseat got out of the car and were immediately spread eagle against the hood.

A fairly bright streetlamp close to the car allowed Bryson, Marisa and Jack to witness the vigorous searches of the two and then the search of the car's empty trunk. A cardboard sign two-feet-long reading, "FOLLOW ME DOC B," was all the police appeared to have found. The two were handcuffed and held at gunpoint on the sidewalk side of their car. When one of the police teams got back into their car and headed toward the 7-Eleven parking lot, Bryson took his cue and pulled the truck out onto the road, heading for the unknown.

# Chapter Twenty-Three

# SPLASH

Jenny walked up and down the hotel's boutique store corridors, mindlessly looking at the overpriced wares in the windows. All were closed by now except the tiny gift shop. She was too nervous to stay in the rooms she had checked into. The adjoining rooms were luxurious, but she had expected more space and maybe a bowl of fruit; she was famished. She bought a Coke, a package of Oreo cookies, and a packet of Advil in the gift shop and headed for the pool.

There were still a few late swimmers, as well as a young athletic kid picking up towels and straightening deck chairs.

She savored the cookies, wishing she had bought three or four packs instead of just one. She popped three Advil and was taking a long swallow of her drink when she saw him. At first she wasn't entirely positive it was him, but then he turned toward the light, giving her a good look at his face and hair. It was definitely her tormentor from the Four Seasons in Miami.

The jerk was sneaking into the hotel lobby from a back door—probably the golf course entrance. With the pop bottle half covering her face, she didn't think he had seen her. Slowly she shifted her head sideways, covering even more of her face with her hand and bottle. He didn't even glance in her direction, but moved instead into the lobby, stopping from time to time to read plaques on walls or to look at artwork. He was putting on a show for someone, but she wasn't sure for whom. He acted like he knew she was there, but didn't want her to see him. When he finally left her sight, she jumped up and ran to the furthest end of the pool area from the lobby. The lounge chair canopies had all been laid flat for the night and the cabana curtains drawn back. The towel kiosk was closed as was the snack bar. She stepped into a recess between the snack bar and the rest-rooms, grabbed her phone out of her purse and tapped in the wanted numbers.

Marisa answered her phone on the first musical ring. "Hello, I can't talk right now, we're in the middle of a . . . ."

"Don't hang up," yelled Jenny. "It's me. The creep who tried to kidnap me before is here!"

"Where is here, this time?" Marisa asked. She was frustrated, not with Jenny but with the GPS and the stupid Florida road signs. Jack had become dizzy again and had crawled into the bed in the sleeper cabin, leaving Marisa to navigate, and they had come up with a new plan.

"I'm in the pool garden of the Breakers Hotel, hiding. I checked into our rooms and was getting something to eat when I saw the creep. This thing has got to stop! Where are you, and how is Jack?"

"If we can find the stupid road, we should be there at the hotel in less than half an hour. Bryson has a plan to get rid of the trailer and maybe your boyfriend too."

Jenny would have laughed if she wasn't so afraid. She had been face-to-face with the blond guy and had sensed the desperation in his actions. She knew that the guy was not going to go away easily, but she was determined to act bravely even if it was a façade.

"Tell you what, Marisa. You get our husbands here safely, and I'll stay in my room with both of them, and you can have this thirty-year-old Blondie all to yourself."

"It's a deal," said Marisa, closing the connection.

Jenny was standing in the darkened breezeway alone, wondering what to do when she heard the voice. "May I help you find something, ma'am?" The voice was close enough to Jenny that she could feel the breath that produced the words.

She surprised herself by not screaming or even jumping

away. Instead she turned and smiled. "Why thank you, I think I dropped a ten-dollar bill here. Do you have a flashlight?" She looked straight into the face of the blond demon.

"So is the friend you are going to share with me as feisty as you?"

Jenny looked down, expecting to see him holding a knife or a gun—maybe she had seen too many Perry Mason or NCIS shows. His hands were empty but hers weren't.

"What do you want?" she asked. "I don't have anything of yours, especially cars, and probably nothing else you really want either. I'm a wrinkled-up old lady."

"I just need to assure myself that your friends in the truck make it here safely, and that when they finally get here, they give me what is rightfully mine. Somebody is trying to change the game plan and you, at the moment, are my only insurance that will assure me of keeping my property. Now, let's get away from these smelly restrooms and go up to your room. By the way, you have good taste in hotels. I was so afraid that you were going to stop at that Quality Inn when you got off the freeway."

Jenny had often been tempted to take a self-defense class, but instead she had paid to have her three daughters take a short course in martial arts before they went off to travel around Europe one summer. They had shared a few of the more memorable tips with their mom, but Jenny had never practiced any of the maneuvers. This night she surprised herself.

Blondie had yet to hurt her, but she retained the memory of his painful grip on her arm and wrist earlier that evening. He was nudging her along with an occasional shoulder bump, past the pool in the direction of the lobby. Near the pool's edge, she stopped and turned to face him, intentionally staring down at her open, and three-quarter full, plastic bottle of soda. When she saw Blondie's eyes go there also, she gave the bottle one good shake then brought it upward, squeezing it at the same time as hard as she could. This forced the cold, effervescent liquid to spew out of the nozzle in a solid stream into her assailant's eyes.

The upward force of the bottle, still tightly gripped in her fist, continued until the sharp edge on the mouth of the bottle struck the man just below his left nostril, tearing away flesh and cartilage. With his eyes incapacitated, he turned away from her, staggering to keep his balance.

Standing firm as her whole body pulsed with the surging of adrenaline, she watched as the demon tried to suppress his cries of agony. Holding both hands over his bleeding face, it was apparent that he didn't know which direction he was moving. Jenny knew she should run, but her soul begged for more revenge. As he staggered, he cursed in a foreign language. Struggling to gain control of his vision and the pain in his face, he moved closer to the deep end of the swimming pool. Here she made her move.

Jenny bent down, taking a hold of the end of a rather heavy metal framed lounge chair and started pushing it toward the blond man. It made a screeching sound as it slid across the cement pool deck. The faster she pushed, the louder and more ear-piercing the sound became. He turned toward her but it was too late.

The chair was moving fast as the lower edge of the heavy metal frame hit his shins just below his kneecaps. The momentum of the fast-moving chair shot his feet and lower legs out from under him, forcing him forward. His arms, trunk and head collapsed, striking the frame of the chair and wrenching his right shoulder on the armrest of the heavy, custom-made furniture. Blondie's entire body then followed the forward motion of the chair still being pushed by the energized Jenny.

The noise caused by the splash of the chair with the man's body on board was heard by several of the hotel employees and guests. A garden supervisor working at the opposite end of the pool area turned to view the scene and immediately recognized the potentially lethal situation. He spoke into his radio, and within seconds, several security men were converging on the area.

Jenny stepped into the shadows of the small snack shop buildings and then walked around the opposite end of the pool, joining the rubbernecking guests all of whom were delighted that there was actually some type of action taking place at the usually stoic hotel. Once the security men had pulled the near-drowned rat from the pool and Jenny had assured herself that Blondie wasn't going to die, she slipped into the lobby and went back to the gift shop for something else to eat and drink.

She was leafing through a Vogue magazine, trying to calm down when the sound of a siren announced the arrival of the Fire and Rescue team. Jenny stayed at the magazine rack until the team of paramedics rolled a gurney past on the way to the pool. A short five minutes later they rushed back out of the lobby toward an awaiting ambulance. On-board the gurney, struggling to free himself from the woven nylon restraints that held him firm, was the tall blond man. He was screaming at the paramedics that he did not want to go to the hospital. The rescue workers were ignoring his pleas. The hotel guests in the lobby, most dressed for dinner in elegant South Beach chic duds, were aghast at the sight of the man's bloodied face and dripping wet clothes.

Jenny followed the signs to the ladies' room and slipped inside. Luckily, she was alone. She looked at herself in the mirror and was astonished that instead of a sixty-year-old, burned-out farm grandmother, she saw a vibrant, elegant, and yes even somewhat foxy female.

When she exited the marble and maple powder room leading back into the main lobby, a greeting of applause from the hotel patrons would not have been a surprise. Instead she was greeted by a female police officer holding a two-way radio and a clipboard. The equally young male officer standing ten feet behind her had his right hand resting on his holstered pistol.

"Hold it right there, madam. I need to talk to you."

Jenny could hear her cell phone ringing at the bottom of her shoulder bag, but now was not the time to reach into it for anything.

"Would you follow me out to the lobby, please?" the female ordered.

There was little doubt that this was a question without an expected positive outcome. As they walked down the hallway into the expansive lobby, they passed a massive gilded mirror. Jenny glanced at herself for the second time in less than five minutes, but this time, she saw an exhausted and older person.

\*\*\*

As Bryson climbed into the driver's seat after a short stop, he became acutely aware that the inside of the truck's cabin was starting to smell like the men's gym locker room at his old Scottsdale High. Both men had gone way too long and done way too much physical exertion since their last shower. Even his wife was dripping wet with sweat. Added to the mix was the smell of blood that lingered on both men's clothes and Jack's turban-like head dressing.

Bryson had been forced to make a drive-by pit stop for Marisa and to pump in a few gallons of diesel. He was still waiting for a phone call from Fritz with further instructions. Who the guys in the Mercedes were, he hadn't a clue.

He still had no sure sense that he was doing the right thing. Since the detainment of the people in the Mercedes and Marisa's last conversation with Jenny, Bryson had been heading the truck and trailer toward Palm Beach and where he remembered the Breakers Hotel was located. Marisa had given up trying to work the GPS and Jack had again crawled into the sleeper cabin. Bryson rolled down the truck's windows to clear the air, but the outside blanket of heavy, wet air swirling through the cab annoyed him as bad as the acrid smell of sweaty scrub clothes.

"When will they call again?" Marisa asked.

"Who knows? Right now I'm too tired to think about it. The whole thing may be finished soon. Maybe we can park the truck in the lot at the hotel, unhook the trailer and then find Jenny. I'll call the car dealer's number in Reno and leave a message as to where he can find his damn trailer and cars. Then maybe, just maybe, we'll be done with it. Can you imagine how fantastic a hot shower and cool sheets will feel? We can order room service and eat steaks and hot fudge sundaes in bed."

As if on cue, the cell phone rang. Marisa picked it up off the console. She flipped it open and then pressed the speaker phone control.

"That was a real cute trick you pulled back at the 7-Eleven," the voice said. It sounded like Fritz, but it had been a while since Bryson had heard his voice and there was lots of static. Marisa was holding the phone and had no idea who it could be. She pointed toward the phone and then handed it to Bryson.

"This is Dr. Bender," Bryson said, taking the phone from his wife. "Have we been playing your stupid games long enough or should I just drive this trailer off into one of these waterways?"

"Whoa, Doc! You wouldn't want to do that now. I'm sure you are getting tired of this load and I understand there have been some problems along the way . . . none of which I had anything to do with. Thanks for getting rid of those jerks in the Mercedes. I'll give you credit; that was slick. Now, we can finish our original deal and you can be on your way. Just to answer your unasked question, those guys who have been interrupting your travel so often are a group of amateur car repo-jerks from Seattle. I did the best I could to get rid of them outside

Reno but they are like junkyard dogs. I think they are gone now. You did great!"

"Who am I speaking to?" Bryson asked, trying to keep his composure and keep the truck in his own lane.

"It's me Doc, Fritz. Those are my company's cars you are hauling. I sure hope you have been taking good care of them."

"Well, we have tried to call you for the last ten days. Why do we suddenly hear from you now?"

"Because you are here, Doc. Right now my GPS tracker in the auto trailer says you are less than twenty miles from where I need the cars delivered."

"You told me Miami; why the change of plans and why all the threats?"

"The threats were from my previous partner. He got nervous and decided he wanted his share *and* mine. He has a couple of other idiots working for him that he didn't tell me about. I understand you may have met them along the way. How 'bout that Indian guy? Was he crazy or what? And like I said a minute ago, good job getting rid of the repo-idiots in the Mercedes."

"So who hijacked the truck and busted up one of your cars?"

"Hold on there, my good friend. I'm not sure I know what you are talking about."

"Forget it for now. What is the plan?" Bryson asked, just wanting to be done with the whole thing. "I'm exhausted and need to get this day over with."

"First things first, Doc. My ex-partner will be pretty bummed if you let somebody get into the truck. He is the one who thinks your daughter is real pretty, but way too young for him. His son says that your friend Jack has a real mean wife. This partner wants to take a close look inside the trailer, and if everything is okay, then you can unhook the trailer and drive away."

"Well, let's get it done!" Bryson nearly screamed into the phone.

Marisa was sitting back in her seat, staring at the phone. Jack had revived himself and had his bandaged head between the curtains.

"Hey, Doc. Don't go getting postal on us now. We are almost done with this project. Look straight ahead of you. Do you see a black Suburban with its flasher lights on?"

"I see it," Bryson answered in a belligerent tone.

"Stay on its bumper and don't think about making any stops at any convenience stores. Also, I want you to keep talking on the phone. Maybe your wife could sing for us. Just don't think about making any phone calls to the police. By the way, I heard the cops up north are looking for a blue Peterbilt that caused a big ruckus at one of the truck stops. When you head back out West, you might consider taking a different route."

Bryson handed the open phone to Marisa so he could downshift and catch up with the black Chevy SUV. He was torn between doing exactly what Fritz told him and going back to the plan he had hatched, using Jack to unhitch the trailer when they stopped at a red light. Jack had been sure he could do it in less than a minute, but Bryson wasn't sure that Jack would be able to crawl out of the truck and up onto the hitch platform, let alone perform the necessary steps to unhook all the lines. He looked at his wife and thought about Madeline and decided their best chance was to follow their instructions and hope for the best. Jenny was one more concern, but his mind was too cluttered and exhausted to even think about her situation.

The closer they got to the oceanfront, the more waterways there were to cross and to follow. They were far off the trucker's beaten path by now. They had read about the Intercoastal Waterway, a channel of connecting canals and rivers extending for thousands of miles down and around the Eastern Seaboard and the Gulf of Mexico. As they passed over the narrow bridges and skirted the deep channels, a new plan grew in Bryson's mind. Back in the days of performing surgery, elbow deep in blood and viscera, he had often faced what appeared to be insurmountable difficulties where an entirely new and innovative surgical plan had to be adopted. At this moment, he definitely needed such a plan.

They passed a road sign that announced a boat dock and landing just two miles ahead. Bryson put the phone on mute and told Marisa to get in the back and gather any valuables from the sleeping cabin and to put them in a black roller carry-on bag. "Don't forget the bundles of money and the gun."

The bundles of money were news to her and she started to protest.

"Just do what you're told; we've only got a couple of minutes."

Next, he picked up the phone. Taking it off mute, he told Fritz he was having problems with his brakes and needed to pull off into a parking area to check the airlines.

"Not so fast, Doc. I told you no funny stuff. Just follow the 'Burb."

"No can do. If I go through the next red light and wipe out someone's car, your cars are going to end up part of a lengthy investigation. Maybe impounded or confiscated. You better let me stop. How about this boat ramp parking lot I see up ahead?"

"Just do it and do it quickly."

The Mangrove View Boatyard and Loading Ramp was a public facility with large parking areas for tow vehicles and long boat trailers. At this late hour most of the day-trippers had finished their runs up and down the waterways.

Bryson did a quick scan of the parking lot. Turning Big Blue in a tight half-circle, he lined the truck and trailer up even with the boat ramp, with the water just sixty feet behind the back doors of the trailer. He gave Jack and Marisa each a confirmatory glance, and when his look was returned with positive nods, he slid the shift lever into reverse and started the truck and trailer backwards towards the murky water's edge.

No sooner had he begun rolling backwards than the black Suburban came screaming around the corner, heading for the truck and trailer. At the speed it was accelerating, Bryson wasn't sure it was going to be able to stop before it ran into the truck. The SUV's lights shining into the driver-side window nearly blinded Bryson, but created a diversion at the same time for both Marisa and Jack to crawl out of the passenger's side door.

On the cell phone, Fritz was screaming.

Once the Suburban did stop, its driver jumped out of the SUV and frantically ran toward Big Blue. Bryson figured he would be carrying a gun but saw nothing except the man's clenched fists and frenzied gestures. Bryson ignored him and kept very slowly backing down the boat-launching ramp toward the water.

*** 

Jack, with Marisa's help, had crawled up onto the hitch platform from the passenger side. He was in the process of detaching one of the two major air pressure brake cables and the electrical cable for the trailer's lights. Once detached, the only thing keeping the truck and trailer together was the mechanical coupler. This could be released from inside the cab. Jack slid the fifteen-inch-long steel pin out of its jacket and banged it three times against the back of the sleeper cab, alerting Bryson. Now he controlled whether to stay attached to the trailer or release it and let it roll backward into the thirty-foot-deep inter-coastal waterway. He would skip putting down the trailer's metal wheels. When Bryson finally stopped the truck, the trailer was on a ten-degree incline, just feet away from the water's edge.

***

The cell phone on the console rang again. Marisa had snapped it shut before she and Jack had left the cab.

"What the heck do you think you are doing?" said Fritz. "Are you retarded? There's twenty-million dollars' worth of cars in that trailer! Stop right where you are and get out of the truck."

Bryson knew that the man standing in the headlights shaking his fists wasn't the voice on the phone, and amid the glare, finally made out the outline of a second big SUV sitting further away in the shadows of the parking lot.

Bryson took a deep breath to calm himself. "Let's just say that I'm tired of listening to you and your idiot friends give instructions. I've decided, being a fair man, to let you have your trailer back but with a few conditions. First off, no more of your bullying threats. One more and your cars go for a swim. Second, I want the payment I am owed for the transport in cash and I want it before I set the brakes on the trailer. I think we agreed on twelve-thousand dollars, but that didn't include the hospital bills and the hazardous duty pay. Just make it an even twenty-thousand. Third, if I ever hear that you have threatened me or any of my friends or family, especially my daughter, ever again, the video we took of the inside of the van and of the dealership in Reno, and the one I'm recording right now, are going straight to my brother-in-law at the FBI office in Las Vegas. Is there any of what I just said that you don't quite understand?"

He waited, but got no answer. "By the way, there was some strange-looking paper blowing around inside the trailer. One of your good ol' buddies tried to take all of it when he hijacked the truck up near Pensacola or wherever we were, but he left some of the loose bills floating around. It looks a lot like funny-money if you know what I mean. I'll bet the FBI would love to get a close look at it along with the VIN numbers of the six cars in the trailer."

As Bryson waited for a response, he heard Marisa and Jack climb back inside the cab. To his surprise, the man standing outside Big Blue turned and walked back to his Suburban and turned off the glaring headlights.

"Listen, Doc," the voice on the phone said, "you are either a lot braver or a lot stupider than I gave you credit for. Your role in this simple transport was to be just that. Transport the cars across the country and pick up your money. It wasn't my plan to have a couple of greedy criminals try to load some extras on board the trailer or to have the cars removed along the way. You did a good job protecting my assets, and so I'm going to reward you. I'm going to tell my associate sitting there in front of you to slowly drive out of the lot and go to a place nearby where he will pick up your money. Then he will bring it back to you and set it at the entrance to the boat ramp. Your job is to keep calm and not do anything stupid. My cars won't do well under water. If they go for a swim, trust me, you and your wife and your partners, and maybe even your daughter, will do some swimming as well."

"Neither will your funny money and drugs and whatever other kind of crap you have hidden in the cars," interrupted Bryson. "You have threatened me for the last time. You have fifteen minutes, and then we're leaving without the trailer."

"Let's be nice, Doc. All those nasty things you are saying are way beyond the plan you need to concern yourself with. Just be patient and sit there for another ten minutes then you can drive off and we won't bother you. Trust me when I say that I have lots of problems to deal with besides you."

The phone went dead. The black Suburban backed away and drove out of the parking lot. Bryson pointed out the other SUV to Jack and Marisa and brought them up to date on the phone conversation.

That's when Marisa made her own decision.

"There is no way that I am going to let those cretins get away with all the things they have done to all of us. You men have had your fun cross-country ride and your adventure with the snakes and Indians and your yummy chicken fried steak, but Jenny and Madeline and I have had nothing but fear and worry, and I, for one, feel ten years older. We are not just going to drive away and let these crooks have their way."

\*\*\*

Marisa moved back into the sleeper and sat on the lower bunk bed. Using her phone, she called Madeline and talked for less than a minute. Once assured her daughter was fine, she called Jenny. That frantic conversation ended with Jenny agreeing to wait for the other three in the room at the Breakers.

After hearing from Jenny, Marisa was even madder than before. Thinking back on Bryson's story about the event at the Home Depot, she made a plan of her own. She fumbled around in the small drawer in the sleeper cab where the men had thrown odds and ends, spoons, extra bolts and loose parts of the truck's interior that had no apparent use, and there she came out with what she was looking for—a practically new box cutter.

She knew that Bryson and Jack would throw a fit if they heard of her plan, so she waited five minutes and then poked her head through the curtains and whispered into Bryson's ear. "I've got to go. I can't use this Porta-Potty with Jack sitting right there. I'll be right back."

Without waiting for an answer, she scampered over Bryson's lap and out of the driver's door. She headed across the narrow boat ramp toward a small, dimly lit block building. Lights surrounding the boat ramp's parking area were scattered and fairly dim but adequate for her to see her way. Marisa heard Bryson holler for her to hurry.

\*\*\*

"How are you doing?" Bryson asked Jack, who was still upright, but had his bandaged head leaning back against the headrest.

"I'm ready for a cheeseburger and a soft pillow. Did Marisa say Jenny was going to order food for us?"

"She didn't, but once we get finished here and headed that way, I'll have Marisa call her and we'll have them empty the kitchen."

It was sixteen minutes by Big Blue's digital clock before the black Suburban turned into the boat ramp parking lot again. The second SUV had been sitting on the far side of the parking area in a shadow the whole time. The Chevy stopped on the far end next to the other vehicle where dome lights went on and then off in both vehicles. The next thing Bryson saw was three men walking across the parking lot toward Big Blue. One of them was carrying a small gym bag and a long flashlight. The other two were empty-handed as best Bryson could tell.

"Do you think they are just going to leave us the money and then walk away?" Jack asked.

Before Bryson could comment, a large Kenworth tractor eased around the corner into the lot and pulled up next to the two SUVs. It kept its engine idling with its lights on bright, giving illumination to the area between it and Big Blue.

"Looks like the transfer carrier is here," said Bryson. "Maybe this thing is going to be okay. Now, where the heck is Marisa?"

Two men walked into a lighted area near Bryson's side of the truck and motioned for him to lower his window. Once in the light, Bryson and Jack could easily recognize the face of Fritz. The slick car dealer from Reno was wearing jeans that were too short for the cowboy boots on his feet; the San Francisco Forty-Niners jersey looked stupid on the man. One of the other men appeared to be a stranger but on closer study looked familiar to Bryson. He had a hair braid threaded through the back of an oversized baseball cap. He looked a lot like a younger version of the Indian who had driven the empty transporter truck back in New Mexico.

"Hey, Doc. How are my cars?" Fritz asked in a strong voice. "I sure hope they don't have any scratches. They go on the auction block day after tomorrow."

"You can spend all night detailing them but not until we are paid and are long gone."

"Well, here is your money. I really am sorry for all the trouble. It really wasn't my fault. Just had greedy business partners who tried to swing the scale in their favor. I hope there are no hard feelings. I'm going to set the money down here on the ground. We are going to put the wheels down on the auto trailer and then when you are comfortable with the money in the bag, just flash your lights and release the hitch. We'll do the rest. Then you can take off. By the way, is your friend there okay?"

A surge of panic suddenly hit Bryson like a kick in the gut when he realized that Marisa had gone off to the restroom and was not back yet. He scanned the area around the block building but couldn't see her. He looked over to ask Jack to go look for her, but Jack had his eyes closed and was obviously in no shape to help.

Fritz turned and waved at the driver of the Kenworth, directing him to head toward them. Showdown time had come.

*\*\**

Marisa had no intention of going into that stinky and poorly lit restroom. Once she disappeared behind the shadow of the building, she headed around the perimeter of the parking lot, ducking behind an occasional boat trailer and a couple of motor homes, neither of which had lights on or any sign of occupancy. The plan in her mind had one goal and one goal only: disable the SUVs. For a suburban housewife who had raised five normal kids and kept a busy doctor healthy and happy for forty years, Marisa was about to transform her everyday housewife life into an entire new persona.

She thought about what she was about to do. Right now the priority was to get the three of them safely and permanently away from this bizarre situation. She had never been afraid of spiders, which was a good thing as she ducked under cobweb-strung trees behind the two SUVs. She was afraid of snakes but hadn't been reminded that there were many types of the critters slithering through the area she had just traversed. Thankfully, she had also not been reminded that the Intercoastal Waterway was literally crawling with alligators.

Marisa crept up behind the black Suburban first and saw no one inside. She bent down by the front tire, and with a quick stroke, sliced the valve stem off of the wheel. The hiss of extruding air broke the stillness of the night but was almost immediately covered by the sound of a big truck engine. She snuck between the front bumper of the Suburban and the other SUV. It looked like a foreign model to her, maybe a Porsche or Land Rover. Wasting no time, she amputated the valve stems on two of the foreign car's wheels and then went back to the Suburban and took off another stem. It was then that she smelled the cigarette smoke and saw a man leaning against the front of the smaller SUV, watching the proceedings in the middle of the lot.

As the big Kenworth started inching toward Big Blue and the boat-launching ramp, Marisa dashed right up behind the moving semi and walked along its blind shadowed side until she was even with the restrooms, where she stepped into another shadow. She counted to ten and then ran out and around Big Blue to the passenger side and hammered on the door for Jack to let her in.

"Where have you been?" Bryson asked, sounding relieved that she was safely back inside.

She didn't answer but crawled into the sleeper cabin, having to crawl over Jack's lap to get there. She slipped the box cutter back into the drawer and then popped her head out from the curtains.

"Jack, why don't you go in the back and lie down. Marisa will help me up here," Bryson ordered. "Marisa, I need you to get out of the cab and go get the bag with the money in it."

"You can't be serious! We don't need their money. Just unhook the trailer and let's get the heck out of here. Let them keep their filthy money. You don't even know if there *is* any money or if it is stolen or even counterfeit."

"Sweetheart, it's the principle of it. If I don't get paid, they are going to think that we are at fault for all the crazy things that have happened."

"Bryson, are you out of your mind? You are exhausted, injured, sleep- and nutrition-deprived and you are facing at least four people who would kill all of us for a Yugo, let alone a truckload of Ferraris. And now you want to prove a principle?"

"Okay, I see your point. You just stay here in the truck and I'll get out and block the tires then . . . "

"Bryson, you are not getting out. Pull the trailer up to the middle of the parking lot where it is flat and then release the thingamajig or hydromagnate . . . whatever you release and drive us out of here."

"Marisa, you don't get it. If I just pull away, the front of the trailer will fall flat on the ground. It is a good idea, however, to pull it back up on level ground."

Bryson yelled out the window to Fritz that he was moving the trailer to a flatter place. Fritz rushed over and picked up the bag then walked around to Marisa's side of the truck, still carrying the gym bag with the supposed money. Marisa put her window down a couple of inches, standing up to reach the opening and spoke to him.

"Hi, I'm the doctor's wife. We don't want anything to damage your precious cars so my husband is going to drive the truck out into the parking lot where it is nice and flat. You can do whatever you do to put the front trailer wheels down and then we are going to leave. You look like a real honest person, so if we get up where it is flat and the trailer is safe, I'll expect you to hand me the bag and then, like I said, we will leave and you can do whatever you need to and get your precious little cars to the little show or the little parade or wherever you need them."

"Tell your husband that we need a key for the padlock," Fritz said.

"Well, he can't get it right now because it is on the key ring with the car keys . . . I mean the truck keys. When we stop and have the bag and you have your little wheels down, then we'll give you the keys. Fair enough? Incidentally, I have my cell phone on speed dial to 911. If you do anything except what you agreed to, I'm punching the button. You've heard how we women like to take over in times of stress . . . sort of like backseat driving . . . well now you are dealing with me. I normally don't like to call people derogatory names but I've saved up a couple of choice anatomical ones just for you and your friends. If you do what I ask you to do, I'll erase them from my mind."

Fritz held out his hand to get her attention. "You don't need to move your truck. Just don't release the brakes until we get the trailer wheels down and blocks behind the wheels."

"We better move it anyway. I think some of those hoses just came loose, all by themselves."

Bryson was amazed and startled at her assertiveness and outright takeover of control. He sank back in the driver's seat and let out a deep breath, which it seemed he had been holding forever. He put the truck in gear and honked the horn. The Kenworth tractor had made a wide turn and was now facing the same direction as Big Blue, apparently ready to pull in to hitch up the trailer the second Bryson released his hitch and pulled away.

Marisa demanded the money and had negotiated a modicum of safe passage for them. She still hadn't shared what else she had done to prevent Fritz and his buddies from following them.

The next five minutes flew by as the mystery men appeared out of the dark to manually put down the parking wheels on the trailer. Fritz, to Marisa's surprise, then stepped up on the running board and tried to pass the green nylon bag through the window opening to her. She had to open the window a bit wider for the bag to fit through, then immediately closed it up tight. She asked Bryson to turn on a dome light then peeked inside the bag. She was again surprised that it was full of small bundles of hundred dollar bills. She reached over to the console and picked up a round key ring holding the two brass keys to the trailer's padlock. She inched down the window just enough to fit the key ring and handed them out the window to Fritz.

Bryson didn't even wait for the man to step off the running board before he had the truck in gear and rolling toward the highway entrance. He didn't look back, but Marisa on the other hand couldn't contain her curiosity, and at one point even crawled across Bryson's lap to get a view of the parking lot behind them.

"Wait until they get ready to leave," Marisa muttered. "They are going to be in for the surprise of their lives."

She crawled back into her seat and fastened the seat belt for the first time all night then said, "Take me home, James," and turned to give her husband a big Cheshire cat grin.

*** 

Bryson had forgotten how different the truck drove without a twenty-thousand-pound trailer behind it. The truck's speed and agility quickly put a sizable distance between them.

They were two or three miles from the boat launch when they were finally forced to stop for a red light. Bryson and Marisa looked at one another. The slightest twinge of a smile began in the corner of Bryson's mouth.

"What did you do?" A twinkle started in his eyes and grew into a curious grin.

"How fast can somebody change two flat tires on a Suburban?"

"You can't be serious? You let the air out of a tire on their Suburban?"

Marisa held up her delicate and previously well-manicured hand. Her nails were scraped and her index fingernail was shattered and split. She unfolded her hand, revealing the four valve stems.

"One would think that for all the money one pays for an SUV these days, they would put stronger valve stems on the tires. Those things cut through like a soft piece of cheese."

The red light turned green and Bryson accelerated, checking his rearview mirrors.

"They won't be close behind," said Marisa. "Also, you might be interested to know that Jack stuffed a half-melted Snickers into the main brake hose fitting. I'll bet it takes them a while to get that out."

They both chuckled, then laughed uncontrollably.

"What's so funny up here?" Jack said as he stuck his bandaged head through the curtain. "You two make it hard for a guy to get a decent nap."

# Chapter Twenty-Four
## LUXURIES AT LAST

The signs for the Breakers Hotel and Spa were nearly every two blocks as they drove east toward the ocean. Bryson made a drive-by at the hotel's grand entrance the first time, not pulling into the covered portico with its crystal chandeliers and livered bellhops. Instead, he drove to a parking lot behind a row of nearby shops and stopped and asked a security guard if it would be possible to leave the truck there overnight. A crisp hundred-dollar bill sealed the deal.

"I'll be back in ten minutes," he told the man.

He made a second circle in front of the hotel but this time stopped in the outer drive and unloaded Marisa's three bags along with his and Jack's duffel bags. A smaller green sports bag joined the pile. A doorman loaded the gear onto a shiny brass trolley and then assisted Bryson as he helped Jack down from the truck. A wheelchair appeared through the massive entrance doors for Jack. After confirming that Jenny had checked them in, Bryson tipped the doorman. He climbed back into the truck and pulled away, toward the hidden parking lot.

**\*\*\***

As Marisa checked the house phone for Jenny's room, she overheard a diamond-encrusted woman with silver-blonde hair and skin that looked like beef jerky say to a man wearing a light purple dinner jacket with a pink-and-white striped silk shirt. "Now I've seen everything at this place, Winston. First the police and ambulances surround the place and now they have turned it into a truck driver's nursing home."

Marisa tried but was unable to restrain herself, so she

turned to the couple and asked, in a faux West Tennessee accent, "'Scuse me, little lady, y'all wouldn't happen to know the phone number for the closest Popeye's fried chicken place, would you? We're just starving and wanted to fetch in something really fancy for dinner. We're hoping they have them tater-tots on special."

"You're finally here? Where is Jack?" Jenny chimed in over the phone.

"What's the room number? We'll be right up."

Marisa wrote the room numbers on the palm of her hand and motioned for a bellman to follow her with the luggage trolley. She pushed the wheelchair herself in spite of a second bellman trying to relieve her of the job. The parade rolled toward the elevator, drawing attention from passers-by.

The reunion at the bedroom door was bittersweet. It took Jenny only one quick minute to realize just how injured and impaired Jack really was. At first she was angry that Bryson hadn't taken him to the hospital again, but then Jack told her to lighten up and to just get him in a hot bathtub and to order them all some food. Uninhibited, he stood up from the wheelchair and was peeling off the smelly, bloodstained scrub clothes as he moved toward the bathroom.

"You might be surprised how well I clean up, darling. I might even get a little frisky once I get cleaned up and load some calories on board," he said, smiling over his shoulder at Jenny and winking at Marisa.

The bellman opened the adjoining room's door for Marisa, and without asking, brought her a bucket of ice. Remembering that Bryson didn't know the room number, she opened her door again to tell the man to send Bryson up to the room.

Marisa opened her carry-on and laid out a few of her essential toiletries, then freshened up. She was shocked at her appearance. The last twelve hours had really taken a toll on her hair, face and body. It made her pause to wonder just how completely wiped out her husband must feel. No sleep, no decent food, maximum stress and constant tension . . . just like a night on call in Labor and Delivery, she remembered.

She had never understood how Bryson had been able to get out of a warm bed in the middle of a cold night, get dressed, drive to the hospital and then perform a life-and-death surgery or difficult delivery where one slight error in judgment could mean the difference between a healthy or a damaged baby.

She could hear bathwater running and Jenny and Jack talking in the adjoining room. The double doors between the rooms were still both open a crack. Jack must have been in the tub because there was an echo and Jenny was raising her voice a bit to be heard over the running water.

Maybe she would run the water into the Jacuzzi tub for Bryson. She was tempted to call room service for something scrumptious to eat, but didn't want to tie up the phone until Bryson knew the room number. She started the bathwater, adding the hotel's foaming bath gel, then sat down on the edge of the bed and waited.

**✳✳✳**

Bryson thought he had found the perfect place to park Big Blue and was just climbing down from the running board when a tiny Cuban man wearing a security guard uniform and a gun belt yelled at him from across the parking lot. This guy wasn't the one he had bribed less than ten minutes ago.

"*No, en posible, señor,*" said the man in a rapid Spanish.

"I don't speak Spanish," Bryson said, hoping the man would give him a break and let him leave the truck. He had already paid off one guard. He even pulled out his wallet again and took out a real twenty-dollar bill, but the little Cuban waved him off as if insulted.

Bryson was too tired to argue, so he pressed the FOB to reopen the truck door. Just as he did so, a black Suburban turned the corner on the main street, screeching tires as it headed toward the hotel entrance. The sight was way too frightening for Bryson to ignore. He reached in the back pocket of his scrubs and pulled out one of the crumpled hundred dollar bills and stuck it in the Cuban's hand.

"Guard the truck. I will be back and move it before they open up in the morning." He opened the pass-through door into the sleeper cab and grabbed the oil rag with its solid steel content, slammed the door and half ran, half hobbled toward the hotel.

Bryson dodged cars and bushes until he had a good view of the front of the hotel lobby. It was Fritz for sure, standing at the bellman's desk, peeling greenbacks off a thick roll to get the information he wanted. Bryson couldn't see anyone else with him. The Suburban stood empty with its warning lights flashing.

There was no way to get into the main part of the hotel without passing through the lobby, but Bryson had an ace up his sleeve. He had Marisa's cell phone in his pocket and it had Jenny's number on the speed dial. He stepped into a lighted corridor and scrolled through a long list of familiar names until he found it. Green button twice . . . he remembered. To his surprise, it was Marisa that answered the phone.

"Where are you? I've got your hot water running in the double tub and I'm ready to order two New York strips with salads and onion rings. You are going to love this room. Remember the huge flat screen TV you said you were going to buy once you got time to watch anything but the news? Well, there is one that comes out of a table at the foot of the bed. You may never want to leave here."

"I need to talk to Jenny," Bryson said, having been as patient as he could possibly be while she appraised the hotel room.

"What for? I'm pretty sure she is in the tub with Jack. There is an open door between the rooms so I could take her the phone."

"No, just go to the bathroom door and ask if there is a back way up to the room. What's the room number?"

"We are in 1604. Jenny is in 1606; just a second."

Bryson could hear Marisa talking and Jenny's voice in the background. He watched Fritz talk to the bellman and then write something on a pad of paper. He passed the guy money and they shook hands. This was not getting any better.

"Bryson, there is an entrance off the pool area with its own elevator. The pool is on the north side of the building. I can look down and see it. Why? What's going on?"

"Listen. Do not open the door for anyone, even room service, until I get there. I'll knock five times and whistle the Hell song. Trust me, this is very important."

✳✳✳

Bryson stayed back in the shadows while he made his next call. He dialed 911 and waited for the operator to pick up. It only took one ring.

"Emergency operator, can I help you?"

"Yes, thank you, a woman here at the Breakers just asked me to call for her. Some tall white guy just knocked her down and stole her purse. She says he groped her too. She just ran after the guy. He's wearing a gold Forty-Niners T-shirt. He is maybe six feet tall and has reddish-brown hair and cowboy boots. I think I see him in the hotel lobby."

"Please stay where you are and do not try to intervene," the bossy woman's voice commanded.

"Lady, I have to leave. You guys can take over." Bryson hung up the phone and moved quickly around the main building toward the pool. To get into the pool area there was a gate that only opened outward and had a key card box alongside. One of the few lucky charms of Bryson's day brought a boy carrying a long water rifle. The kid slung the gate open in front of Bryson and dashed by.

Bryson saw the poolside elevator and rushed in that direction. Punching the button multiple times—as if that would make it come any faster—he heard the distant sound of a siren. The doors opened, unloading two more young kids toting Uzi-like water guns. *The guns nowadays are way cooler than when I was a kid*, Bryson thought. He almost missed the elevator thinking about water guns. His brain was definitely closing down for the night.

Bryson saw the police guard in the next room and breathed a sigh of relief. The man was on his radio and ignored Bryson.

He gave the five knocks on the door but didn't have time to do the whistle before Marisa had the door open and pulled him inside the room.

"Quick, come and look at this," she said, tugging on the sleeve of the borrowed scrub tops.

Bryson followed her to the window on the opposite side of the bed and looked down at the pool area. Three security guys and two policemen were encircling a man who was spread eagle on the grass near the pool. Squinting hard, Bryson could make out the word NINERS splayed across the back of the man's shirt.

"Isn't that the guy from the boat dock parking lot?" Marisa asked. "How could he have possibly gotten here so fast?"

Bryson shrugged and staggered to the bed. He sat on the edge and pried off one of his Wellington boots using the opposite foot. Before Marisa had time to turn back the Chanel print bedspread and move the decorator pillows, he had boosted his whole body onto the bed.

"Whatever it was you did to get rid of that creep sure worked. If you think our story back at the boat dock was something, wait until we get the long version of Jenny's double kidnapping and then her takedown of the guy right there on the pool deck."

She was still watching out the window as Fritz was cuffed, pulled up to his feet and then marched out of sight. "I ordered after you called. I started to fill the tub for you but shut it off when you called. Do you want to eat first or soak in the tub? Bryson?"

She looked toward her husband for an answer but didn't get one. Bryson was sound asleep, his mind and body in complete shutdown. The slow rise and fall of his chest and the rosy color of his cheeks and nose were the only signs of life.

The food arrived half an hour later. Marisa told the man to leave it by the door and that she would get it in a minute. She slipped off the terry cloth robe from the hotel closet and crawled up on the bed next to Bryson, draping the robe over both of their feet. It was morning before she even noticed that she had left all the lights on.

✻✻✻

"Are you two alive in there?" Jack stood in the doorway without his gauze head dressing. He was scrubbed, rested, fed, and decked out in slacks and a silk shirt, which Jenny had proudly splurged on when she was at the hotel in Miami.

Bryson and Marisa lifted their heads off the pillows and stared at him. Marisa was wrapped in the bedspread, but Bryson was still on the top of it wearing his bloody scrubs. He had one sock on and the other was missing. He hadn't showered or shaved for what seemed like days.

"You look like a Havana pimp," Bryson said, slowly lowering his head back onto the pillow.

"Thanks. That's the sweetest thing you have ever said to me. I'm just guessing but I would bet that you two need a few more minutes before you'll be joining us for the breakfast buffet. Jenny is on the phone. When she stops talking to her sister, we'll head down to the restaurant patio and get the four of us a table."

The door clicked closed behind Jack. Bryson and Marisa turned to face each other. "I can't remember anything since I walked in the door last night," Bryson said. "Did you eat our dinner?"

She shook her head as she crawled off the bed and headed toward the bathroom. "Get up and take a shower," she said as she turned the corner. "I'm starving; let's go to breakfast."

Bryson was five minutes into a scalding hot shower when it occurred to him that the only clothes he had were probably in the truck. They had unloaded Marisa and Jack's bags but he had intended to pick out a few things from the pile of rumpled clothes. He couldn't remember. That left him with dirty underwear and a set of hospital scrubs that were anything but clean and fresh. What the heck, he would just wear his scrubs to breakfast. They could find a store later to buy something better.

# Chapter Twenty-Five

# THE TAKE

When Bryson emerged from the steamy bathroom, Marisa was standing over an ironing board, putting the final touches on a pair of golf shorts and an island-style shirt. There on the floor beside her was his travel bag. They had unloaded it from the truck with the other bags after all.

Next to the bag on the floor sat a small cardboard box and a stack of bundled paper; it was the money from the back of the Ferrari. The small green bag Marisa had taken from the boat ramp lay next to it.

"You didn't tell me how well trucking paid," Marisa said. "Maybe I wouldn't have complained so much. Just so you know, the green bag has twenty-thousand dollars in it. This, however," she said pointing to the stack on the floor with her sandal clad foot, "is about three hundred thousand dollars. No wonder those guys were so anxious to get their hands on the trailer."

"I didn't have time to tell you the whole story last night but . . ."

"Get dressed," she said throwing him a pair of briefs, "I want to hear Jack's and your story at the same time. Jenny has a tale of her own to tell. We really ought to hire a court reporter to take notes, or maybe even a newspaper reporter. I'm sure that eventually we'll need to tell the story to someone with a law degree."

Marisa paused before they left the room, gathered up the scattered money and carried it to the closet where she placed it in the electronic safe using her favorite code.

*\*\*\**

Shaved, showered and dressed appropriately, the couples met downstairs at the hotel restaurant on the patio that overlooked the pool and luxurious grounds with its mani-cured trees and hedges and vast beds of late spring flowers. Beyond the gardens lay the sparkling blue Atlantic ocean. A scattering of sail and power boats floated on the horizon.

Jenny led off with her story. She told her tale of assault, near abduction and escape with the help of the football player.

Jack tried to explain the need for the change in location from the original hotel in Miami but was waved off by Jenny as she and Marisa wanted to hear the various stories of the attempted hijacking in Arizona and the real hijacking in northern Florida.

Food was ordered and the men proceeded with their sto-ries, which were often interrupted by the ladies wanting more detail or questioning if there wasn't some embellish-ing of the stories taking place.

Marisa finally came forth, to the amazement of the oth-ers, with her story of sneaking around the dimly lit parking lot and amputating the valve stems of the bad guys' tires. Jokes were shared and updates of everyone's varied injuries, aches and pains were discussed. The waiter interrupted the animated conversation arriving with large plates of steam-ing food. The four started into their breakfasts; they were all starved. After a pause in their brisk eating, Marisa turned to Jenny.

"My husband would like to apologize to you and Jack for all the trouble you've had to go through because of him and his truck."

"What are you talking about?" Bryson said, throwing his head and shoulders back in a defiant manner. "I will do no such thing. Jack and I have had a fantastic adventure, the first of many to come. We fully expect the two of you ladies to join us for the entire length of our next trip. Matter of fact, I'm going to call the freight broker as soon as we have finished breakfast to find out if he has any special transport needs; maybe, a container full of kidnapped Chinese children or a truckload of stolen nuclear missiles. But Jenny, I will apologize for one thing . . . We are truly sorry that you didn't get to ride in the truck with us last night as we evaded the Florida Mafia and the police."

\*\*\*

"You have got to be kidding me," Jack said.

The other three turned to see the object of his concern. There, less than fifty feet away stood two men; one was Fritz.

"That's the blond guy who broke into my room in Miami. The same jerk who tried to kidnap me but went for a swim instead," Jenny said.

The two men were glaring at the couples' table. Even though both men had been detained the night before, right there on the Breakers' property, here they were back to cause more trouble.

While Blondie stayed by the hostess podium, Fritz brazenly walked toward the couples. Bryson quickly stood and walked toward him, nodding at an area of empty tables off in an alcove away from the windows. Fritz took the hint and veered off to join Bryson.

"I thought we saw the last of you last night," Bryson stated, his head held high and his voice firm.

"When we opened the auto trailer last night there seemed to be a few things missing. Most important were some packages belonging to the guy standing by the hostess. He has nothing to do with the cars but trust me, he is very well connected and he is very mad. He wants his property back."

"Whatever was in the trailer is what you got back. If the cars are a little worse for wear, take it up with the guy who hijacked the truck then left my partner for dead. By the way, your friend over there by the door is going to do some hard prison time when Ms. Glen gets done filing all of her complaints. Sexual assault, breaking and entering, kidnapping, plus associating with idiots like you."

"Here is the deal," Fritz said, glancing at the other parties in the room. "My associate seemed to have left a package of important papers in one of the Ferraris. The items are missing. Why they were even put there and who took them, I don't know and really don't care. I just want him out of both of our lives. If he gets those papers back this morning, he will catch the next plane to Vegas and you'll never see him again. If not, then he can be a very dangerous man to me and to the four of you."

Bryson looked him firmly in the eyes and lied. "I haven't a clue what you are even talking about. All we know is that my truck and your whole load of cars were followed the entire way here and that several attempts were made to get into the trailer. I tried to notify you of the problems as they occurred, but you were too busy to return my calls. The padlocks were cut several times. Somebody did finally get inside and whatever they took or broke or scratched is not our fault. So, the bottom line here is for you to tell your buddy over there to leave now and not show his face again, or I will call the police."

"You don't get it, Doc. This isn't some guy who is going to walk away. He wants his packages and he wants them now. We know they aren't in your blue truck cab . . . sorry about the window, by the way. If it's any consolation, your window will cost a tenth of what the Ferrari window will cost me." He gave Bryson a smirk. "Your threats of calling the police are only going to waste the rest of a nice day at the beach for your wives. I paid you for the transport so help me here and help yourself as well. Go to your room or wherever you have the packages and bring them down to the bellman's desk out front. We'll be waiting in a black Suburban, maybe you'll recognize it. The tires and wheels don't quite match."

Bryson had had enough. He walked away from Fritz, heading straight for Blondie. He marched past him, brushing against his shoulder, and then at the last second, turned and slapped the startled man on the face with the flat of his hand. The sharp sound brought the chatter and clatter of the room to immediate silence. With a second motion smooth as a Las Vegas card dealer, Bryson flicked his left index finger into the man's right eye.

Without even breaking stride, Bryson continued into the lobby, heading directly toward the front desk. Cutting in line, Bryson hammered his fist down on the marble countertop to get the desk manager's attention.

"Do you know that there is a pickpocket in the dining room? He just tried to steal my wallet and he assaulted me. I think he is the same man that the police arrested here last night. What kind of habitat for criminals do you manage here?"

The startled manager immediately picked up the phone and spoke into the receiver. In less than twenty seconds, Bryson saw three uniformed security men come out of a door behind the check-in desk and dash toward the dining room. Bryson followed right behind them.

∗∗∗

Entering the dining room, Bryson encountered a scene of pandemonium.

On the opposite side of the dining room, Blondie was standing behind Jack, Jenny and Marisa. He was pointing a small automatic pistol at Jenny's head. He was screaming at the top of his lungs for her to give him the bundles of money or he would shoot all three of them. The security men spread out around the room, but none of them carried a weapon more threatening than a can of mace. Bryson surveyed the rest of the room, searching for Fritz, but he was nowhere in sight.

The hero of the moment turned out to be a newly hired teenage busboy. He was doing a great job keeping the heavy tray balanced over his right shoulder until he rounded the corner from behind a carved Corinthian pillar and ran straight into the back of Blondie.

Glasses, plates and cups hit the stone floor and exploded into sharp, irregular weapons. When the startled Blondie stepped back to gain his balance, he stepped in the middle of a half-eaten plate of Bananas Foster, which caused his left foot to shoot out from under him. That was all gravity needed to take over. It yanked him instantly to the glass-strewn floor like a giant vacuum cleaner sucking down a tuft of feathers. Reaching out to break his fall, the palms of both his hands slapped onto shards of shattered crystal. The small pistol slid across the floor. That was the end of the fight.

The security guards had their mace cans drawn and probably would have sprayed the man had he not rolled over, leaving only his back exposed. Yelling and shouting ensued, causing most of the remaining breakfast guests to scramble for the exit, meals uneaten and checks unpaid.

"Does anybody know this man?" the senior guard asked the remaining onlookers.

Jack took Jenny by the arm and led her toward a veranda door. Marisa and Bryson headed for the main entrance, not even looking back.

"This is ridiculous," Bryson said as they walked slowly through the lobby. "We're never going to get anything to eat."

Marisa looked at him and laughed. "As though that is the worst of our problems?"

∗∗∗

"What sort of shape do you think my truck is going to be in?" Bryson said out loud to himself as he walked the two blocks to the parking lot where he had left Big Blue the night before. Turning the corner leading into the parking area behind a group of boutique shops, he saw his truck shining in the mid-morning sun. There was no one around it, and very few cars were in the parking lot. He had imagined all sorts of damage and at the minimum a shattered window or two. He couldn't believe his eyes as he did a walk-around. There wasn't a scratch on the thing. No broken windows, no sign of forced entry and not even a flat tire. They hadn't found the truck. That was the only explanation. Fritz had been bluffing.

"Maybe—just maybe—they are gone from our lives," he later explained to Marisa and Jack. They were standing alongside Big Blue in the circle drive in front of the hotel. The bellman was loading Jenny's many bags into the storage area behind the sleeper cabin.

She seemed a little put out that there was dust in the storage area but Jack gave her a "settle down" look and she swallowed hard and instructed the bellman appropriately. There was a curious crowd of hotel guests watching the loading and impending departure of "the truckers." Both Jenny and Marisa had become fifteen-minute stars of the hotel staff after the gun assault. The hotel manager had come to offer apologies and to assure them that their meals and stay at the Breakers would be complimentary.

Bryson fired up the engine, and with a friendly wave to the hotel staff and a blast of the air horn, Big Blue headed out to the long entry drive.

"Where to, big boy?" Marisa said, sticking her head out from between the curtains.

"What did you do with the green bag and the paper bundles?" Bryson asked.

"They're right here. What do you say we divide the loot up four ways? That way you men won't be worrying about us blowing your share on fancy clothes."

"Don't ask me," Bryson said. "Jack found the bundles. It's his to spend or share however he sees fit."

"What about it, Jack?" Marisa asked. "Surely you're not going to keep it all for yourself?"

"What in the world are you three talking about?" Jenny asked.

Marisa carefully unwrapped the edge of one of the paper bundles and teased out five or six crisp hundred-dollar bills, handing them to Jenny. "Jack found this in one of the cars the boys hauled."

Jenny took the paper money and looked at each bill with an intense interest but less excitement than any of them had expected. "Don't any of you know that it is a federal crime to hold or transport counterfeit money? This stuff looks pretty good, but it's nothing that a quality laser jet copier couldn't reproduce if one had the right paper. Remember? I worked at the bank for three years during the farm's lean years. The FBI gave us refresher courses every year on the recognition of funny money and this is definitely funny money."

Jack turned sideways in his chair to face his wife. "There was a lot more of the stuff where this came from. The bundles had slid under a blanket or piece of carpet. When I woke up, there were loose bills scattered all over the back of the trailer, and those paper-wrapped bundles were in the back of the Ferrari."

"When I first looked into the car there were twenty or more of the packages," Bryson added.

"Well, if we don't all want to go to prison for a very long time, we need to either get rid of this stuff or go to the nearest FBI office and turn it in. So is this what all of your cross-country escapades and all the assaults and scares were about, or was it really the cars?" Jenny said.

No one spoke for a while, then Marisa presented her hypothesis. "What if your friendly exotic auto dealer was legitimate and really needed to get those six cars across the country to the car show or auction or whatever he needed them here for? Then, what if one of the previous owners had stashed the money in the cars because he needed a safe way to get the money out of Nevada?"

"The two knew each other. I'm sure the blond guy at breakfast helped load the cars into the van in Reno," said Bryson.

"So you guys picked up a trailer with six cars. Each car is worth at least half a million dollars, right?" Marisa went on. "But one or two of the cars are hiding places for some type of contraband. The last article I read would call those cars mules . . . and you two asses . . . for an unknown, but probably large amount, of funny money and whatever else they might have stashed in them."

"Who is to say that all six of the cars weren't loaded with something highly illegal?" Jenny said. "Drugs, gemstones, stolen art? And why hire a novice trucker, like you, Bryson, to haul the Holy Grail of exotic cars across country? Because you were a retired doctor enamored with truck driving and better still you were going to travel with a bored farmer sidekick! Every other veteran trucker would have inspected his load and known something about who he was working for."

Only the throbbing of the diesel engine and the hum of the tires kept the silence from being overpowered as the four of them pondered the situation. They all finally agreed that the threat from Blondie was history. Fritz had his trailer and the cars though they were a little worse for wear. Still, he was the catalyst who had put the deal together and he seemed to be familiar with most of the players, including some mystery third player who also wanted to repo the cars.

"My guess is, that as long as we have the money, we have a nest of hornets flying around our heads, maybe even the heads of our children," Jack said.

They turned onto the freeway, heading north toward Orlando and Jacksonville. The women had inched themselves into the front, Jenny sharing a third of Jack's passenger club chair and Marisa sitting, wedged between the seats, on one of her suitcases with a couple of pillows on top for padding.

"Everyone who tried to get into the back of the trailer must have had a hand in the deal," Bryson said. "There was that girl who caused the wreck in Carson City, then the person who cut the lock when we were eating at the ranch house. They had to be working with the girl in the hardware store."

"How about the Indians, who nearly shot us to steal the cars?" Jack added. "That kid with them last night looked a lot like the guy we saw near Winslow."

"Of course to me, all those Indians look alike," Bryson joked.

"All of you northern Scandinavian immigrants look alike too," chimed in the tan-skinned Jenny, "and don't ever forget it."

"Who hijacked the truck? It wasn't Blondie or the jerks we saw in the Mercedes who wanted us to follow them," Marisa added. "And who called me and threatened Madeline? How could they even know anything about her?"

Again, silence filled the cabin.

"The truck dealer!" Bryson and Jack said in chorus.

"That over-friendly guy in Bozeman. He was a nosey guy and a talker," Bryson added. "We spent time talking and visiting with the guy. We told him about our wives and families. He's the one who set up the transport deal with the car dealer in Reno in the first place."

"So where do we go from here? We can't keep the money and we can't go back to the police in any of these southern towns. They would love to throw us all in jail and the truck for that matter," Jack said.

"Let's go to Washington, D.C., and have a meeting with the real FBI," Jenny said.

Everyone looked at her like she had finally lost it, but as the silence in the cabin lengthened the plan started to make sense.

Jack had certainly suffered the most and should they give up the money, it would be he and Jenny who had the most to lose. Bryson turned to get a glimpse of his wife and when she smiled at him, the first smile he had seen in a while, he nodded in agreement.

"Can we stop at Jamestown and Williamsburg on the way? I've always wanted to go to Yorktown," Jack asked. "We drove right by all those Civil War sites in the South that I had hoped to visit."

Three of them looked at Jack and then all broke out in smiles.

"Then it's off to the J. Edgar Hoover Building we go," said Bryson.

Jack scooted Jenny over so he could reach the navigation controls and plugged in an address—1600 Pennsylvania Avenue, Washington, D.C.

# Chapter Twenty-Six

# THE FEDS

The further up the coast toward Washington, D.C. they got, the less attractive their idea of talking to the authorities became. How would they explain not calling the authorities immediately after the money was discovered? And why leave the scene of the crimes? And how many bogus hundred-dollar bills had Bryson handed out? Maybe they were the ones who would be in big trouble.

Late in the afternoon with the truck rolling smoothly along the freeway somewhere in South Carolina, Jack sat up from his cozy bed and announced that he just remembered that one of his cousin's boys, a kid who had worked on the farm a couple of summers for Jack, had joined the FBI and was living somewhere on the East Coast.

Jenny got on her phone and called an old friend in Idaho. Within twenty minutes Jack's phone rang and Preston was on the other end.

Preston was with the FBI and presently working in the Richmond office. After listening to a preview of Uncle Jack's story, Preston suggested that they all meet in Richmond, Virginia, late the next afternoon. He would make all the arrangements and would call them back.

For Bryson, it started to feel as though the weight of the world was being lifted from his shoulders.

"Hey, I've got a great idea," Bryson said in a loud voice. "The next time we need to stop for fuel we can find a good Southern home-cooking place and get us some fried chicken, or better still, a chicken fried steak."

The other three agreed on the idea of stopping for a hot meal.

"I could go for a crisp salad and a bowl of hot soup," Jenny replied. "But I know how you love to try the local cuisine, so I'm good for anything."

And then the rain began. This storm hit them by surprise. It started with a few invisible gusts of wind that rocked the truck, shaking Marisa out from the back. She popped her head out from behind the curtain. "Bryson, did you fall asleep?"

He didn't answer. He didn't have to. A sheet of wind-driven rain and hailstones smashed into the truck, dropping visibility to less than fifty feet. The noise alone sounded like machine gun fire; the buffeting of the wind gusts shook the six-thousand-pound Peterbilt tractor like a baby's rattle. Bryson's reaction time was a little slow, but he still managed to stop the truck just short of a line of cars slowing as the wall of icy water hit the line of traffic.

"What's up?" Jack said, poking his head through the curtains.

"Just some bad weather. I'll try to get a report on the radio. It doesn't look good for making that hotel in Raleigh in time for dinner." The traffic was at a standstill in both directions.

As they waited, listening to the XM weather broadcast and watching the sheets of rain and dramatic gusts of wind knock down tree branches and rock the cars and trucks around them, they were suddenly startled by the ringing of Bryson's cell phone.

"This is Dr. Bender," he answered in the tone of expectant concern, which he had used for the last thirty years of practice.

The voice on the other end of the phone was unfamiliar to Bryson. It was a man with a foreign accent.

"You don't know me but we have a common acquaintance, a certain automobile dealer in Nevada," the man said. "You have something that I need very badly, and I now in turn have something that I think you would want returned."

And then silence, followed by another voice. "Daddy? It's Madeline. There's a man here who says you are coming by the school to drop off a package."

It was a good thing that they were sitting still in congested traffic. Otherwise, Bryson never could have controlled the truck.

The stranger was immediately back on the phone and in a gentle voice suggested that Bryson change his direction. The man sounded as though he knew exactly where the truck was at the time. He even gave Bryson a couple of helpful directions to shorten the route to Fayetteville, where he demanded Bryson meet him.

"There is a Marriott hotel along the freeway just south of Fayetteville. We can have a happy little family reunion there at about ten tonight. Your lovely daughter is anxious to see you. Don't forget my little packages, and Dr. Bender, don't try anything cute. A close relative of mine just spent six hours in the Palm Beach emergency room having his hands sewn back together. I would hate to have your beautiful daughter here have the same experience with her face."

Then the phone went dead.

Bryson held the phone away from his head. He looked at his wife as tears welled up in his eyes.

"What is it?" Marisa demanded.

"They still want their money. And they have Madeline."

*** 

Raised voices and confused thoughts followed. As the rainstorm passed, so did the confusion. It was replaced with a determined and calculated plan. They would do as the voice on the phone asked, but they would not take the chance that everything would just turn out okay. They would insert their own set of factors into the equation.

"We have got to stop and eat and get fuel. Fayetteville is over six hours from here and he told you ten o'clock, correct?" Jack asked Bryson, who nodded a confirmation. "I want us to find a place close to the hotel he stipulated and drop the three of us off. There is no point in endangering our wives. You can take the money to the jerk, pick up Madeline and then meet us."

Bryson was experiencing the onset of a new major fatigue attack. His adrenaline from the call was wearing off and his having driven all day and the lack of nutritious food and stimulant drink all combined to leave him in a state of stupor.

"I agree with Jack," said Marisa, "except I will stay with you. There isn't room in the truck for five of us anyway. We'll find a hotel near the Marriott and drop off Jack and Jenny."

Jenny didn't comment. Bryson was surprised at Jack's opting out of the action. The problem was that he was too spent to argue. It was all he was going to be able to do to drive the truck the additional miles in rain and heavy traffic. They found a newer truck stop where there was a Wendy's and clean restrooms.

\*\*\*

Jack insisted on staying with the truck to do the fueling while the others washed up and got the food. The second they were out of view, Jack pulled out Jenny's cell phone and called his FBI nephew.

\*\*\*

"How can fast food taste so good going down and then almost immediately make my stomach ache? Kids eat this crap all the time and it doesn't seem to bother them," Jack said.

"It's the onions and the enzymes they put in the stuff that attacks our stomachs. Kids' digestive systems could dissolve nails. Our gall bladders get old and flabby and can't handle anything greasy or spicy."

"Don't believe a word of the dribble he's telling you," Marisa interjected. "He makes up his medical facts as the occasions arise."

For the next few hours Jack insisted that he was fine to do the driving while Bryson lie down on the bed. It took only moments before the doctor was snoring. Marisa and Jenny shared the passenger seat, helping Jack navigate. The miles flew by as the weather got better and the traffic thinned out.

By late in the afternoon Bryson was back behind the wheel as they crossed the state line into North Carolina. There had been no word from Madeline's abductor nor had the four of them dared talk about any possible outcome but a good one. Parting with the money seemed like an easy thing to do.

They pulled off the Interstate onto an access road where they immediately saw the sign for the Marriott where they were supposed to meet the mystery caller and Madeline. A second sign indicated a Hyatt close by.

Jack was taking a second turn at the wheel and seeing the sign, put on the turn signal and slowed near a long flower-lined Hyatt entrance. Rather than turning into the driveway he came to a complete stop. He set the brake and turned on the emergency flasher.

Bryson emerged from the sleeper cabin, rubbing his eyes and taking in the surroundings. "Are you getting out here?" Bryson asked Jack.

"The three of us are," Jack answered, nodding toward the women.

Marisa started to protest but was cut off by Jack raising his hand. "Listen to me for one second. I called my nephew again, and he is having FBI agents stake out the hotel. Kidnapping is a federal crime. All Bryson has to do is drive the truck into the lobby area and identify Madeline and the creeps that are holding her. The FBI will take over from there. Preston insisted that the three of us stay out of the way. I just saw two unmarked government cars pull around us and drive toward the Marriott. Get your purses and carry-on bags and we will go check into the hotel. Bryson, you are supposed to stop in the entrance area and then just sit in the truck until someone talks to you. Do you have your cell phone?"

The three looked at Jack like he had lost his marbles, but slowly realized that he was the only one who had been thinking rationally. They shrugged and followed his instructions. Five minutes later, three of them paraded down a long sidewalk toward the Hyatt entrance. Bryson watched them go and then crawled back into the sleeper cab. He fumbled in the dark to find the correct drawer until his hand found the oil rag with its metallic content. He climbed back into the driver's seat, tucking the gun into a map pocket alongside the seat. He released the brakes and revved up the engine. He slid the gearshift knob into first and let out the clutch. The time was ten o'clock.

\*\*\*

The Marriott parking lot was cut from a virgin forest of oaks and sumacs, leaving many of the largest and most beautiful trees in place. Winding paths meandered around vast flower beds, which trailed off into the dark back toward the Hyatt next door. Bryson had to guide the truck around and through smaller parking areas to get to a space close enough to the massive hotel entrance to be able to see it and still not raise the ire of the hotel security people. In spite of the promise of help from their FBI contact, Bryson was still very nervous. His last short nap left him feeling more in control, and hopefully, able to think quickly.

He parked the truck and shut down the engine, turning off all the lights as the diesel clattered and chugged to a halt. Bryson had been told to sit tight in the truck until given further instructions. The rain had stopped and the truck windows were down, letting the cool night breeze drift through the stuffy cab. Mixed in the breeze was the odor of stale clothes, diesel fuel, traces of the ladies' perfumes and shampoos mixed with the humid smell of flowers and musty grass clippings. An occasional car rolled by on the main road and the sound of frogs and crickets could be heard in the distance.

Patience had never been one of Bryson's virtues. His hand kept slipping into the seat side pocket, feeling for the gun; his head kept turning from side to side at each tiny sound. There were many cars in the parking lot but none appeared occupied. A taxi came down the lane driving too fast for the narrow pathways. It screeched around the corner, slamming on its brakes just in time to avoid hitting the front fender of Big Blue.

The driver screamed an obscenity, blaming the truck for blocking his right of way. As the taxi backed away then shot forward, leaving a pathetic single trail of burned rubber, Bryson felt a stirring at the passenger window. He turned to face the extended arm of a man pointing a shiny silver pistol. The old hawk-nosed man had a nasty grin on his bearded face. He was much older than Bryson had expected. He was standing on the running board leaning into the window, his approach having been covered by the taxi's distracting arrival.

"You must be the good doctor," the man said in a sarcastic tone. His accent was Germanic.

"I want to see my daughter," Bryson answered in a firm but calm tone.

"Not to worry, my friend. She is nearby and will be pleased to see you as well. Now if you would be so kind as to place the packages, which you have been safely holding for me on the passenger seat, then sit back down and fasten your seat belt, I will signal and my colleague will bring your daughter around to the front of the truck. It is a very simple request so please, don't make it difficult."

Bryson studied the man's face. There were no other sounds, nor were there signs of other people around, leaving him with the sense that there was no real option but to do as he was told. He crawled out of the seat and into the back. Marisa had transferred all the paper bundles of money into the green nylon gym bag Fritz had given them. She had kept the twenty-thousand dollars of genuine money received from Fritz safely stashed in her rolling carry-on. Bryson heard the passenger door open and noticed the dome lights come on. By the time he returned from the sleeper cabin, the door was wide open and the man was standing on the ground. He still held the gun pointed in Bryson's direction.

"Oh how nice. You have put it in a handy carrying bag. Now just put it on the seat and sit back down."

Bryson sat on the inside edge of the driver's seat, holding the bag between himself and the open passenger door. "Until I see that my daughter is safe, I'm not moving again."

"You have no option, Doctor. Either you do as I say, or I will simply shoot you and take the bag. I will keep your daughter to do with as I please. Perhaps she can help nurse my son's poor injured hands back to health with her soft, smooth skin."

Bryson could feel his pulse pounding in his temples. His blood pressure had to be at an all-time high but he couldn't concede his need to see Madeline before he handed over his only bargaining tool. He scanned the parking area for any sign of the FBI cars or men; he saw nothing. He slipped his hand into the side pocket of the seat and gripped the gun handle. The green bag hid his hand from view.

"Just let me see her. I don't want your damn counterfeit money. You can take it and be free to leave. Just let me see my daughter first!"

The man looked at him, thinking over the proposal and then he raised the gun, pointing it at Bryson.

"Wait, wait," Bryson murmured, clutching his chest with his left hand. "My chest! The pain is intense. I think I'm having a heart attack!"

He dropped the green bag on the floor of the truck near the gearshift lever, grabbing the gun with his right hand, all the time groaning as he slid to the floor between the truck's large seats. He brought the revolver around as he fell, sliding his right arm under the passenger seat and pointing the gun through the gap between the floor and the bottom of the motorized seat. He waited for the man to move into his line of sight and reach for the green bag.

Bryson snapped the gun safety off and waited. Then, he heard a strange sickening thud. He strained to see beneath the seat but saw only a slight shadow on the open door. The green bag hadn't moved and neither could Bryson. He was wedged between the seats with his right arm pinned under him, his injured shoulder searing with pain. The space between the seats was much narrower than his rushed planning had calculated. His right foot had snagged behind the back of the brake pedal and his left arm was stuck between his chest and the gearshift base. He knew that he could still pull the trigger but he had no target. The next sound he heard shot a chill through his entire body. The driver-side door opened.

"Don't move! I'll come around to help you," came a voice, but it was not the European's.

His mind was playing tricks on him. It sounded like Jack's voice, but he knew it couldn't be. He listened and then heard footsteps on the pavement along the passenger side of the truck. There was a slight movement and then he saw an arm reach up for the assist bar and felt the movement of the truck as a man stepped onto the running board. He squinted to get a direction to fire, but tears had welled up in his eyes from the dust on the floorboard and the excruciating pain in his shoulder. Bryson blinked several times to clear his vision. He had a partial shot, just inches from the person's leg but figured he would have just one clear shot so he waited for the man to step down.

"What in the heck are you doing lying on the floor?" came Jack's voice. Startled, Bryson heard the voice and saw the thigh of the man at the same instant. He squeezed the trigger a millisecond before he realized that it was Jack asking the question.

The gun was less than two feet from the upper leg of the man crawling into the truck's cab. Bryson's mind went blank as the processed information of Jack's arrival reached his motor neurons too late to stop his index finger from contracting. The hammer on the revolver fell with a precise metallic snap, followed by Bryson's reflex jerking of the gun. Pain shot up his hand and arm as his wrist snagged on a bolt holding the seat's motor in place.

There was no report from the gun. No sound of an exploding bullet. The revolver had not fired.

"Are you about done playing around on the ground down there?" Jack asked as he leaned over the seat and looked down at Bryson.

"Jack! It's really you."

"Who did you expect to arrive and save your ass? The Lone Ranger?"

"Where did the European guy with the gun go?" Bryson asked as he wiggled to free his right arm from under the truck's seat.

"Do you mean the guy lying out here on the ground with a giant goose egg on his head? Stop talking and squirming and let me pull you up."

Once upright, Bryson settled into the driver's seat and caught his breath. He could see the body of the man lying face down on the pavement. His questioning eyes turned to Jack for an answer, but the thought was interrupted by a screeching of tires, followed by a loud crashing noise in the direction of the Marriott lobby.

"Follow me!" Jack yelled, walking briskly toward the entrance of the hotel.

Bryson was out of breath and confused. He needed to know who the man on the ground was but the crash needed his attention worse.

A black Ford LTD was blocking the hotel's entrance drive. Its emergency lights were flashing, and all four doors were hanging open. In front of the Ford was a silver Mercedes S-Class sedan. The Mercedes' front end was crumpled into a concrete flower box. Airbags were deployed and steam was wafting out of the radiator. Lying in the back window was a poster-board sign the read, "FOLLOW ME DOC B."

Three men all wearing FBI jackets surrounded the car. One held a weapon. The other two were on radio phones. A man in a black leather coat with blood draining out of his left ear was slumped over the deflated steering wheel airbag.

As Bryson caught up with Jack, they were waved over by an FBI agent in a blue windbreaker. Bryson ran toward the second LTD. Standing beside it, dressed in what must have been her running outfit—shorts, New Balance running shoes and a short-sleeve Duke sweatshirt—was a smiling Madeline.

"Daddy!" she yelled and ran toward her father, the smile replaced with a waterfall of grateful tears.

Police and ambulance sirens could be heard coming from several directions as a crowd of hotel guests and employees grew around the marble entrance. Bryson looked back toward his truck and could see that it was now encircled with more Ford sedans. A tall man wearing handcuffs was being stuffed into the back of one of the vehicles.

Jack joined the father-daughter hug circle, holding one another tight and long.

"Are you hurt, Maddie?"

"Just my wrists are kind of sore. They didn't hurt me. They really never even touched me. They just told me I had to come to meet you or else you and Mom would get arrested. They just put the tape on me when we were here in the parking lot and saw your truck pull into the lot. Is that your truck, Dad? It's gigantic. I want a ride."

The men looked at her and laughed.

\*\*\*

Preston, the lead FBI agent, was standing patiently beside them waiting for the reunion to conclude in order that he could begin to figure out what the heck was going on.

"I thought I left you at the Hyatt with the girls," Bryson said to Jack as the FBI agent questioned Madeline.

"I cut through the adjoining parking lots. Luckily, I stumbled over a round wood tree stake and picked it up. It made a great baseball bat. I hit a home run on that guy's head back there," Jack said, nodding toward Big Blue.

As the crime scene cleared of spectators, Bryson took out his cell phone and called Marisa. Moments later she and Jenny were brought to the Marriott by a Hyatt courtesy car. Maddie and her mom were reunited in a flood of tears and questions.

The Marriott manager offered their executive conference room for the five victims, the local police and the FBI agents to talk. The manager even had soft drinks and a dessert tray delivered to the temporary guests. Marisa sat on a couch, not letting Madeline out of her reach. A paramedic was asked to attend to Bryson's right wrist laceration, which by now had managed to leave trails of blood on him, Madeline and the front of Jack's new shirt. Both arms were now in bandages.

An ambulance had taken the injured man from the Mercedes and the older European man—apparently Blondie's father—off for treatment and then booking.

It took nearly two hours for the police and FBI agents to piece together the five different stories and begin to make sense from all of them. Around midnight, Madeline, being even more assertive and stubborn than her mom, insisted that the FBI men let her parents go to the Hyatt and get some sleep. All agreed to resume the questioning the next morning.

At the Hyatt, Bryson parked Big Blue in an RV space and locked the door with the FOB. He glanced back at the truck as he walked away, giving it a nod of appreciation. Was he going crazy or had he already been there?

# Chapter Twenty-Seven
## FRITZ AGAIN?

The local newspaper delivered with Bryson's room service breakfast had a surprise article on the front page . . . It was a picture of his truck and an interview with the Marriott manager telling of a kidnap-related "FBI SHOOT-OUT" in front of the hotel. Reading deep into the article, one learned that there really were no shots fired but some of the hotel guests did see guns in the hands of the FBI personnel; and that there had even been an ambulance "with lights flashing and its siren at full volume" to attend to the unconscious man found next to the big blue Peterbilt truck.

The women were all still asleep when Jack tapped on the adjoining door and came in to visit with Bryson. Bryson had ordered enough food for an army, and so the men sat on the veranda in the morning sunshine, eating scrambled eggs, sausage and thick, crispy bacon. The orange juice was hand squeezed and ice cold. It was unlike anything they had had to drink the last twelve days. They rehashed parts of the previous night's fiasco.

"What I still don't get," Jack said, "is why the various players along our route across the country didn't coordinate their efforts? The whole thing seems like an exercise in stupidity. Why didn't they just put the money in the trunk of a car and drive it wherever they wanted to go?"

"I think for Fritz it was all about the cars, and the funny money was a surprise to him," Bryson said, stuffing a link sausage in his mouth. "There must be more to the cars than we may ever know. Either they are worth a lot more than we suspect or maybe they're knock-offs being sold as authentic."

"How about we head back down to Florida and attend

the supposed car show and auction?" Jack asked with a gleam in his eye.

Bryson glanced up from his newspaper and studied Jack with his half-shaved head and his three-day growth of beard—his electric shaver battery had died. He wore a new shirt that held the creases of the original packaging. The bags under his eyes looked like purple leather change purses, and yet here he was ready to extend their adventure onto the court of the adversary.

"I think we'd better settle into a resort on the coast, maybe Hilton Head or Amelia Island, and let our wives work on their tans. You need some time to heal and I need to figure out how I'm going to get Big Blue back across the country and still save my marriage. By the way, how is your head feeling today?"

"It's fine. It just looks bad because the nurse in the hospital refused to shave all of my hair. In ten minutes, I have an appointment for a haircut, a shave and one of those girlie-man massages my wife is always drooling about. Maybe I'll get a pedicure too. I'll leave the day's planning up to you and the girls. I'm good for about anything that doesn't involve guns. By the way, didn't I hear the hammer come down on your revolver when you were hiding under the truck seat last night? What were you aiming at?"

The question hung in the air like a dense cloud of cigar smoke distracting Bryson's thinking long after Jack left. He had forgotten all about the gun and pulling the trigger. Why hadn't it fired? Bryson couldn't even remember where he had left the gun.

He showered, shaved and snuck out the door without waking Marisa or Madeline. He left a note that he would be back soon and took the truck keys and his cell phone. If Marisa wanted him she would call. He stopped by the front desk and asked the concierge to arrange a rental car for him. He needed to take Madeline back to Duke, and he wasn't about to ask her or her mom to ride in the truck again.

He picked up an icy cold can of Diet Pepsi at the gift

shop and headed out toward Big Blue. As he walked across the parking lot, he stopped for a minute, looking at Big Blue. He was struck with a deep sense of pride of ownership. In spite of all the troubles it had caused up to this time, he had grown to look at the truck and even the oddball and dangerous experiences as a new beginning.

Bryson walked up to the truck and sat down on the running board. He opened his can of soda and let the early morning sunshine work on his soul. He had loved his life, but the last twelve days were amazing. He was a different man than the last day he had worked in his old office, doing breast exams and PAP smears. His mind was on a different plane. His life now had a meaning that wasn't there when all he was doing was working toward paying the bills.

He thought about his relationship with Marisa and each of his kids. He wondered about Teri and his other employees and what they were doing. Could things ever be the same with Marisa again? She'd had a life of pleasant routines: the house, their meals, her tennis, ladies' organizations and church responsibilities. Would she have a hard time returning to her normal life with him around?

Bryson finished his soda and crushed the can. He stood up, realizing that every muscle and joint in his body was stiff and sore. His hair was long and wavy, and his three-day growth of beard was itching. He thought about joining Jack for a shave and haircut and then doing a few laps in the pool. His life wasn't over and his romance may need rekindling, but he knew just the man to do it.

He turned away from the truck and started back toward the hotel lobby, but then his memory pricked his curiosity and he did a one-eighty and pulled out his truck keys. He opened the door and climbed into the cab. It took an uncomfortable bending motion for him to look under the seat for his gun, but his hand found it and retrieved the heavy revolver, bumping the back of his injured hand again. He held the gun in the light and closely inspected it. Why hadn't the gun fired last night?

He opened the breech and began to spin the cylinder then suddenly stopped it. Slower now, he turned the cylinder. No wonder the gun had not fired and blown a hole in Jack's thigh. There was not a single bullet in it.

*** 

"What do you mean you unloaded the gun?" Bryson queried Marisa as he stood over the enormous bathtub. He was more curious than mad. She was neck-deep in bubbles with fragrant steam filling the room and fogging the mirrors.

"It was inspiration," she returned her answer softly, swishing the bubbles around just enough to enhance his view.

"What do you mean inspiration? What if I would have needed that gun loaded to save you or Madeline?"

"But you didn't need it to save us, or to save yourself, and had it been loaded you probably would have maimed Jack, if not killed him. So, you see, it was inspiration. There is no other way to look at it," she said in a slightly arrogant tone. "By the way, dear, did you notice that this tub is big enough for two people?"

*** 

By late morning, everyone had experienced enough of the Hyatt Hotel's gracious amenities. Madeline was eager to get back to Duke, and the FBI had filled in all the blanks on their reams of questioning forms.

Bryson had a new Cadillac sedan delivered from the local Hertz office, and with Marisa behind the wheel, the three women were prepared to leave for Durham. Bryson and Jack would be back on the Interstate as soon as they got Big Blue's three-thousand-mile tune-up performed at a local Peterbilt service center.

Jenny had made reservations at the Sheraton Resort in Myrtle Beach and the two couples planned to meet there in time for an evening of fine dining. Bryson had made it clear that he was covering all expenses during their travel. Jack had balked, but Jenny, for her part, felt she had earned a queen's vacation.

*** 

Everyone was excited about the day's plans except Fritz. He was hiding behind a grapefruit tree in the Marriott parking lot where he watched with binoculars as the five supervised the loading of luggage into the car. Dr. Bender still had something that Fritz was desperate to retrieve. It wasn't the twenty-thousand dollars of real hundred dollar bills that he had paid Bryson to transport the cars. He couldn't have cared less about that money. It also wasn't about the gym bag full of packets of counterfeit dollars now in the hands of the FBI. It was what he had inadvertently slipped inside the stack of the greenbacks given to Bryson at the boat ramp parking lot.

He couldn't believe he had forgotten that he had hidden it there. He finally remembered after a frantic search through his bags and car. He remembered thinking at the time he filled the cash tote bag, clear back in Reno, that it would be a safe place. He had had no intention of giving any money to the doc.

He hoped it hadn't been noticed. Seeing the luggage loaded into the rental car gave him confidence that retrieving his package would not be a problem. Then he saw the men kiss the women and head for the blue truck, each pulling a small rolling carry-on bag. Who had the stack of money with its special accompaniment?

With the Bender woman driving, the Cadillac pulled around to the area where the truck was parked and then stopped. The doc and his pal were walking around the truck, checking it over. Why couldn't they get on with it so he could follow them? His frustration grew as the truck pulled out of the parking lot and the women followed close behind.

He jumped into his rental car and sped out of the parking lot onto the highway. He caught up with the truck just in time to see the Cadillac turn onto the freeway headed south. The big blue truck continued up the access road toward the main part of Fayetteville. Which way to go? Who had the stack of bills? He flipped a mental coin and when it came up tails, he followed the women.

Fritz was anxious. In his rush to leave the parking lot, the squeal of his car tires caused Madeline to look out the back window.

✳✳✳

"Mom, I think someone is following us. I just saw a car speed out of the parking lot and run someone off the road."

Marisa and Jenny immediately looked backward and picked up on the rapidly approaching car. As they went into the main flow of freeway traffic, the white Lincoln sedan dropped a few cars back and followed them. Marisa changed lanes a couple of times, noting that the Lincoln kept changing lanes as well.

Marisa pulled into the HOV lane and gunned the car, leaving the Lincoln trapped behind a plumbing truck and a cluster of smaller cars.

"Should we call Dad?" Madeline asked.

"They're already ten miles from here," Marisa answered. "Just hang on tight. I'll take care of this. Jenny, when we're about half a mile from the next exit, let me know."

The white car changed into the HOV lane and began to gain on them.

"There's the exit sign," Jenny and Madeline sang out in unison.

Without touching her blinker, Marisa made a fast triple-lane change just in time to shoot off into the exit lane and down the ramp toward an intersection controlled by a red light. She nearly locked up the brakes to come to the required stop. All three women looked back to see an empty strip of asphalt behind them.

"Now what, Mom? He'll just get off at the next exit and track us down."

"Not if we outsmart him. He can't get off the freeway for another two miles," Jenny said with an intensity that surprised the Bender women. "I'm not going to let those jerks ruin another day of our vacation. Unless you have a better idea, Marisa, here's what we should do."

*\*\**

Jack and Bryson found an awesome truckers' service center. The heavy traffic up and down the East Coast freeway system spurred the amount of business that in turn pushed the competitive edge. This place's service area looked like a Lexus showroom, and the waiting area was complete with a circle of leather couches and a bank of five flat-screen TVs, each on a different channel, and a row of Internet-connected computers. Free sandwiches, doughnuts, coffee and soft drinks were served to the drivers by perky waitresses. Bryson noticed a number of women in the waiting lounge and figured they were drivers in their own right. The biggest surprise was that the place was smokeless.

The young service representative who had waited on them estimated about two hours to have their truck greased, the oil changed, washed, detailed and the fuel tanks topped off. Bryson didn't ask for a price, guessing that it would be a lot. Maybe he would pay for it with a few of the crumpled hundred dollar bills he had retrieved from deep in the pocket of the borrowed scrub pants. *Who would know? Nah, forget it*, he told himself.

322 Steven I. Dahl, M.D.

He found a leather armchair off to the side, away from other customers, and opened his rolling travel bag. Jack had wandered off to inspect the long row of semi-tractors. Looking around to be sure that there were no prying eyes close by, Bryson reached into the bag that held his laptop, his shaving kit and a couple of clean golf shirts. Down near the bottom his hand closed around the tape-bound stack of hundred dollar bills. He was again surprised by how thick and heavy this taped bundle was.

Putting the rectangular stack on his lap, he shuffled the end, listening for the sound of one hundred crisp hundred dollars bills whisper through his fingers. He remembered the day he held his first hundred-dollar bill. He was a senior in medical school and had finished a two-month clerkship. It was finally payday. The paymaster had looked over his pay file and then picked up a stack of bills and began counting off fifteen of them—all hundreds. Bryson remembered how the sergeant had looked at him and laughed when he picked up the slippery little pile, spilling half of them on the floor.

As he brushed his fingers over the end of this stack, something didn't compute. A number of the bills in the middle of the stack must be stuck together. Only the outer inch or so on the top and bottom of the pack were free from the clear packing tape that bound the stack.

He looked around again and then reached in his pocket for his pocketknife. He chose the smallest blade and carefully sliced a lengthwise incision on each side of the packet. He laid the knife on a windowsill beside him and separated the top half of the bills from the bottom.

The bills weren't stuck together as he had presumed. The money was all there, but in the middle of the stack was a quarter-inch thick piece of cardboard the was painted green around the edges. The cardboard was wrapped in clear packing tape. Looking at the flat surface, he saw five staggered, perfectly round holes cut through the cardboard. Fitted into each of the five holes was a large gold coin.

Slipping on his glasses, he studied the stamped figures and the writing on the coins. They appeared to be like new, but the inscriptions were definitely ancient. Holding them up to better light, the writing looked to be Egyptian or Arabic.

"What the heck is going on?" he asked himself. Bryson rewrapped the packet of money and stuffed it into the depths of his bag, leaving the cardboard holding the coins in a separate zipper pocket in the inside of the roller bag.

It took longer than estimated to service the truck. Close inspection of the tires found a carefully made slice around the inside edge of the left front tire. It wasn't deep, but appeared intentional. At high speed, more than likely it would have broken down the sidewall of the tire, producing a blowout. The realization that he and Jack had been attacked again made his skin crawl.

Retired, greased, fueled and pristine clean, Big Blue was delivered to the anxious men about three hours from the time of their arrival. They were both restless, worrying about being late for their evening date.

"Can you believe they even laundered the sleeper cab's sheets and pillow cases?" Jack commented as they drove out of the service center toward the freeway. Both men had eaten a fast-food meal during the wait and had also replenished the stock of snacks and drinks in the tiny fridge in the cabin. Their GPS told them they were three and a half hours from Myrtle Beach.

"When you get done with the GPS, take a look at the item in the side zipper pocket of my bag, but be careful with it. It's wrapped in a T-shirt."

Jack unwrapped the surprise item and studied each of the coins. He let out a long whistle as he refolded the coins and listened to Bryson's story of finding them buried in the

324 Steven I. Dahl, M.D.

stack of hundreds. "My guess is that they are ancient Persian. They were probably stolen from some museum or someone's private collection; maybe from the Baghdad museum after the overthrow of Sadam. I'll bet they are worth a lot more than the money they were wrapped up with."

"What do we do with them? Do you want to call your friends at the FBI again and let them know?"

"I don't know about you, but I have had enough of this whole thing for now. How about we proceed with plan A and meet the girls and work on our tans and get in a few rounds of golf. I'll call my nephew when we get home and they can look into it then."

"I'm fine with that plan, but I'll skip the golf. My shoulder is still killing me."

They tried their wives' cell phones, but got only voicemail recordings. Jack finally pooped out and went to the sleeper for a nap. He still wasn't up to driving and his headaches fluctuated in intensity with his blood levels of Advil and Tylenol. He had no sooner fallen asleep than Bryson's cell phone started dancing on the dashboard ledge, its vibrator and Beach Boys' tune snatching his attention.

"Dr. Bender here."

"Fritz, your friendly neighborhood car dealer here," the voice answered in a mocking tone.

"Well, Fritz, what a surprise! Here I thought you would be busy down at the courthouse trying to bail your kidnapping friends out of jail. What can I do for you? Haul another load of counterfeit money, or maybe a trailer full of illegal aliens for you?" Bryson spoke with bravado, but in his gut he had a very uneasy feeling.

"Doc, I hate to interrupt your day, but I believe you have something that belongs to me. Have you spent any of the money I gave you? You know, the money I paid you for transporting the cars?"

"Maybe the FBI got it. They were very interested in everything we had, and everything your sleazy friends had as well." Bryson could feel Jack's head close behind his, obviously trying to overhear more than one side of the conversation.

"Those boys are three-strike felons. They're out of our lives forever. But Doc, I need your cooperation here. I have misplaced something, and I believe you might have it."

As Jack slid into the passenger seat, Bryson handed him the phone, nodding for him to press the speaker phone button.

"What is it that you lost, besides your mind?"

"Doc, that's so rude, and after all, I did to get you a start in the trucking business. I'm going to have to tell our friend in Bozeman, Montana, not to sell you anymore new trucks. Seriously, there was a piece of cardboard wrapped with the generous twenty grand I paid you. It has a few coins from my boyhood coin collection. My grandfather gave those to me. Though they aren't really worth much, they have a lot of sentimental value to me. I know that you have them. Let's arrange a meeting place, your call, someplace convenient to you, so I can pick them up. How easy is that?"

"Maybe you have mixed up the money and given Grandpa's gold coins to somebody else." Bryson said, wanting to get off the phone, but at the same time enjoying having Fritz squirm a little.

"Oh, so you have seen my coins. I didn't mention that they were gold," Fritz said.

Ignoring his slip-up, Bryson asked, "By the way, who arranged for us to be the transporter of the counterfeit money? Was that you or the truck dealer? Maybe it was both of you. That's what we told the FBI. I'm surprised they haven't arrested you yet." Bryson and Jack smiled at one another.

"Here's the deal, Doc. You find my grandfather's coins and I'll give you a little finder's fee to sweeten the deal, and here it is—I'll quit calling you, and you can go on happily trucking down the lonesome road until you die of old age. The alternative deal is that I track you down again—believe me, it isn't that hard; every time you cross a state border your GPS reports where you are. When I find you, I will take back the money and the coins and give you a little something to make that old-age dying thing unnecessary."

"Now that sounds more like the Fritz we know. Tell us, did you go to a special school to learn your trade or is it something one picks up groveling around in the gutter with other low-lifes?" Jack said.

"So it's *we* now. Your friend with the rag on his head came out of his coma, did he? Well, Mister Raghead, maybe you are the one I should be convincing. Your wife's new blond German friend has shared some of your wife's secrets. She is really easy to frighten. Maybe I'll have to approach the two of you old geezers through your wives. Maybe they can convince you that keeping another man's childhood treasures is not a good idea."

"Say, I'm real sorry to end this conversation, but my ear is getting sore and my battery is low. I hope you find whatever you are looking for. And Fritz, don't call us back. If we need your help, we know where your auto business is located," Jack said. With that said he pressed the red button, ending the conversation.

"Can he really track us on our GPS?" Bryson asked Jack.

"His GPS thing was just to confuse us," Jack answered. "Raghead, eh? I've been called a lot of things but never a raghead. So what are we *really* going to do?"

Bryson glanced at Jack and then back at his business of driving.

"Why don't we just forget about Fritz? He hasn't a clue where any of us are. I figure by the time the girls drop off Madeline and make it to the hotel, it will be well into the evening. I don't know about you, but I could use a good calm dinner tonight. I want to make another stab at finding the perfect chicken fried steak."

***

Driving to the campus of Duke University had been a delight. The three women had chatted and laughed. They hadn't seen the white sedan again. They had stopped at a tiny luncheon place and ate fresh seafood salads and blueberry bread pudding.

The women made it to Duke just as the three-forty classes were letting out. Realizing that she was nearly late for an afternoon Zoology lab orientation, Madeline gave her mom and Jenny hugs and kisses and rushed off toward her dorm, two days older and ten years wiser than the last time she had set foot on campus.

Jenny looked at the students making their way down the wide campus paths and expanses of grass. There were small groups of students leaning against trees and sitting cross-legged on the grass, visiting with friends and new acquaintances.

"It almost makes me want to go back to school again," she told Marisa. "Can you imagine having the knowledge you have now and being able to restart your life at age eighteen? Oh, to have my young body back again, not to mention a second look at the field of prospective husbands. I doubt I would choose anyone different . . . you know what I mean? But I could have given a lot of guys a closer inspection."

Both women laughed and then screamed in one breath. The white Lincoln swerved toward them, jumping the curb across the tree-lined median of the divided campus drive. It bounced and bumped over the concrete curbs, then came to an abrupt stop immediately in front of their car, its rear wheels still on the grass. Marisa slammed on the brakes, throwing Jenny into the dashboard, her seat belt having been forgotten in the goodbyes and nostalgia.

Before either woman could refocus on what had happened, Fritz had pulled Marisa's door open and screamed at both women to get out of the car. He reached inside and pushed the trunk release button, popping the trunk lid. He opened the back door and grabbed Marisa's purse, then dumped it upside down onto the rear seat.

"Give me your purse!" he screamed at Jenny. She tossed it over the seat, barely missing his face. He dumped the contents onto the seat. Uttering a vile curse, he screamed at the women, "Stay in the car!"

"Make up your mind, you idiot," Marisa said out loud, but the words were drowned out by the honking horns.

Cars had started to line up behind the Cadillac, unable to get around without crossing the median curb. Fritz quickly went to the back of the car, oblivious to honking horns and yelling out of car windows. He opened the trunk and began to attack the suitcases. He dumped each one onto the floor of the trunk, and then began rummaging through the contents, tossing items back and forth. When he came to the bottom of the first suitcase, having found nothing, he angrily threw the empty bag out onto the pavement. There were four suitcases in the trunk, some large and some small. By the time Fritz rapidly searched through two of them, there was a foot-deep pile of dresses, pants, blouses, undergarments, shoes and toiletries filling the trunk and spilling out onto the ground.

The people in the cars stuck behind Marisa's Cadillac were going crazy watching this idiot. Finally, a tall muscular basketball player type got out of the third car back and approached Fritz. Other drivers were getting out of cars as well and pedestrian students were beginning to gather around, enjoying the ruckus—a change of pace was always welcome on any college campus. Soon, a police siren could be heard approaching the scene.

Fritz went to the open driver's side door again and screamed at the women in a tone that was borderline psychotic. "Where are my coins?"

Neither Marisa nor Jenny had any idea what this mad-man was talking about. They sat frozen in the car.

Fritz was suddenly slung like a rag doll up against a square brick lamppost. The muscular basketball guy put a half-Nelson armlock on him and goose-hopped him around to the driver's door of the white Lincoln. Fritz's head was pushed down into the open doorway of the car and his torso was shoved into the driver's seat. The sirens were getting closer.

"Now drive your car out of our way and don't come back," the basketball guy yelled, still squeezing the back of Fritz's neck in a crushing death grip.

The athlete then stepped away from the car and slammed the door shut. Fritz looked out the window and finally started the car's engine. The Lincoln started moving, its back wheels spinning on the grass of the median until they finally got a grip on the concrete of the curb, rocketing the car forward onto the road.

The young man strolled to the back of Marisa and Jenny's Cadillac where he began picking up the scattered clothes. He placed the three empty suitcases on top of the jumble and forcibly closed the trunk lid. The gathered crowd applauded his action as several of the students took photos with their cell phone cameras.

Smiling at her, the handsome basketball guy said, "I don't know what was going on there, lady, but I'm late for my Organic Chemistry lab, and my professor thinks that the world turns on his clock. Sorry, your husband was so angry."

Jenny looked at Marisa and broke out laughing. "How did you ever hook up with such a young husband?"

Marisa was flabbergasted. She sat staring ahead for a minute, trying to organize her thoughts until the cacoph-ony of car horns behind her made her focus and put the Cadillac into gear. She started driving down the tree-covered boulevard just as three campus police cars approached from the other direction. Minutes later, she and Jenny were turning onto the freeway entrance. Off to the right, they saw the Lincoln pulled over to the side of the road. It was wedged between two local police cars, lights flashing with uniformed officers surrounding the white sedan. At first, Marisa's reaction was to stop and tell the police what the crazy man had done. She even put on her turn signal and slowed the car.

"Don't even think about it!" Jenny said.

# Chapter Twenty-Eight
## KICKING BACK

The Sheraton Hotel and Spa at Myrtle Beach was far more luxurious than any of the four would have dreamed. When the couples were shown to their adjoining Carolina ocean-view suites, they were pleased at the size, décor and views. Their respective suitcases were delivered and large tips were distributed. A time for dinner was agreed upon and reservations were made at a recommended French restaurant overlooking the harbor. "What the heck happened to all our clothes?" Bryson finally mustered the courage to ask.

The ladies had decided not to phone with the news of the bad experience. Now that they were face to face, Marisa and Jenny told their husbands all about their run-in with the maniacal Fritz.

"Well, maybe that's the end of it," Bryson said. "I don't know about you three, but I'm going for a swim before dinner. I had a very mediocre chicken fried steak for lunch and it is still hanging around my middle . . . too much breaded grease. I need exercise!"

"I'm headed for the Jacuzzi tub," said Jenny.

Marisa nodded in agreement. "Hey, I almost forgot to ask—what was that guy Fritz looking for? He kept screaming, 'My coins, I want my coins!'"

Bryson and Jack looked at each other and frowned. Maybe their ordeal wasn't over after all.

### ✳✳✳

When a person has been busy every day of their adult life, it is impossible to slow down and do nothing—well, probably not impossible but definitely difficult—thus by the third day of relaxation on the fairways and poolside lounge chairs of Myrtle Beach, Bryson was starting to get a little stir crazy. He was about to ask for a job at the hotel, helping with the dishes in the kitchen or with the groundskeeper, mowing grass. He had read four novels and every newspaper sold at the gift shop.

Sitting in a soft lounge chair, smeared with sunscreen, he had booted up his laptop and was randomly scanning the news when something caught his eye. He clicked on a teaser headline about stolen museum art and found himself staring in disbelief at a picture of one of the gold coins, which was sitting at that very moment in the electronic safe in his hotel room.

The online article told of a theft from a little known gallery, the Munch Museum in Oslo, Norway. The gallery was building a collection of ancient Mesopotamian metallic artifacts, some of which were deemed to be priceless. The gallery had been broken into six months before, leaving shattered empty display cases. There had been no damage to any of the many wall-hung paintings, including the famous "Scream" by Edvard Munch, which had been stolen years before, but luckily found and returned unharmed.

The article stated that a few pieces of the coin collection were showing up at auctions and the alleged thief was under arrest. The article went on to say that many of the most valuable pieces were still at large. Especially valuable was a set of five solid-gold coins that were believed to have been minted in Babylon sometime during the sixth century B.C. No dollar value was given for the coins but a six figure reward was offered for their safe return.

Bryson hustled off to the resort's business center where he printed a copy of the Internet article as well as a couple of related articles written at the time of the original theft. When he returned to the pool to awaken the slumbering Jack and share the news with him and the wives, the three were gathered around the TV at the pool bar watching a "Breaking News" story about an escape from the city's jail complex. Apparently, a helicopter had dropped a line into the exercise yard and made off with inmates who were awaiting indictment. There on the TV screen were two high-definition pictures of the escapees. Fritz's wide eyes and smiling face was, it seemed, grinning directly at Bryson. Like the following eyes of the Mona Lisa, Bryson couldn't escape Fritz's intimidating stare.

The next morning, Bryson arose early and went to the hotel gift shop to buy each of the various newspapers they carried. He was somewhat surprised, perhaps even disappointed, that there wasn't anything new to learn about Fritz and his devious partners. He did, however, find a follow-up to the story in the Washington Post about the stolen and now missing coins. Norway's Munch Museum claimed that the coins were struck for one of the Kings of Babylon, probably King Nebuchadnezzar II in 630 B.C. The actual value of each of the coins was unknown but the article did say that the Lloyd's of London insurance policy covering the coins was more than five million dollars. The last sentence of the newspaper article again mentioned a substantial reward for the return of the coins.

The biggest problem in life Bryson now faced was what to do with the precious golden coins. If he were to call the FBI again, the four of them would be back in the middle of another tedious investigation, but not telling the authorities about the coins would bring more questions and suspicion down on Bryson, Jack and even the innocent Marisa and Jenny.

Returning the coins to the rightful owners, and possibly collecting a reasonable reward, was beginning to sound like a good idea. How to go about it was a new and very real dilemma. Like so many things one worries about in life, the bad things seldom happen, and the near impossible things are often quite simple.

\*\*\*

Marisa lay in the lounge chair beside the resort's glimmering swimming pool trying to relax and enjoy the day, but instead was watching her husband struggle. He was trying to verbalize their options to her. They could keep the coins in a safe deposit box for a few years and then drop them off anonymously at an art museum, they could call Jack's relative at the FBI and have him take possession of the coins with the agreement that they would not be questioned or prosecuted, or they could go online and anonymously try to collect the reward. After listening to several other even less plausible scenarios, Marisa had finally had enough. Bryson's imagination was getting out of hand, and his sense of reason was failing. She would handle this.

She got up from the comfortable lounge, abandoning her novel and fresh drink. She wrapped herself in her cover-up, ignoring Bryson's continued brainstorms. He suddenly stopped talking, realizing she was gone. Without explanation, she walked barefoot across the poolside deck into the covered cocktail lounging area. There, Marisa beckoned an attendant to bring her a house phone.

With the telephone in hand, she settled into a huge wicker fan-back chair and placed a long-distance information call to the Munch Museum in Oslo, Norway. A Mr. Johaneson answered the phone and listened patiently to Marisa's story. He asked several specific questions about the coins and then put her on hold. When he came back on the phone, he asked her if she could email him a picture of the coins.

"Assuming you have our coins, would it be possible for you to come to Norway to deliver the coins in person?"

Marisa asked the man to hold for a minute. She walked back out to the pool area and stuck her head in Jenny and Jack's cabana. Jack was sound asleep. Jenny was in the middle of the newest vampire novel.

"Hey Jenny," Marisa said, "how about a free trip to Norway?"

At this point in her day-to-day planning, and life for that matter, Jenny was up for just about anything that wasn't forbidden by the Ten Commandments, or involved a truck.

"Why not?" she said. "All the food in my fridge at home is spoiled by now anyway."

Marisa was back on the telephone, and without even conferring with Bryson, made tentative arrangements. She went to the hotel room and retrieved the coins from the safe. She took several pictures of the coins with her cell phone camera then emailed them to the Norwegian museum. Five minutes later her cell rang. Mr. Johaneson's voice was a full octave higher than it had been.

Marisa had become an expert in planning trips. She had always been the Bender family's travel agent. The final arrangements for the trip from Myrtle Beach to Atlanta to Oslo with an open-ended return, were in place, except for the last, biggest problem. Where does one park a two-hundred-thousand dollar, twelve-foot high, ten-thousand-pound semi-truck?

The answer, it turned out, was as easy as a stained, crumpled, hundred-dollar bill. With the truck parked and locked up tight, the four well-fed and rested Westerners crawled into the back of a stretch limo and headed for the airport. A quick run to a nearby mall for some wardrobe additions had been made, and a locking metal briefcase had been purchased to hold the coins.

# Chapter Twenty-Nine
## REWARDS

The first-class compartment in the 777 was fantastic. They were scheduled for a late evening flight directly from Atlanta to Oslo. The quick hop over the North Pole would give them a night to enjoy the airplane's reclining bed-like lounge seats with their new leather smell and velvet soft feel. The food, starting with the pre-take off snacks of hot Godiva chocolate cookies, was exceptional. Everything was looking great until Marisa stood up to retrieve her iPod from the overhead storage bin. She let out a loud gasp that drew the attention of several of the other passengers, including Bryson and Jack.

"What's the matter?" Bryson asked, fumbling with his seat belt latch and then jumping to his feet, spilling his juice in the process. He thought she must have hurt herself closing the bin door.

"Sorry," she apologized to those staring at her. "I'm fine. I just pinched my finger."

The flight attendant was at her side, doting over her and mopping up the spilled juice. Marisa didn't have a chance to say anything to Bryson until the safety announcements, repeated in three languages, were finished and the plane was ready to be pushed away from the jet way.

"What do you mean you think you saw Fritz?" Bryson demanded in a less than hushed tone. "You have got to be wrong. He's on the run from the police. There is no way he would take the chance of getting on an international fight. You have got to be mistaken."

The two were buckled in their seats for takeoff. Silently, they churned over the possibility of their nemesis actually being on the same airplane with them.

Bryson, in spite of how logical his mind used to work, was mentally beating himself back into a basket of jumbled nerves. Leaning back in the deep leather seat merely gave his brain more time to build his wife's probable miss-sighting into another dilemma.

Once the seat belt sign was turned off and the flight attendants were again up and about, Bryson got out of his window seat and bent forward, leaning over Jenny's seat back to share his agony with Jack. Misery loves company, and within moments, Bryson had ruined the peacefulness of the flight for all four of the friends. After lengthy consultation with Jack, he decided that the only reasonable solution was a search of the airplane to get an answer to the mystery.

The wives tried to talk Bryson and Jack out of any kind of action, urging them to sit down and chill out. But the men couldn't be consoled with mere words. They both had to know if Fritz was onboard. Bryson opened his carry-on and retrieved a sharpened pencil. He had read once that a simple sharpened lead pencil could be used as a lethal weapon by plunging the point into the assailant's carotid artery. Next best, Bryson thought, would be to stab the rotten guy right in the eye. No one could put up a serious fight with a pencil sticking out of his eye socket.

As Bryson turned to walk toward the back of the plane, he gripped the pencil in his right hand, holding his arm at his side.

The men each took an aisle in the wide-bodied plane, keeping abreast of one another. They started working their way towards the rear of the plane, examining the faces of every male passenger. The drink carts were already in the aisles and people were up and out of some of the seats. The restrooms were already in use and the first movie of the flight was about to start. Window shades had been pulled down by most of the passengers, creating a visual impairment. Jack made it about halfway to the back of the very long plane. When impeded by serving carts and obese travelers, he gave up, turned around and headed back to his seat in the forward cabin.

Bryson accidentally stepped on the hand of a little boy whose mother had set him on the floor to play, making the boy scream with pain. The nearby flight attendant asked Bryson where he was supposed to be sitting, then curtly sent him back to the front. By the time he fought his way back to his seat, the first course of the meal was being served, and Marisa, Jenny and Jack were well into their salads.

"Did you see him?" Jenny asked out loud from her seat in front of Marisa's.

"It's a zoo back there," was all Bryson mumbled. How was he ever going to be able to relax? Forget the in-flight nap he was planning. He remembered the last time he crossed the Atlantic and had gotten hooked on a Tom Clancy novel and hadn't slept the entire flight. It had taken him four days to get over the jet lag. He couldn't even remember in which city they had spent the first couple of days.

"Crap," he mumbled, as he took a mouthful of wilted lettuce.

***

The new morning sun shone brightly through the windows of the plane as the cabin lights came on and the overhead announcer began working through the safety rules in each of three languages. Bryson was startled at first, and then, gaining consciousness, realized that he had fallen sound asleep.

The first thing he checked was his new metal case, which he found still wedged securely beneath the seat in front of him. Marisa was away from her seat, as was Jenny, probably in the restroom. Jack was still sound asleep.

Bryson combed his hair with his fingers and decided to give the back of the plane one more look. He still had the pencil in his shirt pocket and was alert enough to feel he could deal with Fritz, should he be on the plane. He made his way easily back to the mid-plane restrooms when he saw a man matching the description Marisa had given. The guy was reaching into the overhead bin with his hands on a metal briefcase exactly like the one Bryson had tucked under his own seat—just like the one that held the gold coins. He couldn't make out the man's face, nor did he notice the iPod ear buds trailing down the man's neck, but his build and hair color were identical to Fritz's. Bryson slipped the pencil out of his pocket and approached the man from behind.

"Fritz?" Bryson said in a voice louder than he had intended.

A deathly silence followed. The man gave no sign that he was the object of the name, but continued fussing with his metal case.

Bryson braced himself, sliding the sharply pointed pencil into the palm of his hand and tightening his grip. Then he spoke again. "Fritz, you idiot, how stupid do you have to be to follow us like this? Don't you realize the police are searching for you? You have to be one of the stupidest people I have ever met."

Bryson had the pencil ready for his attack. As the man turned, Bryson cocked his elbow, ready if necessary, to deliver the pencil into Fritz's throat with a powerful thrust.

The man turned his face toward Bryson. "Sir, would you be so kind as to help me lift my briefcase down from this mean old shelf. I tried, but it hurts my shoulders."

Bryson stepped back, staring at the man's face. His hair color and style, his eye color and his lean build all were a dead ringer for Fritz, but this definitely wasn't the Nevada auto trader. Bryson spun on his heels and nearly sprinted toward the front of the plane.

\*\*\*

The museum's limousine was parked in a reserved spot in front of the "Arrivals" door. The livery driver had collected their bags and opened the stretch Mercedes door, nodding toward the car.

"Would you prefer to be delivered to the Intercontinental Hotel now or shall we proceed directly to the museum?" the driver asked as he settled into his seat.

Glances at one another confirmed that getting freshened up at the hotel was a good idea, but delivering the coins and pocketing the reward was a better one. They had all lost too much sleep and energy worrying about the coins.

"No time like the present," Marisa said, smiling at the driver.

"Madame?" he queried, not understanding what the time of day had to do with where he should deliver them.

"Just take us to the museum, please," Bryson said.

The museum itself was a disturbing surprise. It was in a small building in a residential block of apartments. The entry was of simple painted brick and wood and required climbing a set of painted wooden stairs to get to the entrance.

The meeting with the curator and the president of the museum's foundation was held in a long, narrow room with walls carved from teak and lined with shelves displaying old pottery that Bryson thought ought to be thrown away. Beautiful paintings hung in small, poorly lit rooms off the hallway. Bryson got a short glance at "The Scream" as they walked by. He thought it ugly and overrated. There were no display cases indicative of any coin collections.

The curator would have been a shoe-in for the denier in a slasher movie. He was dressed in a tight-fitting black suit and had his hair slicked back with enough grease to pack a truck axle. The foundation president, on the other hand, was wearing a beautiful cashmere three-button suit with a solid-blue tie. He had a friendly smile and spoke near, accent-free English.

The four were offered chilled mineral water and asked to take seats around a wide, oval table whose top appeared to be a solid piece of highly polished petrified tree trunk with a thick beveled glass top. The room was stuffy and claustrophobic.

"I am so glad you are safely here in Oslo," the foundation man began. "We have arranged for you to spend as many days with us as you wish. I hope you will find the hotel, the car and the driver to your satisfaction. Please avail yourselves of them as long as you wish. Now, I am sure you are eager to take care of the business at hand and then begin your visit to our beautiful country. Dr. Bender, would you be so kind as to show us the coins?"

Bryson laid the case on the table and unsnapped the latches. All eyes were on the case as he lifted the lid and removed the two sweaters he had used as packing to prevent the coins from sliding to and fro in the case. Bryson had thoughtfully placed the five gold coins, still imbedded in the cardboard, in an empty Styrofoam egg crate. The curator rolled his eyes when he saw the unprofessional packing, but came to full attention when Bryson opened the featherweight egg carton and removed the heavy coins. With a bit of a grin, he slid the cardboard encasement across the shiny surface toward the two Norwegians.

Both men studied the coins where they lay on the table, touching them only to turn Fritz's makeshift cardboard package over and inspect the back side of the coins.

"Was this the package you found them in?" asked the curator.

"Exactly like that. I didn't replace the clear tape, and have only inspected the surfaces that you now see. The cardboard was in a stack of . . . " Bryson hesitated, not having thought about how much of the story he wanted to tell the men.

"Pardon me," the foundation officer said. "You said in a stack of . . . ?"

"Of cut paper," Bryson said. "Similar to a stack of large greeting cards, about so by so." Bryson motioned the size with his fingers, drawing an imaginary rectangle on the table.

"Are they the real thing?" Jenny asked, impatient with all the preliminary and useless banter.

The curator went to a side table and returned with a felt-lined tray, holding a pair of magnifying loupes and a variety of surgical-appearing instruments. First putting on the eye loupes, he carefully removed the tape. Slipping on a pair of white cotton gloves, he lifted the first of the coins.

The man's slow-motion study of the coins was driving Bryson crazy. Marisa had already stood up and was pondering the various potteries. The chair Bryson was sitting on felt as hard as concrete. The aches and pains of the past weeks were all catching up with him at once. He wished he had thought to get some Advil out of Marisa's purse while they were in the car. Jack and he both slid their chairs back at the same time and stood.

The curator brought a brighter light to the table and a clear liquid to clean the adhesive from the coins. This he did with Q-tips, a millimeter at a time. The tedium of the process was nerve-racking.

Finally, Bryson had had enough. "So what's the story?" he asked.

"Would you like to know the history of the coins?" the curator asked, looking up from his intense study.

"Not really, at least not right now. We want to know if they are the real thing."

"Ja ja, they are the real thing. Ja ja, they are the missing coins. I was looking for any damage, but as you Americans say, they are okee-dokee."

✳✳✳

The next ride in the Mercedes limo was to a solicitor's office a few blocks from the museum. Bryson kept looking over his shoulder, expecting Fritz to show up at any moment.

As yet there had been no mention of the amount of the reward they might receive. The lawyer's office was in a much nicer part of the city and even had its own circular drive and portico. During the lengthy inspection of the coins, neither of the Norwegians had inquired how they had come in possession of the coins. Bryson had concluded that they didn't want to know.

At the solicitor's office, they were ushered into another paneled room and offered more bubbling mineral water. A good twenty minutes later, the solicitor, the curator and the museum foundation president all returned with an elderly female clerk who asked for their passports. She jotted down their numbers and then handed a stack of papers to each of them. Small red X marks were on the papers, and the implication was that they would sign the form which was, to Bryson's dismay, written in Norwegian.

Exhausted, jet-lagged and dying for something cold with ice to drink, Marisa signed her name and begged the others to do the same. The papers were gathered and a brown envelope magically appeared on the table. The solicitor passed out the contents to the four. These were very legible. They were cashier's checks made out to each of the four Americans, written on Barclays Bank in London in the amount of two hundred thousand euros each. A strange aura filled the room. The amount of any reward had never been mentioned. Marisa had never discussed sharing the reward with the Glens. As a matter of fact, she hadn't mentioned sharing it with Bryson either, although that had been her intention. They were all shocked with the amount and that the transaction was accomplished without any discussion. It would appear as though that had been the plan all along.

"How much is this in real money—you know, in American dollars?" Marisa asked the solicitor, never one to let her shyness interfere with getting the facts.

344 Steven I. Dahl, M.D.

"At today's exchange rate, madam, that is approximately three hundred and twenty-thousand American dollars."

"Each?" she mumbled, trying to suppress her exuberance.

"Ja, ja. Each," the solicitor answered in a slightly indignant tone. "Is it not enough? I was told that the amount was agreed upon?"

The four glanced at one another, and in a choir voice said simply, "Yes, it's just right."

Jack pushed his chair away from the table, ending the conversation. "I'm starving, and we need to go to the hotel."

**\*\*\***

They were back in the limo and swiftly cruising down the main boulevard of Oslo toward the Intercontinental Hotel. Not a word was spoken among the four, each clutching their envelope. Each stared out of the window, watching as the sights of the city rolled by.

The luxurious rooms were preregistered for them. By the time the sun should have been setting, they had eaten a scrumptious meal in a real Michelin four-star dining room. Bryson requested that the chef come to the table, and after a lengthy discussion, both had agreed that one of the items on the menu was in fact a version of what Bryson called chicken fried steak. He had of course ordered it and thought it heavenly. As they left the dining room, the head waiter gave him a note from the chef. On the note was the recipe. It was handwritten in English, and underlined was the main ingredient with a warning: *Be certain to use only the best quality and most fresh reindeer flesh for your "Chicken Fried Steak."*

Lying on the cool, soft sheet, Bryson kissed his sleeping wife. The money had not been mentioned by any of the four since they had left the solicitor's office. Fritz also had not been mentioned, although for months to come, Bryson would find himself scanning the newspapers and Internet for news of the recapture of the brilliant forger and auto thief. Bryson's last questioning thought before his mind blanked out was, *What are those coins really worth, and were they real, or another product of a forger's skill coupled with modern science? After all, if we could put a man on the moon, invent a cellular telephone and write and store millions of words and pictures on a flash drive the size of woman's slender finger, could it be that hard for Fritz Krefeld to recreate the wonders of the Garden of Babylon?*

# EPILOGUE

Two weeks later, Bryson received a text message from his accountant. He was standing at a truck stop in North Carolina beside Big Blue, holding the nozzle of the diesel hose. He was watching the pump's digital meter spend his dollars faster than a slot machine. His message stated that a certified letter from the Norwegian government had been received, identifying the reward money as an insurance settlement. This, his accountant promised, would be considered by the IRS as a nontaxable increase. Not a bad payday, especially since it had included twelve days of paid vacation in the magnificent cities of Europe.

Marisa had called the Myrtle Beach hotel that morning, announcing that she and Jenny had arrived safely back home and that it was hot and dry and the two were already planning a weekend in San Diego. They had invited the older grandkids to come along. She was even flying Madeline out to join the family fun. Sea World, Coronado, the Gaslight restaurants and the sandy beaches would be the perfect places to recover from the hardships of their European adventure.

Jack had initially favored heading back home with the wives, but the first softening blow to his resolve was when Bryson received an email from the shipping agent requesting that he call back immediately to talk about a new job. There was a load of factory-new Ferraris sitting on the dock in Philadelphia needing to go to the Ferrari dealer in San Diego as soon as Bryson could make it up there to hook up the enclosed trailer.

Bryson still had to plead with Jack to stick around for the trip. He had listened to Bryson's final sales pitch before agreeing to go:

"Just think, Jack, we can see a whole new part of America. We can take the first two-thirds of the drive through the heartland of our great country. We'll take time to see Constitution Hall and the Liberty Bell, the Baseball Hall of Fame, the Amish country and Museum of Natural History in Chicago. We'll see all those beautiful small towns along the road; the rolling hills, the wavering fields of grain. We'll see the farms with their big red barns, pastures full of cows with their new calves, and Jack, don't forget that we will definitely have the chance for some wonderful eating experiences. I've been told that the Midwest has fantastic home-made pies, and more importantly, some of the world's best chicken fried steak. At least that's what I've been told."

THE END

# About The Author

After thirty years of medical practice and raising five children, *Dr. Steven I. Dahl* and his wife Paula split their time between their homes in the Arizona desert and the mountain peaks of Utah. Humanitarian medical missions in third world countries, spending time with their seventeen grandchildren and writing fiction thrillers fill the retirement years. With his fourth novel penned, he and Paula will be off to Europe for more adventure.

# Acknowledgments

Many heartfelt thanks go out to all who have contributed to the completion of this novel. Foremost, I wish to thank my agent/publisher Lisa Akoury-Ross and Sweet Dreams Publishing of Massachusetts, and my editor Jayne Pupek. Not forgotten, are the many friends and family who have added expertise and enablement. These include, but are not limited to, Margret Rosenhan, Elyssa Bent, Andrea Allen, John and Lyn Glenn, Mary Platt, Dennis Toleman and Julie Lassetter.

Completion of a work of fiction is the fulfillment of a thirty-year goal. It could not have become a reality without the constant encouragement of my wife Paula and the patience of my family.

# Order *Chicken Fried Steak* for Your Friends!

## *Or other books written by Steven I. Dahl, M.D.*

## Simply visit us at:

www.PublishAtSweetDreams.com
and click on the book title
to order online.

## OR: Fill out the form below and mail your order to:

Title: (check which title or both)
- ❐ Chicken Fried Steak: $14.95                      Quantity: _____
- ❐ HOA Gold: $14.95                                      Quantity: _____

Total number of books: _____          Subtotal: _____

Shipping: _____ $7.00

Total: _____

Name: _____

Street: _____

City, State, Zip: _____

Phone or email: _____